8/99

P9-CQF-165

## SWEET DISTRACTION

When Nerissa turned slightly, the sweet aroma of her perfume taunted Hamilton. His hands tightened on the tree branch as he fought the craving to slide his arms around her supple body.

"Look," she whispered, drawing his eyes from the rise and fall of her breasts to a leaf that she held. "This once was no more than a seed. Now it is part of this massive tree. And it all happened when no one was watching but the sunshine and the wind."

"Many things happen when eyes are too busy elsewhere to notice," he said as softly, his voice rough with longing.

Nerissa closed her eyes as his fingers glided from the branch to her arm. She relished the power and the danger of his touch but knew she must not surrender to it. Too much she had heard of Lord Windham's determination to play booty with the heart of any woman who did not shield it carefully. Releasing the branch, she let it snap up into the air. He leapt back.

"You are a minx!" he said with a laugh.

"And you quite the rogue."

"I try." He drew her hand within his arm and led her farther along the twisting path. "When one is encumbered with the reputation of a *roué*, one is expected to act so."

"I doubt that you have ever done as another has wished."

"You see through me too facilely, Miss Dufresne. I shall endeavor to be on my guard against your intuition."

## ELEGANT LOVE STILL FLOURISHES —
### *Wrap yourself in a Zebra Regency Romance.*

A MATCHMAKER'S MATCH                                    (3783, $3.50/$4.50)
by Nina Porter

To save herself from a loveless marriage, Lady Psyche Veringham pretends to be a bluestocking. Resigned to spinsterhood at twenty-three, Psyche sets her keen mind to snaring a husband for her young charge, Amanda. She sets her cap for long-time bachelor, Justin St. James. This man of the world has had his fill of frothy-headed debutantes and turns the tables on Psyche. Can a bluestocking and a man about town find true love?

FIRES IN THE SNOW                                      (3809, $3.99/$4.99)
by Janis Laden

Because of an unhappy occurrence, Diana Ruskin knew that a secure marriage was not in her future. She was content to assist her physician father and follow in his footsteps . . . until now. After meeting Adam, Duke of Marchmaine, Diana's precise world is shattered. She would simply have to avoid the temptation of his gentle touch and stunning physique — and by doing so break her own heart!

FIRST SEASON                                           (3810, $3.50/$4.50)
by Anne Baldwin

When country heiress Laetitia Biddle arrives in London for the Season, she harbors dreams of triumph and applause. Instead, she becomes the laughingstock of drawing rooms and ballrooms, alike. This headstrong miss blames the rakish Lord Wakeford for her miserable debut, and she vows to rise above her many faux pas. Vowing to become an Original, Letty proves that she's more than a match for this eligible, seasoned Lord.

AN UNCOMMON INTRIGUE                                    (3701, $3.99/$4.99)
by Georgina Devon

Miss Mary Elizabeth Sinclair was rather startled when the British Home Office employed her as a spy. Posing as "Tasha," an exotic fortune-teller, she expected to encounter unforeseen dangers. However, nothing could have prepared her for Lord Eric Stewart, her dashing and infuriating partner. Giving her heart to this haughty rogue would be the most reckless hazard of all.

A MADDENING MINX                                       (3702, $3.50/$4.50)
by Mary Kingsley

After a curricle accident, Miss Sarah Chadwick is literally thrust into the arms of Philip Thornton. While other women shy away from Thornton's eyepatch and aloof exterior, Sarah finds herself drawn to discover why this man is physically and emotionally scarred.

# The Fortune Hunter
## Jo Ann Ferguson

**ZEBRA BOOKS**
**KENSINGTON PUBLISHING CORP.**

*For Rob Cohen,*
*Who knows how much she has helped*
*But may not know how much I appreciate it.*
*Thank you so much!*

ZEBRA BOOKS are published by

Kensington Publishing Corp.
475 Park Avenue South
New York, NY 10016

First Printing: June, 1993

Printed in the United States of America

# Chapter One

"I wager your Cirrus can't clear that hedge!" The red-haired man chuckled as he adjusted his navy riding jacket and settled back in his saddle. "Why do you hesitate, Hamilton? Are you afraid to test your fumble-footed nag?"

"I shall leave that idiocy to you, Philip." Hamilton Windham held the reins easily as he watched his brother patting his horse's neck.

"What? You were bragging just yesterday that Cirrus could jump any hedgerow in the shire. That one seems more high and rasping than any of the others we have passed. Do you fear having to prove your words?"

Hamilton tilted back his tall hat as he eyed the hedge. It was high. *Very high,* yet he was sure his white horse could clear the hedgerow with little effort. When he saw Philip's grin, he smiled as well. How his brother enjoyed roasting him! They had been too serious for too long during their extended visit to Bath. It would do them good to kick up their heels.

"I suspect Cirrus could use the exercise," he said with a chuckle.

"And I suspect you shall end up on the ground."

"Do you?"

Philip laughed at his older brother's fierce expression. Hamilton looked every bit the viscount he was from his hair that had the unruly habit of falling into his grey eyes to his shining boots of the same ebony shade. Nothing could detract from the roughly sculptured line of his jaw. He dressed *à la modality*—but not as foppishly as the dandy-set—for his forest green riding jacket accented the breadth of his shoulders before dropping to the waist of his buckskin breeches. His brother preferred such rough clothing for the country.

"I wager a yellow-boy you can't clear that hedge without losing your seat," Philip said.

"Can you afford to part with a guinea, Philip, when you intend to sit at the board of green cloth with us this evening?"

Laughing again, the redhead backed his prancing horse away from the hedge. He motioned toward its awe-inspiring height. "Think of it as setting me on my way to a fortune-filled night."

"Or starting you on such a round of bad luck you must excuse yourself as you did the last time?"

"You know I was behind the wind that night," Philip said. "I'm plump in the pockets today."

"Then I accept your foolish wager, Brother. Your guinea shall be mine before the hour grows much older."

Philip's laugh followed Hamilton as he turned Cirrus along the road. He had to put some distance between himself and the hedge, for the horse needed to build up speed to clear it. With the cool breeze coming from the sea, tempered by the hot sun, it was the perfect day for a ride . . . if he had been in the proper mood for frivolity. He wasn't. He hadn't been in high spirits for more than a year. Maybe this sport would steer his mind away from his troubles.

His whispered command brought Cirrus's ears up

and sent the horse racing toward the hedge. Leaning forward, Hamilton concentrated. He must wait for the exact moment to give the order to jump. Dust burned in his eyes and throat. Even as he shouted to the horse, he could feel Cirrus tense. They rose—the strength of the horse defying the wind—and fell back to earth on the far side of the hedge.

With a victorious cheer, Hamilton turned the horse back toward the road. Again Cirrus cleared the hedge with ease. The horse's sides heaved against Hamilton's legs as he brought him to a stop by Philip.

"Grand horse, isn't he?" Hamilton asked as he leapt from the saddle. He rubbed the horse's nose and smiled as the horse nuzzled him. "I swear he will be—nay, he already is—the best jumper in all of England."

"What a shame that Sir Delwyn wasn't here! With his love of gambling, you could have emptied his pockets of a handful of guineas."

"I shall leave you and the good baronet to your betting. More important matters plague me."

Philip's smile vanished. "Fudge, Hamilton! You agreed we wouldn't speak of your search today. I tire of it, and so, I vow, does everyone else."

"Everyone but the one who leads me on this merry chase." Hamilton ran a hand through his kohl hair before settling his hat back on his head. His grey eyes glittered with determination, straightening his lips, as he remounted. "I must find that thieving cove before he spends another penny of my money. Don't say it, Philip. I know the rogue has been evading me for a year, but I shall find him."

His brother sighed. "You're obsessed with this futile pursuit. I fail to understand why you, who are as rich as a nabob, are haunted by this."

"I prefer to spend my money as *I* wish, not having

it stolen by a slippery chucklehead."

"Not a chucklehead, Hamilton, for he baffled both Father and me."

Hamilton did not reply. His brother was being generous, as usual. The sad truth was that the former Viscount of Windham, their mutual sire, had been empty-headed. Their father had trusted a man who had come to him with a scheme to enhance the family's wealth and prestige. The viscount had believed the man's bangers. Soon the money and the man had disappeared, leaving the elderly viscount lost in shame. He never recovered, his pride dying before he did. At his father's deathbed, Hamilton had vowed to find the thief and make him pay.

If he had not been away in America on business . . . So many times he had thought that, but wishes changed nothing. While his father had entertained the fleecer, Hamilton had been in New England dealing with his father's interests there. Interests? Even now he was tempted to laugh at the presumption of the small textile factories which claimed to be among the finest in the country. They had been poorly managed. Hamilton had altered that by leaving a competent man in charge before being recalled to England by Philip's frantic letter. The old viscount had died within days of Hamilton's arrival, never knowing Hamilton had returned.

Philip had-been able to tell him very little about the man who had hoodwinked their father. His brother had been at Oxford at the time, so he could give Hamilton nothing more than a name, which was probably false, and a sketchy description of the gold-finder and his manservant. The descriptions of one short and the other a bare-bones with thinning hair could have fit dozens of men.

In the past year, Hamilton had assumed the title of the Viscount of Windham and his brother had finished his schooling, but no sign had been found of the thief or of the sovereigns that had vanished with him.

Forcing a smile, Hamilton said, "We should hurry back to Bath. You have that appointment with Cousin Gilbert at teatime."

"And you have that letter to answer." Philip chuckled as his brother grimaced. "Or perhaps you don't want to answer Elinor's missive? Elinor Howe is an obstinate woman. I warned you that you had taken a maggot in your head when you arranged for her to have the house in London. You never did that for any past convenient, so she is right to think you have more than a passing fancy for her."

Hamilton sighed. He had been a blockhead to take Elinor into his house. It proved to the whole world he had lost his heart to the heartless woman, who thought only of how much blunt she could garner from her collection of lovers. *Blast Elinor!* The dashed woman was taking too much time and keeping him from searching for the Bristol man who had stolen his father's life. He hated to waste even a moment on something as unimportant as an unfaithful mistress.

"Damn," he grumbled as he set Cirrus along the twisting road toward Bath. Hearing hoofbeats, he turned to see Philip's sympathetic expression. That irritated him more. He had no desire for the young sprig's compassion. He wanted to forget his troubles.

With a curse, Hamilton set the horse to a run. He aimed Cirrus at the hedgerow edging the road. For a moment, while they had been flying over the hedge, he had been able to banish both Elinor and the thief from his head. He needed to forget them again.

He ordered Cirrus toward the hedge. As they soared over, he saw a woman walking on the far side. He couldn't turn the horse back in midair. Horror

9

blanched the young woman's face. She turned to run, but he knew she could not escape in time.

Twisting his hand in the reins, Hamilton leaned toward the woman. Every muscle strained as he stretched out his riding crop. A vicious shove knocked her off her feet. She struck the ground out of the horse's path. Hamilton's nose hit the bone beneath Cirrus's mane as they landed roughly. Fighting to keep his seat, he jerked back on the reins. The horse neighed a protest, but came to a halt.

Hamilton leapt from the saddle as he heard his brother's shout. The warning had come far too late. He rushed to where the young woman lay facedown in the high grass. Kneeling beside her, he ran his hands along her slender form. He frowned. Her scarlet velvet spenser was torn, and her straw bonnet had cracked along the brim. Hoping those were her only injuries, he carefully turned her onto her back.

His eyes widened as he snarled his prayers backward. This was no farm lass, sneaking away for a tryst in the hedges. She was dressed well. Her bonnet tilted to reveal lashes, as dark as her hair, shadowing her cheeks. Her skin was colorless, save for a reddening bruise on her left cheekbone. Her wine-red lips were parted. Putting his hand near them, he sought the warmth of her breath. He picked up her limp right arm and found her pulse. It was slow, much too slow.

He glanced up as Philip knelt on the far side of the senseless woman. When his brother smoothed her blue muslin dress about her ankles—so it did not reveal an inappropriate, but definitely appealing, length of slender leg—he shook his head in exasperation.

"Philip, you are ever the gentleman. Who else would think of her modesty at a time such as this?"

"Is she hurt?"

"Senseless. I must have pushed her a scrap harder

10

than I should have. I wanted her out of the way of Cirrus's hoofs.''

Philip pulled off his low hat and used it to shade her face from the sun. "She is no antidote. Her hair is as black as Midnight's mane, and she seems as nicely lined—"

"Spare me the comparisons to your dashed horse! Damn! Is she ever going to wake?"

"If you keep shouting, no doubt you'll wake the dead.''

Hamilton glowered at him before leaning over the young woman again. Cautiously and gently, he tapped her unbruised cheek. It was silken smooth and warm. She moaned, but her eyes did not open. Although he wished her no more injury, he slapped her cheek a bit harder.

The dark lashes fluttered, and her sapphire eyes opened. Bafflement filled them and then horror as she looked up at him as if he was no better than a highwayman. She opened her mouth, but the only sound emerging was a soft sob of anguish.

"Try to remain still," he urged. "Regain your senses without haste.'' Over his shoulder, he ordered, "Philip, run and get that canister from Cirrus. There may be some brandy left in it.''

His brother jumped to his feet and hurried to obey. He returned with the opened bottle. Putting his arm beneath the young woman's shoulders, Hamilton tilted her slightly. He tipped the brandy to her lips. When she took a deep drink, she gasped and began to cough. Tears ran along her cheeks, but he ignored them. He gave her a chance to catch her breath, then lifted the bottle to her lips again. This time, she drank without choking. He offered it a third time. She waved it away weakly, and he lowered her to the ground.

"Are you hurt, miss?" asked Philip.

11

Hamilton fired a furious frown at his brother. Where had Philip left his wits this afternoon? Even a blind buzzard would be able to see the woman suffered from more than a fleabite.

"Not bad," she whispered.

When she winced, Hamilton was sure her head ached. His did with a pulse slicing across his skull. He paid his pain no mind. "Can you stand?"

Philip wrung his gloved hands together, threatening the leather. He halted when Hamilton glared at him again.

"Yes."

At the woman's breathy answer, Hamilton did not wait to ask her permission. He put his arm around her slim waist and helped her as she struggled to her feet. He released her, but watched closely while she took a tentative step. She swayed. Cursing, he caught her left arm to keep her on her feet.

Her shriek of pain drained all color from his brother's face. Hamilton disregarded him as the young woman collapsed against him. His arm circled her slender waist, holding her close so she did not fold to the ground again. A sigh battered his teeth, but he refused to release it. Damn! The afternoon had shown every augury of being an escape from trouble . . . until this!

With care, Hamilton examined her arm. She was so fragile. If she'd had the sense God gave a goose . . . He silenced the thought when he saw her swelling wrist.

"This may hurt," he murmured. A delicate scent drifted from her tangled hair as he bent closer, but he kept his attention on making sure she wasn't badly hurt. He had no need of another woman, another complication, in his life.

She gave him no answer.

"I'll endeavor to be careful," Hamilton said.

12

His fingers probed her narrow wrist. She moaned softly, then clamped her lips closed. Reluctant admiration startled him. She might look as dainty as a soap bubble, but she was able to suffer this pain without screeching as Elinor would have.

*Blast Elinor!* He had enough problems right now without her coy smile invading his head.

"Is it broken?" Philip asked. His anxious voice cracked.

"Nothing seems broken."

Hamilton bent again to peek under her splintered bonnet. Her eyes were closed. Twin tears slid along her cheeks, and she shuddered with silent sobs. Damn! It would be easier if she snarled recriminations at him. He was accustomed to Elinor—and other London ladies raging over the merest slight. This stoicism was unnerving.

Philip reached forward to rearrange the battered bonnet that the nameless woman was wearing. This observation reminded Hamilton that they had no idea what her name was.

"Nerissa Dufresne," she whispered to his question. She rested the back of her finely boned hand against her forehead. Closing her eyes, she shuddered so hard Hamilton feared she would shatter. "Forgive me, sir. I fear my head is going to refuse to stay on my shoulders."

"Hamilton, we must get her to a doctor immediately!" gasped Philip.

"No doctor," she said, her voice gaining some strength. "I shall not be leeched when there is nothing wrong with me but a jumbled brain and a few bruises."

Hamilton smiled. "You are plucky, but by all means, you must allow us to escort you to your destination, Miss Dufresne."

"Sir, I can't impose on a stranger," she answered,

13

trying to focus her eyes on him.

"Forgive me, miss, for failing to introduce you only to the butt of my riding crop." Hearing his brother's groan at his crude speech, he added, "I am Hamilton Windham. Your servant, Miss Dufresne. And this is my brother Philip."

"The Viscount of Windham?"

"Does my name mean something to you, Miss Dufresne?"

When she was about to nod her head, Nerissa put her hand up to her bonnet. Her head threatened to fly off and leave her senseless again. She took a deep breath, although nothing could slow the frantic beat of her thudding heart.

"I am familiar with your name, my lord, although, until but a moment past, I was not familiar with you." Her shoulders quivered, but her voice took on repressive accents as she raised her eyes to meet his slate-grey gaze. "Were you all about in the head to be careering through the field like that? I own that I did not see where you came from, but didn't you see me? Are you foxed? I see no signs of that, but why else would you ride roughshod over me?"

Lord Windham's hands tightened about his riding crop. His eyes burned with silver fire, as he replied in a clipped tone, "Miss Dufresne, you wound me to the very heart. I would never ride down a lady. I was jumping Cirrus, and I failed to see you until we were nearly upon you. You should refrain from lurking in the hedgerow."

"Lurking? I assure you that I was not *lurking*. I was taking a walk—a quiet walk, I had hoped—when you knocked me heels over head."

"I saved your life."

"Which would have been in no danger if you hadn't been so feckless as to leap without determining what might lie beyond. Surely that's the first lesson

14

any rider learns. I . . . Oh!"

The last became a groan as Nerissa's legs failed her. Strong arms caught her and drew her with gentleness toward a firm body. She was grateful Lord Windham's actions were more refined than his words.

The adderish edge vanished from Lord Windham's voice. "Miss Dufresne, you are in no condition for a dagger-drawing. Save your angry words for a later time when you may pummel my ears with them. For now, Philip and I will escort you home posthaste. You would be wise to retire to your private chambers until you are steady on your feet."

"You may be right," she whispered, although unwilling to obey his commands. She was put out of countenance by the thought, for she should owe a duty to this handsome stranger. He could have ridden on, but he had paused to be sure she was safe. To be honest, she could not fault him for the accident, for that was truthfully what it had been.

"Can you stand alone while I toss you up into the saddle?"

"I'm not sure." Nerissa hated the weakness in her voice, for she was usually in good point. When she considered what might result if she could not tend to her household, she felt more ill. "But I shall try, my lord."

Lord Windham slowly withdrew his arm from her waist. She was glad he allowed her to hold onto his strong arm until she was sure she was set on her feet. She pressed her hand against the side of her broken bonnet. Her head felt oddly weightless. Closing her eyes helped, for then only darkness spun, not the whole world. She heard Mr. Windham's gasp. She could not reassure the red-haired man. Words were too much for her weakened condition. She had to focus all her strength on trying to remain on her feet.

She wobbled. As his arm swept around her again,

she leaned on Lord Windham, not caring that such intimacy was being forced on her when her senses might vanish anew at any moment. She must not surrender to the raw agony rollicking through her in an obscene quadrille.

"Hamilton," urged the voice she knew belonged to Mr. Windham, "we can't delay. We must get her back to Bath. Help her up, and—"

"How can she ride?" came Lord Windham's impatient voice. "Good God, Philip, she can't stand. Ride to town and get the carriage. The only way we can get her back to Bath with her reputation intact is in it. She can't be seen sitting across my knees as if she was in her infancy."

"I can get a doctor, and—"

"Just go and get the dashed carriage!" he interrupted again. "We can worry about a doctor later."

The sound of hoofs disappearing in the distance pierced Nerissa's pain. Grasping onto the even rhythm, she used it to pull herself out of the void. She gasped and clutched at Lord Windham's lapels as he lifted her into his arms.

"What are you doing?" she cried, then wished she had remained silent, for the sound ached within her head.

"Miss Dufresne," he said in his impatient voice, "I've sent my brother at top speed to get the carriage. We wish to safeguard your reputation. You can't believe I wish to ruin it before the dust of Philip's passage settles to the road again."

"No, I suppose not." She looked at the rigid line of his jaw.

She could tell Lord Windham was furious. At her? She had done nothing wrong, but to have the misfortune to be in his way. Her right hand clenched on his wool coat. These dashed lords believed the world was theirs to do with as they pleased. Pity those

16

who got in their way. Her gaze rose along his sternly carved face. She tensed as she was captured by his grey eyes. Seeing exasperation there, she realized it was centered on himself. She chided herself for her unflattering thoughts. Lord Windham was as distressed by this episode as she was. She wondered if he had been out to enjoy the peace of the Bath countryside as she had. Not that it mattered now. The peace was gone, lost in a detonation of pain.

Nerissa was pleased when Lord Windham set her with care in the lush grass beneath a tree on a hillock a short distance from the hedge. The cool shade offered comfort, and she found the quivers of fear fading. She was glad to be away from the hedgerow, although she knew it was unlikely a second rider would come vaulting over it.

When the viscount offered her another drink from the canister of brandy, Nerissa said, "My head is spinning enough already, my lord."

With a shrug, he took a deep drink and wiped his mouth with the back of his hand. "Mayhap, but you look to be in pain. The brandy will ease that. Take a drink." He put the bottle on the ground next to her. His eyes narrowed when she did not reach for it.

"You are being most kind, my lord."

"Fiddle! I'd do the same for any bedraggled kitten brushed by Cirrus's hoofs."

Nerissa bristled at his curt retort. He *was* high and mighty! "I retract my Spanish coin, my lord. I vow you are a regular ramshackle."

"What a mull!" he grumbled. Sitting next to her on the hillock, he leaned against the tree. His arms folded over his chest, the motion straining the seams at the shoulders of his coat. "Pray do not take umbrage, Miss Dufresne. I meant you no slight, and I am sure you . . . in your generosity . . . meant none to me. I suspect you are not at your best."

17

Touching her straw bonnet's cracked brim, she looked away. Heated tears welled in her eyes again. She did not want to weep before this hard-spirited man. She would not! Yet her head ached; her left arm was aflame with pain; and, with every breath, her body remembered her impact on the earth. Too easily she recalled the sight of the horse soaring toward her and the grass clutching at her silk slippers as she tried to flee.

"Forgive me anew," Lord Windham said in a softer voice. "I do not mean to be uncivil, but I own to being a bit unsettled as well."

Nerissa looked at him. She had accused *him* of being rude when she was allowing herself to forget he had been a victim of this accident also. "You are right. I'm not at my best."

"How do you feel?"

"I have no need of you quacking me. I am a bit battered, but that is all."

"Is your brain about you now?"

When she smiled, her surprise was mirrored in his wide eyes. "The world isn't as skittish as it was." Her smile faded as pain throbbed along her left wrist. The buttons on her gloves strained against the swelling. She cradled it in her other hand and clenched her teeth. She had not guessed anything that had not been broken could hurt so severely.

"Philip will return in only a few minutes with the carriage. Do you live in Bath?"

"Yes."

What he thought of her terse answer, she could not guess. Nor did she care. She simply wanted to be home. There she could surrender to the tears pricking the back of her eyes.

"Are you in much pain?" Lord Windham leaned forward to look at her wrist.

Nerissa pulled away, overwhelmed by his strong

18

shoulders that blocked her view of her aching arm. She gasped as she discovered how precarious her hold on her senses was. The sound became a moan as she was swept by new waves of undulating pain. Again the powerful arms surrounded her, but, as he tried to keep her from crumpling to the ground, the viscount's arm brushed her left wrist. Agony enfolded her, sweeping her into darkness.

# Chapter Two

"I will be fine," Nerissa assured Lord Windham as he handed her from the curricle. She looked past him to the welcome façade of her home. Its greyish-brown stone front was as smooth as the walkway in front of it. Pediments topped the door and the first-floor windows. The ground-floor windows and those on the upper floors were devoid of any decoration. A wrought-iron fence connected the railing by the few stone steps to the next house.

"Miss Dufresne, I can—"

"I shall be quite fine," she said again, not caring that she interrupted the viscount. The rattle of other vehicles along the street nearly drowned out her soft voice. Maybe if she repeated the refrain that she was fine enough times, *she* would believe it.

"Are you sure?" he asked. He kept one foot in the road as he assisted her onto the walkway, but she still had to look up to meet his eyes. No expression marred the marble coolness of his face, and she found it difficult to believe this was the same man who had been so solicitous while they had waited for Mr. Windham to return with the carriage. "You still have very little color in your face. Philip may have been right. Mayhap we should have stopped at the doctor's."

"I shall be all right once I am inside and am able to rest." Struggling to smile, she kept her hand under her left wrist. It pounded with continuous pain. She included Mr. Windham in her weak smile. "Thank you so much for bringing me home."

"I shall help you in if you wish."

Lord Windham's deep voice drew her eyes back to him. If the situation had been different, she would have enjoyed admiring his strong jaw or trying to decipher the emotions in his volatile eyes. Today, she just wanted to rid her life of him and the pain he had caused.

"That's unnecessary, my lord, but thank you again."

He tipped his hat and bowed slightly. "As you wish, Miss Dufresne. I bid you a good afternoon. I leave you with the hope that tomorrow will be a less adventuresome day for you."

"I pray you are correct."

Nerissa fought to keep her pace even. She tried not to think that anyone looking out of a window on the opposite side of Laura Place would guess Miss Dufresne was out of sorts. She lurched forward to grasp the newel post on the steps as if she had been tippling more than a few swallows of brandy. When Lord Windham offered again to assist her, she struggled to laugh aside his concern. The sound was pathetically feeble.

To be honest, she felt completely corkbrained. Her head was too light. Hoping Lord Windham would believe her, she said, "'Tis nothing but a bit of dizziness."

Foolishly she looked back as she spoke. Seeing his narrowed eyes and tight lips, she was sure he found her words the skimble-skamble they were. She feared he thought she found his assistance abhorrent. That was not true, but she had no stamina to explain she wanted to escape from Lord Windham and this whole bizarre experience. Then perhaps the debilitating pain would disappear, too.

Nerissa's feet were weighted as she labored to lift each of them to the first riser. Gripping the rail, she was able to climb the few steps to the door without collapsing. Even so, she was cautious as she faced the carriage to bid the gentlemen a good day. She gasped when she discovered Lord Windham standing directly behind her, his hands outstretched to catch her if she had fallen. Her sigh reverberated excruciatingly through her, adding to her annoyance with the viscount who ignored her wishes.

"I told you I could climb the steps alone, my lord," she whispered, not daring to speak louder, for she feared her head would explode with agony. She would have scowled, but every motion hurt.

"You must forgive me for not wanting to see you take another tumble." She appreciated that he answered lowly. Again he tipped his hat to her. "I bid you *adieu* once more. If you need anything—"

"Goodbye," she murmured. She was being ill-mannered, but she didn't want to continue this encounter.

Lord Windham's pleasant expression faded. He set his hat more firmly on his head as he strode to the curricle. Walking around the vehicle, he untied his white horse. He mounted with an ease that bespoke many hours in the saddle. He nodded coolly toward her before he slapped the reins against the side of the horse's neck and rode away at a speed seldom seen on the sedate street.

Mr. Windham smiled an apology, but said nothing as he gave an order to the horse pulling the carriage. Only when it had rattled away along the street toward the Pulteney Bridge did Nerissa turn to where her front door was opening. She steeled herself for the task of climbing the final step. When her head continued to spin madly, *nothing* could be managed without all her concentration.

"Miss Dufresne, this is quite the kickup! What have you done now?"

At the sharp voice, Nerissa raised her eyes to meet the sunken ones in the household's butler's narrow face. She had not expected compassion from Hadfield, and she received none. The man, who was as lanky as his face was long, regarded her with distaste. That was no surprise either. He seldom failed to find fault with some aspect of her clothing or her mannerisms, and delighted in each opportunity to acquaint her with her latest shortcoming.

"As you can see," Nerissa retorted with uncommon heat, "I was in a bit of an accident. I am also— although it may strike you heart-deep to hear the tidings—relatively unhurt. If you would be so gracious as to step aside, I would prefer to sit."

"Yes, do step aside, Hadfield," came a seconding order in a warm, contralto voice.

Seeing Mrs. Carroll's wrinkled face, Nerissa managed to smile. Unlike the butler, from the moment of Nerissa's arrival, the housekeeper had made her feel welcome in the house on Laura Place. Mrs. Carroll was thin, almost as thin as the butler, who resembled a death's-head on a mop stick. She could have been a long, grey bird, twittering about, chiding the lower servants, seeing to every detail of the household.

"La! Lamb, you have been hurt! Are those bruises on your face?" Mrs. Carroll tipped Nerissa's face, and choked back a cry when the younger woman was nearly rocked from her feet by the faint motion. "What . . . ? No, share the details with me later. First, tell me where you're injured." She aimed a glower at the butler. "Go and alert Mr. Pilcher. He will have sympathy for poor Miss Dufresne."

"Mr. Pilcher said he had no wish to be disturbed this afternoon," argued Hadfield in his most haughty voice.

"He will make an exception when he hears of his sister's accident." Putting her hands on her narrow hips, Mrs. Carroll snapped, "Don't act so high in the instep with me, Hadfield!"

The butler grumbled as he walked away. The only word Nerissa understood was "stepsister". Hadfield was correct. She was his master's stepsister, but the butler's attempts to create a gap between her and her brother had failed . . . Nerissa forgot him as she strove to ignore the torrent of torment along her arm.

Mrs. Carroll whispered, "Lamb, where are you hurt?"

"My left wrist." Nerissa lifted her arm which seemed as heavy as her ironbound legs.

The grey-haired woman urged Nerissa to sit on the padded bench next to the tall-case clock at one side of the foyer. It was harder to move than Nerissa had expected, but easy to sit, sinking into the cushion hidden beneath blue velvet.

The housekeeper took Nerissa's left hand, placing it judiciously on hers. Pain scored Nerissa. The foyer threatened to become a blur of dark wood and the white and black of the checkered floor. She heard Mrs. Carroll order her to take a deep breath. She obeyed and nearly gagged on it as the housekeeper began to undo the buttons along her glove.

"No!"

"Lamb, I must—"

"Just wait a moment," she begged through the agony. "Give me just a moment." She could not battle the pain and Mrs. Carroll's good intentions at the same time.

Mrs. Carroll halted with a soothing coo. "The glove must be cut off. I shall hurt you too much if I try to ease it off."

"You can't cut it off. These are my second-best gloves, Mrs. Carroll."

"And this is your very best left wrist." Her voice

24

gentled. "Come into the parlor, Miss Dufresne. The light is better there. Let's see what we can do about your glove and—more importantly—your poor arm. You can stand, can't you?"

"Of course." Nerissa's words mocked her, for she was not able to set herself on her feet. Grateful for Mrs. Carroll's assistance, she limped into the second largest room on the ground floor. Only her stepbrother's book room was grander.

Easing around a pair of rosewood chairs, Nerissa rested her right hand on one curved back. She needed a minute to gather her senses about her. She gazed across the blue Oriental rug toward the painted sofa with its brass feet, which shone like beacons in the sunlight pouring through the two windows. It urged her forward, but she could not manage to walk the few paces. She dropped into an upholstered chair, her back to the pier glass between the windows, so she did not have to see the damage inflicted on her by a man who had been trying to save her life.

As Mrs. Carroll bent to check Nerissa's wrist, heavy footsteps raced into the room.

"By all that's blue!" came the squeaky, tenor voice that belonged to Nerissa's stepbrother Cole Pilcher. "What adventure have you muddled into this time?"

"Hush, Mr. Pilcher," the housekeeper chided. "Miss Dufresne has been bumped a bit. Come and sit with her."

"Bumped a bit? How did you do that, Nerissa?"

She considered laughing at her brother's outraged dismay. When the ache escalated across her head, she lost her amusement. Through the flood rushing in her ears, she heard Mrs. Carroll whisper she would fetch her scissors.

"I said no!" she gasped, then moaned as her protest hurt her skull.

"The glove must be cut off. I won't cause you more

pain, Miss Dufresne."

Nerissa noted the stubborn set of the housekeeper's chin. Mrs. Carroll seldom argued with her, but, when she did, Nerissa had learned to accede to the housekeeper's wisdom. "As you wish." As dear as every copper had become in their household, she wondered when she could replace the glove and her ruined bonnet. Her spenser could be mended easily . . . again. Leaning back in the chair, she let its softness surround her as she gazed at the iron grate in the fireplace on the opposite wall.

Never had the chock-full room seemed so dear. The collection of furniture had been taken from their country home before she had arranged for Hill's End to be offered for sale. Running her fingers along the worn mahogany arms of the chair, she took a deep breath of beeswax. The scent belonged both to the past and the present. So little connected the two parts of her life. This should not have been a part of her life, but, when Cole's father died, she had come to Bath to oversee her stepbrother's household. She had been alone since her mother had been buried almost a year before her stepfather cocked up his toes, so Nerissa had been delighted to have a chance to be with family again—no matter how tenuous the connection was.

She also had tired of being in dun territory with the odious creditors lining up outside Hill's End's front gate. Although she had promised her mother she would endeavor to hold onto the lands which had belonged to Nerissa's father's family for centuries, the upkeep had become too prohibitive. She had found it easier to obtain an agent to attempt to sell it. Certainly their purse-pinched days would be behind them once the agent found a buyer.

If her stepfather had left them a respectable jointure, she and Cole would not be forced to play nip-farthings. She was bothered more by their dire

26

circumstances than Cole, for her brother usually thought less about money than he did the hour of the day. In that way, Cole could not have been less like his father, for Mr. Pilcher—she never had and never would think of him any other way—had been obsessed with wealth. It had done him little good, for, despite all his boasting about grand plans, he had left his heir with nothing to run the house in Bath that he had inherited at Nerissa's mother's death.

Nerissa sighed. A visit to grassville, with the green aroma that reminded her of Hill's End, always brought forth her frustration with memories that were better forgotten.

"No brandy," Nerissa whispered to contradict her brother's order. Tearing herself away from her discouraging thoughts, she forced a smile. "I may be a bit the worse for the wear, but I shan't drink spirits at such an hour. Tea, Mrs. Carroll, if you will. And please have Frye come down. I may need her assistance to get up the stairs."

"That is the wisest thing I've heard you say, lamb." Mrs. Carroll's voice was stern, but she offered Nerissa a smile before she scurried out of the room.

Cole called after her, "Brandy for me. I need it." He knelt by Nerissa's chair and took her right hand in his pudgy ones. "Dear Nerissa, what happened? I thought you were going for a ride with Annis Ehrlich."

Nerissa looked into his blue eyes that were so much like her own. That there was even this much of a resemblance between her and her stepbrother Cole Pilcher was astounding, because only the marriage of her mother to his widower father had made them brother and sister. While Nerissa was told often that she was the pattern card of her mother, Cole had inherited his father's looks. Stocky and with thinning hair of a sandy color, he stood only a few inches

27

taller than her own spare height. Seldom was he seen without a book in his hands or one propped in front of his nose.

In the months since she had moved to Bath, she had accustomed herself to eating each meal facing his latest manual. She had learned, during those curious meals, more about surveying and geology and transportation than any other woman of two-and-twenty. Her brother was possessed by a dream she could not share, despite her efforts. He longed to build a toll canal from Bristol to London. He had spoken of it during their short time together as children. In the years when they had been kept apart by their parents' acrimonious separation, she had assumed Cole would set aside his childish aspirations. Coming out of short pants had not changed Cole Pilcher. He remained dedicated to achieving his goal.

But he was not an air-dreamer. He was devising his plans with utmost care and attention to the newest scientific developments. Every week, he scanned the *Bath Chronicle* for news about any canal work throughout England. He ordered books from London and memorized each detail.

It was a grand scheme and was certain to leave them swimming in lard, if he made it a reality. There was the singular problem that his father's estate allowed them to live comfortably in the house on Laura Place *only* if Cole supplemented his inheritance with tutoring the children of their wealthier neighbors. That allowed him scant time for the pursuit of his dream. Nerissa wished she could assist him, but she found sewing an onerous chore for which she had no talent, and she had discovered no other work for a woman of her class in Bath.

Nothing was as it should be: Hill's End on the block; Cole's dreams delayed; now this absurd accident. Nerissa winced as she touched a bruise along her temple.

"Oh, dear Sister, you are hurt!" Cole clasped her hand tighter, the motion aggravating the pain in her head. "What a rag-mannered cove I am to be asking you questions when you're struggling to cling to your high health."

"I'm a bit battered, but I assure you that I shall be fine. I don't need you quacking me." All the color drained from Nerissa's cheeks as she recalled making nearly the same retort to Lord Windham less than an hour before.

"Nerissa!"

"I am fine," she repeated, but with a scrap more strength. If she wound herself up with thoughts of the viscount, Cole would be even more determined to unearth every detail. She preferred to forget the embarrassing episode. "I know I look a dashed shabby, but . . ."

Her words faded as Mrs. Carroll bustled into the room. The housekeeper held her scissors like a weapon in her thin hands. Biting her lip, Nerissa balanced her left arm on the chair and watched as the housekeeper cautiously slid the tips of the scissors beneath the leather. The gentle caress of the metal on her swollen wrist detonated within her, turning the room into an endless tunnel, unlit with anything but pain.

Nerissa grabbed on to her senses. She couldn't lose them completely. Then they would smother her with more concern. She felt too bad to suffer that. Hearing Cole begging her to answer him, she tried. It was impossible to form a single word in her pain-ridden mind. Feeling tender hands loosening her broken bonnet, she kept her eyes closed. It was easier not to fight the pain.

"There. All done," the housekeeper murmured. "Ginny?"

Curiosity urged Nerissa to open her eyes as she

heard Mrs. Carroll call to the maid. Ginny held out a metal basin, her eyes wide with dismay as she stared at Nerissa's bruised wrist. The housekeeper wrapped warm, moist clothes about Nerissa's wrist, hiding the swelling and discoloring. The heat lessened the pounding, and Nerissa whispered her thanks.

"'Tis nothing, lamb. Have Frye order a bath when you're ready. I'll see you have plenty of hot water to soothe those bruises. Now just sit and be quiet."

"Yes, Mrs. Carroll," she said so dutifully the housekeeper smiled before she herded Ginny out of the room.

Cole leaned forward. "Nerissa, please set my mind to rest. What happened to you?"

"Annis was unable to go for a ride with me, so I went for a walk by myself."

"By yourself? Are you mad?"

"Don't chide me, Cole. I've no interest in your scolds. I swear my head is going to explode. Where is Hadfield with that tea? Ah, here he comes, and with Frye." Sitting straighter, she was able to smile as her abigail bustled toward her. "Now, Frye, don't take on so. I'm alive as you can see. If I had popped-off, I wouldn't be reprimanding you now."

The square woman bore a stronger resemblance to Nerissa's brother than Nerissa did. Of the same full build, the middle-aged woman's hair was a nondescript color, that Cole always called (with a muffled laugh) dandy grey-russet. The brown strands refused to stay in a proper chignon. Instead it fuzzed about her round face which was lined with dismay. Frye's expression warned Nerissa she must look even worse than she felt.

"Pluck yourself up," Nerissa added when her abigail burst into tears. Deep sobs punctured the room's hush and battered Nerissa's aching head. "Cole, speak to her. She heeds you when she refuses to listen to me."

30

"That is because you make demands that even a shuttlehead would know are impossible to obey."

"Dear Frye," Nerissa tried again, "if I had wanted a watering pot, I would have sent you to the garden. Stop the weeping and bring us some tea."

She sighed. Her words were not easing her abigail's despair. Reaching gingerly for the teapot, Nerissa noticed, for the first time that she still wore her spenser. The idea of removing it sent another aching wave over her. Propriety was unnecessary in the midst of this small crisis. She loaded a cup with sugar and poured in the weak tea her abigail preferred. She shoved the cup into Frye's hands and implored her to sit before she collapsed and complicated the whole situation.

"Advice you should take for yourself, Sister," said Cole past the storm of her abigail's tears.

"I *am* sitting, as you can see. Also I am—as you can see—remaining quiet as Mrs. Carroll commanded." She strained to keep her voice even, but managed that tremendous task. "Help yourself to a cake, Cole, and tell me how you have spent your afternoon. Did you find the geological reports you were looking for this morning?"

He plucked a cake from the tray and wagged it in her direction. "You're trying to fire a gun. I'll tell you about my day *after* you explain what happened to you."

"Annis did not, as I told you, wish to go for a ride, so I decided to take a walk."

"Where?"

"You know me, Cole. I can be a regular butterfly on a summer's day."

Instead of being mollified, her brother put the cake back on the tray. He frowned. "But *where* did you go?"

Nerissa considered demurring, but she suspected Hadfield would be delighted to inform "the young master"—as he insisted on calling Cole, causing her to wonder how the butler referred to her outside her hearing—that she had come home in a curricle with Lord Windham and his brother. That, coupled with her dishevelment, was sure to create more of a to-do in the household. If she wanted some quiet later to soothe her aching head, an explanation was necessary now.

*Blast that man and his horse*, she thought, then sighed. Lord Windham had tried to make amends. She had pushed them aside. She didn't want to be obligated to him, too.

"I went for a trot in the country. I haven't left Bath in weeks. When Annis was unable to go, because her sister demanded that Annis join her at the *couturière*, I decided to go as I had planned. Bath is so small it doesn't take long to reach daisyville."

Cole leapt to his feet. "Have you lost every bit of sense you possessed? You could have met a collector, or worse, out there alone."

"No highwayman would be interested in me when I have nothing of value."

"You should have taken Frye with you."

The abigail looked up in horror. Even when they had lived at Hill's End, Frye had kept close to the main house, budging out-of-doors only when Mrs. Pilcher had insisted Frye serve as a watchdog for Nerissa.

"That's a bag of moonshine! I'm quite capable of walking about in the country." Nerissa smiled when Cole scowled with disagreement. "All right, I concede it might have been a want-witted thing to do."

"It was jobbernowl! Look at you! Nerissa, what happened to you?"

"Lord Windham happened to take a hedge exactly where I was walking."

"Nerissa!" His face became as hueless as hers felt.

"Calm yourself, Cole. I am alive. Lord Windham tells me he pushed me out of the way. I can't attest to that, for I recall nothing of it."

Frye cried, "Fear has wiped the whole from your head!"

"It is over, and . . . except for a few bumps . . . nothing is amiss," Nerissa said quickly to comfort both of them. She would as lief not to explain that the diabolically handsome viscount had knocked her from her feet and from her senses. She did not want Cole demanding that Lord Windham name his friends. From such an affair of honor, her brother was certain to emerge the loser. "Please don't think anymore about it."

"Lord Windham, did you say?" Cole asked as if he had not listened to her last words. He walked from his chair to the hearth, then back, tapping his finger against his receding chin.

"Yes." She started to frown, but halted when the expression added to her misery. "Do you know him?"

"I know *of* him." He clasped his hands behind his back in the pose he always assumed when he was deep in thought. Without looking at her, he said, "He has been in Bath only a short while longer than you. I'm surprised. You'd think he would have returned to Town. Bath's entertainments must be a bore to him."

"The Season is past."

Again Cole acted as if he had not heard her. "His brother was with him? I recall nothing in the *Chronicle* about the viscount's brother's arrival in Bath."

Nerissa exchanged a weak smile with Frye. Unless a tidbit of news had something to do with Cole's canal project, he rarely recalled what he had read in the newspapers even a second afterward.

Reaching up to take his hand, she urged him to sit. "Don't burden yourself with thoughts of the viscount and Mr. Windham. I doubt they will think much about us. I would as lief hear of your work today. Did you find the answer to the problem of the solid rock?"

Cole needed no other prodding to launch into a long, intricate monologue. Letting the confusing terms for canal building surround her, the soothing sound of her brother's voice became a warm blanket to pull around Nerissa. She tried to shut out the anguish. It was nearly impossible, but far easier, she discovered, than forgetting the memory of the intriguing silver sparkle in Lord Windham's eyes.

# Chapter Three

The clatter of wagon wheels and the shouts of the milk lasses in the street woke Nerissa. Lying in her bed while she stared through the filmy curtains which filtered the grey light, she listened to the frantic pace of Laura Place at dawn.

Her head and her body hurt, even the steady pulse of her heart hurt. Running her fingers along the quilted smoothness of her yellow covers, she closed her eyes and tried to think the pain away. That was futile. The ache surrounded her like a dim aura.

When she heard muted sounds from her dressing room, Nerissa knew Frye was skulking about, getting ready for the day. That her abigail was within call soothed her, but staying abed would do nothing but lead to *ennui*. She would be wiser to keep herself busy so she could forget her misery.

Rolling onto her side, she gazed at her room. Brightening sunshine inched across the dull carpet topped by the furniture she had had brought from Hill's End on that bone-setter cart. Nerissa smiled at the mahogany writing desk and the two chairs by the foot of her high poster bed. Everything was decorated in the warm shades of yellow that her mother had laughingly judged too bright for a young lady.

Nerissa slipped out of bed, inching her toes toward

the steps to the floor. Taking a single step, she grabbed for the bedpost. She was as weak as if she was suffering from a fever. She did not move until her heartbeat had slowed from its frantic pace. Only when it was even again did she try a second step. It proved easier than the first, and she soon was able to walk, albeit slowly, about the room.

"Miss Dufresne!" came Frye's surprised reprimand. "Why are you up?"

"It *is* day," she answered reasonably, but added no more when she saw her maid's lips straighten in a frown.

"If you're hungry, I shall have toast and tea brought."

"There is no need to go to such lengths. I am quite capable of going down the stairs. Find my wrapper, will you?"

"Miss Dufresne, I think—"

"For once, Frye," she said sharply, "I don't care a rap what you think. Now are you going to help me, or must I lurch about alone?"

Frye acquiesced, but hovered around Nerissa, continually urging her to return to bed. Nerissa disregarded her abigail's anxiety. Although Frye might be correct—for Nerissa's eyes still had a strange habit of unfocusing when she blinked—she would not stay in bed all day. She was stiff from her bruises, and that would worsen if she did as Frye beseeched. What she needed was a cup of hot coffee and a hotter bath to ease the creak of abused limbs.

When Frye relented enough to bring her her favorite blue wrapper, Nerissa was glad of her abigail's help in putting on the simple garment. She had planned to call on Annis Ehrlich this afternoon, but she would have to send her regrets. How distraught Annis would be when she discovered what had happened! Not that Annis was in any way to blame. Not even Lord Windham was. . . .

*Blast him!* Why must he invade her thoughts when he was out of her life?

"That should do perfectly," Nerissa said as she pointed to a white silk shawl Frye was folding to put in the cupboard.

The plump woman held up the fringed square of shimmering fabric and regarded it with confusion. "Do for what?"

"Do you know how to tie a sling, Frye?"

"I think you should rest before—"

"I am going down to the breakfast parlor. I want to read the newspaper and enjoy my brother's company. Cole will be upset if I remain cloistered here."

"Miss Dufresne—"

"Frye, I'm going down to the breakfast parlor."

The abigail sighed. "As you wish. Can I help you with the sling?"

She started to demur, then nodded.

"I shall try to help you without injuring you more."

Nerissa bit her lower lip as she bent her arm so Frye could drape the material about her. Every motion—even the brush of air against her arm as Frye edged around her to tie the material behind her nape—added to the anguish. She said nothing. To own to it would make her abigail even more insistent that she go back to bed.

Agreeing to return for a bath and a rest after breakfast, Nerissa left her room. The upper hall of the town house was preternaturally quiet in the early morning. Mrs. Carroll must have ordered the maids to stay away from Nerissa's bedroom until she woke. Trust the housekeeper to worry about her! As she walked down the gently curving staircase, she saw a crow-black form in the shadows.

"Good morning, Hadfield," she said quietly.

He looked in her direction, his gaze focusing on her makeshift sling. Without speaking, he walked toward the back of the house. His coarse chuckles drifted to Nerissa.

Outraged, she was tempted to shout after him. Frye had been kind enough to disregard the blackening bruises Nerissa had seen in her glass. Hadfield wanted to put her into a pelter. She refused to give him that satisfaction. However, she would remain silent about his behavior no longer. Cole must listen to her.

Fury strengthened her uneven steps as she entered the light green breakfast parlor. The scent of freshly brewed coffee soothed her. Cook peeked in and offered Nerissa a sympathetic smile. Wiping her hand against her frosty-faced cheeks, the tall woman wore a worried expression when Nerissa ordered only a muffin and jam. Nerissa appreciated her concern, but was too fatigued by the walk down the stairs to want to do anything but sit.

A round table was set in the middle of the cozy room, which was situated to get the most of the morning sun. Cole looked up at the sound of Nerissa's voice. With his cravat untied and his shirt hanging out from his breeches, he held a book close to his nose.

"I see the dogs haven't dined yet," Nerissa said with a smile.

Looking over his shoulder at his drooping shirt ends, he grinned sheepishly and tucked them into his dark brown breeches. His smile vanished when he saw the sling about her arm. Jumping to his feet, he let the book he had been reading fall to the table with a crash. She winced, but her shock was stronger than her pain. Cole was obsessively solicitous of his work materials and never mishandled them.

"Nerissa," he said with a hint of censure in his voice, "you should have sent for breakfast."

"Then I would have missed the chance to speak with you. Isn't today the day the Mortimer boys come

38

for their math lesson?"

He scowled as he pulled out her chair and watched as she cautiously sat. "They come tomorrow. Felix Tucker has his math lesson this morning, and his older brother this afternoon. By the elevens, I wish I didn't have to spend time trying to inspire some thought in those cabbage-heads. No doubt, Felix will be the cherubim he is each week. Not only does he whine, but, last week, he stepped on one of my manuals. I should put my materials out of the reach of his dirty hands."

"Cole, you are much too lenient a tutor."

"If I was a gerund-grinder with Mrs. Tucker's beloved brats, she would send them posthaste to Mr. Kelly's school. We need the bustle if we want to live here. Thank goodness," he added as he pushed the tile and the coffeepot toward her, "I can depend on you to oversee the house. Without you and Hadfield, I don't know what I'd do."

Uneasily, Nerissa said, "I wish to speak to you of Hadfield."

"Oh?" Cole picked up the newspaper which had been folded in the middle of the table. When he opened it, his voice was muffled by the pages. "Is there a problem?"

"He is being more unbearable than usual," she said as she picked up the Pontypool japanned iron coffeepot. Even the bright flowers painted on its side could not bring her out of the dismals. "Cole, if you want my opinion—"

"You know I am always interested in your opinions."

She pulled down the newspaper. When he regarded her in surprise, his toast halfway to his mouth, she said, "We should give Hadfield the bag."

"Dismiss him?" he gasped, sitting straighter. "Hadfield has given years of service to this family. He was my father's closest confidant. How could you suggest we give him his *congé?*"

"I'm tired of his malicious display toward me and toward anyone who calls to see me. Just last week he kept Annis waiting in the foyer for close to a half hour before he announced her."

He smiled and folded his arms on the table. "Nerissa, you know Annis is given to exaggeration."

"Even if he allowed her to wait for five minutes, that is unacceptable."

"I shall speak to him. Will that be satisfactory?"

Nerissa hesitated, then nodded. Even if Cole remembered to reprimand Hadfield, which was as unlikely as snow on a Bath summer morning, the butler would not change his ways. As she stirred sugar into her coffee, being careful not to splatter it on her sling, she decided, that until she was herself again, it was just as well Cole would forget to reprimand the butler, for that would make the situation worse.

If it could get worse.


The afternoon warmth crept into the sitting room as Nerissa read a book of her favorite poetry. Her feet were propped on a footstool. Only by promising Frye she would read quietly had she convinced the abigail to stop flitting in and out of the room like an oversized moth. Quiet was the best prescription for her throbbing head, and she could not achieve it when her maid buzzed about her.

A knock on the door jarred through her skull, but she called for the person to enter. When she saw the butler, her lips tightened. She did not feel ready to fly out at Hadfield, although she knew the confrontation was inevitable. Just not today, she hoped.

"A gentleman named Windham is here to see you, miss," Hadfield said quietly.

Nerissa almost gasped aloud at her odd reaction to

the announcement that Lord Windham was calling. Her fingers were trembling so hard she had to set the book on a table. Her heart was thumping so loud she feared the butler would hear it. Why was *he* here? She had thought Lord Windham was out of her life. She had thought she was glad to be rid of him and his antics, but that failed to explain her sudden flush of pleasure at his call.

She smoothed her pale pink skirt as she stood. The ribbons at the high bodice fluttered around her like capricious butterflies. "Windham?"

"Mr. Philip Windham was the name he gave."

"Please show him in. And, Hadfield, ask Frye to join us." Nerissa sighed as she watched the butler leave. She had been a perfect blockhead to think the viscount would call on her. Even in the midst of her blurred memories of the previous day, she could not help recalling how delighted Lord Windham had been to climb onto his horse and ride away.

Not that she could blame him, for she had been beastly to refuse his assistance as if he had been a leper. With her head clearer today, she realized she would be wise to express her gratitude to Mr. Windham and hope he would convey the message to his brother. Then the episode certainly would be at an end . . . as she wanted. Yet, if that was so, she couldn't understand why that idea distressed her.

When Mrs. Carroll, rather than Hadfield, opened the door for Mr. Windham, Nerissa swallowed her outrage that Hadfield was neglecting his duties again. The butler was more interested in giving a bottle of liquor a black eye and sharing gossip with the kitchen maids. She should not delay another day convincing Cole to fire the butler. She doubted her pleas would do much good, though. She would get the same noncommittal answer she had received each time she broached the subject.

She put the butler from her head as Mr. Windham

crossed the room. His clothes were more formal than the ones he had worn while riding the previous afternoon. With a black coat that announced its excellent tailor by its stylish lines and a red striped waistcoat clashing with his ginger hackles, he wore a sedate shirt and tan breeches. A hint of lace appeared at his wide cuffs when he took the hand she held out to him.

"Miss Dufresne," he said, shaking her hand with gracious gentleness, "I trust you'll forgive this unannounced intrusion. I only wish to reassure myself that you are well."

Motioning for him to sit on the chair next to where she had been reading, she smiled. "You are beyond kindness, Mr. Windham. I can tell you I feel much better than I did yesterday evening."

"Have you seen a doctor?" He grinned as he looked at the lacy sling she wore. He wiped the smile from his face, replacing it with the guilty expression of a naughty lad.

"It isn't necessary."

Mr. Windham cleared his throat, betraying his disquiet. "Don't think me without manners to discuss such a matter when we are little more than the slightest of acquaintances, but I want you to know that my brother and I will be glad to assume any bills you might incur from this unspeakable incident."

"You're generous, Mr. Windham, but I am not a nip cheese."

"I didn't mean to suggest that."

"Of course, you didn't." Nerissa wondered if he was always so eager to apologize for everything he said and did. It made conversation difficult. "I wouldn't begrudge myself the company of a physician if I had needed one. There is nothing a doctor could do for my buffeted head, and my household has taken it upon themselves to see I shall do nothing with my left arm until it is healed to *their* satisfaction. You needn't worry about me."

"Alas, Miss Dufresne, your words only convince me that we have been beneath reproach." He sat where she had indicated, but appeared stiffly uncomfortable. "I know my brother is as distressed about this unfortunate incident as I am. I should have waited for Hamilton to return to Queen Square so we could both look in on you, but I was too anxious to soothe my conscience."

Nerissa smiled dutifully, but she believed Mr. Windham's words no more than he did. Lord Windham probably had dismissed her from his mind as soon as he left Laura Place. That the brothers resided on the finest street in the city was no astounding revelation. They wore their wealth and prestige with an indifference that came from possessing both all their lives.

"Mr. Windham, there was no need for anyone to call with an apology. Both you and his lordship were quite profuse yesterday." Sitting, she tried to ignore the sitting room's frayed furniture. She noticed it only as she saw Mr. Windham glance around the room. No doubt, he was unaccustomed to such shabbiness, but this was her home. She wouldn't have traded it for anything . . . but Hill's End. Grief smothered her at the thought of losing the only home she'd known before this one. Her chin raised as she silenced her misery. "I trust now that you have seen me, you can be satisfied I don't intend to cock up my toes."

He gave her a tentative smile. "If I may be so bold, may I say you look very lovely, Miss Dufresne?"

"A surprise on your part, I am certain. I looked a complete florence yesterday." Nerissa laughed, hoping to put the nervous young man at ease. "I am never at my best with a dirty face and scratched elbows." When he frowned, she hurried to add, "Mr. Windham, please allow me to change the subject to a topic you will find more comfortable. We cannot alter the past, so why should we dwell upon it?"

"If that's your wish."

"It is."

Taking a deep breath, the red-haired man nodded. He clasped and unclasped his fingers. Silence clamped around them. Every tick of the mantel clock seemed too loud.

Finally, after what Nerissa feared was an eternity, Mr. Windham asked, "Have you been in Bath long?"

"A few months. I came here to live with my brother." Nerissa glanced toward the foyer, but, as she should have guessed, Cole's book-room door remained closed. With his students gone for the day, he must be lost, as usual, in his studies. Rather than tell Mr. Windham the truth—for he might think her unmannered not to call her brother out to be introduced—she said, "I hope you will have the opportunity to meet him someday."

"I hope so, too, for, if I may be so presumptuous, I hope you will welcome me calling here again."

Nerissa found it easier to smile. "I would be delighted to have you call whenever you might be in Laura Place. I am at home Wednesday afternoons."

"Then I shall look forward to Wednesday next." Rising, he reached for her hand. Instead of shaking it, he began to lift it toward his lips.

Nerissa had no chance to react to his surprising boldness, for he froze as the door opened after a cursory knock. She was about to chastise Hadfield, but the words vanished, unuttered, as she stared past Mr. Windham to meet grey eyes that twinkled with mocking amusement.

Lord Windham handed Mrs. Carroll his hat and leather gloves. The housekeeper glanced from the viscount to Nerissa, and Nerissa knew her disquiet could not be hidden. Tempted to ask Mrs. Carroll to find Frye and send her to the sitting room, Nerissa remained silent. She could not air her domestic problems before her guests. She wondered what other orders Hadfield had ignored. If only Cole would chastise the impertinent butler! Surely Hadfield would listen to him. But that was unlikely to happen. Cole liked nothing to disturb the serenity in his house, so he would allow the situation to drift along unchanged while he clung to the comfort of his books.

And Nerissa didn't have time to worry about the butler when she was receiving both Windham brothers. She must keep her wits about her if she wanted to be a good hostess and hide the pleasure that had filled her at Lord Windham's arrival.

"Good afternoon, my lord," Nerissa said as she started to rise.

"Please remain seated, Miss Dufresne. I didn't call to disturb your recuperation," he answered in his warm voice that resounded through her like the tolling of a distant church bell.

As his smile swept the iciness from his eyes, Nerissa struggled to still her heart. When Lord Windham turned to his brother, she guessed the viscount did not share the unsettling, but decidedly delightful feeling within her. That thought troubled her more. Had the bump to her head unhinged her brain? She should care little about Lord Windham's sentiments. Standing, for she did not want to be put at a disadvantage by the viscount's impressive height, Nerissa kept a cautious hand on the chair.

"I thought I would find you here, Philip," Lord Windham said. "Have you forgotten the meeting you were supposed to have had at the King's Pump Room nearly an hour ago?"

"The King's Pump Room? Fudge!" Mr. Windham's face bared his astonishment, then his dismay. With an expression that belonged to a chagrined child, he bowed his head toward Nerissa. "Please excuse me, Miss Dufresne. I must go and make my apologies to . . ." Color rose brighter along his face. Again he dipped his head toward her before hurrying out of the room.

A low laugh rumbled over the closing of the door. She looked at Lord Windham. He put his hands in his trousers' pockets as he walked toward her. The motion pushed back the tails of his dark green double-breasted jacket which was open to reveal his silk waistcoat. A fall of lace dropped from his high collar and the perfectly tied white stock which accented the healthy color of his skin. Sunlight glinted off the gold buttons on his wide cuffs and along the front of his coat. His steps were effortless, and she imagined him as a primeval hunter stalking his prey. Stalking her?

Angry at her peculiar fancy, she said, "I did not expect a call from you, too, my lord."

"Forgive the pup, Miss Dufresne," Lord Windham said, as if she had not spoken, "for his lack of manners."

"I find Mr. Windham to be extraordinarily polite."

"Do you?" He paused too near to her.

Nerissa felt overmastered by his height and the breadth of his shoulders which eclipsed the doorway. Telling herself not to be a complete chucklehead, for Lord Windham would be delighted to put her out of curl, she gestured toward the chair where his brother had been sitting.

"Are you asking me to remain, Miss Dufresne?"

"Unless you, too, have a meeting."

"Regrettably, I do, but not for an hour. May I enjoy your company until then?"

"I would appreciate the chance to thank you properly."

"Deuce take it," he said as he motioned for her to sit. When she had, he followed suit. "You are going to stop thanking me for what was without question all my doing, aren't you? I daresay you would thank the hangman for finding a fine choker to set about your neck."

Nerissa frowned at his odd words. This viscount was acting like a rough diamond. "I doubt I would find myself in such a predicament."

He chuckled. "You think I'm a ramshackle fellow when I am only speaking plainly. If it makes you feel better, I accept your gratitude, if you'll accept my apology. Then we shall be done with this accursed happening."

Nerissa smiled in spite of herself. She need not be concerned about an unsteady conversation with this dark-haired man. The glint in his eyes suggested he was a flash at gab, even as it warned her that she must watch each word she chose.

"Ah, a smile. That is much more to the purpose," Lord Windham said. Crossing one brightly shined boot over the knee of his trousers, he leaned back as if she had invited him to run tame through her home. Suddenly he reached toward her and gripped her chin. Tilting her face, he cursed lowly. "I see you have fallen down and trodden upon your eye. This is odd. I must own, although I have landed a few facers in my youth, I never have given a lady a black eye."

"My lord, I assure you. . . ." Nerissa halted herself as his smile broadened. Knowing she should ask him to take his fancy manners from her home, she was startled when her lips tilted in an answering grin.

"Much better. Your smile tells me you are as well as can be expected. I have found, Miss Dufresne, that words are often false, but, upon watching a face with its quirks, the truth can be uncovered."

"I'm astounded. I didn't guess you to possess such rare talents that you could guess my thoughts before I spoke."

He laughed, the sound swirling through her

without the pain of the previous day. Instead it was accompanied by an undeniable happiness at being in the company of this handsome and needle-witted man.

"Such a skill would be of wonder, Miss Dufresne, for it would strip one's opponents as bare as birth. If I possessed such a gift, I wouldn't have needed to follow my brother here. I would have known you are suffering little damage."

"Considering that both of us could have been injured seriously, I think we should count ourselves lucky."

Lord Windham stood. "I can do nothing about your arm, Miss Dufresne, but . . ." Going to the door, he opened it and picked up a round box she had not seen when he entered. He closed the door. As he walked toward her, he held out the box, which was covered with pink silk and topped by a velvet ribbon. "For you."

"For me?" Nerissa flushed when she realized she sounded as if she was still in the schoolroom.

He placed the box in her lap, then—with a grimace as he saw she would have trouble undoing the red bow—he leaned forward to untie it. Lifting off the top, he urged, "Look inside, Miss Dufresne."

Nerissa pushed aside the tissue and pulled out a delicately made straw bonnet that was decorated with feathers and a silk ribbon of the most delicate blue she had ever seen. Its design was of the highest kick.

"If it isn't to your liking, Miss Dufresne," he continued, "you may return it to the millinery shop on—"

"It's lovely," she whispered, not caring that she interrupted him as she admired the fashionable bonnet. It must have cost him dear. "But, my lord, such a gift! I can't accept it!"

"It needs to be worn to be appreciated." He ignored her protests as, with a chuckle, he took the box and set it on the floor. "That is a direct quote from *Madame* de Ramel, the milliner who sold me this bonnet. She was curious about why I was buying this and for whom. You have made me the source of rumors throughout Bath, Miss Dufresne."

"It takes little for scandal to burst into being in Bath."

"That is part of its charm. Now shall we see if this hat is equally charming?"

Lord Windham's smile matched the amusement in his eyes as he settled the bonnet on her head. The long ribbons drooped onto Nerissa's sling, but he was mindful of her injury as he lifted them and tied the silk beneath her chin. Taking a step back, he nodded.

"*Madame* was right. The hat is much lovelier on. Don't think me lathering you, Miss Dufresne, when I say that it is perfect for you." He held out his hand as he pointed toward the looking glass set between the two windows. "Would you like to see how entrancing you look?" He hesitated, then asked in a more serious tone, "Do you need help?" He held out his hand.

Surprised by his considerate question and the warmth swirling through her, Nerissa hesitated. She should let him help her. She would have accepted any other man's assistance without faltering, but Lord Windham was different. She wasn't sure why, but the idea of touching his hand—even so chastely— frightened her. She didn't fear him, but her reaction to him. It was like nothing else she had ever felt.

Disdaining his hand, she stood quickly. Too quickly, she realized, when the room threatened to telescope into blackness. She took carefully calculated steps toward the pier glass. As she stood in front of it, the dark mist slowly faded to reveal her bruised face topped by the stylish hat. Lord Windham was correct. It *was* perfect for her. The ribbons accented the color of her eyes, and the stylish brim shadowed the bruises on her face.

She started to comment, but the words vanished, unspoken, when the mirror revealed Lord Windham standing behind her. His breath warmed her nape as he murmured, "Very nice."

For a moment, she was certain he had no idea how he threatened to overmaster her when he stood so close to her. Then, when she saw the hint of challenge in his smile, she knew he was acutely aware of every motion he made and how it affected those around him. She would not allow him to put her out of countenance with his pranks. When she faced him, she was amazed when he did not step away.

Boldly, he touched the fringe hanging from her sling. "I hope the damage to your arm can be dealt with as swiftly as your hat, Miss Dufresne."

"As I told Mr. Windham, time will be the best healer." Running her other hand along the fringe, she pushed his fingers aside in what she hoped would appear to be a casual motion. "To own the truth," she added, as she turned away, "I wear this to satisfy my anxious abigail. She wishes to see me cosseted in bed with plenty of tea and cookies, as if I was still in short coats. I'd as lief wear this than suffer her distress."

"You are wise." He glanced toward the clock. "Forgive me, but I must end this fascinating meeting, Miss Dufresne. May we continue it at Mr. Rowland's party tomorrow evening?"

"I am afraid not. I wasn't invited."

"Then allow me to rectify that." He smiled as she opened her mouth to protest. "Don't think me a ramshackle cove again. I assure you that I'm not. At least, not now. Rowland is having an open house for those who enjoy playing a few hands of cards. Do you find that a pleasant pastime?"

"Yes," she said, then wished she had remained silent as he took her hand and bowed over it. His skin was not soft like Cole's. Its coarse caress inspired a renewed pulse within her, not of pain, but a sensation as potent. She held her breath as she wondered would he be so brazen as to kiss her fingers as his brother had attempted and what she would do if he did?

Her worries were allayed when he raised his head. "My carriage and I are at your disposal, Miss Dufresne. Shall nine o'clock be convenient for me to call for you?"

Nerissa smiled. He must not guess how bewildered she felt. When had she lost control of the conversation? She must regain mastery of it and herself before Lord Windham called again. If she failed, she did not want to consider what the consequences might be.

# Chapter Four

Rain splattered on the walkway when Nerissa emerged from the carriage. Drawing her shawl closer around the shoulders of her white muslin gown so it covered the lacy sling, she was glad she had left the lovely bonnet Lord Windham had given her yesterday at home. The white chip hat she wore tilted back on her head, revealing too many of the bruises on her face, she realized when a gentleman hurried past, then turned to regard her with an openmouthed gawk. He nearly collided with a wrought-iron fence before turning to vanish into the misty rain.

Nerissa took a deep breath and tried to force a smile. The motion hurt her face, so she gave up the attempt as she went to the door with its curved window above it in the center of Camden Crescent.

The Ehrlich family had lived in the elegant town house since shortly after it had been built. The tall columns along the first and second floor did not match the simplicity of the ground floor. As she stepped out of the rain, Nerissa smiled at the image of an elephant carved in the lintel. Such frivolity did not fit the fancy row of houses, but it suited Annis perfectly.

When the door was opened by a smiling *major domo*, she thought wistfully how wondrous it would be to be greeted each time she returned to Laura Place by such a friendly face. "Good afternoon, Cunliffe. Is Miss Annis at home this afternoon?"

"You know she is always home to you, Miss Dufresne." The short, muscular man, who appeared as though he would be more comfortable in a boxing match than in the navy and scarlet livery of the Ehrlich family, opened the door wider. "I shall . . ."

Nerissa was not to find out what he planned to do, for his words ended in a strangled gurgle as she stepped into the broad entrance hall. With the light from the brass chandelier emphasizing the malevolent colors of her bruises, she was not surprised by his reaction.

He mumbled something and scurried away to find Annis. Touching the puffiness on her cheek, Nerissa sighed. She had no intention of staying hidden in her house until the outward signs of the accident healed.

On the street side of the foyer, small curtains bunched over the top of the tall windows, letting in what little light had oozed through the grey clouds. Two mirrors offered her the opportunity to check her appearance. One was hung between the windows; the other set over a small table placed next to a door that led to another corridor beyond and the servants' stairs to the kitchen in the cellar. As she crossed the wooden floor with its inlaid pattern of circles and flowers, she avoided looking in the mirrors.

"Nerissa!" came a shout from the top of the curving stairs to the left. Annis Ehrlich ran down them at an indecorous pace.

Annis had the misfortune to resemble her dour-faced father instead of her glorious mother. With two older sisters who were the epitome of Mrs. Ehrlich's beauty, Annis had accustomed herself to living in the shadow of their splendor. Not that she was not dainty of ankle or prettily spoken, but Annis's drooping locks and plain features caused people—who did not look close enough—to fail to note her sweet smile and the twinkle of gaiety in her brown eyes.

From the moment Nerissa had been introduced to Annis, she had liked the woman who was nearly of her age. Annis had been kind and acquainted Nerissa with the many and oftentimes strange customs of Bath and its society which were as strict as the *ton* in London. When Annis had included Nerissa in parties hostessed by Annis's recently married sister, she had helped Nerissa to meet the people who had dismissed Cole as not having a spark of spirit to brighten their conversations.

Dressed today in a muslin dress with bishop's sleeves that were decorated with golden ribbons, she hurried forward to take Nerissa's hands in slim fingers. Tears glittered in her wide eyes.

"Oh, my dearest Nerissa, look at you. You have fallen down and trodden on your eye."

"It is rather black, isn't it?" she asked with a smile as they walked up the stairs and into the cozy parlor which looked out over the street. She was glad when she discovered the room was empty. The rest of the Ehrlich family was troublesome at best, and Nerissa was honestly not at her most patient today.

Nerissa laughed as Annis cooed over her with dismay while ringing for tea. Lightly, Nerissa said, "I can vow that I look much worse than I feel today. If you had called yesterday, I could not have said the same."

"Dear me, dear me, look at your face. It has put me quite to the stare. It's nearly the purple shade of the ribbons on your gown. How long will you have to remain quiet before you can come for a ride with me again?" She put her hand to her full bosom. "Dear me, listen to me! How can I speak to you of plans for taking a ride when if we had gone in the carriage yesterday this would never have happened? What kind of friend abandons her dearest bosom bow to go for a walk alone and allows something like this to happen? I swear that I cried myself to sleep last night when Mama told me that you were hurt. If you wish for me to—"

Putting her fingers on Annis's arm to interrupt her, Nerissa said soothingly, "Sit down, and stop babbling. You are making yourself overwrought over nothing. It was but an accident. It could have happened to anyone."

"But it happened to you!" A sigh burst from her. "And 'tis all my doing."

"Nonsense. It was none of your doing. Lord Windham merely—"

"Lord Windham? Hamilton Windham?" Her eyes grew even wider. *"He did this to you?"*

Nerissa sat on a comfortable chair and smiled when Annis pushed an embroidered stool toward her. Setting her feet on it compliantly, she leaned back and said, "It was only an accident."

"'Wastrel Windam' does nothing by accident, if one is to believe *on dits.*"

Nerissa's brow furrowed, but she ignored the pain for the first time. "I find your words unseemly. The viscount was very gracious, Annis. It's unlike you to speak unkindly of someone you don't know." She faltered, her coolness fading into uncertainty. "Or do you know him?"

"Only *of* him." Annis wrung her hands as she perched on the edge of a green silk settee. "It was rumored he would wed Elinor Howe, who was the widow of his best friend." She lowered her voice to a conspiratorial whisper. "They were constantly together in London. Constantly together, if you understand what I mean."

"I understand," she answered emotionlessly.

"Then he set Mrs. Howe aside and came here to Bath. It was most mysterious. You should be grateful you escaped with only an abrased face, for he has made no attachment to any woman since, although he has kept company with many."

She shrugged, trying to appear nonchalant. The words oddly disturbed her, for she had guessed Lord Windham to be a man of honor. Not that such habits would label him anything but a member of the *ton*. The flirtations they enjoyed were nothing like the quiet existence she knew with her brother.

"All I can say is that he was the perfect gentleman with me."

"Gentleman maybe," came a shrill voice from the doorway, "but I doubt if anyone—even you, Nerissa, in your charity—would call Lord Windham perfect."

Nerissa had to struggle to keep from frowning. Janelle Ehrlich was the opposite of her sister. As lovely as the first morning of spring, she had a temper as fiery as August heat and a demeanor as unwelcome as a January sunset. Swaying into the room, her wrapper a delicate shade of pink to accent her golden hair, she dropped next to her sister. A servant followed, carrying a tea tray set for two. Janelle did not wait for the others, but helped herself to a cake and a cup of the steaming tea.

"Do *you* know the viscount?" Nerissa asked, offering Annis a smile when her friend handed her the other cup. She was glad Annis had seen how difficult it would be for her to pick up the cup.

"I have seen him at various gatherings," Janelle said with a superior tilt of her pert nose. "He is a peculiar man, strikingly handsome, I will own, but interested only in those woman whose reputations have become questionable. Mayhap he wishes not to risk another disastrous liaison like the one with Elinor Howe."

Annis laughed shortly. "Do not act so top-lofty, Janelle. You aren't telling us anything that hasn't been poker-talk since last year." With a wink to her friend, she added in a stern tone, "I am sure Nerissa has no interest in hearing the viscount disparaged when he was kind enough to treat her graciously."

Playing with the ribbons that accented the full curves beneath her wrapper, Janelle cooed, "Are you sure of that? Nerissa, you are positively agog with this, aren't you? Did he knock all sense from your skull?"

"I know very little about the viscount, other than reading in the newspaper that he was in attendance at some of the *soirées* about Bath," she had to own, although she hated giving Janelle the upper hand.

With another tilt of her round chin, Janelle laughed. "Oh, Nerissa, you are ever a goose! You are too much like Annis. You think some glorious knight on his white charger will come seeking your heart. You should as lief concentrate on finding a *beau* who will offer you a comfortable life and a family."

"Like your Mr. Oakley?" Annis returned. "What did I hear Mama call him yesterday? Comfortably dull and well-fixed."

"Mr. Oakley is a charming *beau*." Rising, she set the cup back on the table. "Annis, you are so jealous of his attentions to me that you have become intolerable of late."

As her sister flounced out of the room, every inch the wounded soul, Annis chuckled behind her hand. "She is welcome to her Mr. Oakley. He is not comfortably dull. He is *just* dull!" Taking a frosted cake from the plate, she sighed. "Of course, when Mama has succeeded in finding a husband for Janelle, she will turn her matchmaking eye upon me. I have heard her making plans to spend next Season in London. She despairs, I believe, of ever finding me a husband in Bath." A dimple appeared in each cheek. "Mayhap because I have told her there is not one among the lot that I would consider."

Nerissa lowered the teacup. The steam clawed her

aching face. Balancing it on her lap, she asked, "Was what Janelle said true? Lord Windham seemed very much the gentleman both times I spoke with him."

"Both times?" Annis's eyes widened. "He has called on you?"

"Only to ascertain the state of my recovery."

"Will he be calling again?"

Nerissa noted a shadow near the door of the parlor. No doubt, Janelle was eavesdropping, hoping to learn something she could repeat while sipping scandal broth with her friends. She would not give Annis's sister that pleasure. Putting her cup on the table, she rose awkwardly.

Annis's face grew long with dismay. "Nerissa, have I said something to disturb you? Or—and you must think me a beast to forget your injuries—are you in pain?"

"I am fine," she lied, not wanting to reveal the truth. If it reached Frye's ears, her abigail would insist that she remain in bed. "And, of course, you have said nothing to set up my bristles. I have a few errands to run. Would you like to join me?" She glanced toward the door again. "We can enjoy some private prittle-prattle while I shop."

With a smile, Annis nodded. "Private, it shall be."


A potpourri of pungent odors welcomed Nerissa as she and Annis entered a shop near the corner of Great Pulteney and William Streets. Her nose was tickled by bits of the various varieties of snuff that filled Mrs. Peach's shop. As she waited for her eyes to adjust to the darkness, she stared at the clay pots lining the shelves behind the counter.

Annis was surprisingly silent, as she had been since Nerissa had told her that Lord Windham was escorting her to a small party that evening at Mr. Rowland's house. Annis had been scandalized by the invitation and shocked that Nerissa had accepted.

"He is rakehell, Nerissa," she had gasped. "You will ruin your reputation being seen with him."

"He has been nothing but a gentleman to me, and I could see nothing wrong with agreeing to go with him and his brother this evening."

"Frye must be—"

"Frye is putting herself into a stew about everything at the moment." Laughing, she patted her friend's hand. "It is but one evening, and I know he wishes to atone for his thoughtlessness that caused the accident. Could I be so uncivil as to deny him that chance?"

Annis had scowled before replying, "I suppose not." Those were the last words she had uttered.

Nerissa tried not to think of her friend's dismay. Her thoughts should be on what she would purchase. It was useless, for she longed to beg Annis's forgiveness. Her friend only worried that she was doing something jobbernowl.

The shopkeeper's familiar voice interrupted her thoughts. She smiled as she greeted Mrs. Peach.

"Good day, Miss Ehrlich, Miss Dufresne," said Mrs. Peach in her scratchy voice. She stared at Nerissa and choked, "Miss Dufresne!"

"It is nothing," Nerissa answered as she had so many times.

"'Tis a shame," grumbled the old woman, whose hands were stained from the snuff she sold.

"Soon it will be nothing but a memory and an amusing anecdote."

The shopkeeper seemed unconvinced, but turned to speak to Annis. As she listened to her friend reply to the shopkeeper's questions, Nerissa calculated how much she needed to buy and, more importantly, how much she could afford. She frowned as she tried to figure the total in her head.

"So down pinned?" asked a friendly voice behind her.

She smiled when Mr. Windham tipped his topper to her. His clothes were as usual *à la modality*. His coat was of the warmest russet shade and his nankeen pantaloons properly secured under his shoes. As he set his hat back on his head, the gold buttons on his coat flashed in the faint light from the lamp behind the counter.

"What a pleasant surprise!" she exclaimed.

"How kind of you to say that! May I return the kindness and say that it is grand to see you looking so hale?"

"I am glad you think so. Everyone else today has been too solicitous of my health."

He chuckled. "You do not take coddling well, I collect."

"She *should* be coddled after what she suffered!" Annis burst into the conversation and continued before Nerissa could warn her to watch her words. "When that profligate Lord Windham failed to watch where he was going, Nerissa was the one to suffer."

"Annis . . ." Nerissa cautioned.

"You need not defend that ramshackle fellow, Nerissa," her friend returned with fire. "I know he brought you back to Laura Place, but . . ." She turned to include Mr. Windham in her fury. ". . . he thinks to repair the damage with nothing more than an invitation to a rout. Nerissa could have been killed, although she is too generous to speak of it."

Watching Mr. Windham's face, which was for once as blank as his brother's could be, Nerissa wished she could silence her friend. She knew how futile any attempt to quell Annis's righteous rage would be.

"I am certain Lord Windham intended no harm to Miss Dufresne," he said quietly.

"It matters little what he *intended*. Look at her!"

"I have been," he said, his smile returning, "and I

am pleased to see her looking so well. Miss Dufresne, would you be so kind as to introduce me to your friend?"

Nerissa took a deep breath to steady her voice, then said, "Miss Annis Ehrlich, this is Mr. Philip Windham, Lord Windham's brother."

Annis's intense color became ghostly as she pressed her fingertips to her lips. "Mr. Windham, I had no idea . . . I mean, I meant nothing . . ."

"Of course you meant something." His smile softened his words, as he added, "You have every right to come to the defense of your bosom bow, and I must tell you that your fervor is admirable. My brother and I have been haunted by the horror of the injuries Miss Dufresne has suffered." Taking Annis's hand, he shook it gravely. "It is *my* pleasure to make your acquaintance, Miss Ehrlich."

Annis looked at Nerissa for assistance. Nerissa tried to think of something to fill the troublesome silence. She knew her words sounded strained when she said, "We are doing errands, Mr. Windham. What has brought you out on this dreary day?"

"The hope of finding something more pleasant than my own company." His smile broadened, and Nerissa realized this Windham brother had been given a share of the charm his brother possessed. "I believe I have."

Mrs. Peach called, "Miss Dufresne?"

Nerissa hesitated, then realized that Annis was laughing at something Mr. Windham was saying. The tension had vanished with his candor. Leaving them to talk, she gave her order to the shopkeeper. Nerissa watched Mrs. Peach measure out the snuff from the clay jar behind her counter. The sharp smell tickled her nose, but she struggled not to sneeze as the older woman prattled on about what a fine young man Nerissa's brother was to recognize the qualities of Martinique snuff.

"And a packet of Spanish Sabilla, too," Nerissa said when Mrs. Peach had wrapped the package for Cole.

"Your brother is trying some of that brand again? When you did not order it upon your last visit, I thought he had decided it was not to his taste."

Nerissa smiled rather than answered. She guessed Mrs. Peach, who was an avid user of the snuffs she sold, would be outraged if she learned that Nerissa used the finely ground, reddish powder to clean her teeth. Taking her package, she turned and gasped.

Neither Annis nor Mr. Windham was in the shop. Was Annis all about in her head to wander away with a man she had only just met? After the dressing down she had given Nerissa, it seemed impossible.

Rushing out onto the street, Nerissa grimaced when water splashed from a puddle over her half-boots. Her frown became astonishment when she saw her friend standing next to Lord Windham's brother and pointing to something in the shop window next to Mrs. Peach's store. With their heads tipped toward each other, they were chatting as if they enjoyed a deep *amitié*.

Nerissa released the breath she had been holding. Walking to them, she said regretfully, "We told your mother we would return immediately, Annis, so we must bid Mr. Windham *adieu*."

"I trust I shall see you again," Mr. Windham hurried to say as he shook Annis's hand lingeringly. "Mayhap at Rowland's gathering this evening?"

Before she could answer, a laugh sounded behind Nerissa. It sent a trill of pleasure cascading through her. Looking over her shoulder, she hoped her reaction was hidden. It would be cockle-brained of her to allow Lord Windham to discover that she was finding it difficult to ignore how the warmth of his voice and his devilishly charming smile affected her.

"Is this to become a habit, Philip? I am constantly

finding you in the company of Bath's loveliest ladies." Lord Windham smiled.

"Hamilton, I don't believe you know Miss Ehrlich," Mr. Windham said. "Miss Ehrlich, my brother."

The viscount greeted Annis, and they shared the proper nothing-sayings for such a meeting. Only then did he turn to Nerissa. "I did not realize that purple was becoming the shade of choice for a lady's cheeks, but it is most becoming, Miss Dufresne."

"Hamilton!" gasped his shocked brother.

"Do not let him disturb you with his tactlessness, Mr. Windham," Nerissa said as she met the viscount's smile with a steady stare. "He thinks only of trying to send me up to the boughs with his backhanded compliments, but I can assure you that he has failed. I have found that I enjoy being purple-faced to being a red-faced rider who cannot see past the tip of his mount's nose."

Mr. Windham chuckled, ignoring his brother's glower in his direction. Annis laughed lightly, again putting her fingers to her lips, but she was unable to try to halt the merry sound.

"I deserve that trimming, Miss Dufresne," Lord Windham said as he watched his brother stroll with Annis toward the next shop window. "Even after our brief acquaintance, I should know better than to cross words with you. Now I suppose I should ask Miss Ehrlich's pardon. She has certainly caught Philip's eye. I hope that she has not taken snuff at my crude words."

Nerissa could not help laughing when he glanced at the tobacco shop as he apologized. "Fortunately Miss Ehrlich does not take insult easily, my lord, but you would be wise to delay your amends until later. I think Annis is quite as taken by your brother as he is with her. Little we say or do will penetrate the song created by two innocent hearts."

"How astute you are! However, Miss Dufresne, if I may be so bold as to speak of your health again, you should be off your feet. Purple is the sole hue on your face. I have seen dead men with more color in their cheeks." He offered his arm.

She gratefully put her hand on it. Although she had not wished anyone to guess, her head ached as if a dozen gnomes pounded hammers against her skull. His shoulder was tantalizingly close, but she did not dare to rest her cheek against it when they stood on the busy street. She wondered if it would be as soft as she recalled it being when they sat side by side beneath the tree beyond the hedgerow, or if it would be as hard as the muscles in his arm.

If Lord Windham noted how she leaned on him as they walked, he was kind enough to say nothing of it. She was glad, for she had little energy left to engage in another dagger-drawing with him.

When they passed Mr. Windham and Annis, the viscount tapped his brother on the shoulder. Upon getting Philip's attention which had been focused on Annis's charming tale of her sister's latest *fête,* he motioned for them to follow. "It is quick, is it not?" he mused as they continued toward where her carriage waited by the curb.

Nerissa glanced back to be sure that Annis was not lagging behind, becoming so caught up in the first flush of a flirtation that she forgot herself. "If you mean the warmth of attraction, I must agree with you in the case of your brother and my friend. They seemed overmastered by it from the moment they first spoke." She laughed. "*Almost* from the moment they first spoke."

"*Almost from the moment?* Did Philip bowl her over as I did you?"

Nerissa explained the meeting in the shop, then added, "Annis is a dear friend, and she leaps to my defense at every chance."

"I see Philip has set her worries to rest about the accident, and you have to own that he chose a more charming way to meet her than I did to meet you." His voice softened. "I am truly glad to see you out of your house. I trust that means you soon will be regaining the pretty pink in your cheeks. Savage that I am, I have endured the jesting of my good fellows which I so rightly deserve for failing to watch where I set Cirrus. No doubt I shall be forced to suffer their well-placed gibes this evening."

"If you would as lief that I did not attend . . ."

"What a rapper! Of certainty you must attend, Miss Dufresne. There have been cruel rumors of your untimely demise circulating—at my expense, if you wish to know the truth. I beseech you to make your high health known before I find myself in deadly suspense at the end of a hangman's noose."

Nerissa laughed. "My lord, humility doesn't come easily from your lips."

His grey eyes twinkled with mischief as he took her gloved hand between his. She gasped at his forward motion as they stood in the middle of the walkway. A pulse of the same, delightful warmth she had felt when he stood so close to her in the parlor raced along her limbs, coiling through her middle. The slow smile on his expressive lips stirred the gentle heat to a flame.

Without speaking, he brought her hand to his mouth. His ashen gaze threatened to overwhelm her with the passions she could see within it. Her eyes closed when he touched her hand so fleetingly with his lips. All of her being focused on that spot where his breath seeped through her gloves to set her skin afire.

Something struck her sore face, and Nerissa choked back a moan. She opened her eyes to see Lord Windham looking skyward. Lazy drops of rain splashed into the puddle at her feet.

"Allow us to see you and Miss Ehrlich home and out of the storm," he said, his voice once again unemotional.

"That is unnecessary. My carriage is right here." She watched as Annis hurried to climb into the tired-looking carriage with Mr. Windham's assistance.

Lord Windham handed her in as graciously. "Then I bid you a farewell until this evening, Miss Dufresne." He released her hand as his smile included both women. "If you did not believe my words before, I hope that you will now when I say that I look forward to that hour with great anticipation."

"So do I," she answered softly, so softly she was unsure if he heard them as he urged his brother to hurry toward their own carriage. Not that it mattered, for she suspected Lord Windham already had discerned the longings of her rebellious heart which pulsed faster at the thought of spending the evening with him.

# Chapter Five

Hamilton watched Miss Dufresne's carriage drive away through the rain. Stepping back under an awning, he motioned for his brother, who was staring after the vehicle as if his eyes were tied to it.

"Philip!" he called, then laughed. "Miss Ehrlich will have little use for you if you prove you don't have the sense God gave a goose and stand out there in the rain."

With a sheepish grin, his brother trotted beneath the awning. "She is wonderful."

"I am sure she is."

At Hamilton's distant tone, Philip turned to face him. "Is something amiss? I thought you were having a pleasant conversation with Miss Dufresne."

"You can take the carriage home. I will join you later."

"Hamilton . . ."

He forced a smile he hoped would soon be genuine. "I have just a bit of business I need to attend to while you think of what you wish to say to Miss Ehrlich in the note I'm sure you are composing in your head even now."

"I had hoped to ask her to join us this evening at Rowland's," he said in an almost shy voice.

Hamilton cursed silently. After seeing how low

love had brought him, his brother should know better than to get so moony about a woman after a single meeting. He would have to set Philip to rights, but it must be later. He was already late for his meeting.

Bending his head into the drizzle, he strode along the street. It had been a pleasant conversation with Miss Dufresne, and he had been honest when he said he looked forward to seeing her this evening, but that would be the end of the matter. Once the "Polite World" discovered she was up and about, his duty to her would be ended.

If only her blue eyes were not so lustrous and her laugh so enticing. . . . He shook his head. He was no pup like Philip, who was ready to embark upon his first tangle with love. After Elinor had betrayed him, he had forsworn any such webs of sweet deception again. Better it would be for him to concentrate on the true reason he had come to Bath.

The vegetable stalls near the bridge were almost deserted, so Hamilton was able to spot his man immediately. Mallory, if he recalled the name correctly, looked as out of place among the few shoppers as a saddle on a sow. The man, who was bulky and cut off like a weathered stump, did not pause to look at any of the offered wares. Nor did he seek shelter under the roof of one of the stalls from the increasing rain. He stood, as resolute as a street lamp, and stared at the people passing him.

His eyes became dark slits in his full face as Hamilton walked toward him. In lieu of a greeting, Mallory simply nodded. Hamilton motioned toward the street. They would attract less notice if they walked through the surprisingly chilly rain while they talked.

"Arrived on the Mail yesterday," Mallory said with an accent that labelled his birthplace as the heart of

London. "I know what ye want me to be doin', milord."

"You are familiar with what has been unearthed so far?"

He spat into the street and snorted. "Nothin' worthwhile. Can't find a man when all ye do is ask about. Should have sent fer me months ago. Now it'll be harder to find yer man."

"Townsend recommends you highly."

"I be one of 'is best." Mallory hooked his thumbs into the lapels of his wet coat that strained across his full belly. "Not a thief whom I can't take, milord."

Hamilton ignored the round man's boasting. Whether it was true or not mattered little to him. Townsend's Bow Street Runners had an excellent reputation for finding their prey, especially as thief-takers. The last man Hamilton had hired had proven to be a miserable failure. Mallory could be no worse, and there was a chance he might do better, even though the trail had grown cold in Bath.

"I shall expect regular reports on your progress," he said coolly.

"Ye're paying, milord. What ye wants I'll get ye."

"I will let you know where we can meet. Understandably, it would not do for you to appear on the doorstep of my house."

"Understandably." He rubbed his fingers against his unshaven jaw. "As fer an 'ouse, milord . . ."

Hamilton withdrew a handful of coins and dropped them in the man's palm which was lined with dirt. "This should be enough for you to hire a suitable lodging. Send me an address where I can reach you."

"Aye, milord."

The man appeared to be waiting for Hamilton to add more, but he had nothing else to say to the Runner. Mallory's smile faded when Hamilton remained silent, and the shorter man edged away. Hamilton brushed past him to find a hired carriage to take him back to Queen Square. He did not look back.


Mrs. Ehrlich flowed into the room, clicking her tongue at the bedraggled state of her least daughter. With her blond hair, that was laced liberally with silver, half-hidden beneath a frilled mob cap and an elegant gown of white cambric, which displayed her still superb figure, she always delighted in making a grand entrance, no matter how small the audience.

"Annis, look at you! As drenched and bedraggled as yesterday's newspaper."

"Mama!" She ran forward to take her mother's hands. "I have had the most wondrous afternoon."

Mrs. Ehrlich looked past her, still frowning. "And, Nerissa, you are as wet! Have you misplaced every lick of common sense? You both should be soaking in warm tubs before you catch your deaths of cold."

"Mama!" Annis refused to be ignored. "I met a charming man while we were about on our errands."

"How nice for you, my dear. Do bid Nerissa a good afternoon so you can get freshened up before Mr. Oakley calls upon your sister."

"He asked if I would like to join him for a *soirée* this evening."

Nerissa hid her smile when Mrs. Ehrlich opened her mouth to give her daughter another order, then slowly closed it, surprise widening her blue eyes. The startled woman gasped, "You met a man and let him offer you an invitation? Just like that?"

"Mama, Nerissa introduced us."

Mrs. Ehrlich's smile returned, but it was calculating. Nerissa could almost hear the thoughts in Mrs. Ehrlich's head. With Annis's oldest sister married satisfactorily and Janelle soon to be if Mr. Oakley proposed as they expected, a chance meeting could prove a boon to a mother who had anticipated difficulty in finding a man to buckle himself to her youngest, most stubborn daughter.

"How sweet of you, Nerissa," she cooed, all dismay gone from her voice. "You are so kind to do this for Annis when you are in the market for a *beau* yourself."

"Mama!" Exasperation spilled from every pore of Annis's indignant body. She flashed Nerissa an apologetic smile. Nerissa wanted to tell her not to worry. By this time, she was accustomed to Mrs. Ehrlich's single-minded pursuit of a husband for each of her daughters. Nothing else—not even friendships—must be allowed to stand in the way of finding suitable matches for her daughters.

"Hush, Annis," her mother said. "Calm yourself and then tell me about this lucky encounter."

"We were at Mrs. Peach's shop when Mr. Windham—"

"Windham?" Her smile became a furious frown. "Where was your head, Annis? Do you think I would let you be seen in *his* company?"

"Not Lord Windham, Mama. His brother." She sighed and closed her eyes, joy burning brightly on her face. "He is a gentleman, Mama, even forgiving me for my unthinking words about the viscount."

"Which are undoubtedly true."

"Which are no more than poker-talk," Nerissa said quietly. She did not look away when Mrs. Ehrlich affixed her with one of her infamous glowers. Lord Windham had done nothing for her to cause her to disparage him or listen to his name ridiculed.

"This was your idea, I take it." Mrs. Ehrlich's indignity burned in her eyes.

"As Annis said, we met Mr. Windham at Mrs. Peach's shop." She saw no reason to complicate the conversation by adding that the viscount had been present as well. "He spoke with us and was most taken with Annis. You can be sure Annis did nothing to cause you alarm."

"Except considering this untoward invitation—"

"Mama, Mr. Windham simply asked—"

"—which, of course, you cannot accept until Mr. Windham has presented himself to me for my approval." The devious expression returned to her face. "That should prove most interesting."

Annis turned to Nerissa, but Nerissa had no idea what to say. Mrs. Ehrlich would not change her mind on this, for she was determined that each of her daughters would marry a man of first respectability. Leaving Mrs. Ehrlich to contemplate that meeting, Nerissa went to the door with her friend.

"Shall I inform Mr. Windham of your regrets?" she asked, wishing she could find a way to convince Annis not to drop down on herself. So seldom did she see her friend melancholy, she was unsure how to cheer her.

"No," Annis answered with soft sorrow, "I shall send him a note explaining Mama's insistence upon meeting him first."

She smiled. "He will understand. It is *comme il faut.*"

"I hope so." Her eyes began to glow with happiness again and just a hint of her mother's cunning. "I hope Mama understands, too. I intend to see Mr. Windham again—no matter what she decides."


"Miss Dufresne, I cannot believe you intend to go out this evening." Frye folded her arms over the drooping shelf of her breast. Frowning, she regarded her lady from top to bottom.

Except for the fringed sling, she could find

nothing to criticize about her charge's clothes. Although almost a year old, Nerissa's gown was a lovely sprigged muslin of an ephemeral blue. Its high bodice and modest *décolletage* flattered Nerissa's delicate curves. With her hair piled *à la* Sappho about her crown, only the ebony lace draped around her neck to cradle her arm and her bruises marred the image.

Frye's frown became more rigid as her gaze settled on the puffy discoloring on Nerissa's cheek. "Miss Dufresne, are you listening to me?"

"Every word," Nerissa said, smiling as she struggled to draw on her unheeled slippers. Rows of fine lace decorated their silk toes. She never had guessed it would be so difficult to manage otherwise simple tasks with one hand.

"Can I dare to believe that you have reconsidered?"

"Lord Windham would think me to have been born at Hogs Norton if I declined his invitation at this late hour."

"Mrs. Ehrlich refused to let Miss Annis go until she had the opportunity to meet Mr. Windham herself to judge if he is suitable to call upon her daughter. I wish you would introduce the viscount to your brother."

"Cole? Oh, Frye, you know he thinks of nothing but his canal." She laughed merrily. "I would not ask him to concern himself with an invitation to a quiet gathering."

"He is your brother. Lord Windham should have sought his pardon as well as yours for what has happened."

"Nonsense!" She reached for the pink hatbox and lifted the top to remove the beautiful hat.

Frye glanced over Nerissa's shoulder and gasped, "Where did you get that?"

"It was a gift. A get-well gift," she added when Nerissa heard her abigail gasp in horror. "Actually,

Lord Windham purchased it to replace the one ruined in the accident.''

As she cautiously set the hat on her hair, she noticed again how the sides dipped down from the brim to conceal her upper cheeks. While Frye rearranged the ribbons under her chin—for the abigail always had to fiddle with Nerissa's clothes in some way—Nerissa smiled. The silk ribbons around the brim ended with a profusion of bows at the square crown. They would steal anyone's attention from the shadowed contusions on her face.

The rattle of carriage wheels slowing to a stop in front of the house urged her to open the dark blue curtains and peek out. Again Frye chastised her, but Nerissa just laughed lightly. This was the first time she had been invited to a gathering in Bath without being considered an appendage of the Ehrlich family. She would not let her aching arm steal her excitement.

When the housekeeper came to announce that the gentlemen were arriving, Mrs. Carroll's broad smile added to the flutter in Nerissa's center, but she remembered to be cautious as she walked down the stairs with Frye following close behind.

"Mr. Pilcher is in his book room, of course," Mrs. Carroll said in answer to Nerissa's question. "If you wish me to ask Hadfield to get him—I own to not wishing to interrupt Mr. Pilcher myself when he left such specific instructions about not being bothered— I can—''

"No, no," Nerissa said hastily. "If Cole asks where I am, please inform him. I should be home early. I understand this is an informal gathering.''

"Of course.'' The housekeeper looked relieved.

As they reached the foyer, a knock sounded on the door. Mrs. Carroll hurried to pull it open, grumbling about the butler who never seemed about his post. Agreeing with her mutely, Nerissa promised herself to do something about the matter . . . tomorrow.

The least bit of irritation at Hadfield oozed away into silence when Lord Windham entered the wreath of candlelight from the brass light in the middle of the foyer ceiling. The glow gave an auburn glow to his dark hair and brightened the white of his immaculate cravat and breeches. As he reached for her hand and bowed over it politely, she noticed how the navy velvet of his coat was decorated with buttons as bright as his gold vest. His shoes shone with what must have been hours of attention.

"Good evening, my lord," Nerissa said softly, for the quiver in her center had become a tempest of some sensation that was halfway between pleasure and uneasy anticipation.

When he released her hand, she wished she could think of an excuse to offer it to him again. His gentle grip had sent warm rivers of delight up her arm.

Lord Windham stepped aside and smiled. For the first time, she noticed his brother had entered the house as well. She greeted Mr. Windham warmly.

"Were you waiting for us, Miss Dufresne?" asked Lord Windham. "This is a rare pleasure."

"If you wish me to keep you waiting—as apparently you see as the obligation of your acquaintances—you need only to sit and cool your heels by the hearth."

Lord Windham laughed, but Frye frowned at the unseemly words. Nerissa clamped her lips closed. Even her mishap, which had left her bruised and aching, did not give her the excuse of speaking before she thought. She was about to apologize, but her gaze was swallowed by the unexplored depths of Lord Windham's grey eyes. Every thought . . . reasonable or otherwise . . . became jumbled.

"Miss Dufresne," the viscount said with another rumble of laughter, "you are refreshing at the end of this long summer. Don't you think so, Philip?"

The younger man's mouth was twisted, and she

knew he was struggling not to embarrass himself with a laugh. A touch of it escaped as he said, "I have said that since the first."

"Then, as we all are in agreement—a most uncommon circumstance, I suspect—shall we be on our way?" The viscount accepted Nerissa's cape from Mrs. Carroll and settled it on her shoulders, taking care not to jostle her left arm. "May I say also that I am pleased you have chosen to wear this bonnet?"

She let him draw her fingers into his arm and was suffused anew with pleasure. To cover her disquiet with the sensations, she said to Mrs. Carroll, who was standing by the door, "Please ask Cole not to wait up for me. I know he prefers to seek his bed early."

"Yes, Miss Dufresne," she answered dutifully, but Nerissa noted the door did not close immediately as they walked down the steps to the street with Frye in tow. She guessed Mrs. Carroll was enjoying the opportunity to be the first beneath the stairs to have a bit of gossip about Miss Dufresne's life, which had been decidedly boring, up until the past few days.

Only when they were comfortable in the crested carriage—with Frye and Nerissa facing the two men, who politely rode backwards—did Lord Windham say, "I assume Cole is your brother, Miss Dufresne."

"Yes," Nerissa said as she ran her fingers clandestinely along the royal-blue velvet of the carriage's thick seats. Thinking of the uncomfortable cart she had ridden in during the trip from Hill's End, she tried to imagine having this luxury about her all the time. It was impossible. "I came to Bath to manage my brother's household upon the death of our parents."

"Your brother has a reputation for being a recluse."

"He has immersed himself in a project that is very dear to his heart. I respect him for his diligence." She was aware of Frye gauging every word she spoke. No doubt from listening to the same rumors Nerissa had heard, the abigail was not pleased with this evening's plans. After the many times Frye had lambasted her for choosing to sit home instead of taking part in the whirl of Bath's society, Nerissa was astonished at her abigail's disapproval of the viscount and his brother.

Mr. Windham interjected, "May I say, Miss Dufresne, that your color looks much better this evening than even this afternoon? I trust you are feeling more hale."

"As your brother intimated to me today, if purple is a shade signalling high health," she said more sharply than she had intended, for Frye's odd silence was vexing, "then I have it in abundance."

The young man flushed until his brother slapped him companionably on the arm and urged, "Philip, she is funning you. You must learn to tell the difference between Miss Dufresne's jests and the piercing comments that are meant to wound. She seems to favor you only with the former."

"And you, my lord?" she dared to ask.

"I prefer an adder's-tongue to one who would grease my boots with false compliments. Because of that, Miss Dufresne, I suspect you and I shall become good friends."

"I trust so as well."

"Then, yet again, we are in agreement."


Although Lord Windham had told Nerissa the gathering would be a small one, more than forty people crowded the elegant parlor as he escorted her to meet their host. Kirby Rowland was as perfectly groomed as his house, although he was a herring-gutted man, standing a half a head even above Lord Windham. Each movement of his gangly limbs sugggested a masterless marionette. As he adjusted his spectacles on his nose, the gold frames glistened in the lights from the lamps along the friezed wall.

"How kind of you to join us, Miss Dufresne!" he gushed, dipping his balding head over her hand. His bright eyes twinkled merrily behind the lenses. "I believe we met at a *soirée* at Mrs. Ehrlich's house several months ago."

"That is possible," Nerissa answered, then offered an apologetic smile. "I fear I was so nervous that evening I do not recall a single name or face."

"You must feel at ease here. That is the rule of the house. Do find her something to drink, Windham, and introduce her about. I hear Seely coming, and that prattle-bag will soon have my ears ringing."

Lord Windham chuckled under his breath as he led Nerissa toward a table where glasses of wine upon a gold damask cloth awaited the guests. His laugh faded into silence when he looked past her.

Curious what had changed his visage so abruptly, Nerissa turned to see Mr. Windham rushing toward them. The redhead's face was flushed with excitement.

"Hamilton, I was just speaking with Oakley. He heard from a friend, who has an acquaintance highly placed in the War Office, that the casualties at Albuera on the Peninsula were higher than we have been led to believe."

"I am sure the figures have been exaggerated," Lord Windham answered quietly.

"I must ask Rowland to excuse me. I trust you will as well, Miss Dufresne," he added as an afterthought.

Mr. Windham gave her no time to answer before he scurried away like a fox seeking its hole in the hedge. With a quick apology, Lord Windham followed, leaving Nerissa to stand in the middle of the room of strangers and wonder what was amiss.

Nerissa had scant chance to concern herself with

the problems of the Windhams, for a plump man, who introduced himself as Sir Delwyn Seely, quickly included her in a conversation in which he played the sole part. She was required to do no more than smile and nod at the appropriate places. As a half hour, then another passed, she began to fume at Lord Windham who had invited her to this *soirée*, then abandoned her to this man who buffeted her ears with nothing-sayings about places and people she did not know.

Just when she was about to ask the baronet to find a carriage to take her and Frye back to Laura Place, Lord Windham reappeared. He was smiling, but tension made his expression brittle. Instead of an apology, he offered her a glass of ratafia. Curiosity taunted her, but she said nothing as he greeted the pudgy man.

"I am astounded," Sir Delwyn said, unable to let a moment pass in silence, "that Miss Dufresne, who has been treated so horribly by you, Windham, would agree to accompany you here this evening."

"I own that my brain is all jumbled from the accident," Nerissa retorted with a smile as detached as Lord Windham's.

Sir Delwyn laughed, his belly bouncing like a child's ball. "Well said, Miss Dufresne. Your brain may have been jounced, but not your wits. You will need them when you play with us this evening. Why don't you partner with Windham tonight, Miss Dufresne? You are his guest, and you should be witness to his downfall from the good fortune he has been enjoying recently."

"That is unwise of you, Seely," returned the viscount. "I daresay we shall pluck you and Rowland clean of every copper you have."

"Or we shall win the lot." He chuckled again. "We play only for pony, Miss Dufresne, so you need not worry that three gentlemen will take advantage of your gentler ways."

"For pony?" Nerissa gasped, discovering that these men truly did play for more than the halfpence she and her mother had wagered on sunny winter afternoons.

"Nothing more than fifty pounds, Miss Dufresne." Her face must have drained of color, for the rotund man harrumphed and asked them to excuse him.

Nerissa turned to Lord Windham. "My lord, although you did mention this *fête* would include playing cards, you failed to mention certain aspects of your plans this evening to me."

"I assumed you play whist. Was I mistaken?"

"I know the game, of course, but do you mean to suggest that you wish me to join you gentlemen at your table?"

He smiled. "Philip and I had plans to play with our host and the good baronet this evening. However, Philip has seen fit to leave to tend to . . ." His smile wavered, then returned even cooler than before. ". . . to a private matter. I had hoped you might consider taking his place, although I would as lief have asked you instead of having Seely put it to you as a *fait accompli*. If you prefer not to play, or feel that your skills are not appropriate for our table, you need only say that you are not interested."

Nerissa hesitated. Not only did her head ache from the baronet's bibble-babble, but a pain had settled in her shoulder where the scarf cut into it. Her injuries were the perfect excuse to leave early and return to the quiet of the house on Laura Place.

The *too quiet* house, where her brother would be entombed in his book room, and she would have to listen to Hadfield's cruel comments. She had hoped for a night away from that sedentary life, and she had found it tonight. Letting the evening end before it must would be silly.

When she did not answer, Lord Windham took her

hand and led her to a table. He drew out a chair. "Do join us. I need a partner, and, if you wish, I shall stake you a few pounds to begin. Then if fortune smiles on us, and we are successful, you may pay me back at the end of the evening."

"And if I lose?"

"If you lose, it is because I, too, have failed to play well. Don't worry. I do not intend to lose."

Nerissa smiled as she sat and watched him take the chair opposite her. "You are quite cocksure, my lord."

"I have found that luck is mostly skill." His smile became wicked as their host and Seely hurried to the table. When they had greeted Nerissa, he continued, "You will not call a revoke against Miss Dufresne for not shuffling tonight. As you can see, that is quite the impossibility for her tonight."

"Do you feel well enough to play?" asked Mr. Rowland.

As she answered, she felt Lord Windham's gaze on her. "This bruised wrist may offer me the very excuse for any other bad luck that might befall me."

Nerissa was given no more sympathy as the evening progressed rapidly to the rhythm of cards being shuffled and dealt and played and shuffled again. She ignored the growing discomfort of her arm as she tried to balance her cards in her right hand. Concentrating on bidding and which suit was trump, she did not realize how much time had passed until Sir Delwyn tossed his cards into the middle of the table.

"I fear that is all for me," said the baronet with a sigh. "I cannot afford to lose more. Miss Dufresne seems to have continued your luck, Windham. Perhaps tomorrow evening, she would be good enough to be *my* partner."

"Tomorrow night?" Nerissa asked as she stared at the pile of coins in front of her. She had not noticed

81

how it had grown. More than sixty guineas must be glittering by her right hand.

"You shall not give me the chance to win back my losses?" Sir Delwyn asked, his full face long with dismay.

"I don't know. I mean, I never—"

Lord Windham said softly, "Miss Dufresne shall join us again, I am sure."

Looking from his confident smile to the other men's eager expressions, Nerissa faltered as she was about to say that joining them again would be impossible. She had no real reason to decline—no other *soirées* filled her evenings—but she was not pleased that Lord Windham felt he could dictate the course of her life.

The men rose as she did, but stepped aside as Lord Windham came around the table. He offered his arm while he bid their host a good evening. Again Nerissa hesitated, then she put her hand on his arm and walked with him to reclaim their coats.

"You need not be on the high ropes with me," Lord Windham said as he collected her shawl and his tall hat. When he slipped the silk over her shoulders, which were bared by her gown, his fingers lingered. She knew she should pull away, but she did not until she noted the dismay in Frye's sleepy eyes.

"I am not angry with you, my lord."

"Then why so silent? You cannot deny that this evening has been profitable for both of us."

"Here is what you lent me!" she retorted, moving toward the door. "We are quite even, and you shall find, my lord, that you have no reason to impose your plans upon me."

"Why are you flying up to the boughs? I would have guessed that you would be glad instead of in a pelter at the thought of obtaining a bit of change at a diverting game. Unless you are quite different from every other woman I have met, I find it difficult to

82

believe that you can find no use for a few guineas."

Nerissa tried not to think of her fragile financial situation, but his words lured her into thinking what this money could do. The servants could be paid, as well as the butcher. Perhaps even a new lamp for the table in the book room where Cole worked for so many long hours on his dream.

Cole . . .

She looked at her reticule. The fifty guineas she had left would not finance his obsession, but it would help. And if she could win more tomorrow night . . .

"Yes, my lord," Nerissa said, her tone more assured, "I would be delighted to join you tomorrow evening. I trust that you will respect Sir Delwyn's request that I play as his partner."

He pressed the money she had given him into her hand. "Keep this to begin the game tomorrow night."

"My lord, I cannot take your money."

"I doubt if you shall keep it long." His smile was bright with mischief. "It shall be delightful to win my money back from you, Miss Dufresne."

# Chapter Six

"Such a slugabed you are this morning," said Cole with a smile when Nerissa entered the breakfast parlor. He pulled his mother-of-pearl snuff box from his pocket and pinched the snuff between his fingers and inhaled with a smile.

"Is it Wednesday already?" She sighed as she sat at the round table. She managed a weak smile for the maid who placed a cup of steaming coffee in front of her. Nearly a week had passed since she had attended Mr. Rowland's gathering with Lord Windham. Leaning her face into the heat, she said, "I cannot believe that this week has vanished so quickly."

Cole peered around the sheets of the previous day's *Morning Post* from London. "Have you been busy?"

She laughed and reached for the biscuits in the middle of the table. So many times she had been tempted to ask Cole what he would do without her, but she knew the answer. He would muddle through as he did with her assistance. When one was as unconcerned with the passage of time as her stepbrother was, there was no need for someone to keep track of it. Cole's world centered on his dreams.

In the days since her close brush with death, Cole had tried to be anxious about her. Not that he was completely indifferent. When he thought of her suffering, he offered sincere solace and best wishes for a swift recovery. Simply put, he did not often think of anything but his canal project.

On the first morning that she had not worn the sling around her neck, Nerissa had hoped he would notice. He had not. Instead he had given her a description, which had lasted a full hour, of the series of locks that would be necessary at the heart of the canal.

She buttered a biscuit and smiled as he launched into another discourse on his plans. Letting his words wash over her as the water would in his canal, she wished him a good day when he left to meet his students.

Cole was still ensconced in his study when Annis arrived. Glad, for her brother and Annis were as volatile as flint and steel, Nerissa welcomed her friend into her small sitting room on the upper floor of the town house.

"I thought Wednesday would never come," bemoaned Annis as she pulled off her brightly feathered bonnet. "Every afternoon, I must go with Janelle to the *couturière*, and, every evening, I have to sit with her while she flirts with Mr. Oakley. Dash my wigs, but I am bored with her blowing hot and cold on this *beau*. I should not complain." She smiled as she sat on the curved arm settee. "Mama remains fascinated with Janelle and Mr. Oakley, so she has accepted Mr. Windham's request to meet her."

Nerissa reached for the silver teapot which Mrs. Carroll had brought into the sitting room in anticipation of an afternoon of callers. "Why doesn't Janelle make up her mind on Mr. Oakley? I vow, Annis, that neither of your sisters has a suggestion of wit about her."

"But they are beautiful. You are, too, Nerissa, but

you have a gentleness which makes you even more attractive to people." Her long nose wrinkled as she reached for a bull's-eye among the sweetmeats. Chewing on the peppermint, she mused, "Mr. Windham is to meet with Mama tomorrow afternoon. I am sure she will be as charmed with him as I was."

"I trust she will be."

"When you are in his company, does he speak of me?"

Nerissa smiled as she spooned sugar into Annis's cup. "Constantly, so much so that Lord Windham grimaces each time his brother mentions your name."

Before she could add more, Mrs. Carroll knocked on the door and opened it. The housekeeper moved aside as a tall shadow crept across the floor. Hearing a deep voice, Nerissa looked up to see a man dressed in a dark coat and leather breeches as if set for a ride. As her eyes rose along the striped waistcoat, she met amusement in familiar, grey eyes.

"Lord Windham!" She hoped he had not overheard her speak of him. "I did not expect to see you this afternoon."

"Good afternoon, Miss Dufresne." He offered Annis a smile before he added, "And Miss Ehrlich. Philip will be heartsick that he did not join me on this call."

"Will he? How wonderful! Not, my lord, that I wish him to be sad, but—" Annis choked back the rest when Nerissa jabbed her lightly with her elbow. A flush climbed Annis's cheeks.

Lord Windham smiled more broadly. "I understand that you are at home on Wednesday afternoons, Miss Dufresne."

"Yes, of course. Will you join us?" She gestured toward a chair. "We are about to have tea."

"I fear I cannot stay and chat with you ladies." Putting his hand on Nerissa's uninjured arm, he asked, "May I speak with you a moment?"

"Yes, of course," she repeated, but more faintly. Even through his gloves, the heat of his fingers teased her skin. If their few meetings gave any indication to the true man, he was a vexing fellow, with a frightful habit of doing as he saw fit, no matter what others thought. In that way, he was much like Cole, although she could discern no other resemblance between her brother and the forthright viscount.

As they walked out into the upper hall, she battled to regain her composure. She need not act like a goosecap simply because the handsome lord had given her a look-in. He paused before a large window that flooded sunlight across the carpeted floor. Again she noted the red glistening in his ebony hair, but her gaze was drawn to his smile.

"Forgive me for taking you from your friend, Miss Dufresne. I considered sending you a note, but did not trust it to arrive in time."

"Is something wrong?"

He folded his arms across his waistcoat. "There is no need to look so distressed, for the problem is only that Philip may not be able to join us this evening. Perhaps you would ask *your* brother to join us at Rowland's."

Nerissa almost laughed as she tried to imagine Cole at Kirby's house. Within moments of his arrival, he would be pining for his book room and his stacks of papers. She realized with a start that she was unsure if her stepbrother even knew how to play cards.

"It might be wise to consider another partner this evening, my lord," she said quietly.

"But I want you." He chuckled when her eyes widened at his vehemence. "Do not think me crazy, but you have been enjoying such good fortune at the table that I would enjoy sharing it tonight."

"Weren't you the one who said luck is primarily skill?"

"Damn," he said with a sigh, "there's no choice but to drag that young pup from his plans this evening."

"My lord, I never meant for you to insist that Mr. Windham join us, if he needs to be elsewhere."

Lord Hamilton started to answer, then clamped his mouth closed. Abrupt fury glittered in his eye as his lips straightened. Taking a step back, for she feared what would happen if that rage detonated, she gasped when his face altered into a sudden smile.

"Why not? It shall do him good." Tapping his tall beaver into place, he walked toward the stairs.

He paused with his hand on the banister as she asked, "Is something amiss with Mr. Windham?"

"Not yet. . . ." Again he seemed ready to add something more, but did not.

Nerissa hesitated. To probe more deeply would be inappropriate, but she could tell he was not revealing the complete truth. "My lord, if—"

"Don't fret about it. Coming to the party tonight will give him something to think about other than his daunting task of impressing Mrs. Ehrlich so he may call upon his fair Annis. Other matters have delayed him from that interview, but I suspect he will not be able to wait overly long to call."

Nerissa laughed softly as she glanced back at the sitting room. "Annis tells me your brother intends to visit her mother tomorrow. He is right to dread that call."

"He shall learn better before long." Before she could ask him to explain, he added, "I shall see you at nine o'clock then, Miss Dufresne. Or, I should say, *we* shall see you at nine. I trust that will be convenient."

"Yes, of course," she said yet again, but to his back as he went down the stairs. As the door closed behind him, she wondered what the viscount would have done if she had declined his invitation. She suspected she did not want to know.

Nerissa waited impatiently as Frye closed the back of her dress. It was the same gown she had worn several nights before, but her wardrobe was not vast enough for a different gown every evening. That the men never noticed what she wore—other than to give her a hasty compliment as she sat at the card table— should have offered some consolation, but it oddly irritated her.

"Do stand still!" ordered Frye with the irascibility that had been her hallmark for the past week. "I believe the *modiste* makes these closures smaller on every dress."

"If you would rather that I wear the blue one—"

"No, no," the abigail assured her too hastily. "This one is the best."

Nerissa turned to face her. "Why?"

"I . . . I . . ." Frye flushed and walked toward the dressing table.

Nerissa stepped in front of her maid to halt Frye's hurried escape into the dressing room. "What is wrong with you? You seem as nervous as a cat in a kennel."

"May I speak plainly?"

"Frye, you know that I depend on you to do so." She sat in the worn chair by the bed. "How could I have learned half of what I know if I hadn't had you to teach me?"

The older woman's hand clenched on the carved footboard, and her voice trembled. "Miss Dufresne, it appears I have taught you poorly, for it seems that you are learning other lessons. Lessons I had prayed no one I knew and loved—as I love you, for you seem like my own child in my heart—would ever have to learn."

Nerissa leaned forward and put her hand over Frye's, discovering that her abigail's skin was as icy as the pond at Hill's End in midwinter. "Dear Frye, you have me baffled. What have I done to bring you such sorrow? I entreat you to tell me so that I may vow never to do such a thing again."

Frye drew a handkerchief from beneath her long sleeve. Dabbing at her eyes, she raised her head in pitiful defiance. "If you wish to give me my dismissal, I will understand, for what I have to say is horrible beyond belief, yet it must be said. You are no dirty dish, and I would as lief find a position in a scullery than have you do what you are doing with Lord Windham in an effort to save this household."

Nerissa gasped, for Frye's expression of revulsion frightened her. Rising, she put her hand on the older woman's arm again. "Dear Frye, whatever is wrong? Tell me why you are so distressed."

"How can I say such appalling words? You know what else they are saying?"

"I am certain that 'they', as you put it so diplomatically, are saying that the viscount and I have been seen often going into the homes of Mr. Rowland and Sir Delwyn Seely where we spend the evening in seclusion," Nerissa said, keeping her smile hidden.

Frye groaned and hid her face in her hands. "Alas, what did I do wrong? What lesson did I fail to teach you?"

Realizing that her abigail was crying again, Nerissa knelt next to her. She patted Frye's chubby arm and whispered, "Dear Frye, tell me what you fear, so that I may put your mind to ease. I was just funning you."

Color darkened the maid's pale cheeks. "You are a lady of standing, Miss Dufresne, but not of money. If you ruin your reputation, you shall find no decent man to wed you when Lord Windham tires of you and practices his fascinating arts on the next in-nocent maiden who falls prey to his charm. Do not give the gabblemongers the fodder to destroy you, even if you have given him your heart as well as . . ." She shuddered and pressed her hands to her lips.

"You think that I . . . that he . . ." Nerissa's as-tonishment prevented her from saying more.

Frye nodded.

"But why?"

"I found money in your drawer when I was putting away your clean chemises. So much money, and I know you did not have it before *he* began calling with his lavish gifts."

Nerissa rose to sit in the chair and clasped her hands in her lap. "The only gift Lord Windham has given me was the bonnet to replace the one that was ruined. An untoward gift I own, but, as he is a proud man, he hoped the gift would say what he found difficult."

"And the money?"

"I won that playing whist with Lord Windham and his friends. I assure you that, while you are sitting with the others belowstairs, he is not paying me to play anything else with him."

"Miss Dufresne!"

Taking a deep breath, she tried to calm herself. "Was this attack started within this household? If so, you may tell its originator, whom you should know better than to heed, that Lord Windham does not consider me a bit of muslin for his enjoyment. Lord Windham offers me the respect any gentleman should offer a lady." *Except at the card table,* she amended silently.

"I am sorry, but I had to know. When Had . . . when the one who spoke of this sounded so sure, I needed to put my heart to rest."

"You may put your heart to rest as well as reassure everyone in this house and beyond that Lord

Windham and I have only cards in common."

Frye continued to buzz around while Nerissa finished getting dressed, continually apologizing for her lack of faith in her charge. Nerissa did not chide her, for she did not wish to hurt her abigail more. To perdition with Hadfield! His cruelty was now aimed at hurting those she cared for as well as at her. Cole refused to listen to her requests to send him packing, and the only way she could convince him would be to bring him proof. Hadfield was too sly to allow that.

When it was announced that Lord Windham waited below, Nerissa hurried down the stairs. Frye followed, her steps lighter than they had been all day. Nerissa was about to greet the viscount, but halted when she heard a soft click.

She looked toward Cole's book room. The door was ajar. She considered calling to him to come and meet Lord Windham, then changed her mind. Such a meeting was certain to be awkward, for Cole would talk of nothing but his canal. She wanted to avoid any further discomfort this evening.

"How lovely you look tonight," Mr. Windham gushed with his usual graciousness. "Don't you think so, Hamilton?"

"The dress does look better without the bruises to clash with it."

"I'm pleased you think so," Nerissa answered quietly.

Lord Windham's dark brows rose along his forehead, but she said nothing more as he settled her lacy cape over her shoulders.

"The greenhorns are waiting for us to trounce Seely and Rowland tonight," he said as he opened the front door.

"If luck is with us."

"It will be."

Nerissa was about to reply when she heard another muted sound behind her. As she walked out onto the steps, she looked back to see Cole's door was now firmly closed. She wondered what he had hoped to see. A flush climbed her cheeks when she feared he had listened to Hadfield's lies as well. She must set him to rights in the morning.

Hamilton tapped his foot on the marble floor in time with the lush music coming from the opposite end of the room. This was not at all the night he had planned. He had hoped for a rousing game of cards with fevered betting to take his mind off Mallory's first report. Not that the Bow Street Runner had told him anything new. His quarry *had* come to Bath, and there was no sign of him having left. Somewhere in this small city, the man, who had stolen thirty thousand pounds from his father, resided in luxury on that money.

*Blast it!* Seely was drinking himself fuzzy while Rowland was busy playing the lady-killer with Mrs. Monroe and acting as if he was no more than a lad suffering his first calf love.

His eyes narrowed as he saw his brother in intense conversation with Miss Dufresne. She had said scarcely a score of words to him, but seemed eager for his brother's company. That should be all for the good. Yet an emotion he had pledged never to suffer again suffused him, wrenching his gut.

*Blast it!* He had put jealousy behind him when Elinor gave him the bull's-feather with her parade of lovers.

Hamilton was halfway across the room before he realized he was about to charge in on their conversation. Slowing his steps, he heard a loud laugh.

"Quite the primitive, wasn't he? Knocking the poor girl on the head to get her attention?"

He recognized the voice as Seely's, although it was blurred with hazy. His hands curled into fists when he heard Randall Oakley reply.

"He seems to have gotten what he wants. She is living in his pocket." He cursed, then said, "I must speak to Mrs. Ehrlich about urging her youngest to dissolve her friendship with Miss Dufresne. It would not look good for my sister-in-law to be a bosom bow of Windham's natural."

"You think—"

"Without question, Seely. She is as poor as Job's turkey, from what I have heard from Miss Ehrlich. Windham clearly finds her amusing, although I hazard he will tire of her before the fortnight comes to a close."

"I say," Seely said, his voice bright with interest, "that he keeps her for a month."

"I take your wager for . . . shall we say fifty pounds?"

Hamilton stepped forward and smiled. "Can you afford to lose that much, Oakley?"

The beak-nosed man had the sense to look embarrassed, but Seely gave a brandy-faced laugh. The baronet said, "Oakley is well-fixed, Windham. You know that. Otherwise, why would he be allowed to court Miss Ehrlich?" Winking bawdily, he added, "Convince Mrs. Ehrlich of young Philip's plump pockets, and your brother can have her youngest."

"Did you chance upon a windfall, Oakley?" Hamilton asked. "I had heard you were nearly cleaned out on those foolish investments you made in the West Indies."

Oakley scowled and stamped away.

Seely crowed with laughter. "You set his back up for him. He wants no one to know how he managed to impress his future mother-in-law with his worthiness."

Hamilton stared after Oakley. Had his quarry been so close all along? He must have Mallory check to discover if Oakley was buying himself Mrs. Ehrlich's approval with Windham money.

"So tell me," Seely continued, "is it true that Miss Dufresne is leaving her brother's house for yours?"

Hamilton arched a single brow before walking away. He did not wait to hear Seely's fuzzy answer. A smile edged along his lips. These rumors might prove to be most beneficial. If the attention of the *ton* was focused on an *affaire de coeur*, fallacy though it might be, between him and Miss Dufresne, his search could go unnoted, allowing him to discover the truth of Oakley's surprising wherewithal. The right word whispered in the right ear would propel the tale throughout Bath, even though . . .

His gaze returned readily to Miss Dufresne. Her lemon-yellow dress was the perfect foil for her sable hair. Watching her hands move gracefully as she emphasized a point to Philip, he thought of those slight fingers against his arm and his lips. She was alluring, and he could easily surrender to the fantasy of holding her even closer.

With regret, he knew he must halt the hearsay by ignoring it. No matter how much he wished to find the thief, he could not damage Miss Dufresne's reputation.

*Blast it!*

His smile returned as he realized he might be able to salvage something from this increasingly intricate set of circumstances. With a lighter step, he continued across the ballroom.

"Hamilton, where have you been hiding?" his brother asked as he neared.

"I have been looking for my partner at the board of green cloth," he answered with a laugh. "You must allow me to steal Miss Dufresne from you, Philip." Holding out his arm, he asked, "Shall we?"

"Yes, my lord," Nerissa said with a smile. "Will you excuse us, Mr. Windham?"

He grinned broadly. "Never let me be the one to

stand between Dame Fortune and her handmaiden. Good luck to both of you this evening."

"You aren't joining us?" she asked, startled.

"I have other business." He bid them a good evening and walked away.

The fury that had burned in Lord Windham's eyes that afternoon burst forth again as he stared at his brother's back. Knowing she should say nothing, Nerissa asked, "Why isn't Mr. Windham joining us for whist?"

"I will tell you, but not here." Each word was clipped as it pushed past his taut lips.

The music faded into a hush as they climbed the stairs to the room which had been set aside for cards. When they entered, Nerissa was amazed to see it was empty. She turned as she heard the door close.

"My lord, the others—"

"Will be arriving shortly." He leaned against the column edging the door and hooked his thumbs into the waistband of his pantaloons. "I wished a moment to speak with you without other ears listening as they were in your entry foyer this evening."

Nerissa gasped, "You heard . . . ?"

"Only the curiosity of your reclusive brother, which obviously demanded to be satisfied. You should reassure him, Miss Dufresne, that the tales of our intimacy, which are much in the air, are untrue."

Color burned on her cheeks as he spoke so candidly of the whispers she had been unable to disregard this evening. "My lord, mayhap it would be for the best that I am not seen in your company again."

He slowly closed the distance between them. When she would have taken a step back, she found a table blocking her way. Meeting his amused gaze, she lowered herself to a chair at the table. He put his foot on the chair next to hers and leaned forward so his eyes were level with hers.

"I fear that is impossible, for Philip is so taken

with Miss Ehrlich that he will wish to call on you often in the hope that she might be giving you a look-in as well."

"Your brother is not the problem."

"I fear you are mistaken." His finger touched the tip of her chin, and he smiled when her breath caught. "He is indeed one of the problems." As he traced the curve of her jaw, he murmured, "I know you share your brother's curiosity, Miss Dufresne, and are most interested in where my brother flits to while we enjoy the good-fellowship of the card table."

Nerissa wanted to shoot back a fierce retort, but his touch silenced her. She wanted to close her eyes and think only of his coarse skin brushing against her. When she looked up into his eyes, she could not look away. In them, she read frustration and pain. She was astounded that he was willing to bare even this much of himself to her.

"Has he entangled himself in something horrible?"

His laugh had a bitter edge. "You can't guess how right you are. He is arranging to buy the captaincy of a distant cousin who tires of the glory of battle on the Continent."

"Captaincy?" A chill cut through her as she thought of Mr. Windham's bright effervescence against the blight of a battlefield. "Can't you halt him?"

He sighed and shook his head. "It appears not." Taking her hand, he turned it upside down. His finger followed one of the lines in her palm. "There are those who believe a man or a woman can see their future in their hand. Philip, as recklessly, believes this is a way for him to do something of value. While he tells me that my place is among the peers in the House of Lords, he sees his in glorious battle. It does little good to mention that war is seldom glorious."

"Yes if this is what he wants—"

"Are you mad?"

She recoiled from his naked pain. Setting herself on her feet, she said, "If you take that tone with him, I'm not surprised he refuses to listen to you."

He reached to grasp her shoulders, but drew his hand back before he jostled her left arm. Cupping her chin in his hand, he brought her closer. His fingers splayed across her face, awakening sensations she never had guessed could possess such splendor. When her hand rose to the navy velvet of his sleeve, the glow in his eyes deepened to silver.

"Forgive me," he whispered, "for you may be right. If what he wants is this chance for what he calls 'a most magnificent honor', can I tell him no?" The corners of his mouth tilted. "I have told him no on many occasions, but I fear he will listen to his older brother no longer, for he takes great relish in reminding me that I have my own ridiculous goal that obsesses me."

Nerissa asked before she could halt herself, "What is that, my lord?"

"You might find that the whole shall put you in whoops," he said without a smile as he stepped away. Going to the next table, he picked up a deck of cards and shuffled them. "I seek something nowhere near as wondrous as a hero's laurels."

"Are you trying to trip me the double, my lord, with your mystical talk?"

He chuckled. "How your eyes snap when you are in a pelter! I should have exasperated you before this."

"You have!" When Nerissa put her hand to her lips as Lord Windham laughed, she found herself smiling as well.

"Do you mean to suggest, Miss Dufresne, that you find my company distasteful?"

"You are changing the subject, my lord," she said, her smile fading.

"Am I?"

"If you prefer not to speak of this. . . ."

He dropped the cards to the table and took her hand between his broader ones. "How you challenge a man to do what you wish him to! I can understand why your brother stays hidden, for he wishes no one to see the scars where your barbed words have struck him." Sitting again, he drew her down to the chair beside him. "As to your question, Miss Dufresne, I am on a quest. Like the grand knights of yore, I am seeking a nemesis who has betrayed my family's trust."

She flinched as his words brought to mind Janelle's taunt that Nerissa was waiting for a dashing knight to sweep her into a fairy-tale life. "Your family's trust? What do you mean?"

"Exactly what I said. Can it be that you find my story unbelievable?"

"It is unbelievable! This is 1811, not some ancient times when primitive emotions ruled."

He laughed again, but his voice remained taut. "Emotions never change. I would guess a knight riding off on a Crusade felt the same determination I have to find the one who cheated my father out of thirty thousand pounds."

"Cheated?" She glanced about the room.

"Not at a wager, but at a business deal that you would find boring. I am determined to find this man who stole my father's spirit and his life."

In horror, she whispered, "A murderer?"

"You need not be so diabolic in your thoughts, for the fiend did not slay him. Only his deeds did, for my father was a man of uncommon pride."

"Like his sons?"

A smile raced across his face, but his voice remained somber. "To be cheated by a cur, who was beneath his touch, was more than my father could endure. The shame killed him, and I vowed to make the man pay for his crimes."

"That quest has brought you to Bath?"

"Yes, and . . ." His jaw tightened as the sound of footfalls and laughter came from beyond the closed door. "That is why I wished to speak with you alone. I must ask you a favor." Not giving her a chance to reply, he went on, "You have heard the interest, I am sure, in our friendship." A mischievous twinkle betrayed his next words. "Which is deemed to be far warmer than a friendship."

"Yes." She could not halt the faint sound of her voice as he stroked her fingers while he spoke.

"I would, if you will agree, let them continue to think it is more than a friendship." When she started to reply, he put his finger to her lips. "I will call upon you along with Philip and his Annis. Let the *ton* see us in each other's company. Their curiosity will consume them, permitting me to do what I must to find the man who betrayed my father."

"Nothing we say will deter them from their assumptions," she said, but tensed when the door latch rose.

"Then you are agreeable to this?"

She nodded.

Standing, he drew her to her feet. In a low voice that would not reach beyond her ears, he said, "I vow that I shall unearth him with all speed. Then the blackguard will find himself in the midst of his most horrible nightmare as he learns the taste of a Windham's revenge."

# Chapter Seven

Nerissa gripped the banister as she heard a door crash closed on the ground floor. She saw Cole walk away from the front door to where Hadfield was standing in the center of the entrance foyer. Both of them were glowering at the door.

Rushing down the stairs, she gasped, "Cole, what is wrong?" She had never heard him slam the door before.

He snarled, "Everything!"

Taken aback by his vehemence, she put her fingers on his arm. He shook them off and spun to glare at her. Fear pinched at her as she saw for the first time the same terrible choler that she had suffered from his father during the years Mr. Pilcher had shared her mother's house.

"Cole, if there is something I can do . . ."

She realized he was not listening to her. Instead he had turned to the butler. Sharply he said, "I will not suffer that indignity again, Hadfield. If you see any sign of such problems, I wish you to handle them. I know you are familiar with doing so."

"What problem?" Nerissa asked as she glanced from one rigidly set face to the other. Something was dreadfully wrong, and she could not understand why Cole was keeping the truth from her.

"It isn't your concern, Nerissa," her brother returned without looking at her. "Do you understand, Hadfield?"

"I understand you, Mr. Pilcher." Smug satisfaction saturated his voice as he shot a glare in Nerissa's direction. Turning on his heel, he walked toward the back of the house.

"Cole—"

"I do not wish to be disturbed!" he snapped and vanished into his book room.

Nerissa choked back another gasp when that door smashed resoundingly closed. Going to the window by the front door, she peered out. The walkway was empty save for a short, round man who was standing on the opposite side of the street and looking toward the bridge leading into the heart of Bath. A pair of carriages passed, and, when she could see the other side of the street again, he was gone.

Bafflement threaded her forehead. Something had wound up both Cole and Hadfield, but she had no idea what it might be.

Climbing the stairs with the same unseemly speed as she had descended, she went into her room to discover Frye folding chemises and putting them in the cupboard. Frye stopped humming a tuneless song to smile. The abigail's smile drifted away, warning Nerissa that her disquiet was visible on her face.

"Of course, I heard the door close," the older woman said. "Hadfield is always—"

"Cole slammed it."

"Mr. Pilcher? Why?"

Nerissa sat in the chair and drew her feet up beneath her. "I have no idea. I thought you might know. Are there any whispers belowstairs of a problem that Cole has?"

"I know of no problem," Frye said. She shuddered as she folded the last chemise and set it in the drawer.

Closing the door quietly, she added, "Not that I wish to have anything to do with that frightful man's concerns."

Nerissa could not argue with that. She wished she could convince Cole to rid the house of Hadfield. Until then, she must endure the butler's insolent smiles and vicious comments while she tried to puzzle out what was wrong.

Nerissa tilted her parasol, so the white lace dripping off its edge did not obscure her view of the trees, which lined the road leading through the rolling hills out of Bath. Her elbow rested lightly on the scalloped edge of the seat of the phaeton. Annis could not have selected a finer day to celebrate her mother's approval of Mr. Windham with an outing in daisyville. The sun shone with a bright, soft light that added color to the grass and flowers, but did not burn through her bonnet.

"And Mr. Windham can call whenever we are at home," Annis said for at least the tenth time since they had left Town.

"I am so pleased." Nerissa had tried to vary her reply, and she was not sure what she would say the next time Annis voiced her happiness.

"Mama has said I must invite Mr. Windham and his brother to sup some evening soon. Will you come?"

"I will try."

Annis leaned forward. "Do leave Cole at home. I have no wish for Mr. Windham to be bored with his skimble-skamble talk of that canal."

"Miss Ehrlich!" Frye's pursed lips spoke her displeasure as sharply as her words.

With a giggle, Annis said, "Oh, Frye, I knew I could put you in a stew with that comment."

The abigail harrumphed while Nerissa struggled

not to laugh. If Frye took a moment to think, she would know that Cole had no wish to leave his book room for an evening of conversation and dinner.

Her smile wobbled. As Annis continued to prattle about the upcoming party, Nerissa looked ahead to the curve in the road. It was painfully familiar. She was glad the two men rode ahead of them. As insightful as Lord Windham had proven to be, she doubted if she could have hidden her mixed pleasure and dismay as she saw the gate leading to Hill's End. *Her home*, but it was hers only until a buyer could be found. Then everything she had known all her life would be gone.

When Frye patted her hand, Nerissa looked at her abigail. Trust dear Frye to comprehend the depth of her despair. Seeing the sorrow in the older woman's eyes, Nerissa bit her lip to restrain her tears. Hill's End had been home to Frye nearly as long as it had been for Nerissa. Albert Pilcher had stolen almost every one of her father's farthings. Now they must watch strangers take over their home. It was the final insult Albert Pilcher could have heaped on them.

She stared at the stone gate, with its iron arch connecting the pillars, until the road curved to follow the low wall that marked the edge of the property that had been in her family for centuries. Blinking back the tears that she must not allow to fall, she sat straighter when the carriage bounced as the driver turned it onto a rougher road.

Frye muttered something under her breath, but Nerissa did not ask her to repeat her words so they could be understood. She understood all too well, for it had been along this road that she had walked often with her mother and Frye. They had come here to seek May flowers and to look for mistletoe. Nerissa's mother had sat with her on these mossy hummocks and regaled her with tales of the house, which had been built nearly four centuries before.

She said nothing as the carriage was halted, and the coachman jumped down to get the rug from the boot. Lord Windham unlashed the food basket he had attached to his saddle while his brother came to hand them out of the carriage.

Nerissa watched as Annis, delighted as a child, hurried to where the rug was being unrolled, so she could supervise the arrangement of the dishes for their *al fresco* meal. Frye went after her, clucking like an old hen, as she gave orders to the coachman.

Instead of following, Nerissa walked to the top of a knoll. Anguish knotted her middle as she saw the chimneys of Hill's End past the treetops. Trying to imagine others in her home, which was so oddly empty now, was impossible.

"Miss Dufresne, if I have done anything to give you offense, I beg you to forgive me."

At the soft plea, Nerissa looked over her shoulder to see Mr. Windham's sorrowful expression. Although he held a field daisy in his hands, he was rubbing his palms together as if he was trying to rid himself of something distasteful. Attempting a smile, she said, "You have done nothing to cause me to be angry, sir."

"Oh." He said nothing for a moment, then asked, "What has Hamilton done to you?"

Nerissa flinched before realizing he did not mean his question as it had sounded. No one but Frye could comprehend her silence. "Lord Windham's actions have been without complaint," she answered. "Forgive *me* for being so unsociable. I wanted a moment to admire the view."

Mr. Windham hesitated until she was tempted to ask him if he needed help devising his next thought, then he motioned for her to sit on the grass. Squatting next to her, he said, "I am glad you have become friends. Hamilton needs friends."

"He appears to have many."

"Friends?" He shook his head. "Many acquaintances, but his life for the past few years has prohibited him from having friends."

She touched his sleeve, and he met her eyes squarely for the first time. "I know of his determination to find the fleecer who stole your father's money."

"He told you of that?"

"Yes."

"That is a surprise, for he is as shamed by the episode as Father was. Hamilton thinks too much of that. I hope your friendship is the advent of changes for him."

"He thinks of you as well."

"Me?" Mr. Windham's voice cracked on the single word.

Nerissa lowered her parasol and closed it. "Your brother fears for your life if you propel yourself headlong into the war."

Instead of the retort she had expected, Mr. Windham grinned. "This is just the jolly! I knew you would change him from the moment I heard he had bought you that hat."

She touched the brim of the blue bonnet. She had not guessed she must defend the viscount's actions to his brother as she had to so many others. "Lord Windham wished only to replace the hat he had ruined."

"True." He jumped to his feet, his grin returning. "But, Miss Dufresne, he could have sent a message to the milliner's shop and had it delivered to you with an apology. Instead he went to the shop—a place he would usually disdain—and selected the perfect hat for you before delivering it personally." Patting her shoulder, he laughed. "You changed him even before you knew him, Miss Dufresne. He is baring his heart

106

to you as he has no woman since . . ." He gulped and excused himself.

Nerissa was glad that he did not wait for an answer before he went to give the flower to Annis. She would have had nothing to say to him, because his words unsettled her more than she wished to own. *Since Elinor Howe.* That was what Mr. Windham had been about to say.

What sort of woman was Elinor Howe that she could bewitch the viscount, then shun him? She did not want to discover that.

Footsteps against the soft grass urged her to look up. Lord Windham towered over her, his head seemingly brushing the clouds as he smiled. He was dressed as casually as his brother, but she could not help noticing how well his brown riding coat and buckskin breeches matched the lines of his sturdy body.

"Philip said you were enjoying the view and suggested that I should join you," he said as he held out his hand to bring her to her feet.

"Do you always do as your brother suggests?"

"I fear I listen to him no more than he listens to me. Neither of us has heard more than a peep from you today. You have been shockingly quiet, Miss Dufresne."

"I never have had a reputation for having tongue enough for two sets of teeth." When his brows arched, she regretted the barbed words. She had no reason to be angry with Lord Windham, for he was to blame for none of her problems. The man who had brought her such woe was dead, so she had nowhere to focus her frustration. "Forgive me."

He offered his arm, and she put her hand on it. Again she could picture leaning her cheek against his shoulder, savoring his strength, but she guessed he would find such behavior discomfiting.

"There is nothing to forgive you for, although it is

107

clear you are not yourself today." He hesitated, then asked, "Is there something I can do to help?"

Hamilton saw amazement in Nerissa's blue eyes as she faced him. He hid his own. Had he gone queer in the attic? He had no interest in involving himself in Miss Dufresne's difficulties. He had enough of his own. He hoped the evenings with her and Miss Ehrlich and today's outing would persuade his brother to give up his ridiculous plan to buy that blasted commission. Once his brother was settled with a wife and the blackguard who had stolen his father's money was found, Hamilton intended to put the boring life of Bath far behind him.

Yet . . . he could not wrench his gaze from the warm pools of her eyes. His fingers yearned to caress the soft skin of her cheek, which he had first touched so briefly when he woke her from her stupor.

*Sapskull!* he thought viciously. That was what he was if he let himself be lured into the sweet web of another woman's wiles.

"I have been thinking of how things change," she said quietly.

"Just things? Not people?"

A smile swept the darkness from her eyes to leave them as blue as a rain-washed sky. "No, of the changes of time." She stretched to reach a thin branch.

With a laugh, he easily pulled it down, but behind her. Grabbing the other end, he imprisoned her in the small space. She grasped the branch, her fingers brushing his, and the sultry pulse erupted inside him. Her eyes widened, but she did not pull away. That pleased him. He was bored with the coy tricks of the other women he had met since his return from America. She might be very different from Elinor, after all, for Elinor had never tired of coquettish games.

When she turned slightly, the sweet aroma of her

perfume taunted him. His hands tightened on the branch as he fought the craving to slide his arms around her supple body and give freedom to the thoughts that taunted him when he was trying to sleep. So close, her soft contours urged him to let his hands explore what his gaze touched with such hunger as it slipped along the bare skin above her modest *décolletage* and over her bosom that was so perfectly edged by the ribbons of her gown. She was a lovely package, wrapped and waiting for the man who dared the fiery emotions in her blue eyes to discover what waited within her. By all that's blue, she was the most alluring woman he had ever seen!

"Look," she whispered, drawing his eyes unwillingly from the rise and fall of her breasts to a leaf that she held. "This once was no more than a seed. Now it is part of this massive tree." Her head tilted back as she looked up through the branches. "And it all happened when no one was watching but the sunshine and the north wind."

"Many things happen when eyes are too busy elsewhere to notice," he said as softly, his voice rough with the longing he could not govern.

Nerissa closed her eyes as his fingers glided from the branch to her arm. She relished the power and the danger of his touch, but knew she must not surrender to it. Too much she had heard of Lord Windham's determination to play booty with the heart of any woman who did not shield it carefully. Releasing the branch, she let it snap up into the air. He leapt back as the leaves flew past his face.

"You are a minx!" he said with a laugh.

"And you quite the rogue."

"I try." He drew her hand within his arm and led her farther along the twisting path. "When one is encumbered with the reputation of a *roué*, one is expected to act so."

"I doubt that you have ever done as another has wished."

"Philip is right. You see through me too facilely, Miss Dufresne. I shall endeavor to be on my guard against your intuition."

Nerissa lifted the hem of her skirt as he drew her up a small hill toward a copse. Whether it was her hand tightening in his or the soft gasp she had hoped he would not hear, something betrayed her.

He paused and asked, "You don't wish to go in this direction?"

"This direction is fine." She could not tell him of the day when she and Mama first had explored this very thicket. She had been very young, for the outing had been only a week before Mama had married Albert Pilcher.

"If you would as lief return to the others . . ."

"No, I truly want to see what awaits among the trees." Mayhap nothing had changed.

As Lord Windham assisted her up the steep hill, she realized everything had changed. Mama was dead, Hill's End on the block, and she was here with this enigmatic man who intrigued her with such a chaste caress.

Nerissa was glad she had left her parasol by the rug, for the trees had grown even closer than she remembered. As Lord Windham walked ahead of her and held the branches aside for her, she let the shadows suck her into the cool mystery within the copse.

He stopped before a pile of stone that was covered with moss. Beyond the low wall, a hole suggested a dark mystery, save for something which glittered feebly in its depths. She wondered how deep the pool of water might be.

Jabbing at the wall with the toe of his boot, Lord Windham said, "I suspect that this was once a building belonging to a monastery, mayhap to one that was destroyed to raise the house we passed on our way here. You can see what three hundred years of neglect has left." He touched another stone with his boot. It came loose and clattered down the side until it landed with a splash in the water at the bottom. "How easy it is to forget the past when it has been destroyed, even when it surrounds us."

"We must make room for the future, my lord. Perhaps this building was not razed by King Hal's men, but it simply fell into disuse. Who knows? This may be the foundation for nothing more grand than a byre."

"Have you no romance within you? Do you prefer to imagine the lowing of cows to the chants of monks?"

Nerissa laughed and walked with him toward a stone wall. Beyond it, cows nibbled on the grass. "As you know, I enjoy the country, my lord. I would live here always."

"Odd, for I cannot imagine you as a bumpkin." He tapped the feather in the band of her hat. "The cobbles of the city appear more comfortable beneath your feet than this soft sod."

"You are mistaken." Laughing, she whirled away from him, her weightless skirts swirling about her. She held out her arms to embrace the field. "*This*, my lord, is the world I love best."

"Then why do you live in Bath?"

"That is where Cole lives."

"And he needs you?"

Her crystalline laugh rang lightly, soaring within his head with the joy of matins. "Cole would, I fear, be lost without me to oversee his household, but I sneak away to the countryside whenever I can. To feel the tickling of the grass against my stockings and to smell the fresh fodder of a farmer's cuttings may be the most glorious thing I know. Do take a deep breath of it!"

111

She followed her own command. When two broad hands grasped her at the waist, she released the breath in a sharp gasp. She looked up into the viscount's face, which was not marked by his usual, cool smile. The mockery had vanished to be replaced by a naked longing. As her gaze locked with his, the warmth of his palms swept along her sides and drew her closer.

"Lord—"

"Nerissa—for what else can I call you when I hold you in my arms—do you recall that my name is Hamilton? I would take great pleasure in hearing it spoken by your dulcet lips."

Softly she said, "Hamilton, this is not right."

"Why?"

"Why do you ask me that when you know the answer as well as I?" she retorted, but her voice was softened by the delight spreading through her with his hands moving along her back.

He laughed as his finger teased the curve of her cheekbone. "Because I know you will never say 'yes' and 'amen' to everything I say as others do when I ask them such a question. Do you know how unendurable it becomes when Philip agrees with me day after day? I enjoy our dagger-drawing, Nerissa, as much as our times at the card table." His words trailed away as he guided her lips toward his.

Gasping, she turned her face away, but she realized, as he slowly released her, how much she wanted him to kiss her. Not moving away, she met his eyes without compromise. She was astounded to see sorrow in their silvery depths, then asked herself why she was surprised. So easily she understood the remorse of being unable to savor what she longed for with every bit of her being.

He whispered her name. Before she could stop them, her hands slid along his arms to learn the strength hidden beneath his wool coat. When her fingers curved behind his high collar, he drew her back into his arms. She sighed in sweet surrender when she was surrounded by the hard line of his body.

His lips over hers were as demanding as everything else about him, but she answered with her own yearnings for the satisfaction she had dared to dream she could find in his arms. Tearing her breath from her, his kiss sought to strip away every pretense she had devised to hide behind. Her fingers splayed across his back as his hungry mouth feasted on the curve of her cheek, the tip of her nose, even tickling the soft skin of her eyelids. When she laughed softly, he drew away.

She opened her eyes, fearing her honest reaction to his teasing had offended him. When she saw his softened smile, she wondered how she ever had considered this man heartless. She could feel his fervid pulse matching the throbbing of her breathless heart.

Her bonnet fell to the ground as his fingers combed upward through her hair as he claimed her lips anew. Astounded by the gentleness that could not mask his desire, she answered him by leaning closer to him. She wanted more than to feel his hands against her face and her legs brushing his through her skirt. As her breasts grazed his unyielding chest, his arms enveloped her in their strength. She vanished into the sensations of his lips upon her and his fingers exploring her with tender eagerness.

"Damn," he growled under his breath, lifting his lips so little that they skimmed hers as he spoke.

"What is wrong?" She could not imagine what could be amiss when everything was so perfect in his arms.

The soft call of her name in Frye's anxious voice was her answer.

Hamilton smiled. "Your comb-brush is a most

vigilant watchdog. We shall have to make a greater effort to evade her in the future."

His swift kiss seared away her answer, but she guessed he sensed the elation in her heart as she imagined another time—soon—when she could be in his arms again.

# Chapter Eight

Hamilton put down the sheet of paper and stared at the fire burning on the hearth in his sitting room. The spacious room was silent, save for the crackle of the flames and the ticking of the mantel clock set above them. No noise came from the street, for the room was set at the back of the house. Hunching deeper into the red leather chair, he scowled.

What a shuttlehead his brother had become! This long letter from their aunt in York was aglow with her excitement that Philip had decided to join his cousin in the army. With the money Frank garnered from his sale of the captaincy to Philip, he planned to buy himself the rank of colonel. Together they could battle the French scourge on the Continent.

"Blast!" He crumpled the pages and threw them into the fireplace. Somehow he was going to have to convince Philip to see sense. If Miss Ehrlich was not the one to do so. . . .

The door crashed against the wall. He looked up astonished to see Philip charge into the room. His brother's jaw was set at a fierce angle, and his hands jammed into the pockets of his black pantaloons.

"And good afternoon to you," Hamilton said as his brother stamped past him.

Philip snapped, "The Old Tough has made it

clear that she wishes me to have nothing more to do with her daughter.''

"I assume you are speaking of Mrs. Ehrlich?''

"Who else?''

He stood and went to pour his brother a generous serving of brandy. Handing it to Philip, he watched his brother gulp it as if it was no more potent than water. "Who else indeed?'' Hamilton asked as he sat on the arm of the settee. "I trust this means that your visit to the Pump Room with Miss Ehrlich was terminated by her mother's insistence.''

"She would not let me so much as speak with Annis!'' He pounded his fist on a table, threatening to send it crashing to the floor. "I had all I could do not to push past her and search every room of that house for Annis.'' With a curse, he started for the door.

"Where are you going?''

Philip pulled a piece of paper from his pocket and tossed it to his brother. Hamilton had only time to read the salutation before Philip snatched it back. It was their aunt's handwriting. The busybody must have written to Philip at the same time as she had to Hamilton. "It's time I replied to this letter. If I cannot have my dear Annis, I shall not sit here and pine for her. There is a battle I *can* win on the Continent.''

Hamilton shouted after him, but Philip did not slow as he left the room.


Nerissa frowned as a shadow crossed the book she had been reading. She had been so immersed in the story, she had not heard footfalls. Without looking up, she asked, "What is it, Mrs. Carroll?''

"Nerissa, may I be so rude as to interrupt you?'' asked a voice much deeper than the housekeeper's.

"Hamilton!'' She slowly set herself on her feet as

she saw the set of his mouth. Something was wrong, terribly wrong.

"Forgive me for speeding past your housekeeper . . ."

Looking past him, Nerissa saw an out-of-breath Mrs. Carroll in the doorway. She was twisting her apron nervously.

". . . I could not wait to speak with you. I need your help."

Nerissa was astonished, knowing that, for a proud man like Hamilton, it was difficult to speak those words. "What can I do?"

As he began to explain, she nodded. She did not allow him to finish before she was asking the housekeeper to bring her bonnet, so they could do as they must.


"Do you think she will listen?" Nerissa asked as Hamilton handed her down from the closed carriage. The cramp, that had begun in her stomach when Hamilton had told her of his brother's determination to buy the commission with all speed, grew even more painful as they reached the steps to the Ehrlich house.

"I will ensure that she does."

Boldly she took his hand between hers as he had done so often to her. "Hamilton, Mrs. Ehrlich is a single-minded woman. She wishes to see her daughters wed . . . in proper order. Janelle's nuptials are all that concern her now."

"She is sure to see otherwise by the time we are done talking."

He smiled when she arched her brows in an imitation of his most skeptical expression, but his face was grim as the door was opened and they were ushered into the grand entrance foyer. She wished she could mimic his equanimity as they waited to be taken to the parlor. Her fingers clenched and unclenched, and she had to resist wiping their cold dampness against her dress. If they failed in their meeting with Mrs. Ehrlich, there might be no chance to persuade Philip to rethink his plan to join the fight against Napoleon.

Mrs. Ehrlich greeted them with aloof graciousness, but she noticed how Annis's mother's eyes were gauging the cut of Hamilton's coat and the gold buttons on his waistcoat. He had been right in the suspicions he had shared with her in the carriage. Mrs. Ehrlich judged a man by the plumpness of his pockets.

"I am grateful that you could take the time to speak with me this afternoon," he said, bowing politely over her fingers.

The aroma of scented lotions battered Nerissa's nose, and she wondered how much unguent Mrs. Ehrlich used daily to retain her youthful appearance that could not match her youngest daughter's vivacity. She spoke a muted greeting to the woman who had not looked at her after that initial frown.

"It is my pleasure," Mrs. Ehrlich answered, pointing to a settee. "Please sit and make yourself comfortable. I am always delighted to have you call, Lord Windham."

Hamilton bit back a grin. Fortunately for him, Nerissa decided, *he* was not trying to impress his suit upon the fearsome Mrs. Ehrlich. And for Mrs. Ehrlich, as well, for Nerissa was sure the woman had met her equal in stubborn determination in Hamilton. Leaning back against the settee, which was surprisingly comfortable in spite of its fragile appearance, he said, "I trust I need not explain the cause of my visit."

"You are forthright." Her eyes glittered with her scheming thoughts. "So shall I be. Your brother is a fine, young man, my lord, but I wish Annis to enjoy a

Season in Town before she buckles herself into marriage. She is very young, as you have seen. She needs to savor the social whirl before she is settled in some country estate."

Pyramiding his fingers in front of his nose, he said, "That is wise of you, Mrs. Ehrlich. I can assure you that I feel much the same on my brother's behalf. That is why I came to speak with you. It would be wise, most wise, to put a damper on this relationship."

"Hamilton!" Nerissa gasped. "I thought you—"

He ignored her as if she had not spoken. "Philip is only recently down from Oxford. He needs a bit of Town life as well. I am glad to see that we concur on this."

Nerissa interjectd again, "Hamilton—"

"I shall deal with this, my dear," he said, patting her hand in a detached, paternalistic way.

She gave him a fierce scowl. How dare he treat her as if she was no more than a child! When she saw Mrs. Ehrlich's smile fading into dismay, she glanced again at Hamilton. He gave her a surreptitious wink. Holding her lower lip between her teeth, she halted her smile as she realized he had a deception in mind that would best any plan Annis's mother might devise.

"I must think of my brother," he continued.

"Now, my lord," Mrs. Ehrlich said hastily, "there is no need to disconnect them completely."

"I can see no other way. The quicker the separation, the less painful it shall be for all parties." He set one boot on the opposite knee in a casual pose. "A lesson I have discovered to be true in my own life, Mrs. Ehrlich, so I see no other venue than to cut off all dealings between them."

"My lord!" She set herself onto her feet as he rose. "Mayhap we are being a bit impetuous in reaching this decision."

119

"I see nothing impetuous about safeguarding my brother's heart."

As she watched the horror spring into Mrs. Ehrlich's eyes, Nerissa said nothing. The older woman implored him to reconsider, to let his brother know that Annis would welcome his call. Nerissa struggled not to smile when Hamilton agreed with apparent reluctance to let his brother give Annis a look-in the next day. She withheld her laughter until they were seated in the carriage again and driving through the city on their way back to Laura Place.

Hamilton smiled with self-satisfaction at his easy triumph, his feet stretched toward the front of the carriage, his arm draped casually along the back of the seat. He listened to the light sound of her laugh. This would surely convince Philip to reexamine his plans.

"Forgive me," she said, pulling his thoughts back to her. His gaze eagerly strayed to her face when she went on, "I thought you quite dicked in the nob when you started to agree with Mrs. Ehrlich. The poor lady had no idea that you were manipulating her."

"It did go rather well, didn't it?" He chuckled.

She wagged a finger at him. "You shouldn't gloat."

"And why not?"

"Because . . . because . . ." She laughed again. "Mayhap you should. Certainly you had little need for my help. You adroitly dealt with the formidable Mrs. Ehrlich."

"Did you consider that I used this small drama as an excuse to steal you from the all-seeing eyes of your *duenna?*"

"No," she whispered, her voice softening to the husky warmth that swirled within him like a heated wind.

His hand curved around her shoulder, bringing

120

her to face him. "I was certain not even Frye would deny you the chance to leap to the rescue of your bosom bow."

Her fingers rose to his face, and she guided his mouth to hers. As his arm herded her to him, he forgot Annis and Philip. He could think only of the luscious taste of her mouth. When his tongue touched hers, her sharp gasp of pleasure accelerated the throbbing need that ached within him. She softened against him, her body remolding perfectly to his. He delved deeper in her mouth, looking for all the untouched flavors waiting for him. As her fingers clutched his coat, he felt the carriage slow.

Lifting his mouth from hers, he murmured, "We are on Laura Place. I would ask the coachman to take us about the city a while longer, but I must return to tell Philip the good news."

"Go," she said with a smile that stirred the tempest within him. "Stop Philip from making a mistake. There will be other times."

"I promise you that." His smile broadened to match hers. He hoped the rest of the day would go as well. It must, or this small victory he had won for Philip's sake would be no more than bitter ashes amidst his defeat.

Shadows slithered along the ground, malignant and silent. Although carriage wheels rattled on the bridge overhead, only the slap of the water disturbed the blackness beneath its stone arch. Mud stank, wet and undisturbed, on both sides of the river that had been shrunken by summer's passage.

Hamilton waited in silence as he had for the past hour. He was not surprised that Mallory was late, because he suspected the man had scant intelligence. The shuttlehead probably had no idea how to tell time. As the church bells chimed the hour before

121

midnight, he leaned back against the stones and stared out at the city that was settling itself for the night. There were more stars in the sky than lights in the windows he could see. In this section of the city, where men rose with the first light to work, the late hours of the *ton* were unknown.

He heard a hiss, then a curse. It was followed quickly by a splash. With a terse laugh, he reached out a hand to pull the Bow Street Runner from the muddy shallows. Swearing viciously, Mallory shook himself like a dog, spraying both of them with mud.

Wiping the putrid mire from the front of his coat, Hamilton halted as he stared at Mallory's misshapen face. The faint light could not disguise that it was as discolored as Nerissa's had been the day after the accident. The bruises marked both of the man's cheeks and left his right eye swollen shut. "What happened to you?"

"Got jumped."

"By whom?"

"Never got more than a glimpse of the bloody cove's shadow. Thin as an anatomy."

"Tall?" asked Hamilton, unable to keep his eagerness from his voice. Philip had described the thief's accomplice as bald-ribbed and lanky.

"Never saw," he grumbled. "'Appened just this afternoon when I was comin' out of the Cock and Drake. Beat good and thorough, I was."

He recognized the name of the lush-ken, although he had never entered that low tavern himself. "Can you continue?"

"This 'ere be nothin'. I've got beat worse than this."

"So what have you to tell me?"

"I think 'twas a mistake to think yer man be 'ere," Mallory answered. "Can't be in Bath. Mayhap 'e was once, but 'e's gone. The blunt, too."

Hamilton knew his face would betray nothing, not

even in the fiery glare of daylight. His voice was as impassive in the darkness. "Then, Mallory, you need to find out where he has gone to."

"Milord, I've tried, but 'e 'as up and vanished."

"If that was so, you would not have been smashed. You clearly have gotten close to my prey."

"Got no idea where though."

"I wish to hear no excuses, for I have had my ears rung with too many of your bangers. If I had wished only to hear a pretty story, I would not be paying your employer at Bow Street for you to nab this thief for me." From his pocket he pulled a handful of coins which he tossed to the shorter man. "Buy some drinks, and talk to the folks. Someone will have heard of a man coming to Bath with that money."

"Aye," he said with a sigh, but Hamilton could see the greedy glint in his eye. So much like Mrs. Ehrlich's, although that lady would be affronted to be compared to this low creature.

"And one other thing," Hamilton said as the short man started to turn away. "I wish you to investigate Mr. Randall Oakley, who lives on Trim Street near St. John's Gate. It seems he has come into a spill of funds where there presumably was none."

"Aye," Mallory mumbled again.

"Let me know what you find out before the week's end."

Hamilton heard the Runner curse again, but he did not wait to listen to the man's complaints. Climbing the steep embankment to the street, he dragged his dreary spirits after him. He had taken steps to solve the issue of Philip's captaincy today while coming no closer to reaching the goal that had brought them to Bath.

He brushed any hint of dirt from his black cloak as he reached the walkway. This search might prove fruitless, but, until every rock in England had been overturned to discover the whereabouts of the cur who had cheated his father, it must continue. Clearly Mallory was incapable of handling the task alone. The time had come to find another, more competent thief-taker. In the morning, he would pen a letter to Townsend, asking for the services of his best man. In spite of Mallory's assertions, Hamilton suspected this man was not the most competent of the highly praised Bow Street Runners.

*Blast it!* He had spent too long already on this quest which was leading nowhere.

With his hands clasped behind his back and his head down as he ignored the passing traffic, he strode along the walkway. Only when he reached a corner did he realize where he was heading. The windows of Laura Place were bright against the night, although several of the façades were unlit.

He crossed the street where it broadened, leaping aside as a sedan chair cut in front of him, and climbed the three steps to Nerissa's door. No doubt she was asleep at this hour. He smiled as the enticing thought of her curled upon a pillow—his pillow—pulsated deep within him. But he did not want her asleep in his bed. He wanted to feel her mouth beneath his as she swept all thoughts of despair from his head as she had this afternoon when he had held her in the carriage. He wanted her now!

The door vibrated beneath his fist. It came open with a faint squeak of the hinges.

"Is Miss Dufresne in?" he asked, although he knew she must be. Philip had delighted in telling him that Nerissa welcomed no other male callers. That was good, because he wanted her with him tonight, not in the arms of another man.

Hamilton was startled when a spare butler let him in without speaking. He was about to repeat his question when his eyes were caught by a slender shadow on the stairs. If the butler spoke to him, he heard nothing but the renewed rush of pleasure flowing through him as he allowed himself to admire the way the silk Chinese robe outlined Nerissa's curves against the shadows cast by the dim lamp at the upper landing. The blue was several shades lighter than her eyes, which were widening as he stared at her in silence.

A muffled whisper broke his mesmerism, and he looked past Nerissa to see her abigail one step higher on the stairs. Whatever Frye had said brought a frown to Nerissa's face. Shaking her head, Nerissa hurried down the stairs, uncertainty plain on her lovely face.

"Hamilton, is something wrong?"

He glanced past her, but the man who had opened the door had vanished as completely as his hopes of getting an answer to his quest tonight. The poignant reminder of his greatest failure ate at him like an open sore. He took Nerissa's slim hands and stared down into her eyes, which were heavy with fatigue. He longed to see them close in the moment before his mouth claimed hers.

With the greatest effort, he kept his thoughts from intruding on his question. "May a friend of the shortest standing beg the favor of your company for a few minutes?"

"Frye," she said without hesitation and without looking away, "please have some cocoa brought to the parlor. Or would you like something stronger, Hamilton?"

"Brandy for me, Frye," he requested, managing a smile as he saw concern in Nerissa's eyes. It might be as feigned as his own indifference, but it was what he needed to see right now.

His mouth straightened. Elinor had been an expert at showing him what he needed to see at any given moment. So expert had she been that he had been the last to discover her infidelity when she made him the laughingstock of the *ton* before his voyage for America. Had he learned nothing in the years since?

He did not want Elinor in his head tonight. She was gone from his life. Tonight he wanted Nerissa to give him the comfort he had sought so unsuccessfully since Elinor had betrayed him.

When Nerissa gasped, he realized he had tightened his hold on her fingers painfully. "In the parlor," he ordered Frye, not caring that the abigail was staring at him askance as he gave commands as if this was his house.

Nerissa stepped back as Hamilton strode past her. Exchanging a perplexed glance with Frye, she hurried into the parlor after him. The stiff line of his shoulders warned that the conversation would not be an easy one, although she doubted if any in which Hamilton was involved would ever be.

"I did not expect you to knock down my door tonight. I thought you were busy this evening, Hamilton," she said to his back.

He bent to warm his hands over the embers on the hearth, although the night air was not cold. When she saw the line of drying mud on his Hessians, she knew he had not been with his tie-mates at a card table. More grime clung to his cloak that was as black as a starless night.

"I was."

"Doing what?"

"Business, Nerissa."

"Your quest to find that feckless thief," she answered quietly, then realized she would have been wiser to remain silent, for his eyes snapped with steely fury as he whirled to face her.

"Do not probe into things that matter nothing to you."

"But it does matter to me."

The tails of his coat slapped his legs as he walked toward her. The ironic tilt of his brow matched the sarcasm in his voice. "Does it? Pray tell me why?"

"I thought we were friends, Hamilton, and friends

126

share each other's pains as well as triumphs."

When he grasped her shoulders, she heard Frye's gasp, and realized her abigail had followed them into the parlor. She had no time to think of anything else as he asked, "Friends? Is that all you wish to be? Do you wish to forsake this?"

His mouth was not gentle as it captured hers. It was as demanding as every aspect of him, and she knew the danger of relinquishing her will to his strong one. If Annis was correct, and her bosom bow had no reason to lie, once Hamilton was the victor in any chase, he tired of the hunt. She had seen how persistent he was in trying to get what he wanted. He had manipulated Mrs. Ehrlich with the skill of a master today and would do the same to her tonight. Yet, she longed to soften against him, to savor the strength of his hard body, to drown in the rapture of his touch. If she did, she would lose too much. This was a game at which she could never win. She was a widgeon to continue it, but she could not deny herself this delight . . . one last time.

When she put her hands up to push him away, his arm swept around her waist, pulling her tightly to him. His lips left sizzling sparks along her neck, threatening to dissolve her against him. Boldly, his tongue teased the curve of her ear as his breath seared her with its fiery pulse.

His voice was a low growl as he whispered, "Do you want this, Nerissa, or friendship?"

"I don't know," she gasped, struggling to breathe as the longing to draw his mouth back to hers battled her good sense. Blinking, she put her hands on his rough cheeks and brought his face back so she could look up into his hooded eyes. "But I know you need a friend, Hamilton. I would be a friend to you, if you would give me a chance."

She tried to guess what he was thinking, but could read none of the emotions altering his face from its fierce mask. They vanished too quickly as his features grew hard again. Releasing her, he stepped back. His gaze slowly moved along her, as if he was seeking something *she* was hiding. She yearned to tell him that she spoke the truth, but she wondered if he would believe her.

"Friendship is not what I wish from you, Nerissa."

She gripped the back of the chair beside her, for her knees were weak with the emotions washing over her in a fierce wave. Softly she asked, "What do you wish from me?"

"I thought I had made that clear."

The exacting sound of his voice lashed her. This was no profession of affection, but of the desire she had discovered on his lips. Without turning, she whispered, "Frye, will you please see to the cocoa?"

"Miss Dufresne, I must insist—"

"Frye, please." She did not need to see her abigail's face to know that Frye was furious. Later she must soothe Frye, but now she must ascertain why Hamilton was treating her so coldly when his lips had been so lusciously warm.

The door closed behind Frye, leaving them in silence. Nerissa lowered herself carefully to the chair. She no longer trusted her legs to support her. Quietly she asked, "Why are you so angry at me?"

"Angry?" He caught her by the shoulders and brought her to her feet again. Kissing her swiftly, he murmured, "I feel nothing so tepid as anger for you tonight, Nerissa."

She put her hands on his wrists and drew his fingers off her. "Then whom are you angry at?" Her laugh was sharp. "There is no need to ask, is there? You may have saved your brother's life today, but you can think only of vengeance."

"I have to find that accursed sneaksman."

Although she flushed at his crude words, Nerissa retorted, "And then what will you do, Hamilton?

Once you have your revenge, what will you do?"

"Watch what is left of him hang when I hand him over to the authorities."

"And then what?" she asked quietly, not letting him see how his words sickened her nor how she wished he would let her help assuage the pain that was consuming him. "What will you do when you have done all that you can to retaliate against that man?"

He stared at her, and his pain ached within her as if it was her own. She clenched her hands at her side to keep them from reaching out to him. If she let him hold her in rage, she feared she would never rediscover the sweetness she had found in his arms that afternoon. Her sympathy must have shown on her face, for, with a growled farewell, he strode toward the entrance hall.

"Hamilton?" she called to his back.

He did not face her, but stopped.

"Do you have no answer," she asked, "or do you have no answer you wish to share with me?"

For a long moment, she feared he would not answer. Then he turned. No emotion gave life to his hard features. "Do not think to betwattle me with your gentle words and sweet kisses. I was a fool before, but I shan't be one again. Not for you, Nerissa, nor for that damned thief. Good evening."

The door to the street closed loudly in his wake. Nerissa went to the front window and watched him stride purposefully toward the bridge and the city. Blinking back tears, she shivered at the fury in him tonight. She never had seen this side of Hamilton, and the strength of his passions unnerved her.

He had made one thing clear. He trusted her no more than he did any other woman. And why should he when she had been dishonest with him? She longed for more than friendship with him, but she would not be his next light skirt, to be used and left with a few gifts when he turned his eye to another woman.

Quietly, from behind her, Frye asked, "Do you think he will come back?"

"I don't know," she whispered as she stared at the empty street.

"Do you want him to return?"

"I don't know," she repeated, knowing that—if at no other time this evening—she was speaking the truth.

# Chapter Nine

Nerissa stood at the window of her bedroom and watched the rain splatter into the puddles on the stones in front of the house. It was a dismal day that fit her mood. Hamilton had left the house in such a vile state more than three days ago, and she had heard nothing of him since. She had considered calling on Annis to discover if her bosom bow had spoken with Philip, but she had delayed.

Seeing someone happy, even her very best friend, would completely undo her now.

With a sigh, she walked away from the window and sat in the chair where she had left her book, unread. She picked it up and thumbed through it before setting it on her lap again. Although she had errands to tend to this afternoon, she had sent Frye to do them. To speak to their neighbors while she was as melancholy as a gib cat would be a mistake.

"Here you are!"

Nerissa managed a smile as she turned to see Cole in the doorway. His face was alight as he rushed across the room to grasp her hands and bring her to her feet. When she winced as he pulled on her left wrist, he hastily apologized.

"It is nothing," she reassured him as she rubbed her arm.

131

"Come with me! I want you to be the first to see it!"

"Your work on the canal is done?" All thoughts of her grief vanished as she saw the truth on his face.

"The first part." His grin stretched his broad cheeks into a happiness she had not seen on his face since they had exchanged harsh words in the front entry. "Do come, Nerissa. Come and tell me that you think it is wonderful . . . even if it is not."

"It *will* be wonderful, because you did it." She linked her arm with his and walked with him down the stairs and into his cluttered book room.

She usually avoided this room. Not just because it was Cole's sanctuary, but because, more than any other room in the house, it reminded her of Hill's End. Before she had moved to Bath, she had invited her stepbrother to Hill's End to select anything he might be able to use. His book room was crowded with furniture from Hill's End. He had been delighted with the desks and tables that had belonged to Nerissa's father, and she was pleased to see them being used.

Her fingers stroked the corner of a leather writing pad. It was all she could see of the brown material, but, in her deepest memories, she recalled sitting on her father's knee while he wrote at this desk.

She stepped over the piles of books and maps stacked haphazardly on the floor. *Seeing* more of her father's tables was an impossibility when they were covered with many times more books and papers than had fallen to the floor. She was unsure how her stepbrother managed to work in such chaos, but it suited him.

Cole pointed to one table, but she could not guess what he wanted her to see until he jabbed one page with his finger. The crisp paper crackled under his touch as he outlined the grand path of the canal through the hamlets and villages between Bristol and London. As he spoke of the locks and the tolls to be collected, she could imagine the excitement of the settlements when a barge stopped to unload food and merchandise from distant lands.

"It is grand, Cole. Grander than I had guessed. Did you devise this all alone?"

He smiled with satisfaction. "I did look at the preliminary work others have done, but no one has actually drawn all the plans."

"Your hard work shows."

"It is only the beginning. We must go to London, so we can find someone to finance this canal."

"London?" She looked at him, but he was gazing intently at his drawings.

"Of course. Do you think we can find someone with both blunt and an imagination in this provincial city? We shall go to London, and I shall make this more than a dream." Standing straighter, he let the map roll closed with a snap. He gripped it in his pudgy hand. "Otherwise, all this work is nothing but a piece of paper."

"London?" she asked again faintly.

Taking her by the shoulders, he said, "Nerissa, we could travel by the Mail coach. It takes no more than twelve hours from here to London, for it is less than one hundred miles. Think of it! London! I daresay I haven't been in the Metropolis for more than two years, and you have never been there. I could find some financiers, and you . . ." He tapped her on the nose. ". . . you could buy yourself a new pair of gloves."

Turning away so he could not see her expression, she said, "I don't think we can go."

"How can we *not* go? I know I can find some people who would be intrigued by this venture." The excitement in his voice tempered as he added, "Nerissa, I understand that we are not beforehand with the world, but can we be close as wax with our money when this opportunity might obtain us more brass than we could imagine?"

"I cannot make sovereigns appear out of midair."

He kicked a pile of books to the floor, startling her. She backed away as he aimed his foot at another stack. The fury in his eyes reminded her of the night he had slammed the front door . . . and of Hamilton.

"Cole," she said in a soft voice, "you are asking the impossible."

Coldly, he retorted, "I noticed that you have found enough blunt to buy yourself a new hat! Which household account did you bleed that money from?"

Nerissa stared at him, unsure if she was more shocked by his outburst or that he had noticed her new bonnet. Wanting to soothe him before his face became more choleric, she said, "Cole, the bonnet was a gift from Hamilton to replace the one that was ruined when he nearly ran me down."

"Lord Windham?" His brows knit together in rage, and he plowed his way through discarded papers to set his map on a shelf high above the mess.

"What is wrong?" she asked to his back. "Surely you know that Hamilton has been calling here." She almost added that he had spied upon Hamilton and his brother one night, but she did not want to add to his rage.

"You should not be wasting your time and our money on such a frivolous life." He whirled and pointed at her. "Annis Ehrlich! She has put ideas into your head that we can't afford."

"Annis has nothing to do with our situation." Nerissa locked her fingers together in front of her, so he could not see the fury she struggled to keep from her voice. "Nor does Lord Windham. You should know that I would not indulge in any luxury when we have butcher's meat in the kitchen. If I do not pay for that meat, there will be no more brought to us."

For a long moment, she feared that he would continue to shout at her. Then he sighed, and his face regained its normal coloring. "Pardon me. This project has become so important that I fear I am losing my perspective. Instead of deriding you, I should be grateful that you have managed to keep this household solvent."

"I wish I could tell you that I have the wherewithal to take us both on a splendid trip to London, but there is no money beyond what we need to keep the household going." She did not tell him that the servants had not been paid in more than two months. That news would only disturb him more.

"None at all?"

"None at all."

"Impossible!"

"No," she said sadly, "and there shan't be more until Hill's End sells."

When she shook her head, he dropped into a chair by the largest table. He leaned his elbows on the table and covered his face with his hands. She put her fingers on his shoulders, but he shrugged them off.

"Begone, Nerissa," he ordered.

"But, Cole—"

"Just begone!"

Knowing that arguing with him would gain neither of them anything, Nerissa backed toward the door. Pain pierced her as she heard his muffled sobs. He wept not as a child would after learning that a treat would be withheld, but with the anguish of a man who has seen his dreams dashed to dust before he has had a chance to grasp them. Into her memory's ear came the resonance of Hamilton's infuriated voice as he spoke of not being able to succeed at his aspiration of finding the cross-cove who stole his father's money.

Tears blossomed into her eyes. She could not help Hamilton, for he asked for something she must not give him. She wiped her eyes, not wanting anyone to see her pain. Her days were so empty without the anticipation of Hamilton's calls. How many times had she gone to a window to search Laura Place for his carriage or his horse? The number of times she had looked did not matter, for he never had been there.

Even if she could not help Hamilton, there must be a way to aid Cole in reaching past his frustration to find his dream.

*Money!* It was impossible to do without when her brother had such grandiose goals, but they were as full of money as a toad was full of feathers. If she had as much as a sixpence that was not accounted for in the household, she would . . .

Nerissa's eyes widened. There was money that was unaccounted for in the house. She rushed up the stairs at a speed that would have gained her a reprimand from Frye.

Going into her bedroom, she knelt by her dressing table and opened the bottommost drawer. She drew out the small box with fifty guineas in it. They were the ones she had won the first night she played whist with Hamilton and his friends. Her other winnings had been spent to soothe their creditors, but she had saved these for an emergency. Her smile faded as she sat back on her heels. Fifty guineas might as well be a halfpenny, for all the good it did them. They needed much more for a journey to London.

Not only would they require two billets on the eastbound Mail, but Cole's magnificent venture might not be embraced swiftly. While he negotiated with the men he assured her would be interested in bringing the attention of the government onto the project, they must have a place to live in Town. No doubt, entertaining would be part of the contracting of any private financing for the canal. For that, Nerissa must provide food and hire servants, because it would be impossible to take the whole of their household to London.

Fifty guineas would not be enough. She must have

more money if she wished to help Cole make his wish come true. There was only one way, although she had tried to avoid thinking of it, but she could deal with the matter on her way to meet Annis at the *couturière's* shop this afternoon. Humiliating herself by begging might be the sole method to get the money they needed. Closing the box, she reached for the bell by the door, wanting to get the horrible call over.

Mr. Broderick Crimmins leaned back in his chair and scanned his office. The walls were of dark oak, which hid any sunshine that might dare to creep through the tall, thin windows. He liked his office, for it smelled of age and respectability. In his opinion, that was what a solicitor should aspire to at all times. Respectability. Even the word had a grand sound that Mr. Crimmins enjoyed hearing connected to his name.

When voices sounded in the antechamber, he remained sitting at his cluttered desk. There would be no intrusion unless his secretary, Mr. Mann, deemed the visitors worthy of the privilege of entering the inner office. A sour man, Mr. Mann, had proven an asset beyond price to his employer on many occasions. Although Mr. Crimmins wished his secretary would wear something other than the funereal black coat and waistcoat and nankeen trousers to the office, he had no other reason to complain about Mr. Mann.

At a hushed knock, Mr. Crimmins rose. Apparently the caller was a personage of enough importance to obtain Mr. Mann's approval. Tugging at his waistcoat, which had a habit of leaving a gap at the waistband of his breeches, he came forward to greet his client.

Amazement could not be kept from his face as his

scrutiny settled on a delicate form which was topped by a pretty bonnet and swathed in a brightly dyed Kashmir shawl. When the young woman looked up, he tried to smile. His expression wavered, for, although he had met her steady, blue eyes on many occasions, he had learned he could not batter back Miss Dufresne's gaze. He wondered what trouble she was bringing him now. It was his misfortune that his father had been her stepfather's solicitor. He had inherited Miss Dufresne and her problems along with his father's other business.

"Do come in," he urged automatically, aware of his secretary standing by the door. He did not want to appear a fool before Mann. *"On dits* suggested that you were injured rather seriously recently. May I say that you look well?"

Nerissa smiled. The solicitor's words were a welcome acknowledgment that her bruises had faded to mere shadows of their former flamboyance. She sat in the chair that Mr. Crimmins indicated, but she wished he had something other than the too soft chairs in his office. She sank into whichever one she chose, threatening to become lost in the leather while she tried to explain to the solicitor her most recent monetary crisis.

"Thank you, sir. I am sure rumor has made the incident far more harrowing than it truly was."

Returning behind his desk, the young solicitor tried to maintain his cool demeanor while he sat in his chair. Nerissa wondered if he resisted recalling that he had gone to school with her brother for many years. Tales of those earlier times included many escapades that would not fit with the image Mr. Crimmins had created for himself in his darkly paneled cocoon. Or of Cole, she had to own.

"Miss Dufresne, this is a surprise," he said in the emotionless voice he always assumed.

She suspected he thought that tone made him

sound more overmastering, but she usually had to struggle to keep from laughing. Not so today, when she was fighting the blue devils each time Hamilton slipped into her mind. Her hands gripped the strings of her beaded reticule more tightly. Thinking of him was futile, for he clearly had put her from his life as easily as he had the others who had passed through it.

"I did not expect to see you until the quarter's end," Mr. Crimmins continued. "I trust nothing else is amiss with your household now that you have recovered from your mishap."

She released her hold on the bag. Folding her gloved hands primly in front of her, Nerissa forced a smile. "Everything is quite wonderful with our household, Mr. Crimmins, if you wish me to own to the truth. I came to inform you that Mr. Pilcher and I are planning an excursion to London."

"London?" His scowl deepened the ruts along his thin face. "Do you think that is wise?"

"Mr. Crimmins, you know that I am no widgeon. I would not come here to bother you with tales of silly dreams. Mr. Pilcher and I have just decided that furthering his career requires a short sojourn to the Metropolis." Taking a deep breath to prepare herself for the battle she knew was to come, she said, "Because of that, I would ask you to advance us a portion of the money we would receive from the next quarter's household allowance."

"Impossible."

"Mr. Crimmins," Nerissa said quietly, "on numerous occasions, you have implored me to find Mr. Pilcher something worthwhile to do. On every occasion, I have assured you that my brother was involved in a pursuit that would come to fruition at its own rhythm. The opportunity is here at last to culminate his years of study and work."

"Impossible, Miss Dufresne. I cannot give you any brass in advance."

She took another deep breath and slowly expelled it. Flying up to the boughs would gain her nothing from this stolid man. Rational thought worked best with him, as it did with Hamilton.

*Begone,* she shouted silently. *I cannot afford to think of you now when I must think of Cole.* At least, Cole asked for something that wasn't impossible to give. No, another part of her mind answered. What Hamilton wanted would be so very, very easy for her to offer him if he had asked in the carriage on the way back from the interview with Mrs. Ehrlich. Far too easy, she owned. Mayhap it was better that he had not returned, for she feared her longings to be in his arms could betray her.

"Miss Dufresne?"

Mr. Crimmins's impatient voice pulled her back to the problem in front of her. Coolly she said, "You have spoken of the need for our household to become self-supporting. Why are you becoming an addle-plot when we stand on the threshold of achieving that very independence?"

"Your mother's bequest was specific. You would be given a set allowance out of the money Mrs. Pilcher left for you each quarter until it was gone."

And then we will have *nothing,* she thought grimly. Although her stepfather had been as determined to make a fortune as Cole was, he never had made a single effort to do anything but spend her mother's money.

"Mr. Crimmins," she asked, wondering what other argument she could devise to convince the solicitor, "I would think you might see it wise to invest our money now, so that we might have something to live upon after Cole's birthday."

"I cannot change the legacy of your loving father and mother."

Nerissa tried to keep her lips from straightening with loathing. "Loving father" was the last descrip-

140

tion she would have used for Albert Pilcher. The bruises he had left on her during the few years he lived at Hill's End had been more painful than the ones she suffered when she met Hamilton. Reminding herself that it did no good to lambaste the dead, she raised her gaze to meet Mr. Crimmins's colorless eyes.

"Sir, I implore you to reconsider. This proposition is of utmost importance to my brother."

"I am sorry, Miss Dufresne. Even if I thought it was in your best interests to advance you the money—and I speculate that further study into the matter would prove that your plans are unwise—I cannot do as you wish."

Recognizing the finality in his words, Nerissa rose. There was but one more venue to get money for Cole. She did not want to ask the question, but she had no choice. "Have you heard anything from the agent who has Hill's End under the hammer?"

"There has been a query by an interested party. When or if, for I must be honest that it is no more than a query at this point, something becomes more defined, you may be certain that I shall send you such tidings immediately. I collect the price we discussed remains the same."

"We need to have it sold." Her voice almost broke.

"Shall we say ten thousand pounds less then?"

She nodded, for she could not speak the words that were sure to ensure the rapid sale of her beloved home. She bid Mr. Crimmins a good day and walked out of his office. She did not acknowledge his secretary, because she did not want him to see the tears that burned in her eyes. As she hurried down the stairs to the street door, she wondered how she could tell Cole that her last hope to help him had failed. If Mr. Crimmins had agreed to advance but fifty guineas to match the fifty she had, she could have . . .

Nerissa laughed suddenly as she came out into the

watery sunshine. A hundred guineas could have provided for both of them, but, if her brother was careful with those limited funds, fifty guineas would get Cole to London and enable him to meet with prospective backers. She must send him alone. It was not *the* perfect solution, but it was *a* solution.

Her smile disappeared as quickly as the sun behind the clouds that were the steely grey of Hamilton's eyes. She blinked back the hot tears. If only she could bridge the differences between her and the stubborn viscount as easily, but she feared that was impossible.

The *modiste*'s shop was nearly deserted when Nerissa entered. *Madame* DeLeff did not pause in her explanation of the fashion plates that she was showing Annis to greet Nerissa. Nor did Nerissa expect her to leave one of her best customers to speak to her. She had not ordered a new gown since her arrival in Bath.

As soon as the *modiste* went into the back to gather samples, Annis smiled a greeting. "I was beginning to wonder if you had forgotten that we were meeting here today."

"I had to make a few other stops," she hedged, not wanting to reveal the truth of their dire financial predicament to Annis. There was no need to down pin her friend, especially now that she had found a way to help Cole. "Annis, I must ask you a favor."

"Anything." Crossing her hands over her breast, she said, "I owe you so much for helping Hamilton convince Mama to let Philip call."

"I did nothing."

"That is not what Philip says." Her voice dropped to a whisper. "He says if you had not been there, Hamilton would have most certainly put Mama into a pelter. Then there would have been no changing her mind."

Nerissa fingered the thick pages of the book of fashion plates. Speaking of Hamilton made her uneasy. "Annis, please listen and only then tell me if you can do me this favor. Cole needs to go to London."

Her nose wrinkled. "Good! We will be well rid of his dour face."

"He is my stepbrother," she chided gently.

"That does not mean I have to like him. If you did not have the disposition of an angel, Nerissa, you would have seen long ago that he twists whatever he wants out of you."

"Cole?"

Sitting on a bench by the window overlooking the street, Annis shook her head. "Dear Nerissa, you are so blind to him. Because you care so much for family, you cannot see that he thinks only of himself."

"And his project."

"Which will never come to anything."

Nerissa dropped next to her friend. "But it will! He has finished the initial design. Now he must go to find backers to begin the work. That is why I must ask you a favor."

"I shall not sink a farthing into it!"

Again she was shocked by the acrimony in her friend's voice. "Annis, I would not ask such a thing of you. Please listen to me. Cole is going to London, but I shall stay in Bath. However, he is hesitant about me staying here alone. Do you think your mother would allow you to stay with me while he is gone?"

Her friend's dark eyes lit with excitement. "Stay with you? Oh, Nerissa, that would be grand! Janelle has set her cap on Mr. Oakley, and—"

"She has finally decided to marry Mr. Oakley?" Nerissa smiled. "I will own, but only to you, that I find him disgustingly high in the instep for such a boor."

"I agree." Annis's dimples deepened. "Now Mama

can talk only of the preparations for Janelle's betrothal and wedding. I fear I shall go quite mad with all of it buzzing about my head."

"When you wish it was yours?"

"I hope it will be one day soon." Taking Nerissa's hands in hers, she said, "Oh, this shall be the grandest thing we could do. Think what fun we shall have chatting the night away and having our at homes together." She rose and clapped her hands. "And Philip may call with Hamilton to take us about Bath. It shall be grand."

"Do not make any plans that include Hamilton and me."

Annis dismissed Nerissa's words with a wave of her hand. "I know you two have quarrelled, but you must put it behind you."

"I don't think Hamilton wishes that."

"Philip is distressed. You worked so hard to help persuade Mama, and it seems unfair that now you are away from Hamilton."

Nerissa shook her head. "He was the one who left so rudely. I offered him friendship, and he refused it."

"Friendship? Can't you see that the man has a *tendre* for you?"

"Hamilton has no interest in dangling after any woman."

Annis stood and paced the room. "That is odd, for Philip thought you would be the one to help his brother get over his distaste of women."

"Distaste?" She laughed without humor. "Weren't you the one warning me, Annis, that Hamilton has a great deal of interest in the company of women of all sorts?"

"Mayhap distaste was not the correct word." She toyed with a bolt of lace next to the book of fashion plates. Her usual smile was gone, replaced by an intensity that Nerissa had seldom seen on her face. "Philip told me all about how Hamilton was so

144

badly hurt by that Howe woman. She welcomed him in her bed, let him set her up in his house in Town, and then cuckolded him openly when he was away on business. He dares trust no other woman."

"I have seen that." Nerissa rose and walked to the far side of the cozy room. This explained so much of what had happened since she had met Hamilton. His eagerness to lure her into his arms while keeping her away from any other part of his life had come about because he guessed her to be the same as this woman who had hurt him so badly.

"You must help him realize that he has been mistaken, Nerissa."

"But how?"

Annis smiled sadly. "That is something only you can know. Look into your heart, and then I pray that you will find the answer before it is too late."

# Chapter Ten

Nerissa smiled as she rapped on her brother's book-room door. When she heard the muted and disgruntled command to enter, she opened the door.

As she had expected, Cole was bending over a book, his finger tracing the words with his nose less than an inch from the page. Her single suggestion that he might consider eyeglasses to help him with his surfeit of reading had brought her a quick retort of denial. She suspected he did not want to wear blinkers and be teased as a glass-eyes.

He did not pause in his perusal until she lifted his finger from the page. Turning his hand over, she pressed the coins into his palm.

When Cole looked up at her, his eyes widening with amazement, she said, "Now you can go to London, Cole. This should be enough for you to travel and find a cheap place to live as long as you keep from high-eating. If you need me with you in Town, I shall follow when I can."

"I shall be able to manage alone." He dropped the money on top of his book and counted it with the eagerness of a gripe-penny. Without pausing, he added, "Of course, I shall take Hadfield with me. I must present a good image, and a man of any quality has his valet in attendance."

"Of course, you must take him." Nerissa made no effort to hide her happiness. Being rid of the intolerable butler would be well worth the loss of the fifty guineas.

"And what will you do?"

His sharp question startled her. As he stood, secreting the coins in a pocket beneath his rumpled, black coat, she answered, "I have asked Annis to stay with me."

"Annis Ehrlich?" His long nose wrinkled in revulsion. "I don't like the idea of that gabble grinder in my house."

"You will be leaving before she arrives."

"Just be certain she is out before I return."

Nerissa bit her lip to silence her retort. If the truth was known, this house should be hers. Her mother had inherited it from a distant aunt, but Albert Pilcher had laid claim to it as he had to everything else, save for Hill's End, which Nerissa's father had been wise enough to bequeath directly to his daughter.

"When is the Mail leaving for London?" Cole asked.

She told him the information she had gathered while out on her errands. "You have a few hours to pack."

"Let Hadfield know that I will need him to pack for me."

"Cole, I need to—"

"And please send a note to the parents of my students informing that classes are in recess until such time as I return." He pulled a coin from his pocket and tossed it into the air. Catching it gleefully, he added, "With good fortune continuing to smile on me, I shall be done with tutoring the cherubims forever!"

147

"I really have no time to write—"

He whirled to face her. His voice took on a peevish tone as he snapped, "I must hurry to be ready in time to catch the Mail. I would think you could do something to help."

Nerissa stared at him in disbelief, unable to say anything but, "Of course, I want to help you, Cole."

"I know you do." He came around the table, his smile returning. "You have been a great help up until now. It was wrong for Papa to refuse to allow you to come here while he was alive."

Nerissa was glad her brother had turned to scoop up his papers and did not see the dismay on her face. Although there had been no affection between her and her stepfather, she had not guessed Albert Pilcher would be so vulgar as to deny his orphaned stepdaughter a place under his roof. Yet it was no surprise.

In the aftermath of her mother's death, Mr. Pilcher had not so much as bothered to come to the funeral. Instead he had sent a terse note with hypocritical words of grief, showing he was more concerned with the state of his late wife's estate than her death. More than she had been at the time, Nerissa was glad now that her stepfather had stayed away. Although her mother had never said a word against her second husband, Nerissa was sure that Mr. Pilcher had married the widowed Mrs. Dufresne only for the money he had guessed her husband had left her. Finding there was little, he had deserted his wife and stepdaughter and vanished for more than fifteen years.

"Now I must go and ready myself to go to London!" He patted his pocket. "Soon I shall be able to pay you back the fifty pounds with such interest that you will be able to buy dozens of new hats. You will not need to depend on Windham's charity."

"Hamilton was only—"

"I know what he is trying." As if the subject was boring, he changed it abruptly. "Do have Mrs. Carroll see that my extra cravats are pressed neatly before they are packed, Nerissa."

Before she could remind him that she would find it impossible to do half of what he had requested in the short time before he was leaving, she saw Hadfield in the doorway. The butler's expression of disapproval became disgust when Cole rushed to him and told the butler how Nerissa had made it possible for them to go to London.

"The house must be properly closed before we leave," Hadfield said in his coldest voice as he stared at Nerissa.

She watched his lips curl into a smile as Cole answered, "Nerissa is remaining to watch over the house. You and I shall handle the work in London as we have here, Hadfield. I suspect you, too, shall be glad to see Town again."

"Very glad, Mr. Pilcher." He shot Nerissa a triumphant look, but she simply regarded him in silence. His smile wavered when she did not react.

Nerissa was more glad than ever that the hateful man was leaving Bath with Cole. Otherwise, the worthless butler would try to make trouble for her— more trouble than he usually did.

"What is it, Hadfield?" Cole asked sharply when the butler did not obey his order to follow him out of the book room.

The older man appeared surprised that his beloved master would use such a tone with him, but he glowered at Nerissa. She guessed he blamed her for turning Cole against him. Although she was tempted to smile, she did not. She would prove her garret was empty if she did something so idiotic, because the *majordomo* would become even more intolerable

149

upon his return from London.

"A message, Mr. Pilcher."

Holding out his hand, Cole ordered, "Give it over. It might be important."

"It is not for you, sir." Stiffly, he ordered it to Nerissa. "For you, miss."

She took the note he held out with such disdain. Ignoring the butler as Hadfield walked from the room, she gasped when she saw the return address on the envelope. Queen Square!

"What is it?" Cole asked.

"Nothing important." Guilt pinched her, but she did not want to share her uneasiness with Cole when he was so anxious about the trip and the days ahead of him. "Go, and make your arrangements. The Mail will be leaving sooner than you might think."

Her warning was enough to propel him up the stairs at uncommon speed. Sitting in the closest, uncluttered chair, she sighed. She had not wanted Cole lurking nearby while she perused this unexpected letter. He had aimed too many demure hits at Hamilton already, and she wished to hear no more.

She opened the letter and read,

Dear Nerissa,

I am pleased that you agreed for Philip and me to call for you tomorrow afternoon to take you to the Pump Room.

Astonishment swept over her. She had agreed to no such invitation nor had Annis mentioned it, and certainly her friend could not have disguised her delight if she had known of it. What was Hamilton's intention now? She had hoped that this letter would contain an apology or an explanation, but she should have known better.

The last line of the letter only told her that the

150

carriage would arrive for her at exactly one o'clock. It was signed with Hamilton's boldly scrawling signature. She lowered the letter to her lap.

She could hope this was his way of apologizing, but she did not dare to assume anything. She was even less sure of her own feelings. She longed to see Hamilton again, to delight in his touch, to be thrilled by his fiery kisses, but . . .

She rose and folded the letter. First she must see that Cole found a seat on the London-bound Mail. Then she must help Annis get settled here. Only then would she decide what she would do about this astonishing invitation.

Everything worked out as Nerissa had hoped with Annis. Not only was Mrs. Ehrlich delighted to grant permission for her youngest daughter to stay with Nerissa, she went on at more length than usual about the wonders of having the brother of a viscount interested in her dear Annis. Was Janelle listening? Hadn't Mama told her that all her daughters could marry well if they simply had patience?

Leaving Mrs. Ehrlich lambasting Mr. Oakley's name—although she had been thrilled with his attention to Janelle only that morning—Nerissa went with Annis to help her decide what should be brought to Laura Place.

Annis's bedchamber was twice the size of Nerissa's room on Laura Place. Decorated in sedate golds and blues, it was perfectly suited to her friend. Sweeps of frothy material covered every table and draped from the tester bed. The windows were lost behind a sheathing of elegant lace that had yellowed to a warm color. Beneath Nerissa's feet, the thick rug threatened to swallow her thin slippers.

Prattling nonstop, Annis urged Nerissa to sit on

the window seat. She sent her abigail, Horatia, on a dozen errands at once.

"I don't wish to waste a moment of the time we can have at your house," Annis said. "I really was surprised when Mama allowed me to join you. Two young women without a chaperon, after all."

"Your mother knows well that Frye will allow no impropriety."

"True." Her eyes twinkled with happiness. "And you can be sure that Mama will be calling regularly to ascertain from Frye exactly who else is calling on us."

Nerissa hesitated, then said in a somber voice, "I received a letter from Hamilton before I took Cole to the Mail."

"How wonderful!" She hugged Nerissa enthusiastically. When Nerissa stiffened, she pulled back. "Whatever is wrong? Didn't he set things right between you?"

"He wrote only that he and Philip will be escorting us to the Pump Room tomorrow. Did you know of this?"

Annis sat on a chair, her face clouded with confusion. "Philip said nothing of such an invitation."

"Mayhap he knows no more about it than we did." Unable to sit still while she spoke of the disturbing letter, she rose and walked to the far side of the room. She turned to face her friend. "Hamilton may have devised this alone."

"But why?"

"I have no idea." She wrapped her arms around herself, not sure if she was happy or discomposed or both. "All I know is that we are sure to find out tomorrow afternoon."

\*　　　\*　　　\*

Annis hated puzzles. She had owned long ago that she was not as quick at solving such things as her bosom bow Nerissa Dufresne. Yet even Nerissa was unable to guess what would happen when a knock on the door signalled the arrival of Philip and his brother.

Watching Nerissa pace the parlor as she had for the past hour, Annis locked her fingers together in frustration in the lap of her grass-green dress. How could a man, who was as sweet and considerate as Philip Windham, have a brother who could be so prodigiously beastly? If Nerissa had half a brain, she would give Hamilton his *congé* as soon as he walked through the front door.

She sighed. Nerissa would do that no sooner than Annis would push Philip from her life. For some reason that Annis could not fathom, Nerissa was sweet upon the volatile viscount. Sometimes she was certain Hamilton had a cupboard love for Nerissa as well. Then other times—like now—she suspected he cared no more for her friend than he had for any of the other women who had passed through his life.

"They should be here soon," Annis said to fill the silence that was interrupted only by the muffled clatter of carriage wheels on the street.

"Hamilton said they would be here at one o'clock. They shall not arrive a heartbeat before then." Nerissa's faint smile added to the ache in Annis's heart. "He is dismally punctual."

As if to prove her words true, the tall-case clock by the stairs clanged a single time, drowning out the rapping at the door. Nerissa laughed shortly, but Annis had never felt less amused. She knew her friend had slept very little last night, for every time Annis woke, she had heard Nerissa's footfalls in the room across the hall.

Nerissa patted her bosom bow's icy hand before

153

going out in the foyer to see Mrs. Carroll open the door. The housekeeper mumbled something, but Nerissa was sure she would not have understood the most clearly enunciated words as her gaze was caught by Hamilton's uncompromising grey eyes. Something opened within her, a wound that yearned to be healed, a need she could not name, but she could do nothing but stare up into his eyes as he closed the distance between them.

"Nerissa, I would like to speak with you for a moment," he said, his rich, deep voice tolling through her. "Alone."

"My brother's book room is private," she managed to whisper.

"Then may I speak with you there?"

Although she dreaded what he might say to her beyond his brother and Annis's ears, she nodded. She led the way across the foyer, conscious of his eyes watching the sway of the flounces at the hem of her pale, blue skirt.

When she had closed the door, she lit a lamp on one of the tables. His brows lowered as he looked about the messy room, but he said, "I assume the invitation surprised you."

"Very much."

"Honest to the end."

"Is that what this is, Hamilton? The end of our friendship?"

He shook his head. "It would be easier if that was so, but the deception we devised to convince the *élite* to be more interested in our times together than in my search is still necessary."

"So that is why you invited me and Annis to the Pump Room?"

"One of the reasons. I considered, as well, the fact that you are too interested in a match between Philip and Annis to do anything to jeopardize it. You will even spend time in my company to ensure that."

Nerissa was sure her heart would shatter within her, but she kept her chin high. "You need not burden yourself with me, Hamilton. I can assure you that Annis would look with favor upon Philip's suit if he was to present it."

"You are no burden." When he laughed, she stared at him in astonishment. "And I do apologize for my behavior when I was here last."

"You do?"

His hearty laugh bewildered her more. "You are the most blasted woman! You believe me when I jest with you, but discount my words when I speak from the heart."

"Could it be because you speak from the heart so seldom?"

"I have discovered few people truly wish to know what is in a man's soul."

Unwilling to be put off from the truth, she asked, "Were you speaking from the heart the last time you called here?"

"Yes."

Pain buffeted Nerissa as he gave her the answer she had prayed he would not. When she would have turned away, his hands grasped her elbows. Gently he drew her to him. Instead of putting his arm around her, he continued to cup her elbows in his hands.

"Do not look so sad," he said in a raspy whisper. "It is the truth that you are lovely, and I would delight in possessing every inch of you. I would be less than a man if I could look at you with indifference."

"I will not be the way for you to forget another woman's treachery."

"Why are you thinking of another woman when I can think only of you when we stand so close?"

155

"And when we don't?"

When he stared at her, as dumbfounded as she had been moments before, she sighed and drew away. His hesitation told her what no words could. Like Cole, he was obsessed with reaching a goal.

"Nerissa—"

"Do not bother with your loud ones, Hamilton."

He took her hands. "I am not lying when I say that I enjoy the times we have together. Not that they are easy times, for you delight in any chance to turn teasing words into a tiff, but I would like us to be friends, Nerissa."

*"Only friends?"*

"I would have us be more, if *you* would agree." He put his finger to her lips and laughed. "No need for you to fly out at me, for I know you hold the canons of propriety too dear to consider such a relationship."

Nerissa wondered how he could read her thoughts so effortlessly on other matters, but was so mistaken when it came to knowing how desperately she longed to be in his arms, his mouth straining against hers as they sought to give voice to every whisper of passion within them. Although she was sure her broken heart would be rended completely, she said, "Friends we shall be."

Hamilton smiled and stepped over a jumbled collection of books. "So this is your reclusive brother's lair."

"Yes." She blinked back tears that should not be in her eyes when she was getting what she thought she had wanted. Hamilton was back in her life, and he would not ask her to be his natural, to be set aside when he was done with her. She should be pleased, but she was miserable.

He squinted at a small frame on the wall. *"Viam qui nescit, qua deveniat ad mare, Eum oportet amnem quaerere comitem sibi."* He chuckled. "If my

Latin teacher taught me well—and I can tell you that the poor man despaired of me ever sitting still for a single lesson—I believe that says, 'He who knows not the way leading to the sea should make the river his companion.'"

"It is one of Cole's favorite sayings. Plautius, I think." She ran her finger along the edge of one of the tables. To speak of such mundane things when her heart was cramped with sorrow seemed mad, but she struggled to maintain her composure. "He repeated it often when he reached a block in his work."

"So you embroidered it for him to hang on his wall." Folding his arms over the front of his proper brown waistcoat, he said, "You have much affection for your brother, Nerissa. I look forward to the opportunity to meet him."

She was surprised when she could smile honestly. The thought of Hamilton and Cole meeting was humorous. The two men would find each other boring. "He should return from London within a few weeks. Mayhap, if fortune looks with favor on his plans, I shall arrange a small *soirée* to celebrate the beginning of the actual work on his canal."

"Then will you leave Bath?"

As he had before, she was shocked into silence because she had no answer to give him. Neither she nor Cole had ever spoken of what they would do when his dream was achieved. Such changes it would bring to their lives, whether he was successful in Town or not. An icy shiver inched along her back as she thought of what they would do if he found no patrons for his project. There was little money left for them to maintain the house, and, until a buyer put forth money for Hill's End, she could not plan on any income from that quarter.

"We may."

"Believe me, Nerissa," he said, coming around the

157

table and folding her hand in his, "that I shan't look forward to that day."

She gazed up into his eyes and wanted to believe the sentiment in them was genuine. Softly she answered, "Neither will I."

Nerissa was startled to discover two carriages waiting in front of the house. When Hamilton handed her into his sleek curricle, which had been decorated with bright gilt on its sides and its two wheels, she turned to see Philip and Annis sitting in a more sedate gig. Hamilton sat next to her on the red velvet seat and picked up the fringed reins.

Opening her parasol, she asked, "Two carriages simply to go to the Pump Room?"

"We are not going there. It is too beautiful a day to spend inside." He slapped the reins on the back of the horses, but kept them at a decorous pace along the street.

"Then where are we going?"

"I thought that should be a surprise."

"A surprise? You are abducting Annis and me without giving us a clue of where we are going?"

He tilted his tall beaver back on his head as he relaxed against the seat and let the horses go at the sluggish speed of the town traffic. "You need to be more trusting, Nerissa."

"Me?" She shook her head in disbelief. "I am—as I have been told on too many occasions—too trusting."

"Of everyone save me, then, although you may be wise not to trust me. I am sure you have been told that you are caper-witted to trust a swell like me."

"You are no rakehell, Hamilton, although you clearly delight in playing the *rôle*."

"No?"

Tipping the parasol so she could see him without squinting into the bright sunshine, she said, "You delight in any chance to do harm in one's eyes, but you are too engrossed in your quest to find that blackguard to be dangling after any woman's skirts."

She waited for him to own up to her words or deny them, but he asked, "Then why do you show such a lack of trust in me?"

"I would trust you if you could trust me."

His only reply was a lowering of his brows as he frowned. With a sigh, Nerissa leaned back against the seat. Nothing had changed, although she had hoped their conversation in Cole's book room would prove otherwise. Hamilton could profess friendship, but there could be none while he waited for her to betray him.

As the busy streets evolved into soft hills and a nearly empty country road, Hamilton's hand slipped over hers. She looked at him and saw his sad smile.

"It shan't be easy to be as trusting as you are," he said, "but I shall try. You have proven to be a steadfast friend through these taxing days."

"Have you learned anything about the man you seek?"

"I have my suspicions, and I hope they soon will prove fruitful."

Recalling his savage vow to avenge himself on the thief, she shivered at his grim answer.

His laugh contrasted with the dark emotions in his eyes as he added, "My search is no topic for a lovely day like today when I am enjoying your company in this beautiful setting. I thought you would prefer the countryside to the Pump Room."

"Yes," she said, letting his words draw her out of the dank apprehension. Taking a deep breath, she exulted in the scents of flowers and trees before releasing it. She admired the flow of the fields along

159

the hillsides. In the distance, she could see the chimney of a brickworks, but its odious smoke did not reach them. "You know I love the country."

"I know, so I thought we would see as much of it as we could today."

That was the only warning she received before he snapped the whip over the horses' heads. The curricle leapt forward as if the hounds of Hell were snapping at the horses' hoofs. With a gasp, she gripped the side of the vehicle. She heard Hamilton's laugh over the rush of the wind that threatened both her bonnet and parasol. The wheels bounced in a chuckhole, and she grasped Hamilton's arm. If they were upset at this speed, they could be killed.

Putting her hand on his wrist, she drew back on it. He chuckled again, but let her guide his hands to pull on the reins to slow the horses. When they had slowed to a walk and he pulled the curricle beneath the trees on the side of the road, she sagged against the seat.

He held the reins with one hand as his other arm slipped around her shoulders. "You are shaking like a twig in a high wind, Nerissa. I thought you trusted me."

"To break both of our necks?" she retorted heatedly, not caring that each word quaked with her fear.

"To make the day enjoyable for you." When his voice softened to an enticing whisper, she raised her eyes to see the undeniable craving in his. His hand on her shoulders steered her toward his lips. "It shall take Philip and Annis several minutes to catch up with us. We may admire the nature around us, or we may . . ."

His hand swept up her back to press her to him. The familiar, fierce fire exploded within her, but she said, "I thought you wished only to share a friendship with me, Hamilton."

He kissed her right cheek. "Can we not be very special friends?" Teasing the curve of her left cheek with a swift kiss, he murmured, *"Very, very* special friends, my sweet." The tip of his tongue stroked the sensitive skin of her eyelids; she moaned with the longing that captivated her.

As her hand curved around his high collar to bring his mouth to hers, she heard his low laugh, and she knew that he had been correct when he warned her to be wary of trusting him. At the moment when his lips touched hers, she did not care. She might be an air-dreamer, but this rapture was what she wanted . . . no matter what it cost her.

# Chapter Eleven

Children cheered with excitement, and horses rumbled uneasily as Hamilton lifted Nerissa from the curricle to stand next to Annis. Nerissa stared at the collection of silk draped across the ground by the side of the road. Once it was completely inflated, the balloon surely would be as tall as the house on Laura Place. The roar of the flame burning within it threatened to deafen her.

When, with a laugh, Hamilton put his hands over her ears, she drew them away. "It is a lovely roar," she shouted over the noise.

"It is as raucous as a crow at dawn." He turned to watch the balloon thicken and rise as if it was taking life from the heated air within it.

"I have never seen one on the ground before." .

"Then," he said as she put her hand on his proffered arm, "it is time for you to do so."

The ground was soft beneath her slippers. Keeping her parasol over her head, she laughed when two children, who were chasing a brown and black mongrel, raced in front of them. The launching had all the exhilaration of a County Fair day.

The blue and green silk billowed skyward as several men, who were dwarfed by the expanse, worked to get all the material off the ground. They shouted to one another, but their voices were lost amid the flame's thundering howl.

"Amazing," said Philip as the balloon rose off the ground until only its tall, wicker basket clung precariously to the earth.

"I understand they are offering a ride to those daring enough to try it." Hamilton laughed, then asked, "Are you game for an attempt at the sport, Philip?"

"It is risky."

"No riskier than challenging me to jump that blasted hedge."

Philip chuckled and winked at Nerissa. "But you won that wager and much more."

"Then shall we take a flight?"

Nerissa put her hand on Annis's arm, which shook with sudden fear. "I don't think that is such a wise idea."

"Nonsense," Hamilton returned. "It will be delightful. You ladies are welcome to join us."

"No!" gasped Annis. "I shan't do something so want-witted."

Nerissa looked at the balloon and released a silent sigh. To own the truth, she was glad to remain on the ground. Quietly she said, "I shall stay with Annis."

"That leaves you and me, Philip," Hamilton said with another laugh. Taking his brother's arm, he tugged him a half-step toward the balloon. "Let's have a go at it." Hamilton turned his smile on Annis. "And to show your lovely lady that you are truly without fear."

"You need not do this for me," Annis whispered.

"Then do it for the fun," Hamilton said before his brother could reply. "I intend to try it."

Philip hesitated, clearly wanting to go, but unwilling to distress Annis. "Let me give this some thought."

"Bah!" Hamilton sneered. "What thought does it take to step into that basket and ride into the sky?"

Nerissa seized his sleeve. In a low voice, that was nearly swallowed by the rumble, she said, "I think we should let them discuss this alone."

Although she thought he would argue, he nodded. He walked with her in a broad circle around where the men were working to hold the balloon to the ground until they were ready to let it fly.

"Why are you pressuring him into going when he is trying to think of Annis's feelings?" Nerissa asked.

"To prove to him that rushing fearlessly into something dangerous is stupid." At his cold words, she put her hand to her mouth to silence her gasp of horror. Her eyes must have revealed her thoughts, because Hamilton nodded with regret before saying, "He has not changed his mind about buying that commission. Our foray against the formidable Mrs. Ehrlich was for naught."

"So you wish to prove him a coward?"

His eyes glinted dangerously. "Philip is no coward, Nerissa, only misguided in his hopes of finding a hero's glory, when all he might find is a hero's death. I hope this will prove he must think twice before leaping into the fray. If I am correct, he will learn a painless lesson, and I will lose only a few minutes of the day with you."

"And what if he fails to learn it, what do you lose then?" she asked.

"Peace of mind." He clasped his hands behind his back and continued to walk away from the others watching the balloon strain against its anchors.

Nerissa looked from Annis's eager face to Hamilton's back. It was as rigid as the ropes holding the balloon in place. She could not doubt the sincerity of his apprehension about Philip's plans to join the war on the Continent.

Hamilton appeared so alone as he strode through the high grass that had yellowed with the summer heat. Following him, she said, "Hamilton, you can't prevent Philip from doing what he feels he must. To own the truth, you are looking for an answer in the wrong place." She pointed to where his brother had his arm about Annis's shoulder as she leaned her cheek against his coat sleeve. "Let love convince him to see reason."

"I fear Philip has planned this too long to let a dalliance change his mind."

With a barbed laugh, she retorted, "And you think *you* can influence him if Annis cannot? You sadly misjudge what love can do."

"I have learned never to underestimate the havoc love can bring into one's life." His gaze pierced her, daring her to try to hide her thoughts from him when he was being so honest with her. "Those two are a prime example, for I doubt if Philip has told his beloved Annis what he intends to do. If you have not played Tom Tell-Truth with Miss Ehrlich, she has no idea of his ambition to sacrifice his life for his king and Regent."

"I have told her nothing. I thought he would."

"As I feared, Nerissa, you have miscalculated love's determination to make all things perfect. In his attempt to win her heart, my brother has failed to inform Annis that he has already given it to his future career in the army, short though it may be."

"You will drive him away if you don't try to understand his need to live beyond your shadow."

"I have tried to comprehend it, but to no avail."

She raised her chin and grimaced when the brim of her bonnet struck the spines of her parasol.

Hamilton's laugh added to her exasperation. One moment, he was the gentle lover who wooed her with enticing kisses and gentle words. The next, he played the arrogant viscount who discounted the hopes of anyone but himself.

Turning on her heel, she waded back through the tall grass to where Philip and Annis stood. She heard a cheer and looked back over her shoulder to see Hamilton talking to the men overseeing the launching of the balloon. When he climbed into the basket, her heart lurched. She silenced its terrified thump. Let Hamilton be a complete chucklehead! She could talk no sense to him.

Even as she thought that, Nerissa's fingers tightened convulsively on the porcelain handle of her parasol. No matter how intolerable he was—and he was more insufferable than any other person she had ever met—she did not want him to risk his neck on this futile ploy to save his brother's life.

"Hamilton is really going to go!" Philip crowed as she came within earshot. "By the Lord Harry, he is really going!"

"Philip, you need not go," Nerissa hurried to say.

"And let Hamilton get all the glory again?" He shook his head. "I think not." A gentle smile tilted his rigid lips. "Annis, watch from the carriage, for I shall wave to you when we are high above you."

When Annis stood on tiptoe and kissed him lightly on the cheek as she wished him good luck, Nerissa was sure her ears were betwattling her. Annis had been near to tears only minutes ago. Now she was acting as excited about the jaunt as Philip.

She gave Nerissa no chance to ask questions. Grabbing Nerissa's hand, she led her at an uncomely pace to the curricle. "Can you drive this, Nerissa?"

"Yes, but—"

"Philip said to follow the breeze to the east, and we

166

shall be able to meet them when they land on the far side of the hill." She signalled to a man to throw them up into the high seat.

Nerissa gasped as the man seized her around the waist and hefted her as if she was nothing more than a peddler's pack. Sliding along the seat when Annis sat next to her, she did not take the reins her friend held out to her.

"Look!" Annis cried. "There they go!"

The balloon was climbing silently into the eye-searingly blue sky. Nerissa's breath burned in her chest as she watched it go up . . . up . . . ever upward. *Hamilton, you catoller!* She hoped he would return to earth to gloat about how right he had been to challenge his brother in this way.

Annis's eyes sparkled with delight as she urged Nerissa to give chase. "How wondrous!"

"They both are all about in their heads to do this!" Sagging against the seat, she gazed skyward at the dwindling balloon. "You are no better!"

"Do not be such an addle-plot. Philip said nothing could happen. He—" She screamed and pointed to where the balloon was dropping back to earth too swiftly. "No!"

Nerissa seized her friend's arm as they stared in horror at the balloon. It was undeniably out of control. She clasped her hands at her breast as the balloon wobbled toward a copse at the top of the hill.

"Philip!" Annis's cry strained her throat.

Pulling the whip from its holder, Nerissa cracked it over the ears of the horses. They leapt forward, nearly jerking the reins from her hands. She wrapped the leather straps around her wrists as she shouted to the horses to run faster. A cloud of dust flew out behind them as the curricle raced wildly up the steep road.

She struggled to stop the horses. They neighed in

167

terror as the balloon's clamor sounded nearly over their heads. Only Annis's screech was louder as the balloon's basket struck the top of the trees. It hit deeper in the copse, the branches snagging the ropes.

Scrambling from the curricle, Nerissa turned to help her friend down. They lurched out of the way as the terrorized horses reared up and fled along the road, the carriage bouncing after them like a child's toy. Annis's face bleached with horror, but Nerissa kept her from running into the thicket. A dull explosion and a flash flew out from the shadows beneath the trees.

"Philip!" Annis cried again.

Nerissa wanted to ape her panic, but fought the seductive tendrils of hysteria. She raced forward when she saw a man staggering out of the trees. His coat was tattered and scorched.

"Get a cart!" he called. "There are injuries."

Shouts behind Nerissa made her whirl. She saw Annis fall to the ground in a swoon. Torn between helping her and finding out what had happened, she ran back to her friend. She slapped Annis's wrists, then her cheek to bring her back to her senses. Annis's eyes opened, and she moaned. Helping her to sit, Nerissa blinked back the tears in her eyes—sobbing, like Annis, would do no one any good.

"Annis!"

At the shout, Nerissa looked up to see Philip, his cheek scraped and his coat ripped, standing behind her. He pulled Annis to her feet and into his arms.

Nerissa gasped, "Are you hurt? Where is Hamilton?"

"I am fine." He looked back at the copse where the shredded balloon could be seen among the branches. "Thanks to Hamilton."

"Where is he?"

He kept his arm around Annis, but grasped

168

Nerissa's hand. "He should be fine, too."

"Philip!" Why was he choosing now to be as vexing as his brother? "Where is he?"

"Over here," called the voice she had feared she might never hear hoaxing her again.

She ran to where Hamilton was being placed in the back of a filthy pony cart. Seeing his torn pantaloons and the blood flowing along his leg, she fought her head which threatened to float away. This was no time for another fit of vapors.

"How do you fare?" she whispered.

Hamilton gave her a flimsy smile. "Now I can comprehend how you felt, Nerissa, when Cirrus nearly trod over you."

"How could you be so dough-baked?" she cried. "You could have been killed."

"I thought a bit of danger was worth teaching Philip that he was short a sheet to consider purchasing that captaincy. Now look at him! Delighting in Annis's adoration while I suffer from frying in my own grease."

"Mayhap it is time for you to listen to sage advice and let Philip choose what he wishes to do with his life."

"Mayhap you are right." His finger under her chin drew her face toward his. "After all, I have not managed to keep from making a complete muddle of my life."

"You? Owning to a mistake twice in one day?"

"Sarcasm isn't appealing on your lips, although," he added, "your lips are amazingly appealing."

When his mouth touched hers, the sobs beating against her lips burst outward. She clung to him, knowing that he had proved one thing this afternoon with his cockle-brained prank. She was falling in love with this impossible man, who would not want her love.

*　　　*　　　*

Inactivity was intolerable.

Tapping his fingers on the carved wood of his favorite chair in his book room, Hamilton took a sip of brandy and watched the fire on the hearth. Its pretty dance was fine for a background to conversation and cards, but to watch it endlessly was a torment.

He considered ringing for his valet, but Eyre had garnered the habit of being busy elsewhere since the doctor had insisted that Hamilton stay off his injured foot for at least a week. Not that he blamed his valet. In the past seven days, his temper had been short, so short that even Philip had deserted him.

A quick glance at the clock on the mantel told him that the usual hour when Nerissa called had passed. *Blast!* It was Wednesday. She was obliged to stay on Laura Place and hold her at home with Annis Ehrlich.

He propped his chin on his hand and glowered at the flames. Nerissa was the only one who did not treat him as if he was as infirmed as an old horse about to be shot. She would ask him how his ankle did upon her arrival, not every few moments as others did. Instead of puffing out the pillow at his back and asking if he would like some tea, she brought him a glass of brandy and sat with him while he drank. Her quick wit and observations of the activities among *Le Beau Monde* kept him from surrendering to *ennui*.

A rap on the door of his study brought Hamilton's head up. Could this be Nerissa, or was it only Philip, who continued to pop in and out with questions about which cravat to wear that evening and did Hamilton think that pantaloons were too *risqué* for an Assembly in conservative Bath? He hoped it was Nerissa. He wanted to see her saucy smile topped by

170

her eyes that were the blue of a summer sky and her ebony curls surrounding her finely boned face. In his ears, her soft laugh, that was beguiling and bothersome at the same time, sounded.

"Damn," he muttered. He did not need his life mixed up with Nerissa Dufresne's. She was not like the other women who had passed through his days and his nights since Elinor had shamed him, leaving him with only a fond memory of their names and their lips. If he had half a brain, he would put her from his life posthaste.

Philip was not smiling as he peered around the door. "I thought you might be here."

"Where else would I have gone?"

He did not react to Hamilton's sarcasm. Coming into the room, he closed the door behind him. He swallowed roughly, then blurted, "*She* is here."

The emphasis Philip put on the word startled him. He sat straighter in his chair. "*She?* Annis?"

"No."

Hamilton could not halt his smile as he asked, "Then may I collect that Nerissa is calling?"

Philip glanced at the door which opened onto the upper hallway. Softly he said, "Not Nerissa, although I wish she was calling. It's *her*."

The venomous distaste in his brother's voice warned Hamilton exactly who waited below. Philip used that tone only when he spoke of one woman.

Elinor Howe!

Hamilton fisted his hands on the arms of the chair. "Damn, what is Elinor doing here? Doesn't she realize the truth? Whatever scrap of affection there once might have been between us is gone."

"On your side perhaps."

"As there was little on her side to begin with, I can assure you she has not been weeping night after night for the loss of my company." Hamilton set his glass

171

on the table beside his chair. "Do you think she has run out of blunt and intends to kick me for some? Or has she broken the heart of every young fop in the *ton* and wishes to commiserate with me about her misfortune in love?"

Philip locked his fingers behind his dark coat and grumbled, "I never have comprehended why you involved yourself with her after Howe died."

Hamilton did not have to answer as the door came open, as if on cue, to reveal an extraordinarily beautiful woman who was garbed stylishly from the brim of her fluted bonnet to the tips of her satin slippers. No fashion plate could be more elegantly dressed than the full curves of the blonde who held out her arms to him. He said nothing, but that did not lessen her satisfied smile.

"My dearest Hamilton," she gushed as she enveloped him with her embrace and the lush scent of her thick perfume, "I vow I was nearly prostrate with horror when I heard of your accident. How do you do?"

"I would do better if I could breathe."

She laughed, but stepped back. "There I was suffering from the worst tedium in London without you there to laugh with me about all the affectations, and here you are needing someone to entertain you. Darling, you must come back with me as soon as you are hale." Without giving him a chance to reply, she threw her arms around him again. "You missed Priney, the Regent's, first *levée* as Regent last month. It was wondrous, Hamilton. Simply without par, for all the dishes were silver, even for the lowest guest."

"Were you in attendance?" he asked as he drew her arms away and leaned in the other direction. "It was my understanding that no woman whose standing was less than the daughter of an earl was to be invited."

"You know that exceptions are made to all such silly rules." She untied her befeathered bonnet and tossed it to Philip, who regarded it with distaste before dropping it on a table. When she met Hamilton's unwavering gaze, she sighed. "All right, my love. You know I did not attend, but, if you had been decent enough to come to London, you could have taken me. Then you would not have been hurt in that dreadful accident. Whatever was in your mind to do something so muzzy?"

"Philip and I decided it would be fun."

"Oh, Philip," she said with a pout, dismissing the younger man without looking at him. "Everyone, truly everyone, is agog with the fact that you are loitering in this place, Hamilton. Don't you know that Bath is no longer the fashionable site it was when our parents were young?" She dabbed at her eyes with a lace handkerchief. "Oh, my dearest love, forgive me for my thoughtless words! What a muttonhead you must think me when I know that you are here on your quest. Have you found anything?"

Hamilton motioned for her to sit on the sofa. "Elinor, I would have guessed that you might be wise enough to send tidings of your arrival. What if Philip and I had been out of town?"

"Eyre would have received me with his usual gentility, I daresay." She patted the satin cushion next to her. "Dear Hamilton, can you come and sit beside me? I have an ache in my neck from riding across the country. It hurts when I turn it, and you know how I enjoy looking at you." Boldly, she ran her fingers along his thigh. "Have you missed me, my sweet?"

He drew his leg off the stool, leaving her fingers outstretched. "Ratafia, Elinor?"

"After riding in that dreadful Mail—can you

believe that I would have to lower my standards to travel in that horrible drag?—I would prefer something a bit stronger. You do have more of that brandy?" She drew off her lacy gloves and dropped them on the mahogany arm of the settee. "Of course, the hardship of the journey is worth seeing you again. And you, Philip," she added as an afterthought.

Hamilton heard his brother's stifled laugh, but did not look at him as Philip poured Elinor a glass of the sweet wine. He offered it to the blonde. When she regarded it with distaste, Hamilton chuckled.

"It is unlike you to refuse a glass, Elinor," he said coolly.

"My portmanteau should be arriving within the hour. The disgusting creature at the inn probably will steal everything out of it." Elinor laughed, the musical sound reaching to the farthest corner of the room, but neither man responded. "Oh, you do not care a rush that I have brought presents for both of you! I ordered you the most wonderful waistcoat, Philip, of a shade you will never see in this backwater village. A glorious green that is perfect for a ginger-hackled gent like you." Her voice grew sultry as she added, "What I brought you, Hamilton, my dear, I shall show you later . . . in private."

"Am I to assume that you intend to stay here?"

"Certainly." Her eyes widened. "Unless you have done the unbelievable and buckled yourself to some calculating virgin."

Looking at the window, where rain painted ever-changing patterns along the glass, he took a sip of his brandy. With a cold smile, he said, "I can assure you that my marital status remains the same."

"He has missed me, hasn't he, Philip?" She flashed him a brilliant smile. "Do tell me the truth, my dear."

Philip leaned one shoulder against the door frame and shook his head. "Elinor, you know that Hamilton missed you tremendously."

"Aha!" she cried with a victorious smile.

"He missed you as a horse misses a stone in its hoof," he added, laughing. "Once the irritation is gone, he forgets it ever existed."

Elinor scowled, then her smile returned with startling speed. "You are ever the funner. What grand times we shall have together here in this fusty house!"

If she had expected Hamilton to retort heatedly to her insult to his magnificent home, he did not accommodate her. Instead, as he continued to sip his brandy, he scrutinized her with the smile of an indulgent father for a naughty child. Knowing how Elinor hated even a moment of silence, he allowed the quiet to build until he could sense her nerves were taut with irritation.

"I am afraid," he finally said, "that whatever plans you have for this evening must be postponed. Neither Philip nor I shall be at home."

"You are going out when you can barely walk?"

He reached behind his chair and pulled out a walking stick. "This peddler's pony will assist me wherever I wish to go."

"Where are we going, Hamilton?" She clapped her hands. "How sweet of you to have some plans for the very first night of my stay!"

"*I* am going with Philip to Sir Delwyn Seely's house. He is having his weekly rout."

She smiled. "What fun that shall be! I do adore Sir Delwyn. He is such a droll, little man."

"Philip and I are going, *not you.*"

"You would leave me alone when I have come all the way from London to be with you?" She leaned forward to put her hand on his knee. With her eyes wide in an appealing expression, she whispered, "My love, you may not have missed me, but I long to be with you . . . tonight. Surely you recall the first night I spent with you here. It was grand beyond belief."

Hamilton's glance at his brother offered Philip the chance to excuse himself from the increasingly uncomfortable conversation. Philip gave him a smile to wish him good luck in dealing with his former mistress before closing the door.

Hamilton put his glass by Elinor's bonnet on the table, and his gaze was held by the bright ribbons. They were nothing like the ones on the bonnet he had purchased for Nerissa, as Nerissa herself was nothing like Elinor Howe. Admittedly, both women were pleasing to the eye, for Nerissa's dark beauty was as alluring as Elinor's spun gold hair. However, the subtle words plied with the skill of a swordsman enticed him into sharing Nerissa's company again. That subtlety would not be successful with Elinor, for she went after what she wanted openly and ignored those who were more tactful. He must toss delicacy aside.

"Elinor, I thought you understood that there would be nothing between us after you decided that you preferred other company to mine," he said without preamble.

Tears glistened in her dark eyes. "I cannot believe that you are as heartless as you are trying to sound."

"Why are you making me hurt you?"

"Mayhap because I know how much I hurt you."

Once he might have believed the entreaty in her eyes, but no longer. Her skills were as well-practiced as a cyprian's. "Why have you come back? It's been almost seven months since you last bothered me." Folding his arms over his unbuttoned waistcoat which revealed the fall of ruffles at his high collar, he cursed. "Months with nothing to show for it but worthless attempts to uncover the truth! Haven't you learned in all this time that there is no place for any woman in my life while I do what I must to avenge my father's death?"

She rose, putting her arms around his shoulders and placing her cheek against his. "Dearest Hamilton, you know that I am willing to do all you wish to help you find that horrible man. Who else would have waited for you until you returned from your business?"

"You did not wait alone," he said.

She laughed. "Johnny was no more than a friend."

"A very dear one." Again he plucked her hands off him. Shoving them away not ungently, he asked, "Why don't you return to Hurst's bed?"

"He married the Duke of Keyneshire's daughter."

"A new wife does tend to curtail a rake-shame's time with his particular."

"You are being so cruel, Hamilton! Don't you remember who mourned with you when your sainted father died?"

With a laugh, he said, "I recall that you missed the funeral by two hours because you spent the night at a party in Town and could not pull yourself away from Hurst's bed."

"But I wanted to be with you."

"You want many things, Elinor, but having a place in *my* bed is one you will be denied."

"Oh, Hamilton, stop being such a hoaxer. I vow you could make a dog laugh with your jests. You know you want me as much as I want you."

As she pressed her lips to his and her lush body against him, her arms drew him to her. He admired the artistry of her kiss, for Elinor was well-skilled, but he shoved her away.

With a curse, she whirled away from him. "Who is

she?" Elinor demanded, sounding more furious than injured.

"She?" He took a drink of his brandy to wash the flavor of her mouth from his. "You must be more specific."

"The woman you would as lief have in your arms. I can sense someone has come between us."

Hamilton laughed as he put his goblet on the table again. "My dear, you are mistaken. There is no other woman. For, as you should know, my life is filled with matters more important than a tumble in the sheets."

"Enough!" she ordered as she went to the sideboard and opened the brandy. Pouring a generous portion for herself, she selected a chair near his. "There is no need for cruelty when I wish to tell you that it was a mistake for me to leave you before."

"That was no mistake." Relaxing in the chair, he set his aching foot on the stool again. "You know that now as well as you did then. However, Elinor, I would not deny you the haven you seek from the new Mrs. Hurst and all her gabblemongering friends in Town. You are welcome to hide here for as long as you wish, on the lone condition that you do not interfere with my life or Philip's."

"Philip's? Why would I wish to intrude on anything so boring?" Her eyes widened. "Or has he done the impossible and fallen in love?"

"Philip is a fine lad. Simply because he was wise enough to see through your shallow pretense of caring for me—"

"You know my love for you—"

He interrupted her as she had him. "Do be done with your trite bangers, Elinor. I have neither time nor patience to endure them."

Elinor laughed, but he saw her gaze slip toward the door. "I am so delighted to hear of Philip's good

178

news. It is time that one of you made a respectable match."

He lifted his glass in a salute to this woman, who had invaded his life anew, and the woman who remained in his thoughts. Once he rid himself of Elinor, he must banish Nerissa from his life and his thoughts, too. It was time to concentrate on finding that thief. "You can be sure that it shall be him long before me."

# Chapter Twelve

"Hamilton is here!"

Nerissa lowered her book to her lap as Annis rushed into the room, the lilac ribbons of her gown whirling around her like flowers scattered by a breeze. Annis grasped her hands and pulled her to her feet, then ran to ring for Frye.

"You must get dressed!" Annis called over her shoulder as she went into the dressing room.

"Hamilton is here?" she asked, although she knew she sounded like a goosecap. "Annis, the doctor told him to rest for a few more days."

Emerging from Nerissa's dressing room with a dress over each shoulder and two in her arms, she said, "Be that as it may, Hamilton is waiting for you in the foyer. He said that you should be quick, for he does not wish to miss any chance to rout Sir Delwyn at the card table."

Nerissa ignored Annis's shouts at her back as she left the room. Frye gasped when Nerissa passed her on the stairs. The band of white embroidery at the hem of Nerissa's skirt struck her ankles on every step, but she did not slow her furious pace as she crossed the checkered foyer to the parlor door.

"How can you be so want-witted?" she cried.

Hamilton turned awkwardly to face her. The rest

180

of her words dried up and blew away, unuttered. She was overtaken—as she had been so frequently—by the potent emotions in his eyes. He did not fetter them tonight as he leaned on a gold handled walking stick. Every powerful pulse washed over her, threatening to drown her in that grey sea.

"Good evening, Nerissa," he answered calmly.

She stepped into the room. Although Philip stood next to a chair near the hearth, she did not look at him. She admired the sleek cut of Hamilton's black coat and how the lace at his collar emphasized the stubborn angle of his jaw. His dark hair was tousled across his brow. Only the cane suggested he was not enjoying the highest of health.

"The doctor wished for you to rest, Hamilton."

He laughed. "You know I have done nothing but rest for the last week. As you did, I must prove to the 'Polite World' that I have not dropped hooks and am even now supping with Old Scratch himself."

"But to go to Sir Delwyn's hurricane?"

"I shall prop myself on a chair like a rickety, old dowager and indulge in nothing-sayings until Seely decides to empty his pockets of any blunt he wishes to wager." He took a cautious step forward, leaning heavily on the cane. "Will that be satisfactory?"

"Does it matter what I say? You shall do exactly as you please."

Philip's chuckle intruded. "She is correct on that, Hamilton."

"Bah to both of you nay-sayers. Put on your prettiest dress, Nerissa, and let us enjoy some of Seely's hospitality." He pointed past her. "Look, Annis is ready to go even now."

As Philip hurried out into the foyer to greet Annis, Nerissa motioned to a chair. "Sit, and I will get ready."

"Do not be long," he said as he lowered himself to the chair. "You know I dislike waiting."

181

She started to turn to go up the stairs, but her ears noted an edge to his voice that she had never heard before. "Hamilton, are you sure you wish to do this? We can sit here and talk while Philip and Annis—"

"I intend to go to Seely's *soirée* even if you stay here!" Exasperation sparked in his eyes. "Go, and get ready. I have no need of you mewling over me, too."

"Too?"

She was astonished when his gaze avoided hers as he said, "Philip, of course."

As clearly as if he was shouting it, Nerissa knew he was not being truthful. Something was amiss, something he did not mean to share with her. Had his search suffered another setback? He had been so certain he was on the verge of finding the culprit.

She put her hand on his shoulder, offering him consolation. When his fingers reached up to stroke hers in silence, he looked up at her. Again she was surrounded by the raw emotions in his eyes. No man had ever looked at her like this, and she cared little if no other man ever did. But she wanted him to look at her like this again and again and again for the rest of their days.

Was this love? Were these sweet, sultry longings what Byron had written of in his poetry? Never before had she understood, but she believed she did now.

"They would make one think that there is some verity in the idea of love at first sight," said Hamilton, with a strained laugh, as he watched his brother and Annis whirl about to the music of a country dance in the center of the elegant ballroom. It was brightened by the crystal chandeliers at the four corners and a huge one in the center.

"They have seen each other many times," Nerissa reminded him. Sipping on her wine, she stopped her toe from tapping to the music. This quiet corner was truly silent for the first time since their arrival an hour before. Every guest had stopped to discover how Hamilton's ankle did.

He finished his wine and set the glass on the empty chair beside him. "I suspect they will see each other many more times if Philip will forget his idiotic plans."

"Is that what's bothering you tonight?"

"Nothing's bothering me tonight."

She laughed shortly. "Hamilton, I believe I know you well enough now to know when you are discomposed. Is it Philip, or . . . ?" She did not want to speak of his search in the crowded room.

"Have you considered it is nothing more important than the fact that my glass is empty and I enjoy the flavor of Seely's London particular?"

"I would be glad to get you more Madeira if you would be honest with me."

He enfolded her hand in his. "I vow to you that neither Philip's opaque plans or that swindler are much in my thoughts tonight."

Nerissa longed to believe him, but she could not shake her certainty that he was concealing something from her. It was futile to come to points with him when he was so stubborn, so she took his glass and went to have it refilled. She looked back over her shoulder to discover he was watching the door to the foyer intently. She had no idea what or whom he hoped to see.

Philip and Annis were laughing together by the table where the silver wine fountain bubbled brightly. As Nerissa handed the glass to a servant who ladled more wine into it, Philip asked, "How is Hamilton doing? It's most unlike him to sit so complacently."

"He is as friendly as a hungry bear," Nerissa answered.

"That is no surprise. I—" He clamped his lips closed as if he had already said too much.

"Philip, not you, too! Why is Hamilton being so mysterious this evening? He clearly is in a flutter, but he refuses to explain."

"It may be no more than his ankle paining him when he has pressed it too hard."

"It may be no more than that, but I suspect it is much more."

"Philip," Annis said quietly, "if something is amiss, you should not be hiding it from Nerissa. She cares deeply for your brother."

Philip handed her a goblet of wine, then handed one to Nerissa. "I can say no more. It is Hamilton's concern. If he wishes to speak of it, then he will."

"By all that's blue!" Nerissa snapped. "You are as pigheaded as Hamilton!"

She expected him to defend his brother, but instead he muttered, "Damn!"

Astounded, she asked, "What is wrong?"

"Her." He pointed toward the door where a statuesque blonde was smiling as she offered her hand to Sir Delwyn.

Nerissa was baffled. She could see nothing improper about the undeniably beautiful woman, who could have been a pattern card for style, for her gown matched the most recent designs Nerissa had seen at the *modiste*'s shop. The dress was of unblemished white, the silk decorated with wide eyelet lace at the hem and along the sleeves, which were edged with Vandyke. With its deep *décolletage*, the gown accented the tall woman's lovely figure, which was gaining the attention of most of the men in the room.

"I do not believe that I know her," Nerissa said. "Do you, Annis?"

Annis glanced at Philip, then gulped, "I think . . . that is, I thought I might know her, but I must be mistaken."

"You are not mistaken, Annis," Philip answered

with a frown. "I am sure she *is* the very woman you are thinking of."

Nerissa asked, "Why are you two talking in circles? Why are . . . ?" She silenced herself when she saw a man—whom she would be able to identify with ease amid any gathering—hobble to the woman.

Biting her lip, she watched as the woman brazenly slipped her arm around Hamilton and smiled up at him. Neither the viscount or the nameless woman had to speak of the intimacy they had shared . . . and might be planning to share again. The way her body clung to his in a possessive caress announced candidly that they had been lovers.

Ice cramped Nerissa's center, and she mumbled something to Annis and Philip as she put her untouched wine on the table. She did not care a fiddlestick if they thought her rude or mad. All she wanted was to flee from the sight of Hamilton and the woman. Too late, she understood why he had been watching the door. He had hoped to see this woman.

But why had he come to Laura Place and insisted that Nerissa attend this gathering with him? She feared this was his way of ending their times together. Mayhap he had discerned how a *tendre* was growing within her heart for him. He might wish nothing more to do with her.

Nerissa tried to push her way through the crowd toward the opposite side of the room. There might be a door to the garden; she may have seen it when they entered. In the cool of the dark, she might be able to regain her composure. She never reached the door. Caught by the eddies of the crowd, she could only reach the corner where she and Hamilton had been sitting.

Among the guests she heard the same name mentioned again and again. *Elinor Howe.* Elinor Howe was beautiful. Elinor Howe was the pink of

185

the *ton*. Elinor Howe had been Hamilton's bit of muslin. The gabble grinders were speculating, and Nerissa even heard wagering, whether Miss Howe's appearance here tonight meant that she had resumed her place in the viscount's bed.

Tears stung her eyes, each one a brand upon her heart, as she thought of her foolish dreams of being more to Hamilton than a friendly face behind a hand of cards. So little she knew of him, but she found his sharp wit and teasing eyes fascinating. Yet, even while he had been intriguing with her, he must have been arranging for his castoff to return to Bath.

"I thought I might find you hiding here."

Nerissa whirled at the good humor in Hamilton's voice. Looking past him, she discovered he was alone. Had he come to excuse himself from *her* company so he could spend the evening with his mistress? His smile faded, warning her that her thoughts were emblazoned on her face.

She sought what dignity she had remaining. "I did not realize that I was hiding," she returned, hoping the sharp answer would cover her heartache. Aware of the dozens of ears listening to what she said and weighing each to discover her reaction to Mrs. Howe's arrival, she refused to be shamed.

"You seem to be playing least in sight." He offered his arm. "You know I am anxious to meet Rowland and Seely at the card table."

"You want *me* to play cards with you?" Swallowing roughly, she struggled to control her voice. "I thought you might have changed your plans for this evening."

"I do not recall suggesting such a thing." He seemed oblivious to the witnesses to their stilted conversation. "Tonight *you* are *my* partner, Nerissa."

"I had thought you might want another."

"Why?"

She stammered on her answer. "I thought . . . I saw . . ."

"I asked you to join me tonight, Nerissa. You have been enjoying good fortune at the card table. I wish to share in it."

As he led her across the room, his steps uneven, Nerissa was certain every eye was focused on them. She saw Annis's strained face and knew, if there was good fortune to be had that evening, it was unlikely to belong to Nerissa Dufresne.

Hamilton threw his cards down and locked his fingers together on the table as he heard Rowland's chortle. The skinny fool was foxed! Yet, even as he had downed another glass of the baronet's contraband brandy, Rowland had won.

Hamilton reaimed his glower at Nerissa, who had the decency to look properly dismayed at the sudden downturn in her luck. No matter if she was his partner or played against him, she had been costing him blunt any time they had played other than the first night they had sat down with Seely and Rowland. Nincompoop that he was, he continued to allow it!

Between her and Elinor. . . . His fingers closed into a fist on his knee. *Blast that woman!* He should have guessed she would delight in appearing at the party tonight to see what poker-talk she could create. He had guessed correctly! If he had not sent Nerissa to get him a glass of wine when he had, Elinor was certain to have made a scene to mortify Nerissa.

He watched in silence as Nerissa shuffled the cards. Her fingers were as delicate as the rest of her slender form. As she handed the cards to him, so that he might deal them, she brushed his arm with the heavy lace dripping from the short sleeves of her gown. A flush of heat swelled through him, suffocating and demanding release. He thought how easily he could pull her to him and taste the fire on her soft lips. When her eager breath mingled with his, to set their souls into the heart of the flame, he could forget everything else . . . even Elinor.

He dropped the deck onto the table. "Enough for now!"

"Bah, you have a few mints yet to lose, Windham. Why not lose them now?" Rowland laughed drunkenly. "Why not lose them to my best bosom bow . . ." He draped his arm around the baronet, who was obviously on the go himself. ". . . dear Delwyn? We deserve Windham's gold, don't we?"

"I think you have swallowed the hare," said Hamilton as he stood. Leaning on his walking stick, he drew out Nerissa's chair, without asking her if she wanted to leave. Her relief was evident on her face as he bid the other men a good evening.

Only when they walked back into the crowded ballroom did her frown return. "If you have other matters to deal with, Hamilton, I shall find Annis and—"

"Fiddle! I want to speak with you alone."

"I would rather not."

Her soft words added to his exasperation. "Come along! As much as you have cost me tonight, the very least you can do is give me a moment of your undivided attention. You certainly were not thinking of our game tonight."

Without waiting for her to reply, Hamilton led her into the foyer. Her eyes grew round, but she said nothing as he opened a door and ushered her into a cozy sitting room which was hidden beneath the stairs. He gestured for her to sit on the red, leather sofa, then chose a lyre-backed chair facing her. With a sigh, he sat. When she pushed a stool toward him, he gratefully set his aching leg upon it.

"I would appreciate an explanation," he said with another sigh.

"Of what?"

"Your performance at the board of green cloth tonight."

Nerissa laughed to hide her dismay. Hamilton had been correct. Her thoughts had not been upon the cards. "If you recall, whist is a game of chance. Chance failed to smile upon us this evening."

He waved aside her words. "I did not mean that. The game tonight was not such a loss. We did win a few hands, and the company was pleasant until Seely decided to drink out of the island. You said barely two words in a row this evening."

"I had nothing to say." She jutted out her chin in feeble defiance. "As you had nothing to say earlier."

"I think we have much to say."

"You are wrong. I have nothing to say to you now." She rose and looked down at him. "I fear I am keeping you from your companions. If you will excuse me . . ."

He pushed himself to his feet. When he wobbled, she put out her hand to him, but pulled it back before she could touch him. If she did, she was sure she would no longer be able to restrain her tears. Then she would have to own that she had been barely able to see the markings on the cards through the curtain of tears.

"Now I understand. You are in a snit about Elinor appearing here tonight, so you decided to take your revenge on me by letting me lose at the card table."

"If you could think of anything other than your wounded pride, you may recall *I* also lost money at the table tonight. I do not consider your relationship with Mrs. Howe of such consequence that I would toss my money to the winds. If you feel uncomfortable about it, that is your own concern, which clearly you had no interest in sharing with me. I excuse you

189

to return to your incognita. I have no wish for any more of your company."

"*Brava!*" he said, sarcasm thickening his voice. "Such a performance should be strutted upon the boards, Nerissa, but your grand exit is ruined by the fact that you are dependent upon me to see you home."

"Philip would—"

"Be your dashing hero? I am sure of that. Also I am sure you could find other transport in the drawing room. I can name several men among this group who would be very happy to escort you home in the shadows of their closed carriages."

"You are beneath reproach!"

"But I am speaking the truth." He took her hand and drew her back to him. "I know you have no reason to trust me, but believe me when I say that things are not as you may believe."

Nerissa tugged her hand away. "They are not as I believed. I thought you would tell me the truth about something as important as Mrs. Howe."

"I did not ask her to move into Queen Square."

"With you?" She choked. This was even worse than she had feared. She had been an utter widgeon to think Hamilton cared for her. Without saying more, she went to the door.

Hamilton was not surprised when she refrained from slamming the door. Elinor would have crashed it closed so loudly it would have been heard in the servants' quarters on the uppermost floors.

"Damn!" he growled and sat back on the chair. With his ankle as weak as candlewax, he could not give chase without looking like a complete chucklehead.

But that was what he was! Damn Elinor! Damn Nerissa! The game was not worth the candle, but he must deal with both of them. For that, he needed something more fortifying than Frenchified wine.

190

He hoped Seely had some juniper among the port and Malaga, for he would need it before this night came to an end.

Nerissa saw Annis on the far side of the room, her head bent in conversation with Philip. If she told Annis she was not feeling good, surely that would give her the excuse to leave early. And it was the truth . . . her stomach was cramped, and her throat ached from the sobs scratching to escape it.

The only thing that confused her—as it had from the moment she had seen Hamilton and Mrs. Howe—was why he had brought her to Sir Delwny's party when he brazenly had installed his convenient in his house on Queen Square. He could not have hoped to keep such a fact a secret in the small world of Bath society.

"Miss Dufresne?"

At Sir Delwyn's fuddled voice, she sighed and forced a smile. She must let no one know the depth of her anguish at Hamilton's betrayal. Facing him, she said, "Sir Delwyn, I must . . ."

The satisfied smile on the lips of the ravishing blonde standing behind the baronet silenced Nerissa. She did not need to hear Sir Delwyn's stumbling introduction. Nor, she suspected, did Mrs. Howe.

"Miss Dufresne," cooed the older woman, "this is a meeting I have been anticipating greatly since I arrived in Bath this afternoon. Now, for good and all, we are getting to speak. You have been monopolized by my dear Hamilton all evening at the card table."

"Lots of evenings," the baronet said. "Regular tie-mates, they are."

"Is that so?" Mrs. Howe asked. She wafted her fan languidly in front of her face as her cold smile focused on Nerissa. "I suppose you enjoy all sorts of games together, don't you?"

"I am sorry I must be rude, Mrs. Howe," Nerissa said, choosing each word carefully. Even more than before, every ear in the room was aimed at this conversation. No doubt, not a person wished to miss this confrontation. "If you will excuse me, I was about to speak to a dear friend. I have been without manners to leave her this evening."

"Now I understand why Hamilton wished me to remain in Town instead of joining him on Queen Square. How convenient you are for him, my dear!"

Nerissa struggled not to let the woman send her flying up the boughs with her incendiary insults. She bit back her sharp reply when Annis came to stand next to them. The dismayed expression on her friend's face urged Nerissa to recall that stooping to trading demure hits would gain them nothing. She refused to provide entertainment for Sir Delwyn's guests.

When she did not answer, Miss Howe continued, "Such a sweet, silent thing you are! No doubt, he finds you a change from my prattle-box ways. Not that Hamilton would shackle his heart to a bluestocking, you must understand, for he prefers to be entertained by a lady of some imagination." Her smile grew broader. "I am sure you understand quite well what I mean."

"Nerissa, do not listen to her wicked words," urged Annis, firing a furious glower toward Philip.

Philip said nervously, "Elinor, you should not—"

"Oh, Philip," the blonde said, "you are so straitlaced. Always telling me that I should not do anything fun. Why aren't you more like Hamilton?" Her eyelashes fluttered enticingly. "He was always telling me to do things that were ever so much fun."

Nerissa put her hand on his arm to halt his reply. She would not be drawn into pulling caps in front of Sir Delwyn's guests. "Good evening, Mrs. Howe. It has been an indescribable experience to have this opportunity to meet you. I trust you will have an enjoyable sojourn in Bath."

Her serene exit was ruined when Nerissa turned to discover Hamilton behind her. Hating the heat which climbed her cheeks, she hoped no blush betrayed her to those who were listening candidly. She found her gaze held by the steely eyes that seemed to tell her so much and so little at the same time. Again her fingers itched to reach out to him, but she clenched her hands by her side. That did not slow the fires within her as she imagined his arms around her while his lips—which were softening into a secretive smile—caressed hers. Such thoughts were madness when she stood between him and his mistress.

Elinor pushed past her. "Do tell Miss Dufresne good night before we go home." She slipped her arm around Hamilton's.

He lifted her hand off his arm. "We bid *you* good evening, Elinor. If you recall, I escorted Nerissa here this evening. You cannot think that I would abandon her."

"Let Philip take her home while you take me home."

Rage tightened Hamilton's lips. Nerissa was sure Mrs. Howe must be oblivious to everything but her own desires. Otherwise, she would see how she was infuriating him. Mrs. Howe should know that he would not be embarrassed publicly.

When he turned his back on the blonde and bowed his head toward Nerissa, Mrs. Howe's face twisted with a fury that matched Hamilton's fiery emotions.

"Nerissa?" asked Hamilton while he offered his arm to her.

She replied, "You need not—"

"But I wish to see you home," he said in a voice that suggested he would brook no argument.

She put her fingers on his arm. Nerissa knew she had now made an enemy, one as determined to wreak vengeance on her as Hamilton was on the man who had taken his father's money. Nerissa did not look back as she left the room at Hamilton's side. Silence, broken only by whispers as they passed, followed.

No one spoke as they drove with Philip and Annis the short distance to Laura Place. Nerissa stared at her hands which were clasped in her lap, but wished her bonnet would allow her to sneak a glance at Hamilton. The steady rhythm of the street lamps pierced the darkness, but he clung to the shadows, his face hidden from her.

Even when he handed her out, Hamilton remained silent. Philip walked with Annis to the door. Nerissa was about to follow, but she turned to face Hamilton.

"Are you sending her away?" she asked in a whisper.

He did not pretend not to understand. "She has no other place to go."

"Do you still love her?"

"I hope not."

She swallowed roughly, but the lump in her throat refused to be budged. "That is no answer, Hamilton."

"It is the only answer I can give you." His voice grew sharp. "I can tell you, Nerissa, that she matters less to me than nabbing that thief."

"Nothing matters more to you than that, does it?"

"Why are you wasting your breath saying things you know to be true?"

She fought to keep the tears in her eyes as she whispered, "Then I shall say no more to you tonight."

"Nerissa!" he called after her as she climbed the stairs.

For a moment, she considered not turning, but she paused on the top step. Beyond the open door, she could hear Philip murmuring a good night to Annis. Her heart splintered into a dozen painful pieces.

194

How desperately she longed to share that sweetness with Hamilton! He cared only for revenge.

He limped to the railing. Putting his hand on it, he looked up at her. "Nerissa, you know what I must do, and you know I cannot change that."

"Cannot or will not?" When he did not fire back a glib reply, she said, "Until you know the answer to that, you are right. There is no sense in me wasting my breath speaking to you."

"Nerissa!"

This time, she did not turn as she walked into the house and closed the door, shutting him out of her life, but—she feared—not out of her heart.

# Chapter Thirteen

The low ceiling of the tavern swallowed all conversation, leaving the dark room filled with smoke from the hearth and mumbles from the crowd. Depressions in the stone floor were filled with stinking pools. Tables, hidden in every crevice along the uneven walls, offered the perfect place to plan a tryst or a death. At most of them, the patrons were drunk on the cheap gin. However, at the table in the corner farthest from the door to the street, a man in an ebony cape sat with a shorter man. No one approached them, for the fine material of the tall man's cloak bespoke wealth.

Hamilton shrugged aside his cape as he listened to Mallory. When the Bow Street Runner finished with his lengthy, rambling report, Hamilton asked, "So you are certain Oakley played no hand in cheating my father?"

"Not a finger, m'lord," he answered in his thick accent as he drained the blue ruin from his glass and refilled it, spilling some on his hand. Licking it off, he added, "Whatever blunt 'e 'as, and 'tis little, 'e got when an uncle went to his Diet of Worms." He chuckled. "Don't sit down with 'im at the board of green cloth, m'lord. 'E don't 'ave the brass to pay 'is debts."

Hamilton let him prattle on as he glowered into his ale. Damn! He had thought his suspicions about Oakley might prove valuable. They had been nothing but another false lead. He must start over again.

"I want answers!" he said, cutting Mallory off in mid-word. "And I want that thief taken. I have waited long enough for you to do what you vowed you would do before a week passed. It's been more than twice that, and my patience is depleted."

Mallory cringed away from his honed words. The shorter man had recovered from the beating by the unseen assailants, but his face became ruddy with his own outrage. "I've done what I can! Ye've got to give me another chance, milord."

"You have done nothing."

"I tell ye, the man ye want me to take 'as vanished!"

"No man can vanish." Hamilton took a deep drink of his ale and watched Mallory squirm like a lad called before the headmaster. "Even if he has left Bath, which is altogether possible after this delay, there must be some clue or someone who can give us the answer we need. I suggest that, if your past methods have failed to get the answers I need, you try other methods."

Mallory swallowed a mouthful of gin, then scratched his unshaven chin. "There be someone who might be knowin' somethin', but—"

"Do what you must."

"The lass may be quality."

Hamilton hesitated. Inflicting Mallory's brutality on a woman, whether she was gentry or not, was unthinkable. He had seen what the stocky man's bare fists could do when he had walked into this house of waste tonight to discover Mallory with a man at his feet, groaning from a broken jaw. Although Hamilton had no idea what had precipitated the milling— and he had no wish to know—he could not order

Mallory to turn those bunches of fives on a woman.

"Talk to her," he said quietly. "Get some answers."

"And if she don't want to be talkin'?"

He took another drink of the bitter ale, then set his tankard on the table. "If she will not cooperate, Mallory, bring her to me, and I will be sure she tells me everything she knows."

"Aye, milord." He snickered. "And then the lass'll rue the day she first saw ye."

"That she will, for I shall have that man caught."

Not bothering to finish the ale in the filthy glass, Hamilton rose. He dropped a few coins on the table. As Mallory reached for one that was rolling toward the edge, he walked out of the dank tavern. He paused by his carriage and looked at Bath, which was set farther long the Avon. The white buildings glistened in the first light of dawn.

If he returned to Queen Square, Elinor would be a bother . . . even at this hour. He turned to look at the far side of the river where Laura Place was situated. He had no reason to call there. Nerissa had made it clear she wished nothing more to do with him.

His frustration wavered as he remembered the anguish on her face as she slowly closed the door to leave him standing alone on the walkway. He had thought Nerissa understood what even Philip could not. To give up this search now would betray the promise he had made to his father on his deathbed. Vengeance was only secondary to keeping his pledge.

Instead Nerissa had wound herself up as completely as Elinor ever had. Although she had not rung him a regular peal as Elinor delighted in doing, her restrained anger had been even more cutting.

To perdition with both women! Calling up to his coachman, he ordered the man to drive him to one of the gaming-hells in the center of the city. He would put his troubles from his mind with gambling and brandy. That was how he had forgotten Elinor before. That was how he would forget her now. And Nerissa. . . . He flinched again as her face, tears glistening in her sapphire eyes, burst from his memory.

He swore under his breath, then louder, but nothing eased the realization that putting Nerissa out of his life might not be as simple as that. Although it might not be necessary, for clearly she had put him out of hers.

". . . and, without question, we must serve the best champagne we can find. I attended the wedding feast that Lady Gillis sponsored for her niece. The champagne was tasteless. Can you believe that? And she's the wife of an earl!"

Nerissa paid no more attention to Mrs. Ehrlich's words than she had to anything said during the last hour of this interminable call. She stirred her tea, although it had long ago grown cold, and tried not to think of the harsh words she had shared with Hamilton last night. Even now, she could not keep tears from welling into her eyes as she thought of how the pleasant evening had become a disaster.

She had been right to ask Hamilton to stay out of her life, but that thought offered no solace to her grieving heart. During the night, when trying to sleep had been impossible, she had sat by the window and stared out onto the street where she had lost every chance at happiness. She had still been sitting there when dawn was announced by the maids selling milk and eggs in the center of Laura Place.

"Nerissa!"

At Mrs. Ehrlich's impatient tone, which warned

Nerissa this was not the first time Annis's mother had tried to get her attention, Nerissa said softly, "Pardon me, Mrs. Ehrlich. I fear my mind is wandering."

She sniffed derisively. "It is time for you to stop woolgathering, Nerissa. And of what? Lord Windham, no doubt. After all, hasn't that faithless man proven to you that you were a blind buzzard to heed his court promises when he was welcoming his castoff back into his home?"

"Mama!" Annis choked. "That is not the way it is at all. Philip assured me that—"

"Bah!" her mother interrupted. "Of course, Mr. Windham would defend his brother." Tapping a long nail against her powdered cheek, she mused, "I shall have to rethink my permission for him to call upon you."

"Mama!"

"Mrs. Ehrlich," Nerissa said quietly before their quarrel could add to the pain scoring her skull, "Philip Windham should not be punished for his brother's deeds. I believe, as Annis does, that his affection for her is honest and untainted."

Mrs. Ehrlich poured herself another cup of tea and sniffed again. "Do not misunderstand, Nerissa, when I say I have little faith in your judgment in these matters. You have proven you are easily bamboozled." Raising her cup to her lips, she sighed. "Only my concern about leaving you alone on Laura Place prevents me from insisting that Annis return home posthaste. Have you heard from your brother, Nerissa? When does he plan to return to Bath?"

"I received a short message from him only this morning." She did not tell the prying Mrs. Ehrlich that the note had been no longer than two lines to inform Nerissa that Cole had arrived safely in London and expected to be returning before month's end with good news of prospective backers. Whether

200

he had met with them yet he had not bothered to add. "He is doing well. I am sure his project will prove even more successful than any of us imagined."

"That remains to be seen. He is such an air-dreamer, Nerissa, as you are becoming. I would think that—" At the sound of footfalls, she turned to smile a greeting to Janelle and her *fiancé*. "Oh, my dears, how kind of you to join us! I trust you had a delightful sojourn to the Pump Room."

Nerissa exchanged a grimace with Annis. She knew Annis shared her opinion of Randall Oakley. He was disagreeably high in the instep, and Nerissa would have been glad to avoid his company. As the bracket-faced man offered Mrs. Ehrlich a filial buss on the cheek, Janelle twittered an annoying laugh.

"I did not know that you had decided to pay us a call, Annis," Janelle said, envy in every word. Nerissa recalled that Annis's sister had sulked for two days after learning that Annis had been given permission to stay on Laura Place. She suspected Janelle had wanted her younger sister to remain home, so she could parade every moment of the triumph of her betrothal in front of Annis.

Annis answered with quiet dignity, "I enjoy giving Mama a look-in."

"When you are not busy with Windham, I suppose," Mr. Oakley interjected. "He shows a fidelity to you that I would not have guessed any Windham could feel." He chuckled as he sat on a chair beside his future mother-in-law. "But I was silly to think that, wasn't I?" Looking down his long nose at Nerissa, he said, "His brother has shown a great deal of fidelity to a woman who has cuckolded him at every turn."

Not to be left out, Janelle added, "Nerissa, I am so delighted to see you looking so unscathed by your

201

disturbing evening. What I have heard of it!" She pressed her hand to her chest. "You must have a stronger heart than mine to endure such a public humiliation."

Annis instantly set herself on her feet. "Do not try to set Nerissa's back up with your poker-talk, Janelle. Nerissa was not humiliated."

"I would be," her sister insisted, "if my escort's high flyer made such a scene."

"There was no scene," Nerissa said quietly. Setting her cup on the tray, she said, "Thank you for the tea, Mrs. Ehrlich. I hope you will allow us to host you soon on Laura Place."

Janelle refused to be silenced. "Mayhap there was no scene while you were there, Nerissa, but I understand it was quite a piece of work that the guests enjoyed when Lord Windham returned to collect Mrs. Howe."

"He went back to . . . ?" Nerissa halted herself as she saw the gleam in Janelle's eyes. Annis's sister wanted her to react with shock and anger, then she could gloat about having a faithful suitor. Not that she considered Randall Oakley a prize admirer, for he was worth less than a half-farthing.

Mr. Oakley smiled coldly. "It is *on dits* throughout Bath that Lord Windham is enamored with Elinor Howe again. What a gaby he is! Do you think she will play him for the jack as she did before? No doubt, she thinks she can lighten his pockets of some gilt before she goes on to her next paramour."

"Don't say things like that!" cried Annis. "You will hurt Nerissa with your hummers! Hamilton doesn't care a rush for Mrs. Howe, and he has demonstrated that he cares deeply about Nerissa."

"Do not let their insults disturb you, Annis," Nerissa said, rising to her feet. "I thank you for coming to my rescue, but it is not necessary. I judge

202

the source of these statements for what they are. Mr. Oakley and your sister have come in with five eggs, and four of them are rotten with demure hits." Picking up her bonnet, she said, "Again thank you, Mrs. Ehrlich."

With a sob, Annis ran after Nerissa as she went out into the foyer. Nerissa put her arm around her friend and soothed her with trite phrases. Although she longed to be a wet-goose, too, it would gain her nothing but pleasure for those who wished to see her daunted by Elinor Howe's return to Bath.

"Janelle and Mr. Oakley are despicable," Annis choked through her tears. "Why do they want to hurt you?"

"Don't heed them. I shan't." She tied her bonnet under her chin, her fingers freezing on the pretty ribbons as she realized it was the hat Hamilton had given her. Why had she chosen to wear this today? It *did* match the blue sprig linen of her gown and the lace along the ruffles on the sleeve, but she wished to give nobody the idea that she was repining for Hamilton . . . even if it was true.

"Oh, no!" cried Annis.

"What is it?"

She reached up and touched the right side of Nerissa's bonnet. "There is a bare spot right here. You must have lost one of the feathers."

"It doesn't matter." The idea that a missing feather was of importance, when her whole life seemed to be aground, was absurd, but then everything was absurd today. She had given Hamilton his *congé*, while she could think of nothing but seeing him again.

"But it does." Annis motioned to the short butler, who had come forward with their shawls. "Cunliffe, have my green bonnet brought. Miss Dufresne shall wear it while we go to the milliner's shop."

"That is not necessary," Nerissa said while the

butler hurried to obey.

"You cannot be seen on the street with a bonnet that looks like that. What would be thought of you?"

Nerissa knew better than to argue with her bosom bow when Annis took on such repressive accents. Untying her bonnet, she accepted the one that Cunliffe handed to her. She smiled when she saw the amusement in the short man's eyes. She settled the chip hat on the back of her head and tried to make it comfortable. It was slightly too large, but it would do until she could presuade Annis that having a hat that was minus a single feather was no crime.

Annis refused to be persuaded on the matter. She insisted that the carriage take them to *Madame* de Ramel's shop, so that the milliner could repair it posthaste. "After all," she said as they sat in the carriage that bounced along the rough stones of the street, "she may still have more of those wonderful feathers. A few quick stitches, and no one will ever guess that it was damaged."

"There is no hurry."

"But there is. Philip is coming to take me to the theatre tonight." Happiness brightened her face. "We can get your hat fixed, then return home to decide what we will wear."

"I had not planned to go to the theatre this evening."

"Do you and Hamilton have other plans?"

Nerissa could not help but stare at her friend. Her voice had not been quiet when she spoke so sharply to Hamilton last night. With a sigh, she realized that Annis and Philip had been so enraptured with each other that they had noticed nothing else.

"Oh, do come with us," Annis urged.

"I don't think that is possible."

Annis's smile disappeared. "My eyes, Nerissa! Are you going to give up so quickly?"

"Give up?"

She shook her head in bewilderment. "I had thought you possessed a true *tendre* for Hamilton. He seemed to be as taken with you. Then this woman . . ." Her sneer on the word made it sound like an epithet. ". . . comes back into his life, and you are ready to cede him to her without a single question."

"Hamilton is a man, Annis, not something that I own and can keep or give away."

"What of his heart?"

Nerissa looked out the window at the shops they were passing. Dozens of people walked along the street, some arm in arm. Love seemed so simple for other people. Mayhap she had inherited the curse her mother had suffered from . . . falling in love with the wrong man.

"I am beginning to wonder," she answered quietly, turning back to her friend, "if Hamilton has a heart."

"Don't be a cabbage-head! Of course, he has a heart."

"But is there room in it for anything but his yearning for vengeance?"

When Annis stuttered on an answer, Nerissa stared out the window once more. Annis had no answer. Neither did she.

The shop was tiny. The front window and the door filled the whole front. A single chair was set in front of the window, nearly lost in the glare of the sunshine that came through the glass between the diamond mullions. A counter cut the small space in half. It was topped by samples and pieces of lace and flowers that were as brightly dyed as the crimson curtain to the right of the counter.

When a bell over the door tinkled as Nerissa and

Annis entered, a short woman pushed through the curtain to give them a broad smile. *Madame* de Ramel was a plump sprite, who chattered nonstop in a delightful, but barely comprehensible, mixture of French and English. Her greying hair rose in a complex style that had been stylish when Nerissa's mother was young.

When Nerissa explained the problem, the milliner gasped, "A missing feather? Oh, *c'est dommage!*"

"Can you repair it?"

"*Mais, oui.*" She laughed brightly. "Of course. I have many feathers of that *couleur.* Come with me into the back, and you may select the one you like, *mademoiselle.* The feathers are in a box on my worktable."

Annis's eyes shone with excitement as they followed the short woman through the bright splash of curtain. She gasped with delight when they entered a small room that was filled with straw, fabrics, and bright ribbons.

"Look, Nerissa!" she said, picking up a piece of blue silk. "This is the very color of my new gown. What a beautiful turban it would make!"

"And on you, *très belle,*" gushed the milliner. "You must let me make it into a *chapeau* for you."

Nerissa picked up one of the feathers on the table and held it against her bonnet. The tint was a shade too dark. She was reaching for another as the bell over the front door rang again.

"Do stay," urged *Madame* de Ramel over her shoulder as she pushed past the curtain, "until you find the perfect feather, *mademoiselle.* I shall be back as soon as I finish with this customer."

"What do you think?" Annis propped a fake bird over one ear and grinned.

Nerissa started to reply, but motioned her friend to silence when she heard the milliner say, *"Mon*

206

*seigneur, comment allez-vous?*" They must not disrupt *Madame*'s business.

"I am doing well, *Madame*," came the answer in a voice that stiffened Nerissa's back. She whirled to be certain the drape was in place.

Annis whispered, "Isn't that Hamilton?"

"Yes." She closed her eyes as she looked for the strength to maintain her composure. Meeting him had been the last thing she had considered when Annis pressured her to come here, for Philip had been fervent that Hamilton despised the idea of entering such a shop.

"What will you do?"

Nerissa ran her fingers along the feather she had selected. "I shall have *Madame* sew this in place."

"But . . . about Hamilton . . . what . . . ?"

With a taut smile, she said, "I shall bid him a good afternoon."

Ignoring Annis's moan of despair, Nerissa opened the curtain. Neither the milliner nor Hamilton took note of her, for they were looking at a sample book on the counter. She could not keep her gaze from admiring the breadth of his shoulders beneath his riding coat or the way his hair glistened in the bright sunshine. No matter how he vexed her, she longed to hear his laugh and to see his eyes blaze with passion in the moment before his lips touched hers. The shop was so small, that, if she reached out her hand, she could have stroked the firm length of his arm.

"The hat must flatter a woman with light coloring," Hamilton said, without looking away from the book, "and I would like it done by week's end."

Nerissa was sure she had forgotten how to breathe. Elinor Howe was a blonde. If Hamilton was purchasing a hat for her, it must mean that . . . She was not sure what it meant, and she did not want to

207

think of it. All she wished was to be as far away in a place where she could assuage her heart's pain.

*Madame* de Ramel answered hesitantly, "That may not be possible with this hat. It is not as simple as the one you purchased previously."

"It must be this hat. It will suit her perfectly, and it must be done by week's end before we leave for London."

"I shall try, *mon seigneur*." She turned to select another book of samples. "If . . ."

Nerissa met the dismay in the milliner's gaze. When Hamilton turned to see what had disturbed *Madame* de Ramel, his eyes were as devoid of emotion as his face. He said nothing as the flustered milliner ran to Nerissa.

"This feather will be the best match," Nerissa said tonelessly.

"I shall sew it on *immédiatement, Madamoiselle* Dufresne." She lowered her eyes and rushed through the curtain to leave Nerissa alone with Hamilton in the small shop.

Hamilton said nothing as she came around the counter. Leaning his elbow on the top, he continued to watch her with his hooded eyes. She heard a rustle behind her, but did not turn. Some sense, she could not name, told her that Annis was watching through the curtain.

"My bonnet needed fixing," Nerissa said to break the smothering silence.

"So I see." He flicked the garish bow on the side of her borrowed hat. "This is not as becoming on you as the one I selected."

His cold tone struck her as viciously as a blow. Her fingers trembled, wanting to reach out to him, but fearing he would brush them away as heartlessly as he had her words. For the past few weeks, he had been there when she needed someone to listen to her concerns and lighten her heart. Now, when her heart was heaviest, she could not open it to him because he was the cause of her misery.

"Philip wishes," he went on, "to know if you will be joining him and Annis at the theatre this evening."

"And you?"

His smile was as false as the bird Annis had put in her hair. "I had made no plans to attend. To own the truth, I am busy elsewhere this evening."

"You may tell Philip that I will be delighted to join him and Annis tonight."

Astonishment flickered through his eyes, then vanished as he nodded. "I will tell him. He will, no doubt, be pleased."

Nerissa wondered how long they could go on talking like strangers. Only a few days before, she had found rapture in his arms. Now they were as closed as his face, which concealed every thought.

*Madame* de Ramel pushed through the portiere. Her face was certainly not devoid of emotion. Tears bubbled at the corner of her eyes, and her cheeks were spotted with bright pink. Holding out the bonnet, she said nothing.

"Thank you," Nerissa said. "If you will please send the bill to—"

"Me at Queen Square," Hamilton interrupted.

"You need not pay for this repair," Nerissa said.

"It is not my practice to let my gifts create a burden for those who receive them." He turned back to the milliner. "You may enclose it with the hat I will expect to be ready by week's end."

*"Oui, mon seigneur,"* *Madame* de Ramel murmured.

When Hamilton held the door for her and Annis, Nerissa thanked him as quietly as she had the milliner. The sunshine was warm, but it could not touch the iciness in her heart as they stood on the walkway. They were caught in the disquiet that muted even the clatter of carriage wheels and the laughter of children playing among the parked vehicles.

She hid her discomfort while Hamilton handed Annis, then her into her carriage. When she put her hand on the door to pull it closed, he blocked it. She waited for him to speak. He remained silent. Aware of Annis's uneasiness, she knew she should say something, but had no idea what would destroy the wall he had erected between them.

"I trust we shall see you at Sir Delwyn's gathering next week," she whispered, when she could think of nothing else. Even those simple words ached inside her as she thought of not seeing him until the following week.

"Trust?" he said tautly. "Odd you should use that word, Nerissa, when you have yet to learn that trust must be on both sides."

"But you don't trust me." Her laugh was thick with sorrow. "Hamilton, you waited for me to hurt you as she did. You were so sure that I would do that that you decided to prevent it by hurting me first." She pulled the door closed. "You need worry about it no longer. You succeeded, but you shan't hurt me again." When she slapped on the side of the carriage, it rolled out among the traffic.

Annis looked back to see Hamilton watching them, the same blank expression on his face. She wanted to shout to him to race after them, to persuade Nerissa to listen to reason, and to give him another chance to bridge the void of pain. She had never guessed that the viscount could be such a ninny.

*And Nerissa!* Was she all about in the head to speak so cruelly to a man she loved?

Annis understood none of it, but she was determined to get some answers. She must help them heal their hearts before they destroyed them completely. Before it was too late, she would . . .

Sobs filled the carriage. She turned to see Nerissa with her face in her hands. As she gathered Nerissa in her arms and held her while she sobbed, she feared it was too late already.

## Chapter Fourteen

When a knock sounded on the door of Miss Dufresne's private rooms, Frye opened it to discover Mrs. Carroll on the far side. The housekeeper dampened her lips nervously as she glanced toward the stairs.

"Lord Windham is here, Frye." Her voice cracked as she wrung her hands in her apron.

"Tell him that Miss Dufresne is out." She sighed. "At least, it is the truth. I do not think she expected him to continue trying to contact her for so long." Clenching her hands by her side, she asked, "Why can't he see that she will not answer those letters he has sent her? Finally she has come to her senses on this."

Mrs. Carroll lowered her voice to a conspiratorial whisper, although no one else stood in the room. "He does not wish to speak to Miss Dufresne. He asks to speak to you, Frye."

"Me?" The abigail's full face grew long with her baffled frown.

"That is what he said. Smooth as the devil himself, he said, 'Please tell Miss Frye that I would speak with her at her convenience.' What shall I tell him?"

Frye hesitated. In the five days since the afternoon when Miss Dufresne had returned to her room in tears with Miss Ehrlich following and demanding an explanation, the young woman had refused to be at home for Lord Windham. She had received Mr. Windham when he came to call on her and Miss Ehrlich and had gone riding with them to the theatre or into the country, but only when Miss Dufresne could be certain that Lord Windham would not join them.

Miss Ehrlich had been surprisingly reticent about the rift between the viscount and Miss Dufresne. Whispered tales of the return of Lord Windham's mistress to Bath and her spectacular appearance at the Seely townhouse added to the poker-talk muddling about belowstairs. Even Hadfield could not have augmented the fantastic tale that spread through the city in the aftermath of the *soirée*.

Had Miss Dufresne heard the tales that she had demanded that Lord Windham choose between his prime article and her, and he had selected Miss Howe? Had she seen the smiles hidden behind gloved fingers when she did her errands? Had she been hurt by the hearsay that Miss Dufresne was knapped with the viscount's child and was hiding from Society until its birth?

Frye could not guess whether her lady had taken note of any of the various tales. Outwardly, Miss Dufresne remained serene amid the whispers, and appeared delighted by the growing attraction between Miss Ehrlich and Mr. Windham. Frye had discovered no salt staining Miss Dufresne's pillowcases to suggest that she sobbed herself to sleep each night. Only her uncharacteristically callous refusal to speak to Lord Windham suggested the anguish Frye was sure lurked within her lady.

Squaring her stout shoulders, the maid said, "Tell Lord Windham that I shall be down immediately."

"Do you think that is wise?" asked the housekeeper. "Miss Dufresne is adamant about not seeing him."

"*She* is not seeing him, and, Mrs. Carroll," she added in a gentler voice, "I may be able to obtain some answers that will allow us to help her."

Frye paused only long enough to be sure that her appearance was fit to greet a viscount. Tugging at her pale brown dress that tended to bunch at her broad hips, she patted her lackluster hair into place. She smiled as she rounded the banister at the top of the stairs. If Lord Windham thought to bamboozle her by coming the blarney over her, he would discover his error in no time.

In spite of her resolve to maintain the upper hand in the discussion, she hesitated as she reached the base of the stairs. Lord Windham turned to her, a provocative smile on his lips, but it was the cold fire in his eyes that halted Frye as she was about to greet him.

Stepping forward, the viscount nodded as he said, "I thank you for seeing me without delay, Miss Frye. Shall I sound too carney if I suggest that Nerissa might have learned her delightful punctuality from you?"

"If you will follow me, my lord . . ." She hurried into the parlor, away from the man and his easy words that seemed so sincere. They must be no more than loud ones if Miss Dufresne had turned her back on him. Frye was well aware of her charge's fault in trusting those who were least deserving of it.

Her lips tightened as she wondered if Miss Dufresne's eyes would be opened to her stepbrother when he returned home. Mr. Pilcher had, in Frye's opinion, taken advantage of his stepsister, putting the burden of the household on her while he played at his drawings. Miss Dufresne should have been enjoying the swirl of Society instead of worrying about budgets and bills.

When she heard the viscount's assertive footfalls on the floor behind her, Frye warned herself not to think about matters that were unimportant now. She found comfort in the procedure of asking the lord to choose a chair among the collection scattered about the chamber. She selected the one where she usually sat when she joined Miss Dufresne and her guests. When she realized it would force the viscount to regard her from an uncomfortable angle, she wished she could move without appearing as though she was no more than a mooncalf.

Lord Windham smiled as he folded his hands on the knees of his nankeen pantaloons. "You appear ill at ease in my company, Miss Frye. Please be assured that I have not taken the owl with you. Any exasperation I might be harboring is directed at Miss Dufresne. I trust she is not at home this afternoon."

"You are correct. Miss Dufresne is not at home."

"But you are."

"I can tell you, my lord, that nothing you say will convince me to try to woo Miss Dufresne into forgiving you for the distress you have heaped upon her."

He laughed. "I do not expect the impossible from you." Reaching under his dark brown coat, he withdrew a sealed page. "All I ask is that you give this to Miss Dufresne. The other letters I have had delivered here have been returned to me unopened."

Frye did not take the letter. "You have wasted your time calling."

"Only if you refuse to comply with this simple request." He placed the folded page on the arm of her chair. "I must leave Bath tonight for several days, and I wish Miss Dufresne to understand why. Please give her this letter and ask her to read it."

"I shall give it to her, for I would never think of failing to deliver a message to her, but I cannot guarantee that she will read it."

Standing, he said, "I understand. Miss Dufresne's stubborn nature is without par."

"I would not say that."

A slow smile tipped his lips, but his eyes remained frigid. "You may tell Miss Dufresne, as well, that I would not have been so patient about her refusal to see me if I had not been in and out of Bath recently on a business she knows is very important to me. If fortune is with me, it soon shall be finished, and I intend to give her much more of my attention." Giving her no time to reply to his outrageous statement, he added, "Good day, Miss Frye."

The abigail sat in the chair until she heard the door close. Then she picked up the page. Not even Miss Dufresne's name blemished the cream colored vellum. Its very lack of address disturbed her, for it seemed to her that Lord Windham expected his every wish to be satisfied. Dread nibbled at her. This could bode no good for her lady.


"Then she said that she found the waters as tasty as a lemon tart." Annis laughed as she climbed the stairs from the entry foyer with Nerissa. "No wonder dear Philip was struggling not to laugh until we returned to the gig. Dear Nerissa, I swear I was about to fall into whoops myself."

Nerissa smiled absently. True, the discussion at the Pump Room had been amusing, but . . . she sighed silently. Nothing could lighten her spirits when her heart was so weighty. Knowing Annis would be expecting an answer, she managed to say something which sent her friend into another palavering monologue.

Not that she could fault Annis. Since the confrontation at *Madame* de Ramel's shop, Annis had made every effort to keep Nerissa so busy she would have no time to think of Hamilton. The simple truth was that he invaded her thoughts in the middle of a conversation as easily as he did in the middle of the night. Too often, she found herself scanning a gathering, looking for his teasing smile and eyes that taunted her into believing the warmth within them was for her alone.

When they reached the top of the stairs, Frye hurried toward them. Nerissa saw her abigail's troubled expression and interrupted Annis to say, "If you will excuse me, I believe I have some household matters that require my attention."

"Perfect!" Annis hugged her before adding, "I shall take nine winks so I may be bright when Philip returns this evening. We are going to a performance at the Theatre Royal with Janelle and Mr. Oakley. How I wish you would go with us."

Nerissa was able to smile with sincerity. "You know I have no wish to spend even a moment in Mr. Oakley's company."

"Or Janelle's." She laughed. "She has become too much of a good thing since her betrothal was announced. Do go and tend to your duties, Nerissa. I promise I shall remember every detail of the play to share with you when I return."

Nerissa's smile ebbed as she opened the door to her bedroom. When Frye followed her in mutely, she was sure something was wrong. Her abigail seldom failed to ask her where she had been and had she had a good time. Frye's very silence bespoke trouble.

As soon as the door closed behind them, Frye said softly, "Lord Windham stopped by this afternoon."

"Did he?" Nerissa slowly untied the ribbons on her bonnet, keeping her back to her abigail.

Until she had her errant emotions under control, she preferred to keep them hidden. She almost laughed with irony. Not a single person in the household could be indifferent to her ambivalent feelings toward Hamilton. Night after night, she dreamed of being with him, but she could not greet him at her door when he would return home to Mrs. Howe. Then her fantasy would turn to a nightmare as her head was filled with images of the tall blonde laughing at Nerissa's love for a man who preferred Mrs. Howe's easy virtue.

"Miss Dufresne?"

"Yes?"

"He wanted you to have this."

When Frye added nothing more, Nerissa turned to see the sealed letter. She took it gingerly, then tossed it onto the table by her reading chair.

Frye said uneasily, "He asked that you read it."

"I may." Faking a yawn, she said, "Do let me rest, Frye. I never suspected how exhausting it would be to chaperon Annis about Bath."

"You might be wise to read the letter at the very least."

"I shall consider it. Now let me rest before I give a packing-penny to you."

Frye hesitated, then asked, "Miss Dufresne, he seemed very anxious for you to read it. And he said—"

"What did he say?" she asked before she could stop herself. She was acting like a schoolgirl in the throes of her first calf love. Hamilton might feel desire for her, but he would treat her no differently than he had any woman since Mrs. Howe's betrayal. She would not be like those other women.

Frye opened and closed her hands, then locked her fingers together in front of her. "He asked me to tell you. . . . That is, he requested—"

"Do get on with it, Frye!"

"He said that he would have not been so patient with you turning him away if he had not been involved in business that you know is important to him." She swallowed roughly. "Then he plans to turn his attention to you. What does he mean, Miss Dufresne?"

Nerissa turned away again. "I think it is quite clear, Frye."

Frye nodded and scurried out of the room. Nerissa saw her glance back at the letter, fear on her face as if she expected Old Scratch to leap up from it. As the door closed, Nerissa picked up the letter.

She had not wanted to send the others back, but she had. If this was like his last "apology," when he had lured her into forgiving him with an invitation, she must not let herself be tempted to pardon him again.

Even as she thought that, her finger slipped beneath the wax sealing the page. She sat on the chair. She brushed bits of red wax from her lap and glanced out the window, hesitating before she began to read. She had to own that she would want for sense if she let Hamilton invade her life anew. If she did, she was unsure if she could govern her feelings for the intriguing viscount. It was easier to act angry at his crass words than to own to her longings to be in his arms, to feel the throbbing of his heart against her breast, to delight in his tongue stroking hers in an invitation to rapture.

With a soft moan, she forced the enticing thoughts from her head. She must force him just as completely from her mind, but her body refused to obey her. Her hands lifted the letter up, and her eyes revealed each word to her.

My dear Nerissa,

How many letters have I begun this way? You would not know, unless you have kept count of how many you have sent back un-opened. I hope you have acceded to good sense and are reading this one, for I can ascertain no reason to continue to write missives that will go unread.

For the past few days, I have been inundated with Philip's opinions of you and me. To paraphrase them—so I need not run this bottle of ink dry—you are a widgeon. As—he assures me—I am. Mayhap he is correct, but I shall not ask your forgiveness for any offense I might have inflicted upon you because of a promise I made my father while he was taking his last breath. Nor shall I ask why you assumed—as you clearly did—that a visit to a millinery shop was on Elinor's behalf. Tonight, when a lad brings a gift for Annis from her loving Philip, I think you shall realize I was placing that order with the milliner on his behalf. Mayhap, by the time I return from delivering Elinor to Town— where she will be distant enough not to vex me with her demands for what I cannot give her— you will have to come to your senses and will receive me when I call upon you.

I remain, until that time,

Your trusted servant,

Nerissa lowered the letter to her lap as Hamilton's handwriting blurred before her eyes. Happiness flowed into the emptiness inside her.

"Your *trusted* servant," she reread aloud and smiled. Yes, she did trust him, cabbage-head though she might be. If only she could convince him to trust her . . . but mayhap this was a beginning. She hoped that was so.

Nerissa bent her head into the fine mist that was dampening the street and her shawl. It was not far to Laura Place, and she wanted to get inside before it began to rain in earnest. Because she had been going only a short distance along Argyle Street, she had not taken an umbrella to protect her when the massive clouds overhead vented their burden.

Hearing a shout behind her, she looked back to see

a short man pumping his fist angrily at a man, who was driving a wagon along the street. She hurried on, not curious enough about their quarrel to stand in the rain and listen.

A smile tilted her lips. Philip had told her Hamilton was due back in Bath tomorrow. Although she did not know when he might call, she hoped it would be soon. No week had ever passed more slowly than this one.

She paused at the corner of Grove Street to look in the window of a bookstore. So frequently, she had stood here with Cole as they pointed out the books they wished they could read. Cole always selected technical books while she had been partial to Miss Austen's stories and Walter Scott's romantic tales. They seldom purchased anything, for books were a luxury they could scarcely afford.

A drop of rain bounced off her bonnet, and Nerissa knew she could not afford to dally. She went to the curb to cross the street. Looking both ways, she saw the same short man, who had been coming to points with the teamster. He seemed in no hurry. When he saw her looking at him, he stopped and looked in the window of another shop.

Nerissa wove her way through the maze of traffic, and hurried along the walkway. In spite of herself, she looked over her shoulder to see the short man negotiating his way past the carriages and wagons in the street.

When the man crossed the center of Laura Place as she did, Nerissa clutched her bag tighter. He could not be following her. It must be no more than a coincidence. This was a busy street, after all. She looked back and discovered he was closing the distance between them.

Her heart thumped wildly in her ears. Wanting to run, wanting to scream, she did neither. She continued to walk quickly, smiling with relief when she saw the steps to her house.

As she put her hand on the rail, her right arm was grasped. She tried to pull away, but was whirled to face a squat man. His hair fell forward into his narrow eyes, which were regarding her with a lasciviousness that wrenched her stomach.

"Take your hands off me!"

"I be needin' to speak with ye."

"I am sorry," she said primly. "I do not know you, and I do not speak with strangers."

He stepped in front of her, still holding her arm. Hooking a thumb toward the front door, he asked, "Do ye live 'ere?"

She considered lying, but she wanted nothing more at the moment than to get inside the house and close out this horrible man. "Yes."

"Alone?"

"That, sir, is none of your bread and butter." She tried to pull away. When his dirty, cracked nails dug into her arm, she gasped. "You are hurting me."

"I'll be doin' more if ye don't answer me."

Nerissa choked as he thrust his face closer. The scent of cheap gin sickened her. Trying to lean away, she choked back a scream as he abruptly released her, and she fell onto the bottom step.

A tall form stepped between her and the odious man. She released her ragged breath as she looked up at Terry, the house's lone footman. In his hand, he held one of the walking sticks which Cole had inherited from his father, but had never used. As he glowered at the shorter man, he put a hand under her elbow to assist her gently to her feet.

"Begone from here," Nerissa said in a shaky voice.

The short man did not move as he growled, "I know yer 'idin' something, and I'll be findin' out what 'tis. Then ye'll be sorry, ye didn't answer m' questions."

Terry's deep voice rumbled through the increasing

rain. "Begone she said." He emphasized his words with a tap of the walking stick against the iron railing.

The man stamped away, grumbling under his breath.

"Are you all right, Miss Dufresne?" the young man asked.

"Yes," she whispered. She let him take her hand and help her into the house. How fortunate for her that Hadfield was in London with Cole! *He* would have offered her no help and would have enjoyed watching her try to edge past that boorish man.

"What did he want?"

"I don't know." She looked back at the closed door. The man had been insistent that she had some information that he wanted.

"Probably all at sea with too much drink."

"I hope you are right," she answered, but she continued to look over her shoulder at the front door as she climbed the stairs.

Annis had to be calmed from a bout of hysteria when she learned what had happened in front of the house. Giving her a bottle of *sal volatile* to keep her from swooning, Nerissa insisted that her friend sit and sip on a cup of chamomile tea to soothe herself.

Philip watched in uncomfortable silence. His hands were clasped behind the back of his brown coat, and his ruddy brows were wrinkled in concentration. When Nerissa handed him a cup of tea, he perched on the very edge of a chair and said, "Mayhap you should move elsewhere."

"Where?" Nerissa asked. "This is my home." Sorrow twinged through her as she wished she could return to the idyllic setting of Hill's End, but it was impossible.

"There is a room on Queen Square," he said slowly.

She patted his hand, then rose. Her disquiet refused to allow her to sit for more than a single heartbeat. "You are generous to offer, Philip, but you know that is impossible."

"You should come home with me," Annis suggested. "You know Mama wishes we were living at Camden Crescent instead of here."

Nerissa shook her head. She preferred the risk of remaining in her home than suffering the edge of Mrs. Ehrlich's tongue until her brother returned from London. "Cole should be home soon. I simply will be careful until he returns."

"I wish Hamilton was here." A tic accented the tension in Philip's jaw. "He would give that lurcher a few handy blows to teach him not to bother you."

"I can take care of myself."

"Are you certain of that?"

She sighed and tried to give Philip a smile. He was a gentle soul, so gentle she could not envision him wearing a soldier's toggery. "I hope so," she said with every bit of sincerity she could muster.

When, the next morning, Mrs. Carroll announced at the door of the sitting room that Mr. Crimmins would like to speak with Miss Dufresne at her convenience, Nerissa was astonished. The solicitor rarely bestirred himself to go beyond his office.

She wondered what bad tidings the solicitor had to inflict upon her now, but kept her apprehension from her face. "Bring him up. I shall talk to him here."

"What do you think that stodgy paper-skull wants?" Annis asked as the housekeeper hurried away.

"I have no idea."

"He should wait until your brother returns to bother you with any work."

Nerissa smiled. The idea of Cole handling the household's affairs more competently than she could was ludicrous. "I am accustomed to dealing with Mr. Crimmins."

"You do too much." Gathering her needlework, she grimaced. "I shall leave you to this boredom. Let me know when he has left, and we can enjoy a walk before we get ready to go to the Assembly Rooms this evening. I do hope Hamilton is back in Bath in time to join us."

"I hope so, too." When Annis laughed at her fervor, Nerissa could not help smiling. It was impossible to hide the truth that she was anxious to see Hamilton, to smooth over the differences between them, to welcome his lips on hers.

Nerissa's smile lasted until the pompous lawyer bustled into the room moments after Annis had taken her leave. His flamboyantly red waistcoat did not fit with his otherwise somber appearance. Nerissa might have been amused if she had not been so apprehensive about what had drawn him out of his office to call upon her.

"I bring you good news, Miss Dufresne," he said after his unusually effusive greeting. Leaning forward from where he was sitting on the light blue settee, he smiled. "An offer, a very generous offer, if I may be so candid, for Hill's End has been tendered to my office."

"Someone wishes to buy my father's estate?"

"*Your* estate. You must be pleased."

"I am speechless," she said, wondering if he could suspect how true the hackneyed words were. Until the moment he had spoken of a buyer for Hill's End, she had thought he was coming to harangue her for letting Cole go to London.

She looked down at her hands, which were folded in her lap. Her knuckles were bleached as she realized she was about to lose the only home she had known until she came to live with Cole. Strangers would be sitting in the small parlor where her mother had read to her on afternoons, while rain meandered along the uneven, hand-blown glass. Other children would be sleeping in her room, high beneath the front gable. Another family would play ball on the wide expanse of the lawns. A shiver coursed along her back as she realized that the very spot where Hamilton had kissed her on their outing would belong to those strangers. She was losing all she had.

Preoccupied with his own exhilaration over the tidings, Mr. Crimmins mistakenly believed that she was as thrilled. "With your permission, I shall begin the drawing up of the papers for the sale, Miss Dufresne. I shall do it posthaste. If there are no complications—and I fear that there usually are a few in these circumstances—you shall soon find your reticule full of blunt. This should change your financial situation."

"Yes," she said faintly. Shaking herself mentally, she repeated, "Yes, Mr. Crimmins. That will be wonderful. I know that Cole and I shall appreciate having more than a farthing between us."

"May I speak with your stepbrother? There are a few details I wish to acquaint him with."

"Cole is in London."

"How . . . ?"

"Mr. Crimmins," she said primly, irritated by his presumption that she could not understand the procedures for selling Hill's End, "you need concern yourself only with the dispersing of our household quarterly allowance. It is my decision how it will be spent once you have given it to us."

"He went to Town to find backers for those lucubrations of his? Miss Dufresne, I implore you to recall him to Bath immediately. Such canal projects have been tried in the past with little success."

Nerissa wondered where the solicitor had attained

his information on their household. If Hadfield had not left with Cole, she would have accused the butler of spreading tales. There most be another rat squeaking belowstairs. She would set Mrs. Carroll to routing it out as quickly as possible.

"Cole should be returning before month's end," she said in the same formal tone. "I see no reason to curtail his time in London. Although you clearly think otherwise, Mr. Crimmins, Cole's plan has much merit."

"I would caution you not to invest what you might obtain from the sale of Hill's End into that flat move. You will lose everything."

His acrimonious tone amazed her, but she refused to come to points with him. He might think that Cole had been born under a three penny halfpenny planet, but she had to believe that her stepbrother would prove to everyone that he had not wasted his life on this dream.

A dream . . . her unavailing dreams that something would happen to save her home from the block had betrayed her. Hill's End soon would belong to someone else, and her last connection with what had been would be severed.

Standing when he did, she bid him a good afternoon. She watched him walk out the door, then she closed the door. Twisting the lock, she sank into her chair and wept for all she would lose when she signed the papers for Hill's End.

# Chapter Fifteen

Nerissa's fingers were all in a tremble in her evening gloves as she brushed them against the *eau de Nile* crêpe of her gown. The low, square neckline was edged by gold cord to match that on the short sleeves. The skirt was unadorned, but revealed the embroidery on the hem of her petticoat. A demi-train of the same crêpe trailed her down the stairs.

Her smile strained her lips which wanted to quiver as rapidly as her fingers. Tonight—when she should have been thrilled at the chance to see Hamilton again—she had to fight to keep from crying. Although she had known the sale of Hill's End would come about eventually, she still had been unprepared for it.

When she saw only Philip and Annis in the foyer, her smile faltered. Her thoughts must have been clear on her face, because, after exchanging an anxious glance with Annis, Philip hurried forward to greet her.

"Hamilton would want me to express his regrets that he has not returned from London in time for this gathering, Nerissa, but you will still come with us, won't you?" Philip smiled, but his expression seemed in danger of falling into sorrow. Holding his beaver in his hands, he worried the brim with anxious fingers. "I left a message for Hamilton to join us upon his arrival in Bath."

Annis, who was wearing the lovely new hat that had been a gift from an abashed Philip, hurried to say, "Do say yes. You promised me that you would join us tonight when you did not last week. If you do not come with us to the Upper Rooms, I could not bear it. You have not stepped foot out of this house this week to do anything but run errands and post a letter to Cole. Think of the fun we shall have.

"Yes, we shall have a grand time," Philip seconded.

Nerissa held up her hands in mock defeat, because she could not contest her friends who thought only of her happiness. "I shall come along as your watch-dog."

"Nay," he retorted as he bowed in her direction. "Not as Annis's *duenna*, but as my guest as well. I shall be the envy of every man there when I appear with two lovely ladies on my arms."

During the short trip over the Pulteney Bridge and north into the Upper Town, Philip seemed determined to lure Nerissa out of the dismals. To own the truth, she could not think of a single reason why she should not enjoy the evening. He reassured her again and again that Hamilton would rush to the Upper Rooms as soon as he arrived at Queen Square.

"He must surely be eager to see you, Nerissa, especially," he added with a grimace, "after having to endure *her* company for the trip to Town."

"You could speak her name," Annis said, chuckling. "It will not taint you forever."

"You cannot know Elinor Howe well if you say that."

"I have no wish to know her better."

Nerissa silently concurred with her bosom bow. She was glad Mrs. Howe was on the far side of

England, where her nasty words could not hurt them.

When the carriage turned onto Alfred Street and into the carriage entrance to the Upper Rooms, she looked out with interest. So seldom did she come to this part of this city, and she enjoyed the elegance of the buildings which had been built the previous century under the guidance of Mr. Nash. The carriage slowed in front of the elegant overhang that broke the classically designed facade with its three stories of windows marching in perfect precision across it.

The first, furtive raindrops struck the walkway as they hurried into the anteroom. The octagonal room was crowded with those who had come to enjoy the music and dancing in the ballroom, although a few people were drifting toward the eight-sided card room at the opposite end of the antechamber. Sweet scents drifted through the room as the women moved their fans in a silent dance that sent perfume wafting.

Following Philip and Annis toward the ballroom to the left, Nerissa tried to hide her amazement. She had never entered the huge room, which she guessed was more than one hundred feet in length. Portraits covered the walls beneath the rows of Corinthian columns reaching to a soffit still more than ten feet below the coved ceiling. As precisely designed as the exterior, the ballroom's glory focused on five elegant, glass chandeliers lit with hundreds of candles.

Chairs lined the walls, but few people sat. Instead they milled, going from conversation to conversation, seeking the latest news from Bath and beyond. Music came from the galley set high in one long wall. As Nerissa was drawn into the room, she discovered why the women had been rocking their fans in front of their faces. Although the autumnal evening was as warm as the heart of the summer, fires burned on all seven hearths.

While Annis danced a country reel with Philip, Nerissa found herself the center of conversation. The people who came up to her were curious why she was at the Upper Rooms without Hamilton, and where he was, and when he would return, and . . . asked with a glitter of interest in their eyes . . . would she be escorted about Bath by the viscount again.

She was grateful when Philip rescued her from one dowager who was more persistently inquisitive than the others.

Nerissa put her hand on his arm and let him lead her toward the dancers. With a smile, she said, "I thought you would ask Annis for each dance this evening."

"Lady St. John just reminded me that there were many young ladies who might be interested in a dance."

"She thinks you should be interested in her eldest daughter."

He laughed. "Shame on you, Nerissa! You shall have me thinking that I am a rare prize when I was trying to avoid being at outs with her. I know I would have no more chance than a cat in hell without claws if I try to exchange words with that brimstone."

Laughing, as they paused at the end of the line of dancers, Nerissa discovered Annis was partnered by Mr. Goldsmith, her eldest sister's husband. Nerissa had never seen either Philip or Annis so light of heart. Obviously she was not the only one to note that the *tendre* they shared was becoming a deeper affection if Lady St. John was concerned about letting a wealthy catch elude her eldest.

Once she was a part of the dancing, Nerissa was swept into it again and again until tea was served. She danced once more with Philip, then was glad to watch him twirl Annis about the floor. To own the truth, her feet hurt from so much dancing.

She wiggled her toes in her satin slippers and went to the chairs on one side of her room. After this dance, she would persuade Philip and Annis to pause long enough to enjoy a plate of something and some conversation with her.

"Miss Dufresne?" At the sharp, tenor voice, she turned to see a tall man in the livery of the Upper Rooms. He was carrying a tray topped with goblets of champagne, but he did not offer her one. Instead he went on, "Miss Dufresne, I was asked to tell you that a gentleman is waiting most anxiously for you outside."

"In the foyer?"

"By the carriages."

She regarded him in bafflement. Even Hamilton would not ask her to meet him like that, would he? She had to own she never could judge what he might do.

"Did he give you his name?" she asked.

"You don't know who he might be?"

Knowing her cheeks were ablaze with the heat swelling over her at his insinuation, polite though it might be, that she was a *bona roba* if she had more than one gentleman who might ask such a thing of her, she retorted, "Of course, I know who sent the message. Thank you."

He bowed his head and continued across the room with his tray of champagne.

Nerissa looked for Annis and Philip but they had left the dance area, and it was impossible to pick out anyone among the crowd in the room. She hesitated. To leave without telling them would be jobbernowl. Yet if Hamilton was waiting for her—and the more she considered it, the more it seemed his sort of jest—then she would return with Hamilton before she was missed.

Squeezing through the mass of people in the entry,

she edged toward the door. She hoped it was not raining still. The drops of water had stained her gown on the way into the Upper Rooms. Frye would be distressed if Nerissa returned to Laura Place with the dress pocked with water streaks.

Fresh air was intoxicating as Nerissa emerged onto the walkway. Her brow threaded in bafflement when she saw no sign of Hamilton. If this was his idea of a hoax, it was a most unwelcome one.

"Miss Dufresne?"

Nerissa started to reply, but she choked as she stared at the face of the man who had followed her yesterday. She opened her mouth to scream. The sound vanished when something pricked her left side. She looked down to see a small knife pressed to her gown. Its honed edge glittered in the light pouring from the Upper Rooms.

"Be a good girl, and ye'll 'ave no reason to fear this blade." He motioned with his head to the dark beyond the pool of lamplight. "Just walk with me and stow yer jabber."

She nodded, although she wondered if her frozen legs would carry her even a single step. With her heart thuddding in her ears, she had to bite her lip to keep from shrieking a cry of help to the gentleman handing an elderly woman from a nearby carriage. She did not doubt that this horrible man would kill her if she was so want-witted.

Two other shadowy forms appeared as she stepped into the dusk. She had no choice but to let them bind her hands, for the knife remained close to her breast. When the short man chuckled, she whispered, "Why are you doing this?"

"Answers, Miss Dufresne," he said with another laugh. "I want answers, and ye've got them."

"Answers to what?"

Instead of explaining, he made a motion with the

233

knife. She stepped backward, then choked as a cloth was stuffed into her mouth and tied behind her bonnet. A burlap bag was whipped over her head. The material scraped her bare skin as she took a deep breath to scream. The sound disappeared into a moan when pain exploded across her head, hurling her into a darkness deeper than the night.

For a moment, as she emerged from the pit of pain, Nerissa was unsure where . . . or even when . . . she was. She had suffered this agony when the horse had leapt the hedge, landing almost directly on top of her. Was she just waking from that? Enmeshed in excruciating torment, her brain refused to form a single, coherent thought.

Hands lifted her, and she heard the rumble of deep voices. Fear washed over her, as cold as a wintry wave breaking from the sea. She opened her eyes, but could see nothing. When her nose was tickled by roughness that was draped over it, she tried to raise her hand to push the material away. She could not move it.

Horror propelled all confusion out of her mind. The short man and his cronies! *They were abducting her!* She struggled to scream, but her mouth was dry and sore from the fabric wrapped around her head. Only her feet were free. She flailed them, but to no avail.

She heard a door open. She was set on her feet, and she heard voices coming toward her. Desperately she longed to screech for aid, but she was helpless. She sneezed as the bag was pulled off her aching head. The sound nearly obliterated the savage curse in a voice she recognized too easily.

In disbelief, Nerissa looked across the small room to see Hamilton standing by an unlit hearth. His clothes were as ebony as the soot on the stones, but the fury in his eyes was blacker still. What was he doing here with these squires of the pad? Had they abducted him, too? She could not believe that, for he was unbound, and she could not imagine Hamilton being held against his will so docilely.

Hamilton repeated the vicious words, then ordered, "Untie her. Mallory, did you lose what small amount of brains you were given?"

"Milord, I told ye I'd get the lass. She—"

"Enough! Untie her!"

Nerissa winced as the gag was undone, tugging her hair painfully again. When the short man, the man Hamilton had called Mallory, held up his knife, she tried to scream. No sound emerged from her arid throat. He cursed more fiercely than Hamilton had, but sliced through the twine binding her hands.

She took a single step toward Hamilton, then raced to him. He drew her into his arms and stroked her back. She surrendered to the tears of terror that had burned her throat.

Hamilton looked over her head, his mouth a slash of rage in his austere face. When fear quaked along Nerissa's slender body, his hand fisted at his side. Who had been the greater thick—him for hiring Mallory or the incompetent Bow Street Runner? As her tears dampened his shirt, he said, "Hush, my sweet, it was nothing but a mistake."

"Mistake?" choked Mallory. "Milord, ye 'ave got to be listenin' to me on this."

"Mallory, your service to me is completed." He silenced the Runner's blustery retort with, "I suggest you leave for London on the morning Mail."

"Ye should heed me!"

"I have seen enough of your mistakes not to want to listen to the telling of another. It was bad enough when you could not find facts that were clearly visible in front of your ugly face, but to abduct Miss

Dufresne. . . ." His words vanished into a growl, for he would not speak his thoughts in Nerissa's hearing.

A sneer pulled at the short man's lips. "Fry in yer own grease then."

Hamilton simply stared at Mallory. The shorter man's eyes looked away first. With a shout, Mallory called to his comrades, and they slunk out of the small room.

Drawing Nerissa back a half step, he looked for any damage those addled coves might have inflicted upon her. Tendrils of hair draped along her shoulders, that were bared by her gown, and one sleeve was ripped. Otherwise she seemed unharmed.

From beneath his coat, he pulled a flask. A wry grin tipped his lips as he recalled offering her a drink from this very flask on the day they met. Unlike before, she did not hesitate as she held it to her lips. She took no more than a sip before handing it back to him.

"Let's get out of here," he murmured as he closed the flask and put it back under his coat.

"Where are we?"

"The back room of a tavern less than a league out of Bath." He kept his arm around her as he steered her toward the door. She wobbled on every step.

"Out of Bath?" she whispered, her eyes widening in shock. "Annis . . . Philip . . ."

"We will return posthaste to Town to prove to them that you are safe."

"Yes, we must hurry."

When she took another step toward the door, she nearly collapsed. Hamilton caught her shoulders before she could fall. Leaning her against his chest, he bent and slipped his arm beneath her knees. He lifted her until her head rested on his shoulder.

"Thank you," she breathed.

As they came out into the inn's cluttered yard, Hamilton kept his cloak about her. Mallory's stupidity must not compromise her more than it already had. A whistle to his coachman brought his closed carriage to the broken gate. As he climbed in, settling Nerissa carefully on the seat, he called the man to get them back to Bath with the best possible speed.

Nerissa sighed as she let the seat enfold her in safety. Even when the carriage rocked forward, as the coachman plied the tommy to the horses, she did not move. Only when Hamilton held out his handkerchief did she realize she was weeping.

"Nerissa, did they hurt you?"

She wiped the linen against her eyes. "They were as gentle as I could expect from knights of the road."

He smiled coolly. "They were not highwaymen, but Bow Street Runners."

"Why would a Bow Street Runner wish to abduct me?"

"Because Mallory has a knock in his cradle. He thought he could deceive me into paying him what I promised him if he was able to take the thief I seek."

"You hired him?" She sat straighter and turned to him, although she could see nothing of his face in the darkness. "To help you find the fleecer?"

"Townsend's Bow Street Runners have an excellent reputation as thief-takers. 'Twas my misfortune to be saddled with one who was both incompetent and a gooseberry."

"But why did he abduct *me?*"

With a shrug, he said, "Mayhap he wished to distract me from noting his shoddy work by bringing me the prettiest woman in Bath as a gift."

"I doubt I could be considered anywhere near pretty tonight. I must look a complete rump."

"You look beautiful to these eyes that have not

237

been able to enjoy looking at you for so long."

Her own laugh surprised her. "Hamilton, you cannot see me. It is too dark."

"Then I must use another sense to admire your loveliness. The sense of touch, mayhap?"

His hand glided along her shoulders to bring her to him. As her trembling fingers rose along his arms, she moved even closer. She wanted . . . no, she needed to be wrapped in his arms as he helped her put all thoughts of anything but this craving from her head.

"But this is not enough," he said with the impish lilt in his voice that always signalled mischief.

"No?" she returned in the same tone.

"Mayhap I should try the sense of hearing."

"Do you wish to hear that I am pleased you have come back to Bath?"

"Alone?"

She laughed again. "Most definitely, I am pleased you have come back alone."

"That," he said with a scintillating smile she could see even in the darkness, "is better, but still not enough. Do you think the sense of smell would help?"

She could do nothing but giggle when he nuzzled her neck with the tip of his nose. Then, as his heated breath caressed her skin, she clutched tighter to his shoulders. His hand slipped to her waist, and he boldly stroked its gentle curve.

"Is that better?" he rasped, the humor gone from his voice. "Mayhap it is, but it still doesn't serve the purpose. That leaves only the sense of taste."

"Yes," she whispered as her fingers combed upward through his silky hair. "Taste me."

When his tongue teased the half-circle of her ear, she shivered with unexpected pleasure. She had been so certain he would kiss her. She wanted him to kiss her. She wanted that with every beat of her heart. As his breath tickled her ear, she moaned his name with the longing that had been pent-up within her.

Enthralled by his mouth sampling the sensitive skin along her neck, each gentle nibble a separate ecstasy, she let him lean her back into the soft velvet seat. She drew him over her, not wanting to let a moment of the delight evade her. The strength of his body pressed down upon her, introducing her to every virile angle.

She guided his mouth to hers, no longer able to wait to feel its eager caress on her. His tongue parried with hers, daring her to be as bold. She gasped deep within his mouth when his fingers swept over her breast. Rapture rended her, threatening to shred her into a dozen fragments of delight.

A sudden bounce of the carriage made Nerissa clutch his coat. She opened her eyes to see the flash of a street lamp. Its light burned into her, adding to the ache in her skull that she had forgotten for those brief, wondrous moments.

"Bath," Hamilton murmured, and she heard his regret as he sat, drawing her up into his arms.

She said nothing as she leaned her cheek against his chest. The steady beat of his heart soothed her, and she closed her eyes, letting the happiness soar through her. In his arms, she could forget her worries about Cole and his work in London and the anguish of selling Hill's End. In his arms, she thought only of the rough wool of his coat and the scent of his skin and the fascination of his gaze capturing hers.

As the carriage slowed, Hamilton leaned out and shouted to a lad loitering by the door to the Upper Rooms. He tossed the boy a coin and asked him to find Philip Windham inside the Assembly. If the boy brought Mr. Windham and his companion to the carriage, there would be a yellow-boy for him. The lad raced into the building.

Nerissa tried to straighten her bonnet, but she feared the brim had been broken. When Hamilton chuckled, she looked up at him, not sure what he found so amusing.

"I see I shall be indebted to you for another hat. This is becoming a habit, Nerissa."

"This was not your fault," she said as she tugged at one side.

"But this is." He lifted her bonnet from her hair and turned it so she could see the shattered back. In the dim light from the doorway, his smile took on a devilish tilt. "And I would gladly buy you a new hat, any time you wish, in exchange for your kisses."

A shout kept her from having to stammer an answer, because she had not been sure what to say. Philip nearly ripped the door open.

"Nerissa! Thank goodness, you are safe. We have been searching every inch of the Upper Rooms for you. We . . . Hamilton!"

Instead of explaining to his flabbergasted brother, Hamilton said only, "Get your carriage, Philip, and follow us to Laura Place. I think all of us have had enough excitement for one night."

Philip nodded, astonishing Nerissa, for she doubted if she could have restrained her curiosity so readily. When he stepped back, she saw the tension lining his face. She suddenly wanted nothing more than for the four of them to sit in her parlor and enjoy a cup of tea while they laughed together over her misadventure.

As soon as she walked into the foyer, listening to Hamilton explain quickly what had happened to his brother, Nerissa knew she would be denied that simple pleasure. Mrs. Carroll was standing by the staircase, her apron thrown up over her face as she wept. Beside her, Frye was wringing her hands in dismay. The rest of the staff, from the cook to the footman, were clustered around them.

"Miss Dufresne!" cried Frye, and pushed past the others as Nerissa hid her ruined hat behind her. She discovered she needed not have worried about her abigail noticing its battered state, because Frye gasped, "It's terrible! So terrible!"

"What is terrible?"

*"That!"*

Nerissa turned as the older woman pointed to the far side of the foyer. With a gasp, she tossed her hat to the floor and ran to the open door of Cole's book room. She stopped, paralyzed with shock, as she stared about the room. Every drawer had been emptied, every book pulled from the shelves. When she saw the torn sheets scattered on the floor, she pressed her fingers to her lips. All of Cole's work . . . everything he had struggled to design since he had been in short pants . . . all of it was ruined!

Behind her, Annis moaned, "Who would do such a thing?"

"Mallory clearly has had a busy evening," Hamilton said as he bent to pick up a tattered book. He closed it and set it on an otherwise empty shelf.

Philip straightened from where he had been righting a chair. "Mallory? The calf's head who stole Nerissa tonight? Damn you, Hamilton!"

Nerissa turned to stare at the younger man in astonishment. Annis put her hand on Philip's arm, but he refused to be calmed. Grabbing a book from the floor, he shook it in Hamilton's face. Nerissa was startled when Hamilton did not push it away.

"This!" Philip snapped, barely able to spit out each word past his stiff lips. "This is what your desire for revenge has wrought! You have lowered yourself

241

to hiring thugs to abet you in this worthless scheme to find thirty thousand pounds that you truly have no need of. Are you happy with what your obsession has brought you?"

Nerissa took the book and set it on a table. "Enough, Philip. What is done is done. Tomorrow, Frye," she added to her wide-eyed abigail, who was being oddly reticent, "we will see what we can do to clean this up. I don't want Cole to see this." Turning to the housekeeper, who was still crying loudly, she said, "Mrs. Carroll?"

"Yes?" She dabbed at her eyes with the corner of her apron.

"Please have some tea . . ." She looked at Hamilton and smiled sadly. ". . . and some brandy brought to my sitting room. Then see that everyone is calmed down."

"Yes, Miss Dufresne." Backing out of the room, she herded the other servants toward the kitchen.

Frye stayed long enough to ask, "Shall I have the Watch alerted?"

"If you wish," Nerissa answered, "although I don't think we need to worry about this happening again."

When Annis and Philip started up the stairs, Hamilton put his hand on Nerissa's arm and drew her back into the room. He closed the door and turned her to face him.

"Don't be so naïve," he warned in a low voice. "Mallory may not be finished."

Panic flitted through her. "You think he might come back?"

"We cannot be certain until I hear from Townsend that he has sent Mallory on another assignment. Until I do or until your brother returns from London, you should come to Windham Park."

"Windham Park?" she gasped. "But, Hamilton,

that's impossible! If I were to go with you there—"

"*Blast convention!*" His fingers curved along the side of her face and tilted her eyes up so she could not avoid the fierce emotions in his. "You have had a harrowing experience, Nerissa, and you need to get away from the poker-talk that is sure to flutter about Bath in the wake of this evening."

"No one saw us."

"Except Lady St. John who was coming out of the Upper Rooms as Philip let out his roar."

Nerissa blanched. The countess was an incurable gossip. "But to go with you alone would ruin what little reputation I may have left."

His voice softened to a husky whisper. "As much as I would delight in having you all to myself, we shall not be alone. Philip will go with us, and as he would not be able to pull himself from Annis's company for even a moment, she must come also." Gently he brushed her cheek with his fingertip. "I do own to having sympathy for them, for I know the torment of being far from the side of one who fills my thoughts."

She watched his lips form each word and had to struggle to think of anything but their warmth against her mouth. "Mrs. Ehrlich will never agree to Annis traveling under those circumstances."

"Then we shall invite all of the 'Polite World' to the Park to join us."

"How will that prevent the gossip?"

His arm swept around her waist, and he tugged her to him. "If my suspicions are correct, Philip has set his cap on your bosom bow and will ask her to marry up with him any day."

"He has given up his plans to buy that commission?"

"I can't be certain of that, for soldiers are allowed a wife." As his hand stroked her back, sending new flurries of fierce need along her, he said against her

243

ear, "A visit to the country with his beloved might persuade Philip to rethink his plans. Then the *élite* can enjoy talking about him and Annis while I convince you to use your tasty lips for other purposes."

As his mouth slanted across hers, she knew she was ready to agree to anything he wanted, as long as they could share this glorious enchantment. She knew, as well, how dangerous it would be to lose more than her heart to him, and she wondered if she risked more by staying in Bath or going to Windham Park.

# Chapter Sixteen

Beyond the dressing-room window, the gardens of Windham Park spread outward in every direction. Sunlight sparkled brightly on a pool which had a fountain in its heart. Water sprayed skyward more than fifteen feet before falling back into itself. Surrounded on every side by flowering bushes and topiary, the garden was sure to offer more delights to anyone who wandered through it.

The curved roof of a Grecian-style temple could be seen on the far side of a stand of tall trees. When they had driven up to the magnificent house, Nerissa had noticed that it was set in a rose garden. The vines were past flowering, but she could imagine their glorious colors in the spring.

Windham Park was even more incredible than Nerissa had guessed from passing it on the road leading south from Bath. The front façade was a castellated fantasy with a square Norman tower amid the more gently rounded towers at every corner. Bay windows jutted out from the house at every angle and rose from the ground to the battlement-furnished parapets at the top. The country home announced the wealth and prestige of Hamilton's title that went back, unscathed by dishonor, into the dim reaches of history.

But she was not thinking of the grand staircase hall or the smooth lawns as she stared out of the window in the bedchamber she had been given to use. She stared past the temple and the orchards and the brook meandering at its edge to the distant hills that were faded to a purplish-blue. Among them, Hill's End was situated. She would trade all this elegance for her home, which would not be hers much longer.

"Everything is unpacked," Frye said as she closed the door to the cupboard.

Nerissa turned from the window, letting the yellow drapes fall back into place. Frye was a dull spot among the exuberant colors of the main bedchamber, on the other side of the door, for the Chinese silk wallpaper was a dazzling tapestry. A matching fabric swathed the bed, which seemed dwarfed by the rest of the chamber. A hearth, with a carved, black marble mantel, was topped by the small statues which were set on the tables and chests along the walls. Even the collection of furniture could not hide the Oriental rug.

"Would you like some tea to take the dust of the road from your throat?" Frye continued, fluttering around the dressing room like an oversized songbird.

"I think that would be a good idea now that I have bathed." She smiled. "I didn't want to appear in that august hall tonight for dinner looking like a dirty urchin."

A knock on the door to the hallway rang against the high ceiling like distant thunder. Frye motioned for her to stay where she was. "I shall answer it. You need to rest, Miss Dufresne."

Nerissa nodded. Frye had been even more solicitous of her than usual since her abigail discovered the lump on Nerissa's head this morning while brushing her hair. Not satisfied until she heard every detail of the distressing evening, Frye had been surprisingly pleased with Hamilton's invitation to the country.

"I doubted the wisdom of two young women living alone like this," Frye had said with her favorite frown. "'Tis a wonder you have not come to trouble before this. I shall arrange for any messages from Mr. Pilcher to be forwarded to Windham Park, so you may know when it is prudent to return to Bath."

Quarreling with Frye was the last thing Nerissa had wanted to do, so she had listened quietly and looked properly chagrined. She would do the same now, because Frye's advice was wise. Her head still ached, and she could not keep her hands from trembling when she thought of her abduction.

The rapping continued, growing more persistent. "Do go quickly and answer the door, Frye, before our caller wears the skin right off his or her knuckles."

Frye hurried through the bedchamber to the door to the hallway, and opened it only enough to peer around it. When she saw Miss Ehrlich on the far side, she ushered the young woman in with a smile. Miss Ehrlich was attired in a pink gown and a blue silk bonnet with a pert feather on one side.

Frye started to explain that Miss Dufresne was preparing to rest when the door to the dressing room came ajar to reveal Miss Dufresne pulling on her wrapper. Just as she was about to chide her lady for coming out into the bedchamber when she had no idea who might be calling, Frye heard Miss Ehrlich gulp back a sob.

"I must speak with you, Nerissa," choked Miss Ehrlich and looked at Frye beseechingly.

"Excuse us, Frye," Nerissa said.

The abigail did not hesitate. The mottled color of Miss Ehrlich's face warned that she was about to cascade into tears. With a sigh, the maid went out of the room. Miss Dufresne had handled crises more appalling in the past few days than a young wet-goose.

Thinking much the same thing, Nerissa urged Annis to sit on the window seat. With her silk wrapper rustling beneath her as she also sat, Nerissa said, "Pluck up, Annis, and tell me what is amiss."

"'Tis Philip."

"Philip?" Such an answer was one she had least expected, especially when Annis was wearing the hat that Philip had given her. She patted her friend's hand. "Annis, you know that breezes are part—"

"We have not had an argument. 'Tis . . . 'tis . . ." She collapsed into more sobs.

Putting her arm around Annis's quivering shoulders, she murmured, "If Philip said something to you that distresses you, you should know—after watching your sisters being wooed—that such misunderstandings are usually quick in passing. Philip is a fine man. He would not do anything to hurt you intentionally."

"He is a wonderful man." Tears oozed from her dark eyes as she whispered, "I believe I love him."

"That is no surprise." Nerissa smiled gently. "Not to me or to anyone who has seen you two together, but that does not make it any less wonderful, for it is increasingly obvious that he has a *tendre* for you."

Annis raised her eyes, and Nerissa saw the grief in them. "Then how could he do *this* to me?"

"Do what?"

"This awful thing."

"Awful?" she choked as horror filled her. Had she been too lenient in her attention to Annis and her gallant admirer? Her promise to Mrs. Ehrlich to keep close watch on her youngest daughter careered through her head like a taunting refrain that refused to be forgotten. Certainly she should have been able to trust Philip with Annis, for he had been unable to hide his admiration for her.

248

With a quiver of dismay, she rose. She rubbed her suddenly icy hands together as she listened to Annis's weeping. Charmed by Philip's gentle smile, had she let herself be betwattled into forgetting that he shared Hamilton's sire? The strong emotions that coursed through the viscount must boil within the younger man's blood, too. If he had compromised Annis and now was determined to—

"Enough!" she snapped to herself. In the same sharp voice, she demanded, "Annis, tell me what Philip has done to turn you into a watering pot!"

Annis looked up, startled in mid-sob by Nerissa's adder's tongue. Blinking rapidly, each motion freeing yet another tear, she choked, "He is planning to buy a commission and go off to the War."

"I know."

"You knew," she gasped, her eyes wide with recriminations, "and you did not tell me?"

Nerissa said quietly, "It was not my place to speak of such a matter, for I could not know the current course of Philip's thoughts. I was sure that, if he had intentions to continue with such a plan, he would speak to you of it posthaste. It appears he has done that." She leaned her head against the embroidered wool on the tester bed. "Hamilton so hoped he would set aside this opaque ambition."

She hid her face in her hands as she sobbed anew. "I do not want him to do such an insane thing. Talk to him, Nerissa. He admires you. He will listen to you."

"If he refuses to listen to you and Hamilton, why would he heed anything I say?" she asked as she sat again.

With her hands damp with her tears, Annis grasped Nerissa's fingers. She begged, "Please speak to Philip. He admires your common sense greatly, Nerissa." A hint of a smile teased the corners of her quivering lips. "Philip spoke to me, only minutes before he revealed his horrendous intent to buy that commission, of his delight with your taming of his brother."

"I have done no such thing. Hamilton has been a gentleman from the onset."

"To you mayhap, but you know what is said about—"

"I know!" She set herself on her feet and raised her chin. "I know what has been said, and I vow I wish to hear no more of it."

Annis clapped her hands in amusement, although her cheeks still shone with tears. "Oh, you *do* love him, don't you? You love him as much as I love Philip." Her smile crumpled. "Oh, Nerissa, you must convince Philip to rethink this idiocy."

"I shall try."

"Today. *Now!*"

Nerissa smiled as she put her hand to the deep *décolletage* of her dressing gown. "Dear Annis, I am hardly dressed appropriately to speak with Philip now, but I shall endeavor to speak to him today."

"Before dinner?" she asked with childish stubbornness.

"I will try."


In spite of her promise, Nerissa had no time to seek out Philip before dinner. She had planned to rest for only a few minutes, but the lack of sleep the night before and the hectic preparations for their journey had worn her out. She might have slept the whole evening away if Frye had not come to rouse her with a gentle shake.

Hurriedly dressing in her favorite blue Indian muslin gown, she was impatient while Frye twisted her hair high on her head, leaving only a few wisps to curl about her face. A bandeau of blue silk, which was decorated with pearls and lace, encircled her face.

The passage seemed empty when Nerissa emerged from her bedchamber. Shadows hung over the tables along the walls and obscured the paintings within the gilt frames. No sound came from the lower floor, giving her the feeling that she was alone in the massive house. When a hand settled on her arm, a shriek burst from her throat.

She whirled to see Hamilton standing behind her. From his stylishly tied cravat and the ruffles dropping onto his silk waistcoat of nearly the same blue as her gown to his pristine, white breeches, he was dressed *à la modality*. Only his somber expression marred the flawlessness.

"Hamilton, you frightened me," she whispered.

"Forgive me. I should not be sneaking up on you, knowing what you have endured."

"Speak no more of it." She slipped her arms beneath his black coat and rested her cheek against his chest. As his arms surrounded her, she whispered, "I was already unsettled, for Philip told Annis of his plans to join the army on the Peninsula."

"Damn him for a cabbage-head!" he snapped. Putting his thumbs under her chin, he tilted her head back gently. "We must find a way to convince him to see the sense of changing his mind."

"That may no longer be possible."

"Anything is possible until one hops off the perch and is buried." A slow smile drifted from his lips to his eyes. "By tonight, the rest of our party will have arrived from Bath. I think I shall suggest that we celebrate our first day in the country with a hunt."

"A hunt? What good will chasing a fox about the Park do?"

"You can leave that to me. What I need you to do is to convince Annis to ride to the hounds tomorrow."

Nerissa shook her head. "I don't think that is a good idea. Annis is not a competent rider."

"I was hoping you would say that."

"What do you have planned?" she asked, unable to halt her smile as she saw the mischievous angle of his.

"You shall see on the morrow, my sweet." In the moment before his mouth covered hers, he whispered, "With luck, we shall hear no more of these absurd plans to battle the frogs."

Nerissa emerged from the double doors of the ancient manor house to see all the hunters gathered in the courtyard in anticipation of the excitement to come. Grey light filtered through the clouds clinging to the eastern horizon, and a cool hint of autumn brushed the loose tendrils of her hair back from her face.

As she walked toward where the men were discussing past hunts and commenting on the skills of the foxhounds in the pack, she carried the bulk of her long skirt over her arm to reveal her high-lows which were tightly laced about her ankles. She tucked her riding crop under her arm and pulled at her high cravat, which echoed the ones the men wore daily, and wondered why they allowed themselves to be coerced by style into donning something so uncomfortable . . . and why she had.

Nerissa looked past the baying hounds and the men, who were placing eager wagers about which of them would kill the prey, to see Philip checking the gab-string on the horse Nerissa knew was for Annis. Sure that the bridle was firmly in place, he turned as she walked toward him. Tipping his hat toward her, he smiled.

"An excellent hunt it shall be," gushed Philip as he drew on his riding gloves. "And to think that you have convinced Annis to ride with us, Nerissa! I own that I knew you were a woman of rare charm from the first moment that I saw you."

"I was quite senseless at the time, as you should recall."

Color rose along his face, and Nerissa instantly regretted her unthinking retort. When she hurried to apologize, he waved aside her words.

"'Tis I who spoke as if I was cockle-brained. Only a ramshackle cove would remind you of that accident. Forgive me, Nerissa."

"I cannot forgive you when there is no need for an apology from you." Dampening her lips, she lowered her voice. "Philip, may I speak to you alone for a moment?"

"Of what?"

"Of Annis."

He brightened as if a candle had been lighted within him. "Such a treasure! How can I thank you enough for introducing us, Nerissa? Surely fate must have urged me to enter that snuff shop. What else could explain the fortune that brought her into my life?"

Hamilton's laugh intruded. "An eager mother seeking a match for her daughter? Surely you have been afflicted with too many of those types of meetings." He wore his pinks with style, for the riding jacket might have been designed with his lithe form in mind. Dropping nearly to the tops of his boots, which were rolled down to reveal their canvas interiors, the coat opened to expose his gold waistcoat and buckskin breeches. He carried a long flintlock rifle. When Nerissa regarded it with curiosity, he smiled. "A memento from my journey to America. Weapons, not much different from this one, served to outfox our army. I daresay I can turn the tables by outfoxing a brace of foxes with this."

"You sound as if you admire America."

"It is an interesting place. Had I been the younger son, I must admit that I might have considered staying there for a while." As he paused in front of a mottled grey horse, he said, "I am glad, however, that I returned. I did not guess what challenges there would be before me."

"Don't speak of your quest today."

"You clearly are thinking more of it today than I am, for I was speaking of the challenge of dealing with a lovely woman named Nerissa Dufresne."

"Hamilton, you will put her to the blush," Philip chided with a laugh. "I have. . . . Annis!" His smile widened as he rushed forward to take her hands. "You look lovely this morning."

"Indeed you do," Nerissa added as she admired the fashionable cut of her friend's gold habit. The color added fire to her hair, but nothing glowed more than her happy eyes while she let Philip throw her up in the saddle.

Nerissa sighed. Not once last evening had she had a chance to speak with Philip alone. When Hamilton had spoken of his guests, she had not guessed he had invited everyone who had attended Sir Delwyn Seely's weekly gatherings. Each of the guests was eager to discover the truth behind the rumors of what had happened the night before they left Bath, so she was kept busy deflecting their questions with Hamilton's help.

"Don't worry," Hamilton murmured as he came to stand next to her.

"How can I help it? Look at how wondrously happy Annis looks. If he goes, she will be shattered."

"He won't go."

"There are some things even you can't halt, Hamilton."

He laughed. "Clearly there are some things you still have yet to learn, and it behooves me to teach you today."

Although she was certain—or, at least, she thought she was certain—he spoke only of Annis and Philip, the glint in his eyes warned that his words might

254

possess a double meaning. A warm silkiness wrapped around her heart and oozed throughout her. Her hand rose toward him before she could halt it.

Smiling, he lifted it to his lips. Even through her riding gloves, the heat of his mouth seared her skin, flooding her with molten flame. "Nerissa," he whispered, "there are so many things I would take pleasure in teaching you."

"Hamilton . . ."

"Hamilton!" The shout drowned out the rest of her words. Looking past him, she saw Sir Delwyn signalling to him that the master of the foxhounds was ready with the mixed pack to set them to the scent.

"Your horse and my guests are waiting, Nerissa." The sound of her given name on his lips always gave it a musical potency that she had never imagined it could possess. Twirling through her in a sweet melody, his voice caressed her. She took a half-step toward him, wanting to feel more than his voice, but halted when she heard the baronet bellow again.

Hamilton led her to a grey mottled horse. "I hope this will do. I gave the stable's most passive mount to Annis. I thought you might wish something with a bit more spirit."

"Yes." As he tossed her up into the saddle, she adjusted her skirts around her. Softly she asked, "Hamilton, what do you have planned?"

"You shall see." He swung easily onto his horse. "Just follow me and Cirrus at the best pace you can."

The rest of Nerissa's questions went as unanswered as her first one, for the master of the hounds was putting the hounds to the line. The whippers-in were struggling to restrain the dogs who were eager for the run, because the day was perfect for a burning scent, which would lead the dogs on a fast run after the beast.

Within minutes, the hounds came out of the covert

as if someone had fired them from a pistol. Baying their zealous song, they raced away from the copse toward the open field. The whippers-in followed closely to be sure that none of the skirters strayed from the main pack. With a shout, the huntsmen called for the riders to follow.

Nerissa slapped her hand on her horse, delighting in the chase. As she saw the lead thrusters—Hamilton among them—clear a fence easily, she looked back for Annis. Her eyes widened when she realized her friend was racing across the field like a varmint.

"Annis!" she cried, striking the horse with the small whip again. Her friend could not manage a horse at that speed. She was sure to come to a cropper if the beast tried to take the timber as the other riders were doing.

She plied the whip again and again to the horse, but it could not catch Annis's mount, which had skirted a fence and was running even faster. Shrieking Annis's name, she heard other shouts. She could not tell who was calling to her. She did not care. She only wanted to halt that runaway horse before Annis fell and was hurt.

Turning her horse, so it would intercept Annis's, she goaded it with her heels. It took the fence with ease. Dirt sprayed her as the horse cut across the field.

Suddenly a flash of white raced in front of her. She pulled back on the reins. When her horse reared, she clung to them. She could not fall. The horse's hoofs might come down on her. Pain jarred her as her mount dropped back to the ground. Whipping the reins around her wrists, she drew back on them more slowly to keep the horse under control. The beast slowed, quivering as much as she was.

She took several deep breaths, then looked across the field to see another rider overtaking Annis. A ragged sigh of relief allowed her shoulders to sag as the rider—whom she could identify even from across the field by his ginger-hackles as Philip—helped Annis slow her horse. When Annis flung her arms around him, he lifted her from her mount and set her on his knees.

Hearing hoofbeats, she turned in the saddle to see Hamilton on his white horse riding toward the fence. Cirrus cleared the rails with no effort. For one moment, the man and the horse were framed by the clouds. She could believe they were one; a Centaur climbing to the heights of its mythical aerie. Landing with an ease that suggested the fence had been nothing for them to master, the horse kept on, its stride unbroken, until Hamilton slowed it to a stop beside her. He held out her hat, which she had not realized she had lost in her mad dash to save Annis.

Rudely she snatched it from his hands. "Have you gone queer in your attic?" she gasped. "Cutting me off like that! I could have been thrown!"

"You could have been killed," he answered quietly.

"I know. If—"

"If you had kept riding neck-or-nothing in that direction." Taking her horse's halter, he drew her a few paces forward.

Nerissa gasped as she saw the sharp drop. She had not stopped to think there might be a ha-ha in this field. If she had continued speeding to Annis's rescue, the sunken fence could have been a deathtrap for her, because it was too wide for the horse to jump.

The baying of the hounds took a fevered pitch, but she paid the hunt no mind. When Hamilton slid from his saddle and assisted her to the ground, she was glad he kept his arm around her. Her knees were no more solid than the illusion created by the ha-ha.

"Thank you for rescuing me again," she whispered.

"As always, it was my pleasure." He grinned as he looked toward the far side of the field. "After all, everything seems to have come about as we had hoped. The fox is being given a good run, and Philip may be thinking that Annis might need him here more than on the far side of the Channel."

In amazement, she edged from beneath his arm. She leaned on the horse as she gasped, "You planned this? Did you stop to think that Annis might be killed? I told you she has scant skill as a rider. She could have—"

*"Blast it!"* His eyes narrowed into steely slits. "I did not plan for her mount to run away. To own the truth, I had no idea the beast could go any faster than a walk. The hounds must have frightened it." Gripping her shoulders, he pulled her back into his arms. "Do you think I would have endangered her life in an attempt to convince Philip not to endanger his?"

"I—"

"Trust me," he growled. "For once, Nerissa, trust me."

"I do trust you. What I do not trust are the obsessions which consume you and Philip."

His arm dropped to encircle her waist. "You are wise, my sweet, for I am most untrustworthy when I hold you like this."

"That is not what I meant, Hamilton. How can you expect your brother to heed you when you are as senseless in your pursuit as he is in his?"

He laughed at her cool reply. "The only pursuit that intrigues me at this moment is my pursuit of you."

He silenced her with his lips over hers. As his fingers curled upward to caress her with the intimacy that had bewitched her in the carriage, she moaned against his mouth. Eddies of ecstasy swirled outward from his fingertips, making her aware of every inch

258

of her pressed to him. His brazen hands swept along her and settled on her hips as he delved deep into her mouth to urge her even closer.

She was sure she would explode with the passion building within her. It flowed in a fiery flood to the very tips of her toes as she stroked the firm muscles of his back. Slipping up beneath his coat, she delighted in the warm stickiness of his waistcoat against his skin. As much as she wanted him to touch her, she yearned to touch him. The craving became an agony that was ready to engulf her.

"Damn," he whispered as he drew away from her.

She was about to ask what could possibly be wrong when he was bringing her dreams to life. Her question was forestalled by the sound of the hunt coming back toward them. "Already?" she whispered.

"I would have put that fox in my pocket to plant him a while longer, if I had guessed they would capture the creature so quickly." He laughed and tugged her back against him. "Let them see the sweet vixen I have captured with a kiss."

"Is that what I am to you, Lord Wastrel Windham? A trophy from your prowls?"

He chuckled. "I wondered how long it would take before you heard that horrendous name which was inflicted upon me by my so-called friends one night when we all overshot with gin." His smile faded as he asked, "What do you think, Nerissa? Do you think I care so little for you?"

The shouts of the riders came closer, sparing her from having to answer. Instead she asked, "Will you throw me up, Hamilton?"

"For a price."

"A price?" she asked, then smiled as she stood on tiptoe to kiss his cheek. "That, my dear Hamilton, is the payment for helping a lady mount when the hunt is bearing down upon her."

He pulled her into his arms and whispered, "That may be the initial payment, but you must post your payments in full later, my sweet."

Not caring what he meant, wanting only the stolen rapture of his arms, she dissolved into his feverish kiss to the rhythm of two hearts pulsating as one.

# Chapter Seventeen

Nerissa had never guessed that any man could flush as red as Philip did when he returned to the house with Annis. Hamilton's guests cheered when he rode into the yard in front of the stable, Annis still perched on his knees.

"Fine job, Windham!" shouted a male voice she could not put a name to.

"Couldn't have done better myself," said Rowland, a hint of jealousy in his voice.

"Wasn't that the most romantic thing you have ever seen?" gushed a plump lady.

Nerissa smiled as Philip's ears turned even pinker, but she noted that Hamilton's grin was even wider. Although such a spectacular rescue had not been part of his plan—and she vowed to ask him later to explain what he had intended—he was right. The results were the same. Philip was receiving the lauds he had hoped to win on the Continent. She wondered if this would be enough to induce him to stay in England.

"He seems quite uncomfortable," she whispered to Hamilton.

He squeezed her shoulders and laughed. "Let him discover that playing the hero can be a wretched experience."

"Why are you so cynical?" She looked up at him, grasping her hat to keep it from falling off again. Without pins to hold it in place, the hat tilted to one side of her disheveled hair. "Isn't this what you wanted?"

"Among other things." His smile stole her breath from her, for it told her that the kiss in the field was only a prelude to what he wanted to offer her today.

"Nerissa?" called Annis weakly.

Nerissa ran to where the still shaking Annis was being helped to the ground. She took Annis into the house and up the stairs to her room. When Annis moaned about her fearful ride, Nerissa said, "Hush. Do not think of it. You are safe now."

Opening the door to Annis's room, she called for Horatia. The abigail nodded to Nerissa's curt orders to have a bath brought for Miss Ehrlich.

"No," Annis interrupted, "I shall not go to bed for the rest of the day. Philip will be sick with worry if I don't return for the hunt breakfast."

"You should rest."

"Once I am certain he will also."

Nerissa saw the joy on Horatia's face and knew the abigail was delighted with the affection between Annis and Philip. She knew, as well, that it was fruitless to fly out at Annis on this. Leaving Annis to her abigail's ministrations, she returned to her own room.

Frye was pacing the floor as Nerissa entered. Before Nerissa could explain what had happened during the ride, Frye held out a letter. "This just arrived for you."

When she saw the familiar handwriting, Nerissa gasped, "Cole!"

"What is it?" asked Frye.

Laughing, she chided, "Give me a moment to open it, so I can see what it says." She cracked the sealing wax and opened the page. "He's coming home. He should be in Bath within two or three days."

"Then we must return to Bath tomorrow to have the house ready." The abigail hesitated, then asked, "Does he say anything about success for that project of his?"

"No. Mayhap it did not go as he had hoped." She sighed and folded the page.

Frye said consolingly, "It is not so horrid, Miss Dufresne. He can continue his teaching, and you will have the funds from Hill's End."

"I had hoped, if he was successful, that the sale could be halted."

"I know."

Nerissa smiled sadly at her abigail, who understood so much even when she said so little. Holding the page to her breast, she closed her eyes to keep her tears from falling. Her last hope of keeping strangers from beneath the roof of Hill's End depended on what tidings Cole brought with him from Town. Minutes ago, she had been in Hamilton's arms, and she had dreamed of always being that happy. Now she wondered if she ever would escape from this misery.

As Nerissa came down the stairs, glad to be dressed in a simple muslin gown instead of the cumbersome habit that threatened to trip her on every step, Sir Delwyn's jolly laugh rang out through the lower hall. She saw him standing next to Hamilton.

"There she is," the baronet crowed, "the loveliest lady to ever grace Windham Park. What do you say, Windham?"

"I'd say you are foxed," Hamilton replied as he smiled at Nerissa.

He laughed. "I am not so altogethery that I cannot appreciate beauty when it comes floating down that staircase."

Hamilton accepted a cup of the hunt's punch from one of the servants, and came forward to offer Nerissa it and his arm. "I think," he said softly, "the only thing Seely found on that ride was the bottom of a bottle, but I have to agree with him on this. You do look ravishing." His voice became raw with desire. "Mayhap because ravishing you is so much on my mind."

"Hamilton . . ."

"What?" he asked in the same low whisper.

She drew away from him and went to where Annis was clinging to Philip's arm. Feeling Hamilton's gaze in her back, she dared not turn. No longer could she trust herself not to throw herself in his arms and beg him to dry the tears she yearned to cry. That she could not trust herself seemed the greatest irony, when she had spoken so often to Hamilton of trust.

"I owe you thanks, too, Nerissa," Annis gushed as she threw her arms around Nerissa. "If your shout had not alerted Philip, I dare not think what might have happened to me."

"I am glad you are safe," she answered, glad also to be able to fall back on banalities.

"Wasn't Philip so brave?" Annis continued as they walked into what once had been the great hall of the manor. "If he had not swooped down to rescue me as he did, I don't know what I would have done. Dear Philip, I hope I can count on you *whenever* I need help."

"Whenever," he said, kissing her hand fervently.

Nerissa knew this would be the perfect time to broach the topic of his commission, but could not. Annis and Philip seemed so happy in the midst of their friends, and she could not destroy that. Leaving them to talk alone, she went into the great hall. After a quick breakfast, she would retire to her room to sort out the confusion in her mind and in her heart.

The huge room contained nearly fifty people, but

it did not seem crowded. A long oak table had darkened with time to near black. It was edged with benches, but, at one end of the table, an elaborately carved chair marked the seat of the manor's lord. Overhead, in the smoke-stained rafters, which were more than forty feet from the floor, twin banners waved. One was the British flag. She guessed the other design of a boar and a lion was the herald crest of the Windham family. Aromas from the food, spread out for the hunt breakfast, should have been inviting, but, although she was hungry, she could not imagine putting food into her cramped stomach.

Nerissa took a single muffin and tried to eat it while she listened to the tales, which became more outrageous on each telling, and wondered which one among them had killed the fox. She suspected it had been the huntsman.

Sir Delwyn pushed past two of the other guests to say in a voice that carried to the farthest corner of the room, "We missed you, Miss Dufresne, at the kill. However, you had a very exciting ride."

"I would have preferred it to be quieter, and I am pleased that Annis is unhurt."

"Thanks to young Philip. Who would have guessed that young hemp could be such a champion?"

"You should look more closely at Philip," she replied stiffly, not adding it would behoove the baronet to take a closer look when he was not wrapped in warm flannel. "There is much more to him than you might see on first examination."

Sir Delwyn refused to be daunted by her wigging. "And you had an enjoyable ride," he added with a wink, "with his brother, I assume." Chuckling, he walked away, pausing only enough to clap Hamilton on the back as he passed him. He turned and winked at Nerissa again.

Nerissa stared after the baronet in horror. Within

moments, the stout man would be regaling Hamilton's guests with his guess of what had kept Hamilton and her from rejoining the hunt. This was the very gossip they had hoped to avoid by leaving Bath. She wondered how she could have been so stupid. To return—rumpled and smiling—with Hamilton to the manor house was paramount to an announcement that they had taken the time away from prying eyes to savor a tryst in a hedgerow.

"Do not let that duddering rake disturb you with his poker-talk," Hamilton said as he put his hand on her arm. "Seely has more hair than wit, and he has little hair."

"If Frye hears—"

"Your abigail has heard worse, I am sure." When she started to turn away, he cursed. "Nerissa, if you expect me to apologize for kissing you, you shall have an eternity to wait. I cannot regret a moment of any time I have held you, except for the fact that each has come to an end. Nor can I doubt that you feel the same when you burn like an ember in my arms."

The heat that had been climbing her face vanished as a more fierce flame glowed in her heart. His words enticed her into forgetting that he might intend to make her one of his *à suivre* flirtations. As his fingers teased the length of her arm, ruffling her short sleeve, she longed to run her hand up the front of his ruffled shirt. Her fingers recalled the strength of his body, and she needed to feel it once more.

"Why are you fighting this passion we could share?" he asked in a rumbling whisper.

"Because I am afraid of what will happen if I don't."

"And what horrible thing do you fear will happen? Why can't you believe, as I do, that our passion will be splendid?" He moved a half-pace closer to her.

Nerissa backed away, unable to speak the truth she had never owned even to herself. If she succumbed to her desires for Hamilton's caresses, she might prove to be as want-witted as her mother had been when she had been seduced into marrying Albert Pilcher. One of her earliest memories had been of a pledge never to repeat her mother's mistake. It was a pledge she must keep, no matter how much it broke her heart.

Late that afternoon, Nerissa sat in a chair by the window in the glorious bedroom. Her feet were tucked beneath her, her elbow on the arm of the chair, her chin propped on her hand, as she stared out the window. She listened while Frye hummed to herself as she puttered about the room, finishing their packing for the trip the next day, readying Nerissa's clothes for the evening, and supervising the maids as they filled Nerissa's bath. She had hoped to keep her disquiet to herself, but she realized how silly that hope was when Frye came to sit next to her.

"Miss Dufresne, if speaking of it would help, your words would go no farther than my ears."

"I know," she said quietly, "but I have nothing to say."

Frye continued to grumble while Nerissa bathed and then dressed in her best gown of white cambric. Pulling light blue ribbons, which matched the ones at the high bodice of Nerissa's gown and along its hem, through Nerissa's upswept hair, the abigail attempted to discover what had happened that had sent Nerissa to hide in her room while the rest of the guests enjoyed the entertainments provided by Lord Windham.

Finally Nerissa said, "You will have to save your questions, Frye."

"For what? For you to avoid answering them later? Miss Dufresne, if you want my opinion—"

"I don't right now."

"I would say you either have had a falling out with

the viscount or a falling in."

Nerissa faltered as she was putting on her gloves. Baffled, she asked, "What do you mean? A falling in? What is that?"

The abigail's frown did not waver. "A falling in love, Miss Dufresne. You know how caper-witted that would be! Lord Windham has been kind to you, I own, but, knowing what I do of his past, he will have no appropriate intentions. When you assured me you were only friends, I could permit this to continue, but now . . ." She shook her head and turned away. "I shall be glad when we are ensconced in our house on Laura Place again."

Nerissa stared after her abigail as Frye went into the dressing room. In a whisper, she answered, "So will I."

The grand salon of Windham Park had been awakened from its dusty, drowsy sleep to sparkle in the day's last light. The room, set into the largest circular tower, rose to a round window in the top of the dome that was decorated with friezes of the classical gods and goddesses enjoying an *al fresco* gathering while Pan and his pipers provided music. Carved cornices edged the dome with a garden of flowers, each different from the one next to it. Gilt shimmered on the columns edging each door and decorated the walls.

Music was muted beneath conversation as Nerissa walked into the room. She heard upshot laughter and wondered if the men had continued to indulge in their brandy all day. A smile pulled at her stiff lips when she saw Annis and Philip sitting together, holding hands and talking softly.

"The very picture of young love, aren't they?"

She turned slowly to face Hamilton, whose face above his forest green coat was set in stern lines.

Although she longed to ease the rift between them, she must be cautious to ignore her heart, which begged her to give it to him. "We need to talk," she said, not caring if he reviled her for her scaly behavior earlier.

"So we do." Taking her hand, Hamilton said, "Come with me. A walk about the garden shall give us some privacy. I do not wish to share our words with this collection of shuttleheads, who are rapidly traveling into the province of Bacchus."

She looked back to Philip and Annis. Annis's soft giggle slipped surreptitiously through the rumbled conversations. "I promised Mrs. Ehrlich I would keep a close eye on Annis."

Hamilton stroked her fingers as he led her to the opposite end of the room. "I believe the inimitable Mrs. Ehrlich shall be pleased beyond measure when she learns of this evening's events."

"You mean . . . ?" She turned to see Philip holding Annis's hand and whispering to her with an expression of fearful anticipation. "Oh, how wonderful! I had despaired of him ever making his decision. Does this mean he has set aside his plans to join the army?"

"He wrote to our aunt this very afternoon informing her of his change of heart." He laughed wryly. "He has exchanged it for Annis's, I suspect."

"This is wonderful. I must—"

Laughing, Hamilton tightened his hand around hers. "Give poor Philip a moment to put the question to her. He must speak of his heart-smitten longings with sentiment. He shall use poetry, unlike the simple question I would ask, if I ever was such a perfect blockhead to allow myself to be caught in such a situation."

Her heart contracted with painful sorrow. Was this Hamilton's way of telling her he had not changed his plans for his life? She might be important to him *now*, but that would change when the next intriguing miss entered his life.

"Hamilton, I should—"

Again he interrupted her as he tugged on her hand and walked toward the garden door. "We need to talk away from these curious ears."

Causing a scene would complete the undoing of her reputation. She cursed the canons of propriety, which gave her little choice but to go with him out into the cool air.

The sunset was radiant, dampening the light of the candles which stretched its weak fingers across the grass. Scents of dew-washed shrubs were pungent on the evening breeze that reshaped Nerissa's dress to her body.

As he led her past the glow from the grand salon, she asked, "Is that all you aspire to be, Hamilton? A here-and-thereian who bounces through life and never lands anywhere?" She found it easy to look into his silver eyes. Seeing the merriment glowing there, she added, "Is that why you disdained the Season in Town to come to Bath?"

"If you have not forgotten in your excitement over Philip's proposal—which I find most unlike you— you know why I spent this summer in Bath."

She shivered. "I never forget that, not since . . . Forgive me," she added in a stronger voice. "I did not mean to remind you of the disheartening state of your search for that blackguard."

"No need for you to apologize, for I assure you that it is never distant from my mind." He smiled as he seated her on a white, cast-iron bench that circled a tree. "Yet only to you can I speak of this, for Philip is as disdainful of my quest as I was of his scheme to seek glory."

"You have many who care for you." *Although no one could love you as I do!*

"But no one whom I can trust." With a laugh, he

said, "Do not look so sad when my brother's future is about to be settled to his satisfaction and mine."

She folded her hands in her lap, locking her fingers together to keep them from reaching for him. As she opened her mouth to speak, he put his finger to her lips.

"My sweet," he said in the soft, husky tone that she adored, "you must stop worrying about what others will think of your actions and of mine, and consider only what you and I think of them."

Meeting his gaze without compromise, she spoke the words clamoring within her heart. "I have thought often of that today, Hamilton."

"Have you?"

Her heart contracted as she wished he would be as honest with her. Then she realized he might be. He simply did not feel the love she did. If she asked him whether he deemed her more important than the procession of women who had shared his past, she feared he would laugh.

Chubby arms were flung around her neck, halting her before she could speak. Looking over her shoulder, she saw Annis's grin in the moment before Annis cried, "The most glorious thing has happened! Philip has asked me to be his wife."

"And what did you say?" Hamilton asked.

She stared at him, taken aback for a moment. Then she giggled. "I told him yes, of course!"

Nerissa laughed as she hugged Annis, then turned to Philip. A shy smile tipped his lips, and she wondered how two brothers could be so alike and so different. Both Windhams sought out what they wanted and stalked it with a vengeance, but Philip hid his convictions behind a gentle nature.

When Philip squeezed her hand swiftly, Nerissa said, "There can be no more perfect match than you two. Are you going to announce it this evening?"

"Oh, no!" gasped Annis, her voice as shocked as if

Nerissa had suggested she and Philip cuckold the parson. "Mama must grant her approval."

"Which she shall certainly do in double-quick time," said Hamilton with a laugh. Signalling to a servant, who had wandered out into the garden, he ordered champagne to be brought. "Tonight we shall celebrate love." His gaze turned to Nerissa, and she saw the promise there as he added in a whisper only she could hear, "In all its forms."

Moonlight streaked the upper corridor. Only the fact that so many of the guests had risen at dawn for the hunt had brought the gathering in the grand salon to an end before the sunrise. As Nerissa walked along the stone floor, she yawned behind her fingers.

Hamilton laughed lowly, puffing the scent of champagne in her direction. "This fast life may be too much for you."

"I would as lief blame that second bottle of champagne."

"A bit of drink is good for you." He paused and turned to face her.

"But the pop fills my head with bubbles." She looked up at him and swayed. Giggling softly, she leaned back against the wall.

He did not laugh as he took a step toward her. "I want you to know that I was not being honest with you earlier," he whispered as he leaned his hands on either side of her head.

She tried not to hold her breath as she was encompassed by the strength of his presence. Although she could have slipped beneath the velvet-covered steel of his arm and fled to her room farther along the dusky hall, she continued to look up into his mysterious eyes. Not even the dim light could steal the fire from them.

When he touched her bare shoulder with a single fingertip, she quivered, unable to curb the warmth flowing from his skin to hers. She gasped as his finger lazily traced the lace along the *décolletage* of her gown. The sound became a soft sigh of delight as his finger paused directly over her rapidly beating heart.

"I was false," he whispered, "when I spoke of having only my quest on my mind. I do think of one other thing unceasingly. Are you curious about what it might be?"

"No," she answered as softly, "for I daresay it is what plagues me when I find it impossible to sleep."

His low laugh careened through her, setting her whole being to beating with the pulse of her eager heart. "I find it intriguing to think of you awake on Laura Place while I sit before my hearth on Queen Square, wishing you were beside me." His hand twisted through her hair and loosened it to send it cascading along her back in an ebony river. "I would feel your soft tresses against my skin like this."

"Not exactly like this." She felt heat climbing her face at her unthinking words. Yet, even the flame of embarrassment was not as potent as the yearning which burned within her.

He smiled with a slow seductiveness that threatened to buckle her knees as she imagined his lips against hers again. "Then you must show me what sweet fantasies you enjoy when you fail to find sleep."

She needed no further invitation, for the champagne spun through her head, washing away every reason why she should not give life to her longings. Her hands ran up the green velvet of his coat, rediscovering the strong sinews hidden beneath it. Curving her hands around his high collar, she sifted her fingers upward through the thick waves of his

273

hair. Each strand was a separate caress against her trembling touch.

He pulled her to him, his mouth seizing hers with a craving that refused to be ignored. She clung to him, softening as he held her in an iron prison from which she never longed to flee. Feeling his firm chest against her, she delighted in his lips coursing across her cheek then slipping in a tantalizing torment along her neck. Each touch, each moist spark burning into her skin, urged her to set aside every thought but of this moment.

When he reached past her, she gasped as the wall fell away. Hearing his throaty laugh, she looked over her shoulder to see that he had done nothing more than open a door. Her heart halted in mid-beat as she stared at the palatial bedchamber, and knew this huge room with the bed encased in red velvet at its far end was his.

Taking her hand, he drew her into the soft glow of a single candle that soon would be gutting itself in its sea of wax. She was sure she was drowning, as inevitably as that tallow, when he pulled her again into his arms and pushed the door closed.

Nerissa tugged away from him and stopped the door from shutting. Gripping its edge, she whispered, "I cannot be what you wish me to be."

"What do you think I wish you to be?" When she hesitated, he drew away and slammed his hands into his pockets. His voice grew sharp. "Why are you obsessed with Elinor? Is it her ghost whose chill I feel between us?"

She shook her head, glad she could speak the truth. "You tell me she is no longer a part of your life. I believe that, for I have no reason to disbelieve you. Hamilton, you know as well that you have no place in your life for me."

The twinkle returned to his eyes as he reached to sweep her against him again. "I can think of a place for you at this very moment, my sweet."

Although she put her hands on his arms to push away, she had no chance to retort before his mouth found hers again. She ceded herself to the pleasure. To fight it any longer was absurd. This was what she wanted, more than she wanted Hill's End, more than she wanted success for Cole, more than she wanted anything else she could imagine.

In a single smooth motion, he slipped his arm beneath her legs and lifted her into his arms while he kicked the door closed. Her arms wrapped around his shoulders as he carried her to the grand width of his bed. As he leaned her back on the crimson velvet of the coverlet, the flames on the hearth cast their flickering silhouettes against the opposite wall. The two forms merged into one as she drew him down to lie next to her.

He whispered her name in the moment before his lips brushed hers. This gentle, almost chaste touch was not what she ached for. When she brought his mouth back to hers, she heard his low groan of desire. It resonated within her like something alive, emblazoning the fire in her most private depths.

He pressed her back into the bed, and she gasped hungrily against his mouth. When he stroked her leg, luring it to entwine with his, she was certain no sensation could be more wondrous. She discovered how mistaken she was when, drawing her sleeve along her arm, he bared her breast to his questing mouth. Fiery flicks of his tongue teased its very tip. Her whole body quivered before the sensuous assault. The heat of his mouth and the flush of his breath etched rapture into her.

Wanting to give him the same pleasure, she grazed his ear with her tongue. A tremor raced along him and through her as he framed her face with his hands. His kisses were feverish with craving as he brought her up to sit between his knees.

The hooks along the back of her gown fell away before his eager fingers. Rising to kneel in front of him, she smiled as she let her dress drop into a pool of silk on his legs. She loosened her stays and tossed them aside. Her eyes closed when he ran his fingers along her bared breasts, cupping them in his broad palms. Bending toward her, he tasted her sensitive skin.

"Hamilton," she whispered, unable to say more when she was ablaze with the need that was becoming an agony.

With a low laugh, he drew her trembling fingers to his cravat. Her attempts to undo it were hampered by his frenzied kisses. Throwing it and his collar aside, she opened the front of his shirt to reveal the firm skin she had imagined caressing so often.

"A moment," he murmured as he pulled off his coat and kicked off his shoes. Removing his waistcoat, he added, "I vow I would not have been a slave to fashion tonight if I could have guessed you would make me a slave of the passion I long to rouse within you." The devilish glow returned to his eyes as he grasped her hands and brought them to the buttons of his breeches. "Or shall I make you my slave tonight?"

"Hamilton, teach me what I need to know."

He brushed her hair aside and nibbled the curve of her shoulder. In a voice thick with craving, he whispered, "My pleasure, my sweet, my pleasure."

Recklessly, she undid the buttons on his breeches. Her breath caught as he stepped out of them, and she saw the most virile angles of his body. She brought him back down into the bed and gasped when each wiry hair across his chest stroked her. Meeting him, mouth to mouth, she became lost in the roiling sensations as he slid her silk stockings along her legs. Her back arched to keep him close to her when he removed the last of her clothes.

As if he had never touched her before, he began a slow exploration of her, his mouth lingering against her skin while she writhed with ungovernable longing. His hand slid along her hip to her knee, then edged along the inside of her thigh. She clutched his shoulders as the rapture became unbearable and his fingers sought higher.

"Feel how much I want you," he breathed against her skin.

She could not answer. Words had lost all meaning. She pressed against him as he initiated her to the enchantment within her own body. Each motion, each touch, each kiss threatened to consume her. Caught in a vortex, she opened her eyes to see him rising above her. She slipped her arms around him, bringing his mouth back to hers as he brought them together.

The raging storm whirled around her . . . through her . . . and through him. They were *one* in the ecstasy. When the explosion ignited within her, she heard his gasp. She knew, with her last, coherent thought, that the splendor of this moment was well worth whatever it might cost her.

# Chapter Eighteen

Something tickled Nerissa's nose, drawing her out of her luscious dream of Hamilton holding her close. She brushed it away and burrowed back into the pillow. Mayhap if she did not open her eyes, she could recapture the delight.

Her nose wrinkled when the itch returned. She rubbed the back of her hand on it. She frowned as the ticklish sensation transferred to her hand.

Opening her eyes, she saw a strand of her hair propped in front of her face. Past it, a white shirt was only half-buttoned and revealed a strong chest. She raised her eyes to Hamilton's smile.

"Are you always so late abed?" he asked as he sat next to her, his arm resting on the pillow on the far side of her head.

"What time is it?" The bed curtains blocked the windows, and she could not guess the hour from the way the sunlight swept across the rug.

"Nearly midday."

He chuckled when she regarded him in astonishment. As she sat, keeping the cover modestly against her, although there was no part of her he had not explored intimately during the night, he did not move. No more than a shadow's breadth separated them.

With a voracious moan, he swept her into his arms and against his mouth. She released the covers as her hands slipped beneath his open shirt. Even though he had given her little time for sleep that night, the need to touch him had not diminished.

"You are sweet," he whispered. "I think I shall keep you here with me the rest of the day."

"I can't." Sliding her legs over the side of the bed, she reached for the clothes she had tossed aside during the night.

"Why not?" He ran a finger along her bare leg as she pulled on her chemise and stockings.

"I must return to Bath."

"Today?"

She smiled as she heard the dismay in his voice. She knew that feeling too well, for she hated the thought of even a moment away from him. Dressing quickly, she tied her stays in place as best she could. "Cole sent a letter to let me know he intends to return before the week is out. I must be there to welcome him home."

"You do not need to go back."

Nerissa pulled her gown over her head and settled it into place. As he hooked it closed, she whispered, "What do you mean?"

"I thought you might wish to stay here with me." He sat on the edge of the bed. "Or we can return to Queen Square, if you wish."

Walking away, she put her hand on one of the columns, marking the bed's alcove. She did not face him as she said, "You are asking the impossible."

"Why?" He turned her to him. Encircling her face with his hands, he asked, "My sweet, do you wish never again to share what we had here?"

She drew his hands away from her face and held them in hers. "Hamilton, don't ask me such silly questions. Staying with you would be the most glorious thing I could imagine, but I am not like Mrs. Howe."

"Blast Elinor! I have forgotten her, Nerissa. Why can't you?"

"You have *not* forgotten her."

"Nerissa, I assure you—"

As he had so many times, she interrupted him. "You carry her in your heart, even when you hold me. Her legacy of pain still resides there. As your father was betrayed by that thief, you were betrayed by the first woman you dared to love."

Hamilton watched her cross the room to where a full-length mirror was set by a window. She pulled a chair in front of it and sat down to try to rearrange her messed hair.

"Only Philip has learned to trust again," she continued, "and he has won the prize he values more than pride or vengeance. He has won Annis's love."

"Be glad for them, but I cannot offer you the same."

"I know."

"You know?" He had not thought she would be the one to shock him this morning. As she brushed her hair back and tied it with a blue ribbon, he stroked her slender shoulders. He looked into the reflection of her eyes in the glass.

Her fingers settled on his, and she smiled into the glass. "Dear Hamilton, I love you." She laughed gently. "No, you need not look so stricken. I do not ask you to say the same back to me until you can say those words with genuine sentiment."

He whirled her around on the chair and bent until his eyes were even with hers. "There is no room in my life for you now. Until I have done as I vowed, I must think of nothing else."

When she rose, he stepped back. She crossed the room and found her slippers. Pulling them on, she said, "Do not make the same mistake you feared Philip would make. Do not throw your life away on something that may be only a meaningless posturing."

"This vow means everything to me."

"Then," she said quietly, as she walked toward him, "I feel sorry for you, Hamilton. Some day, you may find that conveyancer. You shall have hunted down your fortune and gotten your vengeance." She stood on tiptoe and kissed his cheek that was rough with morning whiskers. "I hope that will be enough for you."

She gave him no time to retort as she went to the door, opened it, and shut it softly behind her. It was just as well, because, for once, he had no quick retort.

"And, of course, you must stand up with me, although Janelle is beside herself with envy that I shall be married at Windham Park," Annis said as she picked up one of the cards in the pattern book and tilted it. "Do you think this would make a lovely wedding dress, Nerissa?"

Nerissa smiled and said absently, "It would look lovely on you."

"You are being too generous. *Madame* would much prefer to be making a wedding gown for you." She leaned forward and smiled. "You have been oddly reticent since we returned from Windham Park. Are you sure you aren't concealing something from me? I saw how Hamilton was looking at you when we were in the country."

Nerissa put down the book that she had not realized she was holding, and walked to look out on the street beyond her sitting-room window. She hoped Annis could not guess how hard it was to hide the truth. She loved Hamilton with every inch of her being. Only his need to avenge his father's humiliation had prevented him from saying the same to her. *Hadn't it?* She must believe that, or she was sure she would shatter and babble the truth.

The past two days had been the longest she had ever endured. Annis had moved back to Camden Crescent in preparation for Cole's homecoming, but that was not the reason Nerissa suffered such a void in her life. She had hoped Hamilton could convince his guests to return to Bath quickly, but that had not happened. Although she had been sucked into the whirl of excitement as Philip had come into Town long enough to garner Mrs. Ehrlich's approval of his suit, each hour seemed more interminable than the previous one.

How many goose's gazettes had she spoken? Frye believed that Nerissa had spent that last night at Windham Park with Annis, planning the wedding. She never had been false with her abigail before, and it disturbed her deeply.

With a sigh, she looked at the table by the window. On it were the papers she must sign in order to sell Hill's End. They had been waiting for her upon her return to Bath, but she had not signed them yet. Once she did, she surrendered her last hope of a miracle preventing the sale.

"Nerissa?"

At Annis's discomposed voice, Nerissa gave her friend a smile. "You are seeing the whole world in the rosy glow of the love you share with Philip. You would be wise not to allow it to deceive you into seeing things that are not true."

"Don't try to trip me the double!" Annis set herself on her feet and folded her arms across her bosom, looking for the first time like her formidable mother. "My eyes can see quite clearly. More clearly than ever before, if you wish to know the truth. You love Hamilton."

"I would be spoony to fall in love with a man who makes it no secret that he wishes to enjoy his bachelor's fare, wouldn't I?"

Annis's face toppled into a mask of sorrow. Running to Nerissa, she took her hands and drew her to sit on the window bench. "Oh, my dearest Nerissa, how do you endure loving a man who refuses to own that he loves you, too?"

Nerissa could not silence the sobs that erupted from her heart. As Annis held her, whispering words of consolation, Nerissa wept for the only remaining dream she had. She feared the dream of loving Hamilton was as doomed as all the other hopes she had dared to cherish.

"The Mail should have been in Bath hours ago." Vexation tainted Frye's voice as she strode along the walkway. "It may simply be delayed, or Mr. Pilcher may have decided to take it tomorrow."

"Yes."

"Miss Dufresne, are you listening to me? Will you slow down?"

Nerissa pulled her shawl closer to her chin. A raw wind made the day unseasonably cool, and she wanted nothing more than to get back to Laura Place. Not only could she get a cup of hot tea, but she would not have to chance meeting someone who had been at Windham Park. If she saw one of Hamilton's guests, she would know that Hamilton was back in Bath, too, although he had not called.

Frye could not hide her satisfaction that he had not come to Laura Place. Nor had she allowed Nerissa to wait for him to give her a look-in. She had insisted on her charge accompanying her on errands every afternoon, even chilly ones like today.

"I am listening to you, Frye," she answered irritably. "And I am hurrying because I am cold."

"You are becoming just like your brother," the abigail chided. "Only you do not walk about with your nose in a book to warn us of when you are off among your dreams. Now, I was saying. . . ."

Nerissa tried to listen as Frye prattled on about the latest *contretemps* at the butcher's shop, but she did not care a rush that Mr. Young was charging a penny more for a pound of mutton. Suddenly Frye's voice rose to a shriek just as Nerissa was stepping into the street to their house.

Nerissa looked to her left to see a carriage bearing down on her. Leaping back onto the walkway, she gasped as the vehicle came to a stop only inches from where she had been standing. She closed her eyes while she fought her shivers of dismay. Becoming lost in her thoughts was proving to be a deadly pastime. She heard a squeak from the carriage, followed by assertive footsteps.

"Are you unhurt? Damn, how could you be so stupid?" The voice and the anger were both endearingly familiar, and she opened her eyes to see Hamilton's face, which was as grey as his eyes that flashed with fury.

Her knees threatened to buckle, and she reached out to clutch his arms, then halted her hands. To touch him—especially at that moment when every nerve was so raw—would undo her completely.

"The least you could do," he snapped, "is to say that you are sorry for scaring nigh to a year off my life!"

"I am sorry." She could force her voice no louder than a whisper as she swayed.

Hamilton cursed and caught her before she could fall. "Blast it, Nerissa, what would you do if I wasn't about to save you?"

"I would not need saving if you didn't drive at such a speed along this busy street."

When he chuckled, she opened her eyes to see his scintillating smile. "You *are* unhurt, for you flay me most fiercely with words when you are in a snit."

"I am *not* in a snit." She started to ease out of his arms, but they refused to release her. "Hamilton, we are on the street."

"I know that." He put his lips against her bonnet as he whispered, "And I know I can go no longer without you in my bed."

"Hamilton, I . . ." She started to laugh as he affixed an angelic expression on his face. The false humility would not have bamboozled anyone. When he joined in her laughter, she added, "You shall never change."

"You are wrong, my sweet." He stepped back and locked his hands behind his dark coat. "I would like to give you an opportunity to prove how wrong you are and let you own to that mistake this evening, if you would consent to be my guest for dinner."

"I would be delighted to—"

"Miss Dufresne, your brother might be arriving tonight," Frye said, annoyance returning to her voice. "What would he think if you were not there to greet him?"

Nerissa pulled her gaze away from Hamilton's smile. She had forgotten that her abigail stood behind her. With a sigh, she said, "Frye is correct. If Cole returns tonight, he will be anxious to share his news of his journey to London."

"Bring him with you."

"He will be exhausted, Lord Windham," Frye said in her most repressive accents. "I am sure you can understand that after your recent sojourn to Town." She flashed Nerissa a glance as if she was proud of bringing the reminder of Mrs. Howe into the conversation.

"Mayhap I should decline." Nerissa sighed silently, wishing she could ask Hamilton what he meant by his cryptic words.

His thumb grazed her jaw as he tilted her face upward. "Nerissa, we need to speak together."

"I know, but it must wait."

"I am not sure I can wait. Do you know that you

have made me queer in the attic with longings which would put you to the blush if I was so brazen to speak of them on the walkway?"

"I have thought endlessly of you," she breathed, knowing that to be false when he touched her was as inconceivable as not thinking of him. When she raised her hand toward his face, not caring that they stood in public view, her arm was grasped.

She whirled to see Frye's scowl, which transformed her face into a furious mask. "Come along, Miss Dufresne. You do not want to have your brother arrive home before you."

"Frye, he cannot enter the house without us seeing him."

"Miss Dufresne!"

"Go along with your comb-brush, who is trying to brush you away from me." Hamilton grinned, but Frye's frown pulled her face into deeper ruts. Bowing his head toward them, he went on, "I shall call tomorrow, Nerissa. Mayhap a bit early, so we may have some time for conversation that is not laced with recriminations and thwarted desires. As tomorrow is Wednesday, I collect that you will have your usual at home."

"She may not," Frye snapped.

"I will," Nerissa said tautly. Pulling her arm out of Frye's chubby hand, she smiled at Hamilton before turning to continue along the walkway with her abigail. She looked back to see him standing alone by his carriage. The anguish in her heart matched what she had seen in his eyes.

Frye wasted no time lambasting Nerissa for lacking sense. As they entered the house, she said, "I thought you had seen reason when you rid yourself of Lord Windham upon our return from the country. Now, when he comes home by weeping cross—most falsely, too, if you wish my opinion—you flirt with him on the street as if you were the cheapest wench.

Can't you see that he intends to be your ruin?"

"You would find fault with a fat goose!" Nerissa shot back. "Lord Windham is my friend." She almost stumbled on the words, which were no longer the truth, but continued gamely. "I do not like being told that I cannot speak to a friend while out on my errands."

Frye put her packages on a bench in the foyer. "You must own that you consider him far more than a cap acquaintance."

"Of course, but, Frye, you should not listen to the poker-talk. Hamilton is a gentleman." *Even when we are in his bed,* she thought, for she could imagine no lover more gentle than Hamilton. She silenced the rebellious beat of her heart as she eagerly recalled his enticing touch.

"If your mother was still alive, she would give me my absence without leave for allowing you to go about with no *duenna* other than Miss Ehrlich, who clearly was too interested in Lord Windham's brother to pay much mind to anything else." Frye fiercely untied the ribbons on her bonnet. "Gull that I am, I thought you would be immune to his charm after he brought that dasher to Bath."

Nerissa said, "I told you that I do not want Mrs. Howe mentioned in this house. I—" She halted herself as she saw a shadow moving on the upper floor. "Cole!"

She ran up the steps to embrace her brother. When he drew quickly away, she recalled how he disliked such shows of affection.

"It is grand to see you again, Nerissa," he said.

"I was thinking much the same." She laughed lightly. "Let me look at you! It seems as if it has been an eternity since I last saw you."

London had created little outward change in her brother. As she had seen him so often when he rose in the morning or after hours of working in his book room, his shirtends hung out of his breeches, and his stockings belonged to two parishes, for one was a creamy white and the other a nubby brown. The only alteration might be a few extra pounds he had added while away.

"I have so many things to tell you, and you must have even more to tell me," she went on. "But you first. How did your trip go?"

"Instead of me telling you, let me show you," he said with a grin.

"Show me what?"

"My backers." His grin stretched his full face.

"You have backers?" She gripped his arm. "That is wonderful!"

He led the way down the stairs, taking them two at a time. Nerissa arched an eyebrow at Frye, who was watching in disbelief. Neither of them had ever seen her brother so animated. His journey clearly had been a success. She was glad she had not signed the papers for Hill's End.

Opening the door to the parlor, which she had not noticed was closed, he called, "Hadfield, did you bring that brandy to toast our return?"

Nerissa tensed. She had forgotten that when Cole came back to Bath, Hadfield would also. This was sure to signify a return to his disruptive tales and troublesome ways belowstairs.

Hadfield was not the only person in the parlor. Two people were standing by the hearth, warming themselves after the long trip from Town. They had their backs to her. The man was as broad-shouldered as Hamilton, but his body was thick with age. Grey tinted his hair which was cut stylish to brush the nape of his high collar. His stylish rust-colored coat was covered with the dust that dimmed the polish of his boots. The golden-haired woman's dark green spenser was frosted with dirt. When the door to the street opened to reveal two lads bringing in a heavy trunk and a portmanteau, she was shocked that Cole's backers must be staying with them.

Why had he failed to tell her that? She had expected that they would find suitable lodgings at the Sydney Hotel at the end of Great Pulteney Street. Glancing back into the foyer, she motioned to a serving lass. She whispered hurried instructions to have Mrs. Carroll have two rooms. . . . Were their guests husband and wife? No matter. It was better to have two rooms freshened and prepared for Mr. Pilcher's friends. With a curtsy, the lass rushed to obey.

Cole looked past his guests to smile at Nerissa. "My friends, come and meet my sister. Nerissa, this is Sir Jerrold Cathcart."

The tall man turned, his eyes widening along with his smile. He grabbed her hand and bowed over it. "This is indeed a pleasure, Miss Dufresne. A great, great pleasure."

"Thank you," she said, overmastered by the flood of emotion in his incredibly deep voice. "I am as pleased to meet you and . . ."

Nerissa's voice faded as she looked past the baronet to his companion. Hearing words, as if from the opposite side of a field, she stared at a face she had hoped never to see again.

"No need for an introduction, my dear Cole. Your stepsister and I have already met." Elinor Howe offered her a cool smile as she slipped her arm through Cole's. "How do you do, Nerissa?"

# Chapter Nineteen

Feeling all at sea, Nerissa did not move. The echo of her words to Frye taunted her. She had not wanted to hear Elinor Howe's name. Now the blonde had somehow inveigled her way into Cole's life. In desperation, she looked to her brother. His smile, however, was fading as he aimed a glower at her like she had seldom seen on his plump face. Knowing he could not understand her reluctance to greet Mrs. Howe, he must be ready to fly off the hooks at her.

Nerissa dampened her lips. "Mrs. Howe, welcome back to Bath."

"My dear," the older woman said, "you must call me 'Elinor'. After all, we shall be getting to know each other very well."

Ignoring Elinor's triumphant smile, Nerissa turned to the baronet. "I hope your trip to Bath was without incident, Sir Jerrold."

Cathcart caught her hand again and bent over it as he raised it to his lips. With a boyish grin, he said, "I would say any discomfort was worth the delight of finding such a paragon at the end of our journey. Pilcher, you have been wise to hide your sister. You must bring her with us to Town when we return. I know dear Elinor would enjoy firing her off, and mayhap I could convince my sister to get you an invitation to Almack's, Miss Dufresne. Then you could have your pick of the young bucks who will be clamoring to leg-shackle themselves to the sister of England's most wealthy canal builder." He dug his elbow into Cole's side. "Maybe get yourself a duke or a marquess for a brother-in-law, eh? One of them would not be averse to marrying a commoner when she stands to have as much money as all of us soon shall have."

"I think that is a fabulous inspiration," purred Elinor. "I would be happy to find Nerissa the perfect husband."

"Miss Dufresne, may I interrupt for a moment?"

At Frye's cool question, Nerissa wanted to fling her arms around her abigail and thank her for rescuing her from this impossible situation. Struggling to keep her own voice serene, Nerissa asked, "What is it, Frye?"

"A small matter. It should not take long, but it needs your attention."

"Run along," said Cole with a magnanimous wave of his hand. "While you tend to arrangements for a fine meal for us this evening, we shall drink a toast to the future of this venture."

Nerissa clenched her hands at Cole's cavalier behavior. She was not accustomed to being ordered about in her own home, but, as she saw Elinor's broadening smile of satisfaction, she wondered how many other things were about to change for the worse.


"Alas, what shall we do?"

"Cease the moaning, Frye," Nerissa said as she went to her desk in her sitting room. "Give me a chance to think."

"That is the same woman who came to live with Lord Windham, isn't it?"

"Forget Elinor!"

"But it is the same woman, isn't it?"

Nerissa turned on her chair to see tears rolling along the grooves in Frye's wide face. Leaping to her feet, she ran to her abigail. She urged the older woman to sit on a chair and brought her a glass of Madeira. Frye's hands shook so fiercely that Nerissa feared she would spill the wine all over herself.

"Dear Frye, I do not understand yet all that is going on, but I hope Hamilton will."

"Not him!" Frye grasped Nerissa's hand. "Do not make matters more critical by involving him. He is sure to side with that dasher downstairs."

Nerissa knelt by Frye's chair. "Hamilton may have some idea of how Elinor Howe came to be in Cole's company. I must protect my brother from her greed."

"Greed? What could she want of Mr. Pilcher? He does not have two farthings to rub together. If you had not been so generous with the few pennies your sainted mother left you, he would have starved in the streets long ago."

"I must find out why she is so interested in Cole, and, for that, I need Hamilton's help."

"'Tis a bad idea."

"It is the only one I have."

Frye opened her mouth to retort, then nodded with reluctance. Taking a deep drink of the sweet wine, she put the glass on a table and rose. "And I shall endeavor to learn what tales Hadfield has brought back from London with him. Mayhap in the midst of his bangers, there will be a kernel of truth."

Nerissa returned to her writing desk. Taking out a sheet of paper and ink, she did not hesitate as she wrote a request for Hamilton to call as soon as he could. She reread the note. Desperation rang through every word, although she had explained nothing. She rang for a maid and asked her to have the letter delivered posthaste to Lord Windham at Queen Square.

When the door closed again, Nerissa dropped into her chair and stared out the window at the square below. It looked dismal beneath the lowering sky, and she felt the same.

At a knock, she called, "Come in, Frye."

"It is not Frye," returned a melodic voice.

Nerissa leapt to her feet as Elinor entered. She stared at Elinor's lovely dress. Its pale pinks and golds shimmered as if the gown was alive, even as it accented her perfect figure. With her hair brushed high on her head and a glass of wine in her hand, she looked as if she had been transported from the midst of an assembly.

Elinor closed the door behind her and motioned for Nerissa to sit again. "I believe you and I have a crow to pluck between us."

Nerissa had no choice but to be gracious when the blonde was her brother's guest. "I doubt if there is any way we can alter the situation, but I will be honest enough to say that I would have preferred to see Old Nick himself as lief you in my house."

"Cole's house."

She flinched at Elinor's terse answer. That was a truth Nerissa did not want to own to when her whole world was topsy-turvy. She had no home beyond this dependency on Cole, who apparently had been changed more than she had guessed by his short sojourn in London.

"My dear," Elinor continued as she lowered herself gracefully to the settee, "you are but a child in so many ways. How many *beaux* did you have calling on you before Hamilton arrived in your life?"

She flushed, but did not lower her eyes. "I think that is no bread and butter of yours."

"But it is." She smiled as she took a sip. Looking over the goblet, she said, "You are Cole's sister, so it behooves me to know everything about you."

"I wish to know no more about *you* than I have already heard."

"Shall I tell you what I know already about you?"

Nerissa shook her head and rose. "I have no wish to hear my name disparaged."

"But there is nothing disparaging about it." She stood and wandered about the room, looking at the portraits on the wall and each piece of furniture as if she was judging its worth. "My dear, you have been nothing less than a saint. Cole tells me that, while your mother was ill for several years, you never strayed from her side."

"It was my wish to remain there and ease her last days instead of engaging in frivolous flirtations."

"Please understand that nothing I say is meant to take a stone from your mother's cairn. You were right to be such a loving daughter." She gave a genteel shiver. "I understand the limitations posed upon one by an ailing connection. I spent many months sitting by the bed of my dying husband. Then he hopped off, and I was a young widow with a fortune to spend and with no one to share it. I know you consider me no better than an easy virtue—for I would guess that your ears have been filled with many intriguing rumors about me—but, to own the truth, I had only one paramour before Hamilton."

"And how many while he believed you cared for him *alone?*"

Elinor smiled as she paused by the window. Running her hand along the table, she looked out onto the street. "You are as conventional as dear Hamilton and, I suspect, as eager to be rid of the confines of those conventions."

Nerissa walked toward the door to put as much space as possible between them. "I have no interest in the prurient facets of your past. As long as you are my brother's guest, I shall treat you with courtesy, but ask no more of me."

"I do not intend to leave until we smooth this between us." Sitting on the window bench, she clasped her long fingers in her lap and regarded Nerissa evenly. "I am not evil personified."

"You hurt Hamilton."

"What a brave maiden you are to jump to the defense of your dashing knight!" Her lips curled in a smile. "Or do I mistakenly call you a maiden?"

Nerissa tried to keep her face from betraying her as she said, "Your demure hits will not endear you to Cole. He prefers a quiet house."

"My dear, you need not entertain me with out and outers. I know Hamilton well." She rose, holding her hands behind her back, as her smile grew more predatory. "I know him very well, so I can guess exactly what he has asked of you and exactly what you have given him. He is a devilishly charming man." Crossing the room, she cupped Nerissa's chin in her hand. "Fear not, my dear. The tales of your indiscretions shall not precede you to London. I have promised Cole to help you make an excellent marriage, and I find it very wise always to do what I promise Cole I will."

Nerissa turned away, unable to endure the jubilation in Elinor's eyes. "You are no better than a *demi mondaine*."

Elinor did not take offense, but simply continued to smile. "A woman on her own has scant place in this world. I have no interest to spend the rest of my years declining into the shadows as a dowager at Almack's. Better I should attach myself to a man who shares my ambitions."

"If you mean Cole, I warn you that I shall do what I can to convince him that it would be a mistake to tangle his life more with yours."

"I am afraid there is nothing you can do to halt me. I do not waste my time doing battle over things I think I cannot win, but I have won your brother's heart."

"You have bought it, you mean."

Her musical laugh could not hide her satisfaction. "One can buy only what is available for a price, my dear Nerissa. He has his price, as I suspect you do. What would you be willing to pay to win Hamilton's heart? Would you sacrifice your reputation? Have you already?" With another laugh, she opened the door. "Think on it, my dear, and you shall see that you are not so dissimilar to me."

"You are wrong. We are very unlike."

"Mayhap, but rumor can suggest differently, if it becomes known that you have replaced me in Hamilton's bed." Her nonchalant pose vanished as she smiled icily. "Try to stop me from my plans with your brother, and you shall learn how quickly you can lose everything."

Elinor walked out and closed the door, leaving Nerissa to stare after her in horror.


Pacing in front of the window of her sitting room, Nerissa stared out at the street, where rain was falling to puddle in every depression in the road. It had been more than a day since she had sent the message to Hamilton, but he had not come to Laura Place to discover why she had sent him the urgent note.

A twinge raced through her each time she recalled how he had told her he had changed. Although she had dared to hope that meant he had come to trust her, an irritating whisper in the back of her mind suggested that his change of heart had come from his longing to end everything between them. She recalled every rumor she had heard of his disinterest in any lasting relationship.

"Nerissa?"

She turned to see Cole behind her. Lost in her gloomy thoughts, she had not heard him approach.

"Oh, Cole! I am so glad you are alone. I want to talk to you."

"Any conversation must wait." He clutched her arm and tugged toward the door. "Crimmins is waiting in the parlor to speak with us."

"Mr. Crimmins? Here again?"

He smiled as if he was humoring a silly child. "Nerissa, put aside your parochial thoughts. Crimmins, like anyone else who has looked down his nose at me, is learning to listen when I demand his attention."

"Why are you letting Elinor put such thoughts into your head? Until the canal proves to be a success—"

His laugh halted her, but scorn filled his voice. "I ask you this final time not to besmirch Elinor's name. She is a rare treasure, and I will not listen to your jealousy. Come along, Nerissa. Crimmins is anxious to get the matter of Hill's End's sale completed."

"How do you know about that?"

"This is my house. Everything that happens under this roof is of my concern. You would be wise to learn that."

Nerissa bit back her reply as he steered her out of the room and down the stairs. Seeing Hadfield's broad smile on his narrow face, she kept her head high. She would provide the butler with no more pleasure at her own expense.

Pulling her arm out of Cole's grip, she held out her hand to the solicitor, who leapt to his feet as they entered. "Good afternoon, Mr. Crimmins."

"A very good afternoon," he agreed. He waited for her to sit, then pulled out a sheaf of papers from beneath his coat. Setting them next to a bottle of ink on a low table beside her, he said, "Please sign here, Miss Dufresne."

Nerissa gasped when she saw the fine flourishes of

Mr. Crimmins's secretary's writing. She recognized the first few words on the top of the first page. This was the contract to initiate the sale of Hill's End that he had sent for her perusal. She had not been able to bring herself to read it before Cole's arrival, and, since his homecoming, she had not given it a thought.

She looked from the solicitor to Cole. Both men were smiling as broadly as Hadfield had. "How did this get returned to your office? I left it . . ." Her lips grew taut as she recalled how Elinor had investigated everything in the room yesterday. The blonde must have pilfered the papers and taken them to Cole. That explained how her brother knew of the upcoming sale, but she did not understand why Elinor would do such a thing.

"Please sign, Miss Dufresne," Mr. Crimmins repeated.

"I would like an opportunity to study it more fully."

Mr. Crimmins said, with a touch of exasperation, "The buyer is very anxious to have the deal completed. If you tarry, you may lose this chance to rid yourself of that estate. Aren't you tired of being out at the elbows?"

"I prefer to read it."

Cole snapped, "Do sign it, Nerissa, and be done with this whimpering. After all, it is nothing more than the procedures to release the money the buyer has already put in escrow for the binder."

"Who is the buyer?" she asked.

Mr. Crimmins looked down his long nose at her. "Even if I was privy to that information, I would be restricted from telling you. Are you going to sign it, Miss Dufresne, so we may get on to the rest of our business?"

"Rest of our business?" The twinge of disquiet inside her burst into a cramp of fear.

"The matters of the future of *this* household."

Nerissa lowered her gaze to the papers in front of her. Mr. Crimmins needed to say no more. Although Cole had been able to find a well-fixed backer for his canal, that did not change their situation on Laura Place. She tried to swallow the lump of congealed tears in her throat as she signed the bottom of the last page, knowing they must avoid bankruptcy.

The solicitor grabbed the pages before the ink had a chance to dry. Folding them, he put them under his coat as he sat on the settee. The gleam in his eyes warned her that he was already considering how he would spend his share of this transaction.

When Cole took a chair across from him, Mr. Crimmins held out a sheet of paper. "As you requested, your inheritance has been deposited in an account in your name in the Bank of England."

"Inheritance?" Nerissa gasped. "I thought your father died penniless."

Cole took the sheet and smiled as he perused it. He slipped it beneath his waistcoat. "You are wrong. He left me a jointure of thirty thousand pounds."

"Thirty thousand pounds?" she repeated in disbelief. It must be a coincidence that Albert Pilcher had bequeathed his son the exact amount stolen from Hamilton's father. She wanted to believe that, but she could not. Albert Pilcher had cheated her mother out of every penny with his beguiling ways. She suspected the late Lord Windham had been his victim as well.

"You always misjudged my father, Nerissa. Like me, he was a man of many talents."

"Thievery and lies!"

He rose and said coldly, "That is enough, Nerissa." Without giving her an opportunity to answer, he went on, "And thank you, Crimmins, for your assistance in this matter. I collect you will have the rest of the paperwork for the sale of Hill's End completed with all due speed. We wish to stay no longer in Bath than is necessary."

"Then you will, I gather, be selling this house, too?"

"Yes," he answered.

"No!" Nerissa turned to her brother. "Cole, you cannot put this house on the block. With Hill's End sold, we would have no place else to go."

"We shall be able to live anywhere we wish once my canal is completed." He patted his waistcoat. "Now that is assured. Thank you, Crimmins."

The solicitor mumbled a good day as he left the room. Cole shut the parlor door behind him. Nerissa was sure he was going to give her an explanation, but instead he said, "I have had my eyes opened, Nerissa, and I care little for what I see of your uncomely behavior."

"I have done nothing of which I should be ashamed."

"It is not your place to question the decisions I have made with Crimmins on your behalf. I leave you to your concerns for the household as I share the good tidings of my inheritance with Elinor."

Jumping to her feet, she cried, "Cole, that money is not yours!"

"On the contrary, it is mine and mine alone."

"Your father stole it!"

His smile disappeared as he seized her arm and shook her. "I shall hear no more of that, Nerissa. My father was a grand inspiration to me."

"How?" she whispered, although her ears rang with his rough behavior. "You have toiled all your life to reach a goal. He never worked a day in his life."

"My father worked very hard."

"But his ill-gotten gains should not be used to help finance your canal. Cole, it is sure to bring the taint of misfortune to your project."

"The canal already is a greater success than I had ever hoped." He smirked slyly. "Cathcart has proven to be very, very generous in his enthusiasm."

"*You are bronzing him!*" she whispered, not wanting to believe that she had allowed herself to be taken in as completely as the baronet. "You never intended to build that canal, did you?"

"How can you say that, dear sister? Haven't I spent years designing it? Do you think I would do all that work for nothing?"

"It would not be for nothing. You will have Sir Jerrold's money. How many others have you bamboozled into believing that you propose to go through with this windmill in your head when all you wish to do is fleece them as readily as your father did?"

He raised his hand, but, when she continued to regard him without cringing, he lowered it. "I shall hear no more insults to my father."

"No," she returned fiercely, "but you shall hear them of you. When I tell—"

With a curse, he shoved her back into the chair. "You shall tell no one anything. Unless I give you permission otherwise, you shall remain in your rooms and receive no callers until we leave for Town."

"I shall *not* be a prisoner in my own house."

"This is, as I should not need to remind you, my house. I shall have the profits from its sale as well as what small bit of brass you shall receive from the sale of that rickety hovel in the country."

Shock struck her as viciously as any blow. "Cole, you cannot be serious. Hill's End is mine."

"I am serious as I assume the duties of a brother to watch over your finances." He laughed, then said, "Oh, and, by the by, Nerissa, I believe this is yours." He tossed a piece of paper in her lap.

When she picked it up, she gasped, stunned anew

301

by his duplicity. It was the note she had written to Hamilton.

"Hadfield is having a message delivered to Lord Windham that you will be unable to see him again." His smile was icy. "I am sure you understand the wisdom of that, sister dear."

"I understand none of this." She stood and crumpled the note in her hand. "And I shall have nothing to do with your beastly plans."

"But you will, Nerissa." He motioned with feigned graciousness toward the door. "You have no other choice."


Glasses clinked as Cole, Elinor, and Sir Jerrold made yet another toast to their good fortune. Nerissa sat, her glass untasted on a table in front of her, and tried to think of a way to speak to the baronet alone. He seemed a gentle soul, who had allowed himself to become enmeshed in Cole's evil scheme to empty his pockets of every sparkle of gold.

Cole's laughter faded as Hadfield came into the room. Motioning for the butler to come to him, he said nothing as Hadfield bent to whisper in his ear. Cole's eyes widened, then narrowed as he smiled. "By all means, Hadfield, show our caller in. It would be most impolite to leave him cooling his heels in the foyer."

Nerissa recognized the sound of the forceful footfalls instantly. Jumping to her feet, she gasped, "Hamilton!"

Hamilton swore silently as he saw Elinor with her arm draped about a strange man's shoulders. Not that he cared a rush if the man wished to buy his old boots. What he cared about was discovering why Nerissa had sent him such an unfeeling message. He suspected it had something to do with Elinor Howe, but said only, "Good evening, Nerissa. And to you,

Cathcart. Elinor, you are looking good."

"As you are, Hamilton dear."

He turned to Cole. "Sir, I do not believe we have met."

"I am Nerissa's brother," the strange man said.

He looked again at Nerissa. She was worrying the lace on her gown, warning him that she was distressed. "Your servant, Mr. Dufresne."

"Hamilton—"

Her brother interrupted her curtly. "Now, Nerissa, why don't you go and chat with Elinor and let us men tend to business?"

"Yes," Elinor cooed, taking Nerissa's hand. "We shall leave you to your brandy and conversation. Good evening, gentlemen." She murmured something to Nerissa. Although Hamilton could not hear the words, he saw Nerissa stiffen. She did not look at him as she went with Elinor from the room.

"Pilcher, get the man some brandy," crowed Cathcart.

"Pilcher?" asked Hamilton.

"I am Nerissa's stepbrother." He splashed brandy in a glass and handed it to Hamilton.

Hamilton's eyes slitted. *Pilcher!* The name had taunted him across the years, but he had surmised that the man who had cheated his father out of thirty thousand pounds would have used a false name. The thief had been more bold than he had guessed, or else this was an uncommon coincidence.

*Coincidence?* That Pilcher was here in Bath, exactly where the trail had led? Or that Nerissa was connected to him? His hands fisted at his sides. Mallory had tried to show him that Nerissa was part of this when the Bow Street Runner abducted her from the Upper Rooms. Beef-brained that he was, Hamilton had not heeded the thief-taker.

"My error," he said emotionlessly. What a widgeon he had been to trust the very woman who had used her wiles to seduce him into giving up his search!

"How kind of you to give us a look-in," Cathcart spouted as he held up his empty glass of brandy to have it refilled. "More for me, too, Pilcher. Have you decided to invest in our canal project as well, Windham? With my money and Pilcher's recent bequest from his late father, we soon shall be the envy of every man in England."

"A bequest?" Hamilton turned back to Pilcher. Cathcart was as full as a goat, so there would be no persuading him now to listen to the good sense of ending any business relationship with Pilcher. "Congratulations, Pilcher, and I applaud you as well for finding a godfather for your project with such speed. Surely you should be able to get approval from the government now that you have golden grease to help you obtain your permits with good speed."

"No need to worry about investors at this point, for we have all the gilt we need to begin. My dear sister Nerissa has agreed to invest the money she has received on the dirty acres her mother left her."

"Is that so?"

"Windham, I—" Pilcher was interrupted by the front door opening again.

Looking over his shoulder, Hamilton saw his brother and Annis enter. They must have grown tired of waiting in the carriage on the chilly night. Had Annis been a part of this scheme, too? No, he decided instantly. As quickly as her face betrayed every emotion, Annis couldn't have kept the plot hidden.

Philip's gaze settled on Cole. A queer expression stole the gentleness from his face. Woodenly he greeted Elinor, who had returned from "escorting" Nerissa, and Sir Jerrold. He nodded to the terse words of Hamilton's introduction of Nerissa's brother. Annis started to chatter, but became silent when no one else answered.

When a bald-rib man came forward to take Philip's hat, Hamilton saw his brother recoil. That told him all he needed to know. He struggled to control the rage boiling within him. Seeing Pilcher had stirred his suspicions, but Philip's countenance when he saw the servant, who had tried to keep his face averted when he ushered Hamilton into the house, confirmed them. Philip's depiction of Pilcher's servant matched this skulking creature exactly.

He had been as much of a sammy as his father had been, although his betrayer had been a beautiful woman, who lit his soul when he held her soft form in his arms. Fury raged through him as he wondered how many other men Nerissa might have flirted with so sweetly . . . before she focused her cunning on him. She had been nearly as successful as her stepfather had been with Hamilton's father. Even as she had been chiding him for not failing to trust her, she had been playing him for the jack.

When his brother gripped his arm, Hamilton aimed a scowl in Philip's direction. This was not the time for a confrontation. First he must get a few answers from Nerissa. Then he would have his vengeance . . . finally.

# *Chapter Twenty*

Frye opened the door to Nerissa's sitting room and peeked around it like a frightened child. "Are you alone?"

Nerissa gave her abigail a watery smile. Wiping the tears from her face, she nodded. No one had come into her room, save Frye, since she had been banished there last night. "Of course."

Opening the door wider, Frye stepped aside. Nerissa whispered Annis's name as her friend raced across the room and flung her arms around her.

Trying to soothe Annis's tears when she was still fighting her own, Nerissa whispered, "I am so happy to see you. Why did Cole let you in to see me? He despises you as much as he does Hamilton."

Annis waited until Frye had pulled the drapes closed before she said, "I sneaked into the house." Holding Nerissa's cool hands in hers, she cried, "Oh, Nerissa, what has gone wrong?"

"Hush," she murmured, glancing toward where Frye had gone to stand guard on the door to the hallway. "If someone was to hear—"

"I waited until I saw your brother and Mrs. Howe leave."

"Cole learns things even when he is not in the house." With a shiver, she wrapped her arms around herself. "Hadfield is eager to carry tales to him."

"That is why I arranged with Frye to come in through the kitchen."

Nerissa looked past Annis to her abigail and flashed her a smile of thanks. She should have known that Frye would not accept Cole's cruel edicts without protest. "Do you know what was said between Cole and Hamilton last night? Cole will tell me nothing."

"Philip tells me he shares Hamilton's suspicion that your stepfather is the man they seek."

"I share it as well. Cole learned yesterday that he has inherited thirty thousand pounds."

"The amount stolen from their father!"

"I am sure only part of that money is from the late Lord Windham. Some is probably my mother's. The rest must belong to Albert Pilcher's other victims, for he seldom could hold onto money for very long. He enjoyed lavishing it on luxury for himself."

"Now your brother will lavish it on Elinor Howe."

Not caring about Cole and his bit of muslin, she whispered, "Cole sent Hamilton a message filled with plumpers, but I fear that Hamilton believes I wish nothing more to do with him."

"Hamilton rails if your name is mentioned." Annis's large eyes filled with tears. "He is the pattern card of a man suffering from a broken heart. I am certain, as I have been of nothing else in my life, that he loves you dearly."

"But he believes I would plot with Cole to betray him?"

"He has been betrayed once by a woman he dared to love."

"I am not Elinor Howe!"

Annis smiled sadly. "I know that, and so would Hamilton if his pride was not so badly wounded. He considers himself a complete chucklehead for failing to listen to that Bow Street Runner he hired."

"Why should he have guessed that my family was

involved?" She grasped Annis's hands. "If I had known of Mr. Pilcher's connection to this matter, I would have told Hamilton immediately."

"I know that, and so will Hamilton . . . eventually. Give him time, Nerissa. Philip and I have been trying to convince him to listen to us."

She rose and rubbed her icy hands together. "I have no time to give him. Cole and Elinor have made plans for us to take the eastbound Mail tomorrow morning. They are eager to see what price they can obtain for me on the Marriage Mart."

"But you love Hamilton!"

"Do you think that matters to them?"

Annis moaned, "Oh, this is even more horrible than I had thought. If you wish, I can take a note to Hamilton."

Her laugh was sullied by sarcasm. "What is the use? He will not heed what I write when his mind has been so poisoned by Cole's insinuations."

"I must be able to do something. There must be some way you can convince Hamilton that you played no part in this."

"There is only tonight. If Hamilton would call . . ."

"But he won't. This is the night of Sir Delwyn's weekly rout. You know he will go, if only to prove to the 'Polite World' that he is indifferent to the pain he is suffering."

"Sir Delwyn's rout?" Nerissa's smile became genuine. She might be queer in her attic to be thinking such thoughts, but she had only tonight to coax Hamilton into listening to the truth.

"What is it?" asked Annis.

Nerissa stooped to whisper to Annis what she needed her bosom bow to do for her. She urged Annis to be careful. If they made a single mistake, Cole would not give her a second chance to try to regain her happiness.

*     *     *

"This is madness!" Frye repeated for the fifth time.

Nerissa looked up from where she was counting the money that Mrs. Carroll had picked up at the solicitor's office less than two hours before. As Nerissa had hoped, Mr. Crimmins saw nothing amiss in the request from Cole's housekeper. She shoved it into her reticule and glanced anxiously toward the door.

She leapt to her feet, holding the bag behind her, when the portal opened. She sighed with relief when the housekeeper ushered two cloaked figures into the room. Mrs. Carroll shut the door and exchanged a fearful frown with Frye.

Annis slipped off the hood of her ebony cloak and motioned for her companion to do the same. Her abigail, Horatia, nodded and untied the ribbons holding her bright red cape closed.

"It is raining, thank goodness," Annis said with a soft laugh. "It was the best excuse to wear these heavy cloaks."

Nerissa smiled her thanks to Horatia as the abigail handed her the red mantle. Annis's abigail wore the same fearful expression as Frye. Throwing it around her, she said, "Now, Frye, you are to let no one in here—not even Cole."

"Be careful, Miss Dufresne," she beseeched.

"I shall." Taking Annis's hand, she slipped out into the upper hall with her friend and Mrs. Carroll.

She walked behind Annis as a proper abigail would, but wished her friend would hurry. At any moment, they might be discovered. She listened to Mrs. Carroll and Annis trying to prattle as if nothing was amiss. They scurried down the stairs. Nerissa followed, hunched into her cape,

"What are *you* doing here?" came Hadfield's hateful voice.

Mrs. Carroll intruded to say, "Miss Ehrlich did not realize that Mr. Pilcher had insisted that his sister rest before their journey tomorrow."

"Miss Dufresne has no interest in speaking with you." Peeking out from beneath her hood, Nerissa saw the butler's smile grow more sly. "In fact, Miss Ehrlich, she gave me a message to pass on to you."

"Then do so." The *hauteur* in Annis's voice startled Nerissa, but she concealed her reaction beneath the bright red cloak.

"Miss Dufresne wishes me to tell you that she will not respond to any letters you might consider sending her in Town."

"Then I shall not write her any! Come along, Horatia. We need not stay where we are not wanted."

Nerissa did not linger to see Hadfield's astonishment at his apparent, easy victory turn into satisfaction. When the door slammed nearly on her heels, she hurried down the wet steps.

"He is even ruder than usual!" Annis muttered as they rushed along the walkway toward her carriage. "I hope the first thing you do when this succeeds is to dismiss that man."

Drawing the cloak around her, Nerissa shivered. "If I succeed."


Hamilton glowered at the other guests attending Sir Delwyn's weekly gathering. None of them paused to speak to him as they hurried past, their eyes averted. No doubt, by this time, each one had been entertained by the poker-talk bolting through Bath. Only a shuttlehead would quiz a man about the fact he had been deceived by the mutual efforts of two former mistresses.

Dancing, their faces fixed in a perpetual expression of bliss, Philip and Annis had avoided him since their arrival. That pleased him, because he was

310

annoyed by their continual attempts to persuade him that Nerissa Dufresne was not involved up to her pretty nose in her stepfamily's conspiracies.

*Blast it!* She sneaked into his mind each time he let down his guard. He did not want to think about her soft mouth or the way she had felt so perfect in his arms. He had put Elinor Howe out of his life. He would do the same with Nerissa Dufresne.

Turning his back on the dance floor, Hamilton strode toward the stairs. The door to the room where card tables were filling up beckoned him to find a surcease for the agony in his heart. Sitting at an empty table, he picked up a pack of cards and began shuffling them. He nodded to Sir Delwyn, when his host came to sit with him, but his eyes widened in surprise as his brother sat at the table as well. He had thought Philip would spend the rest of the evening twirling Annis about the other room.

A slender shadow crept over his hands, and he looked up to see pretty, blue eyes that were dim with sorrow. His fingers tightened on the cards as he stared at Nerissa. Although she wore her blue dress that flattered her, her face was colorless. Watching the baronet leap to his feet, he remained sitting.

Nerissa took the chair their host held out for her, but said nothing. He knew she was waiting for him to speak or look at her again . . . or rise and leave. He did nothing but continue to shuffle the cards.

"What stakes are we playing for, my lord?" she asked quietly.

He ignored her formality. "As we have played for a guinea a point in the past, I would collect that—"

"I think it is time we raised the stakes. Shall we say a century a point?"

Hamilton arched a single brow at his brother, who was still making every effort to avoid his eyes. Was this Nerissa's final insult to him? She planned to play cards with him with the money stolen from his father. He would be damned to perdition before he let her take another penny. If she was opaque enough to challenge him, she would learn the cost of his revenge personally.

He noticed how her hands trembled as she gathered up the cards he was dealing to her. In spite of himself, his gaze stroked the curve of her hueless cheek. He could too easily recall its warmth against his naked chest as she slept within his arms. When he admired the slender length of her fingers as she held her cards competently, his skin tingled with the longing to savor them against him.

*Blast it! He would not be love's singleton again.* He refused to be connived into assuming her innocence was anything but the skills of a consummate actress.

In spite of himself, he gasped when, with a smile, she drew from her reticule a stack of pound notes. Hearing an echoing rumble of whispered comments whirling around them, he looked up to discover a half-dozen observers, who had been drawn to the table by the high-stakes game. She did not appear to notice as she leaned forward and set half of the pound notes in front of Philip.

"A wedding gift," she said, her voice quivering.

"Nerissa, I could not accept such a generous gift," Philip choked.

She looked directly at Hamilton while she said, as he had remarked to her the first night they had played cards, "If fortune smiles on us and we are successful, you may pay me back at the end of the evening."

"But we cannot count on such good fortune! I cannot take your money."

Quietly, she said, "Either you will take it, or Cole shall. I would as lief you had it."

Hamilton clenched his jaw until it hurt. This woman had no honor, for she was stealing from her fellow conveyancers. Not that he should care a fig if they had a falling-out among them. Irritably, he said, "Make up your mind, Philip. The books are growing impatient."

Philip looked from the cards to his brother's taut scowl, then to Nerissa, whose face—for the first time since Hamilton had met her—was blank of emotion. "I am in," he said quietly.

"Then, as suggested," Nerissa said, "we shall play for one hundred pounds per point. Shall we begin?"

Hamilton concentrated on his game, ignoring the onlookers who grew in number with every hand. No one at the table spoke unless it was necessary. He did not have to peek at the tally Sir Delwyn was keeping to know that Nerissa and Philip were losing badly, but her only reaction was the increased shaking of her hands.

Suddenly, Nerissa placed her cards on the table. "I have enough losses for tonight, so I would be wise to give my chair to another." She pulled another handful of pound notes from her bag and stood. "I think this shall cover my debt. Good evening, gentlemen." She hesitated, then said more softly, "And goodbye."

The baronet gasped as she turned to leave, "But, Miss Dufresne, you and young Philip have lost almost thirty thousand pounds between you."

Hamilton paid no attention to the fury of whispers around them as he set himself on his feet. Pushing past the curious guests, he seized Nerissa's arm. He whirled her to face him. He cursed when he saw tears glistening on her cheeks.

Nerissa defied her hands which ached to sweep up along his arms to clasp behind his nape. Then she would press her form to him as he teased her lips with the tantalizing flavors of his mouth.

"My lord," she whispered, daunted by the savagery burning in his eyes, "I have paid my debt to you and

Sir Delwyn. Please grant me the chance to take my leave now."

"You may have paid your debt to Seely," he retorted, "but you have not repaid me completely."

Fear pierced her, as the tempestuous emotions in his eyes struck her. He had said more than once he would do anything to gain his vengeance against the man whose schemes had led to his father's death. She was more certain than she had ever been that he meant exactly that.

In the same cold voice, he said, "We can discuss your debts to me in the book room."

A flame scorched her cheeks as she saw the smiling glances aimed in their direction. His words, coupled with the rumors that Annis had warned her were on the lips of everyone in Bath, suggested that the squaring of the debts between Lord Windham and Miss Dufresne would be settled in a most intimate way. Taking her hand, he turned her toward the stairs beyond the ballroom.

When his fingers touched hers, she forgot everyone else in the room. The fire that had been searing her face surged through her. Again she fought the longing to feel him closer as she walked with him down the stairs and toward the study. He closed the door behind them. She flinched when she heard him latch it, for she knew he intended to keep her from fleeing from this discussion.

"Why?" he asked without preamble. "Or do you wish me to believe it is simply coincidence that you have lost nearly thirty thousand pounds?"

"My stepbrother stole your money. I wished to return it to you."

"Only half. Seely was my partner tonight, so he gets half."

Nerissa sank to a settee as she held her hand over her heart, which had abruptly forgotten how to beat. "If you were to explain—"

"Seely wins so infrequently that he treasures what he can take away from the board of green cloth."

Drawing out her handkerchief, she wiped her damp cheeks. She would not be a watering pot, for that would gain her no sympathy from Hamilton. "Hamilton, I swear to you that I had no knowledge of Albert Pilcher's actions before yesterday. Blockhead that I was, I thought the only one he cheated out of money was my mother."

"So you wish me to believe you got that money tonight from Pilcher?"

"My father left my mother and me a small country estate. When I could no longer afford its upkeep—for, as I told you, Albert Pilcher stole more from my mother than he did from your father—I hired an agent to seek out a buyer. He found one, and the money I lost to you tonight was what I received after my solicitor took his share." She grimaced as she recalled that Mr. Crimmins had considered half of the proceeds a fair amount for overseeing the arrangements.

Again she hoped he would lower the frigid wall he had raised between them. She wanted his arms enveloping her as she rested against his heart. Instead he asked, "And your stepbrother?"

"I wish to say nothing of him."

He put his foot on the table by her and leaned forward to rest his hand on the back of the settee behind her. With his face so close to hers, he asked, "Why?"

"Hamilton, please take the money I lost, and be done with it."

"Will your brother return the rest of my money to me?"

"No!" She surged to her feet, but his hand on her arm kept her from bolting to the door. "Hamilton, I have given you every penny I have. Isn't that enough for you?"

"I want more."

Slowly she faced him, still hoping to see some compassion on his features, but they were as callous as her brother's heart. "I just told you. I have nothing else of value unless you wish to take me to London and offer me on the Marriage Mart to the highest bidder as Cole plans."

"And Elinor, I surmise." His terse laugh lashed her. "However, I pledge to you that they shall be unsuccessful, for you and I know the truth that you have no place among those maidens, who are seeking a husband."

Anguish sliced into her. "Hamilton, please, let this be the end. You have had your vengeance, although I fear you have gained it from a person who has been as wronged as you were."

"I do not want vengeance."

"You don't want vengeance?" she asked, astounded.

His arm swept around her waist, and he herded her against him. As his fingers curved along her cheek, his voice deepened to a husky whisper, "I want you. I want you here with me, not being paraded before the inlaid bachelors of Town."

She did not dare to believe what her ears told her she was hearing, but she drew away from the sweetness of his arms. "I told you that I have not changed, and I haven't. I will not repay my stepfather's debt to you by becoming your natural."

"Nerissa—"

She gave him no chance to finish. "I shall find a way to repay you the rest of the money."

"How?"

"I don't know. No doubt, Cole and Elinor will want whatever money they can get from the sale of the house in Bath, so I cannot hope for help from them. What I had tonight was only the binder I got on my mother's lands, but Cole is certain to see that I get no more money from the sale of Hill's End. Mayhap—"

His sudden laugh silenced her. "Hill's End? That's the name of the *terra firma* your father left you?"

"Yes, but why . . . ?"

With another laugh, he tapped her reticule. "It truly was my money you played with."

"*You* bought Hill's End?" She stared at him, more baffled than before. "But why? You have Windham Park. Why would you want Hill's End?"

"I purchased it for Philip and his bride-to-be as a bribe for him not to buy that commission. Do you think Annis Ehrlich Windham will enjoy living there?"

Tears filled her eyes, but they were tears of happiness. There would be no strangers residing at Hill's End. Instead dear friends would live there. "I doubt it," she said honestly. "The house is drafty."

"But it is convenient to Windham Park, so that you may call there often after we are married."

"*Married?*" Happiness twisted inside her, leaving her breathless. "You want to *marry me?*"

Slipping his arm around her waist again, he whispered, "Never have I been able to trust my heart, and—when it urged me to listen while it spoke of you—I refused to heed it. I as lief harkened to the small voice that warned me away from any woman who might demand every part of me when I wanted to give so little. You, who offered so much when you had nothing, were irresistible." His hand slid up her back to press her to him. "You know I love you, don't you?"

She gave her fingers free rein to stroke his strong shoulders. "Yes, and I love you, Hamilton."

"Then why shouldn't we get married?" He laughed as his fingers played along her cheek. "To think that I hunted for a fortune and found you instead. The sweetest vengeance is that Albert Pilcher did not destroy us, for, through him, we have found love."

"Is that why you wish to marry me? To get the ultimate revenge?"

With a throaty laugh, he whispered, "No, what I want is this." His mouth covered hers, and, surrendering her lips to him, she melted into the fires of ecstasy that always would rage within her when he touched her.

Broderick Crimmins tossed the page down in disgust. He had known that Miss Nerissa Dufresne was going to be a source of trouble since the first time he saw her. He had warned Cole Pilcher to keep his stepsister far away from him, but Pilcher had not listened.

Just this morning, he had received a letter from Lord Windham's solicitor informing him that there would be legal steps taken to recover money from Mr. Albert Pilcher's estate because of fraud perpetrated against the present viscount's father. Now this note!

Tapping his fingers on the page, he ignored the opening paragraph which had pleased him, for Lord Windham was withdrawing his claim against the Pilcher estate and Cole Pilcher. The rest outraged him. Even without looking at the page, he could recall the words:

As Miss Dufresne shall become my wife before the month is out, I am returning the paperwork for the completion of the sale of Hill's End to you unsigned. There is little need for me to purchase what shall be mine when we are wed. I trust you shall return your share of the proceeds of the initial payment to my solicitor immediately.

Dashed woman!

Then he smiled as he reached for the folder with

318

the Pilcher name on it. There was always a way of getting his money back. Opening it, he began to peruse the columns of numbers. Then he called his secretary. He wasn't after a fortune, after all. And just yesterday, he had heard that after getting a hefty amount of money from an investor for his canal project, Cole Pilcher was planning to buckle himself to Elinor Howe and go off to a fine life in London. Before he left, Pilcher could afford to give some blunt to his solicitor . . . just to even things a bit.

# About the Author

JO ANN FERGUSON was born and raised in Salem, New York and now resides in Massachusetts with her husband and three children. After earning a B.A. in history, Jo Ann proudly served two years as a second lieutenant in the Army. While stationed at Fort Dix, New Jersey, she was awarded the Army Commendation Medal.

Now working as a full time writer, Jo Ann also teaches creative writing at Brown University; and in 1992, she was awarded an arts grant for teaching.

Her work with the Romance Writers of America also keeps her very busy. She has served as conference coordinator and now holds the position of RWA National Vice-President.

Jo Ann Ferguson also writes under the pseudonym Rebecca North.